The Legacy of Catfish continues through

LILLY

Madelyn Bennett Edwards

Printers KDP and IngramSpark
Book design by Mark Reid and Lorna Reid at AuthorPackages.com
Edited by JT Hill and Jessica Jacobs
Photography by Brenda Oliver Vessels

Library of Congress Cataloging-in-Publication Data
Names: Edwards, Madelyn Bennett, author
ISBN: 978-0-9994027-4-0

Subjects: Coming of age, romance, race relations, Jim Crow, 1960s, KKK, LSU, Southern University, Sarah Lawrence, Louisiana, Cajun

Manufactured in the United States of America
First Edition - Copyrighted Material

Acknowledgements

Judge Billy Bennett (my brother), Paula Rosenblatt, MACP and Lisa Mezzetti, (my friends) for your patience in reading my manuscript and making beautiful red ink marks throughout.

JT Hill, editor extraordinaire.
Lori Hill, webmaster extraordinaire.
For John Yewell and Mimi Herman, Writeaways, France and Italy hosts extraordinaire

Mark and Lorna Reid of AuthorPackages for cover and interior design, and all the extras that got this book to print.

Embark Literary Journal for recognizing Catfish.

Taryn Hutchison, writing partner, friend, endorser.

For those who hosted book signings and launches, especially: Mike Dempsey, Laura Hope-Gill, Lenoir Rhyne University in Asheville, NC; Van and Catherine Roy, Baileys in Marksville, LA; Brenda Vessels in Beaumont. For the Louisiana Book Festival in Baton Rouge and the SWLA in Lake Charles. For Avoyelles Charter School and for the book clubs who read Catfish and those who invited me to your meetings.

For all of you who believed in me enough to order and read Catfish. My family: children and step children: Lulie, David, Paul, Gretchen, Anna, Sean, Christopher, Kristine, Lee; my brothers Johnny and Billy, and my sister, Sally, and my other sister, Angela; my cousin Letty, special friends, Tanya, Kate, Clare, Jane, Jeralie, Laurie, Bev, and so many more…

For those of you who posted reviews on Amazon and who emailed me, friends and strangers alike, to tell me that my stories and characters meant something to you that you could see, feel, smell, taste, and touch the things I put on the page. That feedback kept me writing on days when I didn't want to.

For everyone who reads my blogs and comments. Thank you. I wouldn't write them otherwise.

It's because all of you that I continue to write.

For Gene.
Who serves and protects so I can write books. You are amazing.

For God
Who believes in me even when I don't.

Table of Contents

Part One: 1974

∽ Chapter One ∽

∽

Union Station

UNION STATION WAS BUSTLING with people walking in every direction as I searched for the arrival gate from Chicago. The next arrival was scheduled for 9:30 AM, an hour away, so I found a seat on a bench and waited. I was nervous and excited at the same time. I remember tapping my foot on the tiled floor and hearing the patter as though it came from someone else's shoe. I absent-mindedly pushed the cuticles on my fingernails, trying hard not to bite them. This was a habit I'd had as a child that I'd fall back into now and again, but today was the wrong time to lapse. I wanted my nails to be perfect when Rodney slid the gold band on the fourth finger of my left hand.

I had taken a train from New York City to DC on Tuesday night; he was to arrive from Chicago Wednesday and I wasn't sure what time, but I wanted to be there, waiting. I was filled with anticipation as I held my small valise that held a beige suit and matching heels I'd bought to wear to the courthouse for our small ceremony. I wanted to look perfect when I became Mrs. Rodney Thibault.

I heard the announcement over the loudspeaker that the train from Chicago had arrived, but I didn't need the alert; I was standing near the arrival door waiting. I would be the first person he would see when he entered the terminal.

People began walking through the doorway, some with briefcases, some carrying luggage, a few with only a newspaper or a magazine. Most were men dressed in suits and ties, looking distinguished and purposeful. It was as if I had X-ray vision and could see through each individual because none of them were Rodney. I watched as the last person sauntered in and looked both ways, then marched towards baggage claim. The attendant closed the door, locked it, and attached a gold strap from one silver four-foot post to another so no one could get near the gate. I had to move back as she completed her task.

The next train would arrive at noon. I went to the bathroom, found the coffee vendor and bought a cup of coffee, a danish, and a book—*Carrie,* by a new author named Stephen King. It had surged to the top of the bestseller list out of nowhere and, as a wannabe writer, I was interested in books that were selling well. I became engrossed in the story of a high school girl who seeks revenge on students who bully and humiliate her. It was futuristic, projecting the plot into 1979, five years away. Carrie, the bullied teen, discovers she has telekinetic powers. I wasn't much for science fiction or gore, but the story sucked me in and I was jerked from my reading trance when the announcer said, "…from Chicago arriving at…" I was on my feet and standing at the door before the intercom completed its message.

This time there were a number of couples and a few women traveling alone who filed into the terminal. I noticed that more of the arriving passengers carried luggage and those who did not seemed in a hurry to get to baggage claim. I looked for the tallest to arrive, someone with dark curly hair and big hazel eyes with amber flecks. He might be wearing a baseball cap so I searched for a navy cap with "Cowboys" stamped in white across the forehead. I thought he could be at the end of the line because he was like that—someone who would let everyone else go first—or he might be carrying a bag or two for an elderly lady.

No one with that description came into the terminal. I thought he would be on the next train, which arrived at 3:30 PM, but he wasn't. And he wasn't on the 6:00 PM either.

I concentrated on my coffee and the *Washington Post*, which was filled with news of the Nixon White House and the scandals being uncovered by reporters Carl Bernstein and Bob Woodward. It was all about a robbery at the Democratic headquarters located in the Watergate Towers.

I wasn't interested in politics in those days, but I followed the gossip surrounding the president and the way he'd fired the independent special prosecutor, Archibald Cox, who was investigating the Watergate scandal. It was called the Saturday Night Massacre and ended with the resignation of the attorney general and his deputy. Impeachment hearings had begun at the beginning of May and there were reports of testimony given to the House Judiciary Committee.

At 7:45 PM, the loudspeaker announced a Chicago arrival. I didn't look up this time. I didn't stand at the doorway when the passengers entered from the tracks. Instead, I sat on the bench across the way and peered over the top of my newspaper as if by acting nonchalant, my jitters would go away. I took deep breaths and thought how I wished I knew some of the new-age concepts of transcendental meditation but I'd always thought that stuff was bunk. Now I wasn't so sure, especially when Rodney was not on the 7:45 PM.

The last arrival from Chicago was at midnight. I would wait to see if he was on it, and if not, I'd call his parents' house in Jean Ville and find out whether they'd heard from him. I'd fallen asleep when the loudspeaker announced the midnight train and I jerked to a seated position on the bench. I stood and stretched, and took a few steps towards the entrance from the tracks.

Only about thirty or forty passengers came into the terminal. They were all sleepy-eyed and stumbling as though awakened from a deep sleep, as I had been. I watched each individual and looked them up and down, noticing what they wore, the cases they carried, the books and newspapers and magazines under their arms, and I started to cry.

I walked to the payphone to call the Thibaults in Jean Ville, Louisiana. I picked up the receiver then glanced at the clock hanging above me. It was too late to phone anyone so I went back to my bench and slept fitfully. When the 6:00 AM train arrived from Chicago I didn't look up. It was Thursday and I'd been at the train station for more than 24 hours.

My nerves were shot. I visualized Rodney every way a dead man could be, and had convinced myself he would never arrive. If he were alive, I figured he had chickened out or had been detained by the promise of an easier life with a woman of his own race. A woman named Annette.

I thought back to our time together only ten days before.

*

In Rodney's eight-year-old sports car, we crossed the Atchafalaya River Bridge—the border between Toussaint and Pointe Coupée Parishes, in South Louisiana. Pine trees, so tall I couldn't see the tops, whizzed by and an occasional magnolia with a few white blooms waiting to pop open came into view. Once we were out of Toussaint Parish I took a deep breath, my first since we'd left our hometown of Jean Ville. I could smell the sweet fragrance of azaleas through the windows, opened a few inches to let in fresh air, humid and thick.

We had not spoken the entire thirty minutes from Jean Ville and it dawned on me that, other than the evening before, when Rodney drove me three blocks to Dr. David Switzer's house for stitches across my cheekbone, this was the first time I'd been in his car with him. His new, used 1966 metallic-blue Mustang fastback was clean, as though no one had ever ridden in the passenger seat where the canvas belt crossed my lap.

After we crossed the bridge into Lettsworth, I reached over and touched Rodney's hand. He squeezed mine and glanced at me with a smile, then looked back at the road.

Our first words were about what we should do when we arrived in Baton Rouge. My plane left for New York the next day and Rodney was going to try to get a ticket to fly with me. We couldn't go into the airport together given the ever-present colored, white entrance debacle. He thought the best thing would be to take me to the apartment he shared with his brother, Jeffrey, close to the Southern University campus, which was near the Baton Rouge airport. I would wait there while he went to buy a ticket.

*

I was sitting at the small, round dining table in the man-cave apartment that smelled of sweat and feet when I heard a key turn in the door. I panicked. Rodney had only been gone five or ten minutes and I had my thesis spread out in front of me, attempting to make the final edits. The door swung open and a good-looking guy—taller than Rodney, and thinner—ducked through the doorway and froze with one hand on the doorknob, the other on the strap across his shoulder that was attached to a navy backpack. We both became deer-in-the-headlights metaphors.

It took a few minutes before I noticed a pretty, light brown-skinned girl standing behind the guy. She was so small compared to him that she looked like a waif, hovering, as though wondering if he'd move out the way so she could get out of the blazing Louisiana heat. She squeezed in between him and the doorframe and now there were three of us, bug-eyed and seemingly terrified.

"Ummm," he said. "I... uh... um... I'm... um... Jeffrey."

"Oh," was all I could muster. My long red hair, which I liked to call strawberry blonde, was draped over my books and papers, and I peered at the pair with one eye before putting my pen down and tucking one side of the thick mane behind my ear. Still, I stared sideways, my head bent over my papers.

"And you?"

"Susanna Burton. Susie."

"Oh," he said. The girl stood there like she was watching a movie. "Where's Rodney?"

"Airport."

"Oh." They didn't move. Neither did I.

A fly buzzed in over the girl's head and lit on Jeffrey's blue baseball cap, "Jaguars" stamped in gold letters across the front. The girl watched it. It flew around him and buzzed near his ear. He let go of the doorknob and swatted at the fly. The door slammed behind them with a loud thud in the quiet, thinking space. I was the intruder, but I didn't feel that way, so I just sat there and waited for one of them to say something polite, accepting, understanding.

I'd forgotten how I looked—a bandage across my cheek and a black, swollen eye.

"Are you okay?" The girl asked.

"Sure. Why?"

"Well, I mean. What happened?"

"Huh?"

"Look, let's try to get this started again," the tall guy said. "I'm Jeffrey, Rodney's brother. It's a pleasure to finally meet you. Rod's told me about you."

"He has?" I stood up and smoothed the knit shirt tucked into my hip-hugger slacks, then extended my hand. "Susie. Nice to know you, too." His long fingers wrapped around my hand and reminded me of Catfish — cotton candy on one side, chocolate on the other. Tears sprang to my eyes.

"I saw you at Catfish's funeral," he said. "I'm sorry we didn't meet then."

"Me, too. My dad was there." I don't know why I said that and, afterwards, I took a deep breath as if to erase the last four words that hung in the air and thought about Catfish.

He was a tall, skinny man who walked in front of our house on South Jefferson Street when I was growing up with my three brothers. My mother told us we couldn't talk to him because he lived in the Quarters and was, "One of them," whatever that meant.

We'd caught a turtle in the ditch in front of our house after a big rain, and when Catfish stopped by that afternoon to play his harmonica, I asked him if he wanted it. James, Will, and I were on a mission to discover whether it were true that colored people ate turtles, and we found out that afternoon.

Catfish explained to me how he would cook it, but what I didn't expect was that over the months and years I would become entranced by the dark-skinned man's willingness to share himself freely, to love unconditionally, and to treat me with a kindness unlike any I'd known. It was very different from the way my father had raised me—with fear, threats, and beatings.

Catfish had taught me to believe in myself for the first time.

I remember looking into his ink-dark eyes and wondering where the bottoms were, and when he laughed, he bent forward, grabbed his belly and bellowed from deep inside. After meeting Catfish that day I would wait for him to walk by our house in the afternoons as he marched home from his job at the slaughterhouse. He taught me how to appreciate the little things in life: the sweet scent of wisteria in bloom, the buzzing of grass bees around my ankles, the freshness of a summer rain, and the taste of honeysuckle picked from the vine.

When Catfish retired from his job and no longer walked in front of our house, I started stealing off to the Quarters to see him. That's when he began telling me stories about his grandparents and parents, and the people who lived on Shadowland plantation before, during, and after the Civil War.

I loved his stories, and I loved the way he told them. After hearing the first few "Catfish tales", I decided I would be a writer one day and the first book I'd write would be Catfish's stories.

I was startled and brought back to the present by Rodney's brother. Jeffrey.

"Yeah. Well… um… This is Sarah."

"Hi, Sarah. Nice to meet you." She looked shocked. Obviously, neither Jeffrey nor Rodney had mentioned me to her. She looked at Jeffrey, then back at me, and nodded but didn't shake the hand that I'd extended in anticipation.

"Yeah. Right," she said.

"Sarah," Jeffrey said.

"Well. Maybe someone could fill me in."

"Rod will be back soon," I said. "You can ask him."

"Looks like he rescued you from something," Jeffrey was making an attempt at small talk, trying to get us two skittish females to cooperate.

"Something like that," I said. "I forgot about my face. Sorry."

"Yeah. Well, as long as Rod didn't do it," Jeffrey's bad joke was followed by a chuckle that made me feel sorry for him. He was trying to break through the thick fog of mistrust that hovered in the air, and neither Sarah nor I helped him.

"Rod would never." I sat back down at the table. The couple stood there like they didn't know what to do.

"Want something to drink?" Jeffrey started for the kitchen behind me.

"No thanks," I said.

"How 'bout you, Sarah?"

"Sure. I'll get it myself." She followed him. I could hear them whispering in the space behind the counter that separated me and the small, round table in the dining area from the kitchen. I couldn't concentrate on my work, so I closed the book, gathered the papers, and made a neat stack on the edge of the table.

The smell of coffee filled the air; a rich aroma laced with chicory that reminded me there were some things I missed about Louisiana when I was in New York. Not many, but some—boiled crawfish, cochon de lait, jambalaya, and that wonderful southern drawl, mixed with a Cajun accent that was balm to my ears. The heat and humidity, though, I didn't miss. Nor did I miss the busybodies who run their mouths, like my parents or Jim Crow or the Klan.

The sound of an electric percolator and Sarah and Jeffrey's whispers became commonplace as I sat alone and wondered how to disappear. I have this habit I don't pay much attention to—I put my face in my hands when I'm thinking—so I guess that's how they found me when they sat down at the table, three cups of coffee, sugar, and cream appearing out of nowhere: a pow-wow of sorts.

"Sarah and I are engaged," Jeffrey said. I looked up with my chin in my hands.

"Congratulations. Have you set a date?"

"We both have two more years of law school before we seal the deal." He reached over and took her hand, holding it on the table so I could see it. They looked at each other in a sweet, endearing sort of way.

Jeffrey reminded me of Rod, though he seemed more soft-spoken and very serious. Sarah was lovely, with flawless skin and dark hair ironed straight with a bit of a flip where it hit her shoulders. Her nails were painted hot pink and she had a small, gold stud in the side of her nose and dangling earrings in both ears. She wore pedal pushers and flip-flops, a contrast to the ornate jewelry but nicely put together with a salmon-colored sleeveless silk blouse.

"Where are you from, Sarah?" I asked.

"Mississippi, on the coast. It's a small town called Waveland."

"I know Waveland," I said. "We used to go to Biloxi on vacation and my mother would tell us stories about spending summers in Waveland."

Silence. *Okay,* I thought. *If they want to know about me, they'll have to ask. I'm not about to offer up my life story, especially to this girl who seemed put off by my presence.*

"Look," I said. "This is obviously uncomfortable for all of us. Let's just wait for Rodney to get back and iron it all out."

"What's to iron out?" Jeffrey asked. Sarah punched him in the side with her elbow. We sat and sipped our coffee and tried not to look at each other, although I knew they were staring at the side of my face and my puffy, dark, left eye. I slipped on my sunglasses to hide my grotesque face and they both blushed and looked at their coffee cups, shifting their eyes to look at each other sideways. I opened my book and started to flip through the typed papers in the manila folder beside it. I clicked the top of the ballpoint pen and made notes in the margins. I didn't mean to be rude, but I wasn't sure what else to do.

It seemed like forever before Rodney walked into the apartment. He stood in the doorway and took in the scene: me bent over papers I couldn't see because I was wearing sunglasses, Jeffrey and Sarah nursing empty coffee cups, no one talking.

"Jeff. Sarah. Hi," Rodney said. He walked into the room. His presence filled the space and I wanted to jump into his arms, but I sat still and stared at him, longing for him to reach for me and hold me. I felt so vulnerable.

Jeffrey got up and the two guys grabbed each other's right hands, tapped their chests together and wrapped their left arms around the other's neck. When they pulled apart, they slid their hands along the other guy's inner arm and cupped their fingers together like choirboys singing a solo. Today we'd call it a "Bro-Hug." Back then, I didn't know what it was.

Rodney gave Sarah a peck on the cheek from behind her chair. He looked at me as though he didn't know how to fold me into the scenario and, after a pause, he took off his cap and pulled me out of my chair and into his arms.

I started to cry. I'm not sure why. I just know I felt safe once he folded his long arms around me, my head on his chest, his breath on the top of my head, little kisses in my hair. He rubbed my back and whispered to me, "It's okay. I'll take care of you." I believed him.

Eventually, we all sat around in the living room to talk. Rodney and I sat on the sofa next to each other holding hands, my head on his shoulder. I didn't have anything to say. I was a spectator of a conversation of which I was the subject.

Sarah was crying because she was sad for someone called Annette and thought Rodney and I had ruined everyone's plans. Rodney tried to explain that he had never led Annette to believe there was any future for their relationship. Sarah contended it was by innuendo. Jeffrey said there were too many law students in the room.

They laughed, argued politely, and Sarah cried. No one seemed to notice I was there, listening to them talk about Rodney and another girl. It hurt, but his arms were around me and my head was on his body and I could hear his heartbeat. Every now and then he pecked the top of my head, rubbed my leg, patted my shoulder. That's what kept me from hysteria.

"Are you going to tell Annette or should I?" Sarah asked. "She's my best friend."

"Of course I'm going to tell her," Rodney said. "I'd like to talk to Susie about it first."

Rodney stood up and pulled me to my feet. "We're going for a drive." I grabbed my purse and he followed me out the door, his hand on my back, guiding me towards his Mustang. When we closed both doors of the car and he started the engine I began to cry, hard. He drove without speaking. In just a few minutes we were parked on a levee watching tugboats push barges down the Mississippi River.

"Listen, baby. We need to talk about some things."

"You mean Annette?"

"Forget Annette. That's over. I'll handle that. We need to talk about New York."

"Aren't you going to explain Annette?"

"Do you want to explain your love life over the past six years?"

"Uh, no. You're right. It doesn't matter."

"That's my girl." He squeezed my leg, then he put both his hands on the steering wheel and stared out the front windshield. "Look, they won't sell me an airline ticket." He told me there was a seat on my plane for him, that is until they looked at his driver's license. He presumed his race precluded him from getting the ticket. I was disappointed, but I guess I knew things wouldn't go smoothly. After all, they never had.

"I really have to get back to New York, Rod." I explained that I had to turn in my thesis, complete one final exam, and attend commencement for graduate school the following week. He said that since he couldn't fly out with me, he'd like to stay in Baton Rouge for a week and graduate with his law school class. His parents would want to see him walk across the stage and receive his law degree.

"This isn't the end of the world," he said, as though trying to convince himself that he was right. "I can take the train up next week, after graduation. That will give me some time to resign from my job, get my transcripts together, and tie up some loose ends."

"Like Annette?"

"Like Annette. And other things. I can leave next Sunday; a week from today."

"I've heard horror stories about Negroes on trains in the South." I was trying to stop crying, unsuccessfully. "And then there's my dad. What if he finds out before you get out of Louisiana?"

"I'll be discreet. How would he find out?" I didn't answer, but we both knew there was an informant in the close-knit circle of people who knew when we saw each other. We still hadn't uncovered the leak. "The only people who'll know are my family and Sarah. They won't tell."

"Still…"

"I'll go straight to Chicago," he said. "Once I'm in Illinois, out of the South, I'll be fine."

"How will we stay in touch? How will I know when you'll be in New York, where to meet you?"

"I'll call your apartment. We'll work it out."

"I'm afraid to leave you here, Rod. I'm afraid I'll never see you again." I stared out the windshield. He patted my shoulder but didn't respond. There was nothing he could say.

*

We stopped by his apartment and I stayed in the car while he went inside to get my books, then we drove to a hotel on Airline Highway. It was the same one we'd been to three years before, when we'd said goodbye. I had an intense feeling of déjà vu wondering whether it was an omen and that this was goodbye, again.

It had been a long time since we'd made love and I felt embarrassed, as though it were the first time. I shouldn't have worried.

A soft light filtered in around the sides of the heavy drapes that covered the long window over the air-conditioning unit and from the lamps on either side of the bed. The way the light, or lack of it, hit Rodney's face, the way his teeth seemed so white in the semi-darkness, and the glow that came from within him, through his eyes, was radiant, almost ethereal. His touch felt brand new and old hat at the same time.

He slid his hands down my arms from where they emerged from my sleeveless blouse, and when he reached my hands he curled his fingers through mine and pulled me close to him, wrapping all four of our arms around my back. My head tucked under his chin and he kissed the top of my head, then the top of my ear, then my neck. I trembled and let out a deep, throaty moan. He moved his lips down my throat to the opening of my shirt and blew softly where he had just kissed my skin. The cool sensation on the hot kiss took me to a new place. I let my head fall back so he could reach my chest. He let go of one of my hands and used his long fingers to unbutton the top few buttons of my blouse and kissed my cleavage.

Ribbons of light touched the side of his face when he moved back to look at me. His touch, his lips, his look and the way the light played on the amber specks in his green eyes entranced me. When he bent to kiss my lips I almost fell into his embrace and he had to catch me to keep me from sliding to the floor. He was conscious of my swollen face and the pain his kisses might cause, so he was tender and gentle. With the back of his hand, he stroked the side of my face that didn't have stitches and a bandage.

"Does it hurt?"

"Only when I think about it."

"I can help you forget about it for a little while."

"Promise?"

What is it about making love to the person you adore that makes you feel complete? When I lay against him, my head on his shoulder, his arms around me, I marveled at the whole of him; of Rodney, of this person who could make me feel so loved that I could forget everything else. He held me all night and we slept in spurts. The next morning, we dressed quietly and he took me to the airport.

I was petrified to go to New York without him, afraid I'd never see him again.

Rodney looked so handsome as he stood in the Baton Rouge airport and watched me board my flight to New York. He told me not to worry, he'd take care of everything, and we would be married in Washington DC the following week and live in New York where mixed-race marriages were accepted.

Yet a fat tear rolled down his cheek as he stood at the gate and watched me walk down the jet way.

He called every day that week. The last time was from a pay phone in Baton Rouge. He told me that he was about to board the train for Chicago, then to DC.

"I'm almost there!" His voice was bright and excited. In my imagination I could see his eyes light up, the way they always did when he had something positive to say. "In a few days you'll be Susie Thibault." I loved the sound of his voice, the upbeat tone he seemed to have in everything he did and said.

God, how I loved that guy—that gorgeous, wonderful, perfect person.

⌒ Chapter Two ⌒

⌒

New York

THE CABBIE DROVE THROUGH Queens and passed through the stately gates at St. John's University onto a green-leafed, tree-lined drive with massive stone buildings on either side. He dropped me in front of the apartment building provided by the university for me and other graduate assistants, where I had lived for the past three years. I loved the spiritual feeling of the campus and the serenity I felt walking across the lawns from one cross-topped building to the next to attend and teach classes.

But I didn't feel serene the day I returned from the train station in DC without Rodney.

Where was he? Why didn't he show up? I just wanted to be near the phone if and when he called.

My tiny unit on the second floor had one bedroom, a small bath, and a combined kitchen and living area. I'd gradually added my own touches and when I opened the door with my key, I looked at my little home with new eyes. What would Rodney think when he got here? The door slammed behind me and I felt a cloak of angst envelop me. *If* he got here.

I had so many secrets. Would he still love me and want me once he knew?

I had to tell him. We couldn't build a future with the past hanging over our lives. I sat down hard in the pillowed chair near the front door and dropped my overnight bag and purse on the floor next to me. Where would I start? The baby? Merrick? Josh? Gavin?

Then it dawned on me that I may never see Rodney again. It hadn't been that long since the Klan tried to kill his dad and left a warning: "Leave the white girl alone." That's what had ended our relationship three years back. Had it happened again?

The phone rang and I jumped up, scared out of my thoughts.

*

I thought back to ten days before when I'd first arrived back in New York after leaving Rodney at the airport in Baton Rouge. When I had entered my apartment that afternoon, the phone was ringing.

"Hi, beautiful," he said when I answered.

"Please get here, Rod. I'm so afraid something will happen to keep you from me."

"Tell me you love me and I'll make that promise."

"Do I have to say the words?"

"Yes. I need to hear them, so you'd better get used to saying them. Now, practice."

"I, uh, you know I do, Rod."

"Say it, Baby."

"I, uh, love you."

"Good job. I love you, Chére." He called me lots of pet names. Chére, which sounded like *sha,* and meant *dear one* in Cajun French, was probably my favorite, but I'd never told him that. "See you in a week."

After we'd hung up, I thought of all of the questions I wanted to ask. Had he talked to Annette? Had he told his parents? Had he quit his job? Then I remembered I'd been with him that morning at the airport in Baton Rouge. How much could he have accomplished in such a short time?

Later he told me everything—that he'd gone straight to New

Iberia to see Annette and, hard as it was, he'd broken things off. In the process, he'd broken her heart. I knew it must have been torture for him to hurt her, or anyone, especially someone who loved him.

I had to do the same thing—break up with Merrick, only Merrick was expecting it, wasn't he? After all, he was married and he must have realized that once I finished graduate school it would be over between us, right?

It had been Monday afternoon when we met at a sidewalk cafe close to campus, a few blocks from Merrick's writers' retreat where we had gone once or twice a week for the past three years. He was happy to see me but appalled by my bruises and bandages. I had forgotten how bad I looked until I saw the expression on his face when he sat down across from me at the little table for two.

"What the hell, Susie?"

"Oh, this? It'll heal. No worries."

"What the devil happened to you?"

"I don't want to talk about it, okay?" He was quiet for a minute. He looked at my face and tried to see behind my dark glasses, which didn't totally hide the swollen eye and purple circle that crept under the lenses. He calmed his voice and spoke in a fatherly tone.

"Susie. Please tell me what happened. I've never seen anyone so, well, so, uh…" He was never at a loss for words, so I almost laughed. Instead, I finished his sentence.

"Beat up?"

"Yes."

"The price of going home." How could I tell him that my own dad beat me up? For me it was almost normal, something that my father had done to me since I was little: lose his temper and take it out on me. Once he beat me so badly I spent a month in the hospital and had the last sacraments administered because they thought I was going to die.

This last time had been different, though; I'd fought back. I'd gone home for Catfish's funeral and my dad accused me of humiliating him in front of a hundred voters. We'd been to the Quarters for the burial and a cochon de lait dinner when he saw me speak to Rodney and suggested it embarrassed him to see me speak to a colored boy in public.

He'd slapped me so hard I fell against the footboard of the bed in the room that had once been mine and now belonged to my baby sister, Sissy. I slid to the floor and before I knew what happened he was on top of me, kicking and slapping. On impulse, I caught one of his feet with both my hands and threw his leg in the air with all my might. He staggered backwards, lost his balance and almost fell.

By the time he got his bearings, I was on my feet and he hit me in the face with his fist to keep me from running out the door. I staggered backwards and a strange darkness came over me. All the anger I'd felt for years bubbled up and I sucker-kicked him in the balls, hard. When he bent over to grab himself I reared back like a runner taking off from a starting block and pushed off hard with my foot, my knee cramming him in the face.

There was a loud crunch when it connected with his forehead and he toppled backwards onto the thick, blue carpet. Blood spurted from above his eye. I grabbed my purse and overnight bag and ran from the room, through the front door, and down the sidewalk while he yelled after me.

Dr. David Switzer, who lived across the street, opened his front door and walked briskly towards the road as he yelled at my dad who, by then, was standing on his front porch. I ran down South Jefferson Street and was only a few blocks from the Quarters.

Later, Rodney had taken me to Dr. Switzer's house and he stitched my face and congratulated me on fighting back. He'd offered to help Rodney and me run away together and to keep the Klan and my dad from hurting Rodney's family once we were gone.

Those were my thoughts as I looked across the table at Merrick, who looked confused, as if trying to understand how I could have been beaten so badly.

"I guess that explains why you didn't go home to Louisiana the entire three years of graduate school—that is, until your grandfather died." Merrick had been my professor, mentor, lover. I'd told him Catfish was my grandfather.

"Sort of. Can we talk about other things?" I couldn't tell Merrick what had happened.

"Let me get adjusted to looking at you like this." We ordered hot tea and sat stirring honey and lemon into the darkening liquid, dipping the tea bags over and over, squeezing the excess out and removing them from the cups, the steam and tea fragrance wafting into the space between us. We each took a sip.

"I have my thesis with me. I'd like to leave it with you and ask when I can take my last final exam?"

"Okay. Tomorrow? Will that work? Are you prepared?"

"Yes. I'll do fine, although I haven't been able to concentrate very much this past week."

"Hmmm. Anything I can do to help?"

"No, I'll be fine." We sipped our tea and I listened to the chatter of the other customers, horns blowing on the street, and the roar of a bus as it barreled down Utopia Parkway. Through it all I spotted a red bird perched in an oak tree in front of the entrance to park. It tweeted, then listened for a reply, and reminded me of sitting in the lush St. Augustine grass with my best friend Marianne, our backs resting against the outside of the old barn in the Quarters, Catfish asleep on his porch. Red birds called to each other—mating calls, love calls.

I thought of Rodney. I thought of what I needed to say to Merrick. My face hurt. I strained to see out of my one fully-opened eye, dark sunglasses masking the space between me and this kind man who had made the past three years bearable.

"Merrick." I talked into my cup. He reached across the table and, with his two forefingers under my chin, lifted my face to make me look at him. I kept my eyes downcast. He lifted my chin higher.

"Susie, you're scaring me."

"Merrick. I'm done with graduate school. I need to move on. You understand, don't you?"

"Move on where?"

"Well, I'm going to look for a job in the city. I have to be out of my apartment by the end of June."

"But us. I mean, we can still see each other, right?"

"I need a clean break, Merrick. You knew this would end."

"No. I didn't. I don't want to lose you. Can't we work things out?"

"I'm not like you, Merrick. I can't handle more than one relationship at a time."

"Oh. Is there someone else?"

"Yes."

"How did that happen so fast? Last week we were fine?"

"An old boyfriend."

"Did he do this to you?"

"NO! Never."

"Then who?"

"I don't want to talk about that. I want to talk about us." We bickered but didn't argue. Merrick had too much class for that. When we parted he said he was still hopeful things would work out between us. I knew they wouldn't, but I let him dream on.

*

I was remembering all these things as I walked into my apartment after spending the night at Union Station waiting for Rodney, who

31

never showed up.

I answered the ringing phone.

"Hi. It's Mari." Marianne Massey was not only my best friend, but also my half-sister, thanks to my dad's clandestine relationship with our help, Tootsie, Marianne's mother and Catfish's daughter.

"Mari! Have you heard from Rodney? He didn't show up in DC" I knew she heard the panic in my voice and she tried to calm me before she told me what she knew about Rodney. Marianne and Rodney were as close as brother and sister. They considered themselves cousins since Rodney's Uncle Bo was married to Marianne's Aunt Jesse. Marianne was as worried about him as I was.

Marianne said Rodney's law school graduation went off without a hitch. He was at the train station the next morning, ticket in hand.

"Yes, he called to tell me he'd be in Chicago the next day and would stay with a cousin overnight" I started to cry. "He said he wanted me to meet him in Washington on Wednesday so we could be married. But he never showed up."

Marianne explained that after Rodney hung up the phone with me and headed to the waiting area for the train to Chicago, two men grabbed him from behind.

"They slipped their arms under Rodney's armpits and practically lifted him off the floor and carried him down the hall and out the front doors." She was talking fast and I had to hold the phone close to my ear to catch every word. "A pickup truck was at the door of the train station, and the men threw Rodney into the cab, squeezing him between two burly guys with baseball caps and sunglasses." Marianne said that the driver of the truck took off while the man sitting shotgun tied a bandana through Rodney's mouth, gagging him. Then the guy slipped a dark sack, like a pillow case, over Rodney's head, secured it around his neck, and tied his wrists together in his lap.

"They were almost out of Baton Rouge when Rodney heard a siren and the driver of the pickup said, 'Oh, shit.' They pulled over and the driver got out. The man next to Rodney pushed a gun into his side and pulled Rodney's head down."

Marianne said that two state troopers met the driver on the side of the truck. One of the troopers argued with the driver and told him to get back in the vehicle while the other trooper started towards the passenger side. Two men in the bed of the truck stood up with guns.

"The cop yelled at them to get on their stomachs and when he reached the window on the passenger's side, the man with the gun on Rodney turned and shot at the cop, but missed. From what Rodney's dad told me, there was a gun fight—two cops, four armed outlaws, and Rodney, with a sack over his head and his hands tied together, lying across the bench seat of the truck."

She said the newspaper report told how the cop on the street shot the two guys in the bed of the truck when they came up shooting. The truck driver didn't have time to get his gun out of the cab in time, so the trooper trapped him against the truck and handcuffed him while he held the two wounded men at gunpoint. The other trooper returned fire and killed the man who held Rodney captive and a bullet hit Rodney's shoulder.

"At some point, two ambulances arrived followed by back-up police officers." Marianne said. "They took Rodney to the hospital against his pleas to drop him at the train station. The men in the back of the truck were also taken to the hospital and I don't know what ever happened to them."

Marianne said Ray Thibault told her that Rod told him the story when they drove to Jackson, Mississippi.

"Mississippi?"

"Wait; there's more," Marianne said.

She told me that the Klan had gotten Jeffrey. Confused about which brother was Rodney, the group of eight men from Jean Ville decided to split up and get them both. After all, they were Mulattoes and Senator Burton, my dad, said one of them had been fooling around with his daughter.

Rodney's dad, Ray, owned the Esso gas station in Jean Ville and Rodney and Jeffrey helped him out whenever they were home. Ray told Marianne that the Klan picked Jeffrey up Saturday night in Jean Ville after he closed the station.

"The men pulled a sack over Jeffrey's head, tied his ankles together and his arms behind his back, then hog-tied him by looping the tied hands and feet through a rope around his neck while he lay on his stomach in the back of a pickup," Mari told me. "He fought to keep his limbs in the 'up' position so the weight wouldn't pull on the noose and strangle him." Marianne said the men drove Jeffrey to First Bridge, a wooded area near the Indian reservation in Jean Ville, where they put him in a wheelbarrow and pushed him deep into the thicket, threw the rope that held his arms, legs and neck together over a tree and left him there.

"If they'd taken him anywhere else, he'd be dead, but he was close to the St. Matthew Quarters and Joe Edgars was walking home from the grocery store. He saw the Klan leaving First Bridge in a truck," Marianne told me. "Joe said he ran through the woods so they wouldn't see him and ran directly into the tree where Jeffrey was hanging."

Rodney's dad told Marianne that, for once, he was glad Joe Edgars was a hoodlum, because he had a knife on his belt and cut Jeffrey down. He said his son was barely breathing and that Joe left Jeffrey on the ground and ran to the first house in the St. Matthew Quarter for help. The preacher's wife, Miss Camellia, called the sheriff and then she called Ray.

"I got there first," Ray told Marianne. "I still don't know whether the sheriff ever arrived. I took Jeffrey straight to Dr. David's house because it was only a few blocks away. Jeffrey wasn't breathing by the time we got there, so Dr. David did mouth-to-mouth and my boy finally took a breath."

"They aren't sure how long he'd gone without oxygen, and that's the big problem," Marianne sighed and finally paused. Then she started to cry because Jeffrey had not regained consciousness since he'd arrived at Jean Ville General Hospital Saturday night. "Five days."

I didn't know what to say. Marianne was spent from telling me the story and she still had not given me any information about Rodney, except to say, "Jackson, Mississippi?" Did he know about Jeffrey? Was he alive?

"How's Rodney? Is he still in the hospital in Baton Rouge? Where is he?" I was frantic, but Marianne said she'd told me everything she knew, that Ray didn't know what happened to Rodney after he jumped out of the car in Jackson, which confused me even more.

She said she would call me when she had more information. I was hysterical when I hung up the phone. I could picture Jeffrey and Sarah from only a week ago—so alive, so in love, so full of hope and promise. Just like me… and Rodney. I tried not to think of Rodney with a bullet through his shoulder, bleeding, maybe dying.

*

I waited another week for Marianne to call me with news, any news. Finally, unable to hold onto my patience any longer I picked up the phone and called her. Tootsie answered.

"Hi, Toot. I need to talk to Marianne." I was curt and short, nervous, not in the mood for small talk.

"Susie. How you doing?" Tootsie drawled on in her southern-Negro cadence, slow as honey dripping from a cone.

"Tootsie, I really need to talk to Marianne. It's important."

"She's at work, Susie. Want me to tell her to call you back?"

Marianne was a nurse at Jean Ville General Hospital. I didn't know what shift she was working.

"Please." I hung up before I burst out crying.

By the time Marianne called me back that night I was into my second glass of wine, pacing my small apartment, crying and scratching the welts that had broken out on my arms.

"Hi, it's me. Look. I saw Ray at the hospital tonight. Jeffrey is still in a coma and it doesn't look good. They aren't sure how much swelling he has on the brain. Only time will tell." She was crying and I could tell she was more worried about Jeffrey than about Rodney. I didn't speak, just let her cry it out and get hold of her thoughts.

"So, Ray told me what happened to Rodney last week. He picked Rodney up at the Baton Rouge jail and drove him to Jackson. Ray said he had a plan to get Rodney out of the South before the Klan got to him like they'd gotten to Jeffrey."

Marianne said Ray banged his car up with a hammer and, somehow, got a black eye. He would go to the sheriff of Hinds County in Jackson and say they'd been attacked by Klan members and that they beat him and took Rodney.

"That way the sheriff would be looking for Rodney, even though Rodney would be long gone." Marianne said.

"Ray said they didn't talk much during the four-hour drive to Jackson from Baton Rouge that night but that Rodney asked Ray about Jeffrey's condition. Rod asked his dad to call your apartment and give you any news, and you would relay it to Rodney when he calls you every day." Marianne took a deep breath and paused.

"Only he hasn't called me once, and it's been almost two weeks." I tried to hear what Marianne said through her sobs.

"About an hour out of Jackson, Ray said they realized they were being followed. Rodney watched a black Ford Fairlane trail Ray's grey Buick on Highway 64," Marianne said. "When Ray slowed to turn off the main highway onto the farm road that led into the west end of Jackson, Rodney jumped out with his backpack strapped on his back, holding his duffle bag to soften the blow. He landed in a ditch, and that's the last time Ray or anyone has seen or heard from him."

"Did Ray go through with his plan with the sheriff in Jackson?" I was confused and scared.

"Yes, but he said it hasn't gone anywhere. The authorities in Mississippi are worse than the ones in Louisiana." Marianne stopped talking and I could hear her inhale sharply, as though trying to catch her breath. We were both quiet for the longest time while I thought of questions to ask her, but couldn't come up with any.

*

The next day, I picked up my mail at the university post office. Rodney's familiar handwriting stretched across a long, white envelope. I ripped it open and read it standing near my post box.

June 12, 1974
Dear Susie,

I'm safe for now, with a friend, but I can't tell anyone where I am because I'm being followed and threatened, and the phone where I'm staying is tapped, so no phone calls, either.

After I last spoke with you, some guys grabbed me and I was shot, not seriously, and put in jail. Dad bailed me out. I don't know if you've talked to anyone and know what happened to Jeffrey. He's in bad shape... in a coma, the last I heard. I'm really worried. I wanted to go to Jean Ville to see him but Dad said the Klan and a posse your dad organized had the hospital staked out.

I asked my dad how anyone found out about us and he told me your dad knew. I questioned dad about that and he said, "Bob Burton is not the saint everyone thinks he is," and that he's a dangerous man. Dad told me that even though they were supposed to be friends, that friendship had been based on ulterior motives of your dad. My dad said your dad was anti-Klan until he found out about us.

That made me think.

What happened next is a story movies are made from. I'll try to write you again to tell you about it but I want to get this letter in the mail now, while I have someone who can take it to the post office.

I love you more than anything. Don't give up on me.

Yours forever,

Rod

I held the letter with both hands against my chest. At least he was safe, for now, or at least he was when he wrote the letter.

I looked at the postmark on the envelope. It had been mailed from Jackson a week before. If the phones were tapped and he couldn't go out in public to mail a letter, was he really in a safe place?

~ Chapter Three ~

~

Catfish

THE SUMMER HEAT ROSE from the pavement and was oppressive by mid-afternoon while I pounded the pavement looking for an apartment. I labored over the decision—was this for me or for us? I wanted Rodney's input. What would he like? Would Queens be right for him?

I'd go back to my university apartment during the hot afternoons and try to keep busy. All morning while I was out, I really wanted to be near the telephone.

I packed boxes of dishes and art I had collected over the years as well as all my personal items. The apartment where I had lived for three years was furnished, so other than one over-stuffed chair with an ottoman and a couple of side tables and lamps, I didn't have much to move. I'd saved some money and could afford to buy a new sofa and a bed, but I wanted Rodney to help me pick them out.

I didn't have school projects, papers to grade, or assignments with due dates and I needed to stay busy so I tried to organize the stories Catfish had told me through the years. I'd promised him I would write them all down and publish a book that would show the world what slavery and post-Civil War life had been like.

He didn't get to tell me all his stories.

I ran to the Quarters the afternoon following his funeral, with a bloody nose and a gash on my face where my dad had hit me. I sneaked into Catfish's house and looked around his living space for the first time. It occurred to me that in all the years I'd visited with Catfish on his back porch, he'd never invited me inside.

I remember running my hand over the four-drawer chest in his small bedroom with pictures of Martin Luther King and John F. Kennedy hanging above it. Without thinking, I had opened the drawers in his bureau, looking for a handkerchief to stop the blood running down my face from my cut cheek.

In the bottom right drawer was a yellow legal pad with "STORIES" printed on the front. I started to slowly flip through the pages. On each page was a caption in block print. "Annie," "Mr. Van," "Mr. Henry," "Alabama," "Mama." And other names: "Audrey," Bessie," "Maureen," "Big Bugger," "Lizzie," "George." Each had a one-page explanation of who they were, approximate dates they were born and died, and a list of good and bad traits. Halfway through the tablet, the pages became blank, but I kept flipping, faster, driven to find something of Catfish I needed.

On the very last page, "Suzanah," was printed at the top.

I sat on the edge of his small bed and read the words made of painstaking letters that squiggled and curved and dropped below the lines. I knew this was his last attempt at writing and that his aged hands strained to form the sentences.

Suzanah,

I tried to make some more stories for you so when you come back I can remember what to tell you. I know you gonna come back. I hope these help your book.

I missed you while you been up North at school.

Love, Cat.

I remember holding the tablet to my chest and wrapping both arms around it and myself. The stories he'd told me and the ones he'd left me to imagine on my own were rich with history and truth that he wanted people to know.

It's difficult to explain how and why I loved Catfish so much. He was gentle, kind, and wise, and had I never known him I would not have understood what a father and grandfather should be; all I had to go on was my dad. I had no grandparents. Through Catfish I learned that the way my dad treated me was not normal or acceptable. It took years for me to understand and it was only through the gentle relationship Catfish offered me and the stories he told me that I came to that realization.

I wished Catfish were here, with his wisdom and subtle, provocative probing that made me think and feel things deep within. I missed him. I missed Tootsie and Marianne and felt disconnected from the people who truly loved me.

I thought about my times with Tootsie on Catfish's porch, especially after the funeral when I ran there for respite after my dad beat me and cut my face open. I'd confronted Tootsie about having an affair with my dad for some twenty- odd years. It struck me how powerless she felt against my dad and all white men.

I felt bad for her; bad for all people who were made to feel powerless because of their race or gender or economic station. I had felt powerless against my dad from the time I was a little girl. He was a bully and his emotional and physical abuse had made me cower and feel afraid all the time.

I told Tootsie she needed to stop seeing my dad.

"I know." Tootsie didn't look at me when we talked about my dad. "I tole him so many times to stop coming around, but he wait a month or so, and start up again. I'm afraid of him. I see what he do to you."

Tootsie had been my family's housekeeper since I'd been about three or four months old. My mother called her *the help,* which seemed demeaning and certainly didn't describe what she was to our family. She had raised me, loved me, and nurtured me more than my own mother, and I adored her even though Tootsie and my dad had been having an affair for years.

My dad, Bob Burton—former mayor, former state senator! And the help! And Marianne was a product of that clandestine relationship, only my dad ignored her completely.

Rodney had explained to me that colored women had been taken advantage of by white men for centuries and that these women were powerless to turn them down. I felt both anger and pity for Tootsie. I felt only anger for my dad.

*

We sat and rocked for a while. Tootsie's brothers, Tom and Sam, and her sister's husband, Bo were sitting on the same chairs where the men who roasted the pig at Catfish's funeral had sat that day. Now that everyone was gone and darkness set in, the men watched a barbecue grill made from a big barrel that someone had welded iron legs onto. Many of the younger children ran and played in the yard while some were in the cane fields and a few watched TV inside Tootsie's cabin.

"Sitting here with the family all around makes me miss my daddy," Tootsie said, as if talking to herself.

"I miss Catfish, too." I was staring at the pipe on the side of the bar-b-que barrel. No smoke was coming out, but the men were gathered around it as though they had a full meal over the coals inside. They seemed to be reminiscing about Catfish, too.

"He was something, Catfish was. A good daddy. You know he never lifted a hand to any of us. Now Mama, she would switch us with those stinging branches off the pecan trees, but Daddy, no, he never raised his voice or his hand." Tootsie was rocking slowly and I could tell she was thinking about something. I waited until she was ready to talk.

"Did he ever tell you how he got his name, 'Catfish'? It's kinda funny." Tootsie chuckled and rocked, her eyes almost closed as if dreaming.

Catfish: by Tootsie
Told in 1974

First time his daddy take him fishing he was about two, and Sam was maybe five. They went to the coulée, over by that little airstrip, but the airport wasn't there then. Catfish's daddy put a worm on a hook and handed Daddy the pole while he baited his own hook and one for Sam. Catfish's cork went under before the other two had they lines in the water and he took to screaming. Daddy dropped the pole and started to run. My granddaddy grabbed the pole just as it was about to get pulled in the water while Sam run after Catfish.

Granddaddy fought with that fish for a while and finally pulled him on the bank and, don't you know, it was a big ole mudfish—one of those bottom feeders that look like a catfish but no white person would eat one of those. They taste like mud and no telling what those fish eat at the bottom of the river.

Granddaddy wanted to throw that fish back in the water but my daddy took to crying and begging his daddy not to throw it back.

"We only keep what we can eat," his daddy say.

"I'll eat it," Catfish say. He was crying and carrying on. So his daddy say okay and put that ole mudfish in the bucket. While Sam and they daddy fished, my daddy tended that mudfish. He went dug up some worms and put them in that water. He put some leaves in there. He added fresh water ever now and then. Later that day when they walked home they had a string of perch in one bucket and that ole mudfish in the other. By then the mudfish was Catfish's pet fish and he named him "Cat." My granddaddy and Sam thought that was so funny, but it weren't funny when Granddaddy took a hammer to the head of that ole

fish and kilt it so he could skin it, because my daddy had promised he would eat it.

Catfish cried and cried when his daddy kilt that ole mudfish, and Sam laughed and laughed and started teasing my daddy and saying, "Daddy killed Cat. Daddy killed Cat." And my daddy just kept on crying. Then his daddy say, "Look, son, it was nothing but an ole mudfish."

"No it weren't," my daddy say. "It was a catfish, and his name was Cat." Well Sam thought that was so funny and he took to teasing my daddy and calling him "Catfish." That nickname didn't really set in at first, but what happened was, after that day, my daddy was determined to catch another mudfish like the one he named Cat; so he'd beg his daddy to take him fishing ever day.

Every time they went fishing he'd say, "I'm gonna catch me a catfish." By the time he was six or seven, his daddy would let him go fishing with Sam and the two of them would compete for who could catch a catfish. And my daddy, he always caught one or two of them ole mudfish, but Sam, he'd catch perches and breams, and the kind of fish good to eat. But all my daddy wanted to catch was a catfish.

When they'd come back from fishing Sam would tease him and call him, Catfish; and soon, everyone started calling him that. To the day he died my daddy love to eat him some fried catfish; and he don't care, mudfish or catfish, he would eat it all the same, dipped in batter and fried golden. And you couldn't tell the difference when my daddy cooked them fish. They all delicious.

Tootsie took a deep breath and stopped rocking. She looked out at the pecan grove as if she could see Catfish picking pecans with his grandchildren. Tears ran down her face, unchecked. I thought about Catfish, too and gave us both quiet space to grieve in silence. Finally, she started to talk again

On Sundays after church, my daddy would go fishing while the others was in Sunday school, 'cause he didn't have to go since he went to school during the week. One day he set his bucket upside down on the bank of the river and flung his line in the water and, fore you knew it, he was tangled up. He look around the big oak tree where he was sitting and there was a girl holding a cane pole and she was just a'cussing because she was tangled up with something. When they started to pull on they lines, they realized they was tangled with each other.

They put they poles on the bank and pulled on the lines 'til they came up entwined together and there was a little catfish on one of the hooks. Because they were so tangled, it was hard to say whose hook the fish was caught on so my daddy, being the gentleman he was, say that it was hers, and he would take it off the hook for her if she'd tell him her name.

"Alabama," she say. Well, Catfish thought she was pulling his leg.

"No, I said your name."

"Alabama."

"That's the name of a state, not a person."

"Well, it's the name of this person." Now she was mad and she say she would have stormed off except her fishing line was tangled with his and she wasn't going home without her fishing pole. By the time they got untangled they was almost friends.

"What's your name," Alabama asked my daddy.

"Catfish," he say.

"That ain't no name. That's a fish. What's your real name?"

"Name is Catfish. That's what everybody call me."

"I ain't calling no growed man 'Catfish' so if you want me to talk to you again, you need to tell me your given name."

"Given name, Peter. Peter Massey. But no one calls me that, and I don't answer to it because it reminds me of a rabbit and I'd rather be a fish." My daddy was serious, but Alabama, she took to laughing and couldn't stop. At first that made Catfish mad, but then he saw the fun in

it and he start laughing, too. Soon the two of them is laughing and joking and carrying on and it wasn't three weeks later they was shacking up in the spare cabin at the end of the row and talking about getting married.

The way I hear tell, they got married when mama was expecting Sam. Then it went from there. And they was always just perfect together. Mama had a big mouth and would gossip and tell stories and she talked real loud. Daddy, he was quiet and he never tole nothing on no one. And he was so gentle, where Mama, she could be fierce.

Yeah, I was blessed with a good mama and daddy and I wish they was still here.

I watched Tootsie rock and stare at the sun setting in fingers of gold and pink over the top of the cane fields, and knew she didn't realize she had just told me that story.

*

I sat at my desk and reread the story Tootsie had told me and tried not to think about losing Rodney.

The stress got the best of me. I went days without eating. I couldn't sleep but a couple of hours without waking up in a sweat, having nightmares, screaming in my dreams.

I'd been back in New York for three weeks and had to be out of the graduate students' apartment before the first of July, ten days. I felt pressure pulling me both ways—out of the life I'd been in, but afraid to go into my new life without Rodney.

After not hearing from him for more than two weeks, the phone rang one evening just as I walked in the door. I dropped everything—my purse, groceries, apartment pamphlets—and ran to the phone without closing the door. The outside heat followed me in as I bolted for the receiver on the wall just inside the kitchen.

"Hello," I breathed heavily into the phone. "Rod, is that you?"

"Susanna? Is this Susanna Burton?" It was a familiar male voice, but not Rodney's. I couldn't breathe. I slid down to the floor with my back against the wall, legs flayed out in front of me.

"Yes. This is Susie Burton."

"This is Ray Thibault, Rod..."

"Yes, sir. I know who you are. Is Rodney okay?"

"Well, that's why I'm calling you. I thought maybe you could answer that question. He told me he would be calling you regularly and that I could check with you to find out..."

"I got a short letter. It was written last week. Do you want me to read it to you?"

"Please." Ray Thibault was breathing a stressful sort of breath. I read the letter to him, every word.

Dead silence. Neither of us could talk. It seemed he knew something I didn't, but wouldn't tell me.

I heard a dial tone. I don't know how long I sat there unable to move. Later, after I had picked up the broken eggs and shattered mayonnaise off the floor and hung up the receiver, I thought about calling Mr. Thibault back. But I couldn't bring myself to do it because if I found out Rodney was gone, I'd have to stop hoping— and hope was all I had left, all I'd ever had when it came to Rodney Thibault.

Another week passed, a month since we'd parted at the Baton Rouge airport. I had to move out of my apartment.

I found a place on 179th Street near Utopia Park. It was shady, had lots of sidewalks for walking, and I knew the area. The apartment itself was a one bedroom, but twice the size of the one I'd lived in for three years at the university.

I finished packing and arranged for a couple of friends with pickup trucks to help transport my things to the new place. I went to the university post office and filled out a form to transfer my mail to my new post office address near Utopia Parkway. I couldn't give my physical address to anyone. I was afraid.

I shopped for a bed and a sofa, and scheduled delivery.

I lost weight and my skin broke out in hives. I itched all over and had an insatiable thirst. I was not well.

~ Chapter Four ~

~

The Job

O NCE I WAS SETTLED in my new place and had a new phone number, I called Marianne. I couldn't stand to wait any longer for news about Rodney. Mari told me that Jeffrey was still in a coma and that the doctors didn't know whether he'd ever come out of it. She said they had no news about Rodney.

I hung up and paced my new apartment, boxes everywhere that needed unpacking. I'd slept on my new mattress for two nights without putting sheets on it.

Meanwhile, I needed a job. My savings wouldn't hold out forever. I had no choice but to talk to Merrick Harper and enlist his help. We met for coffee the morning after I moved.

"There's a lot you don't know about me, Merrick," I started. He didn't say anything, just looked at me with longing. "And there's lots I don't know about you. And we can keep it that way. But I need your help."

"Susie. You know I'll do anything for you."

"I have to be honest with you. This is not about us seeing each other again. It's about you helping me get a job. And it's about you helping me keep my whereabouts secret."

"You talk like you're in trouble." There was fatherly concern in his voice.

"I'm okay, I think. I've moved out of my apartment and have a new place, but no one knows where I live, and no one can find out, except for, well…"

"Okay. So how can I help?"

"Rodney, that's his name. The man I'm going to marry. Anyway, he knows your name. I've told him about you, that you were my department head and friend. When he gets to New York and he can't find me, I think he'll find you."

"So you trust me? You're going to give me your address and trust me?"

"I have to trust you, Merrick. I don't have anyone else." I started to cry. "When I say no one else can know my address, I mean, *no one*. That includes my parents, siblings, friends. No one. Can you do that for me?" I was desperate or I wouldn't have gone to him.

I tried to explain to Merrick that my dad was against my relationship with Rodney and might come looking for me. Merrick was—well, he was surprised, to say the least. He kept staring at me, blinking every now and then as if he could change the picture. But he was kind and, in the end, although he didn't truly understand, he agreed to help me.

"I love you, Susie. You know that."

"You can't love two people."

"Yes you can. You'll understand when you have children, that you don't stop loving one of them when another one comes along." I thought about that, and I thought about the little girl I had given birth to—whose name I didn't know. And I thought about how much I loved Rodney.

"But that doesn't pertain to loving two women, or two men."

"You can't understand," he said. He looked sad, but accepting.

I went back to my apartment, aware that I needed to be careful. All the years I'd lived in New York I'd felt hidden among the masses. Suddenly I no longer felt safe.

Merrick called to set up a meeting for me with the president of Shilling House Publishing, the company that had published the two textbooks he'd written. It wasn't my dream job—I wanted to work with a company that published novels and memoirs—but I needed a job.

The company was on Manton Street in the Jamaica area, just south of St. John's University, and, on a nice day I could walk there from my new place or take the subway. They hired me right away.

I wanted to be a writer and I dreamed of having a publisher fall in love with the Catfish stories. As bereft as I was, I continued to work on them because I think those stories and my connection to Catfish were my sanity during insane times.

Catfish had been particularly interested in the Vans—white folks who owned Shadowland Plantation. His dad felt beholden to Mr. Gordon Van who had been kind and generous to the Masseys.

I could still picture Catfish, the last time I sat on his porch and he rocked back and forth in that old rocking chair, his eyes half-closed against the bright sunlight, with several of his grandchildren jumping rope and chasing chickens in the dusty yard. In my mind, his voice was as fresh as if I were still sitting next to him in the straight-backed chair with the torn green Naugahyde seat.

The stories about Mr. Gordon resonated with me because, although he owned slaves, he was kind to them and treated them like human beings, not like chattel. One of the stories I couldn't get off my mind was one Catfish told me about how white men on the plantation abused the slaves until the Mr. Gordon took over after his father, Mr. Shelton Van, died. I wondered how much had really changed. As recently as a few weeks ago, more than one hundred years since the end of slavery, white men tried to kill Jeffrey and chase Rodney like hunted animals, simply because they were colored and Rodney loved a white girl.

Catfish had rocked back and forth and told the story as though he had a small audience sitting around him, animated but serious.

New Plantation Owner
1855
It was about 1855 and Mr. Gordon Van was, maybe 35, and he'd been living the life of a wealthy bachelor. He'd finished college in some highfalutin place called Harvard and gone on to a school called Oxford, in England, to study poetry and such. He didn't want to come back to South Louisiana to run a plantation, but he didn't have no choice after his daddy died suddenly—seeing as how he just had one sister and she was married and living in North Louisiana on her husband's plantation. So, Mr. Gordon Van, he made the best of it.

Mr. Gordon Van was a tall man with long legs and arms, dignified and masculine, handsome with blonde hair, blue eyes, and high cheekbones with indentions below them. A cleft chin jutted from under wide, thin lips that were quick to smile and show straight, white teeth. His stature demanded respect and spoke volumes about his status, yet he was thoughtful and gentle, a man who seemed different than most plantation owners in South Louisiana. His time up North and in Europe taught him a great deal about tolerance and humanity. He had difficulty understanding slavery in the Deep South. It went against his nature.

According to my granddaddy and daddy, Mr. Gordon was kind and generous, but he was also a shrewd businessman. He saw flaws in the men who ran his plantation.

"What are you doing?" he asked Buckley, the overseer, one afternoon when he saw him whipping up on a slave in the field.

"I'm just letting this nigger know who's boss here!" Buckley said without turning to look at Mr. Van.

"Put that whip down!" Mr. Van tole ole Buckley, but Sherman Buckley kept on striking the slave, his shirt already in shreds.

"I said stop!" Mr. Van jumped from his horse and grabbed Buckley's wrist as he slung it back to strike another blow. "We don't whip our slaves!" He took the whip from the foreman.

"What?" Sherman turned towards Mr. Van and reached for his whip. Mr. Van held it up and away.

"I said!" Van screamed, distinct and loud. "We will not whip our slaves!"

"You going to have trouble unless you show these niggers who's boss." Buckley's face was red and he was fiery mad.

"Get on your horse, round up the other men and meet me at the house!" Van swung his leg over the sorrel's saddle and was about to take off towards the plantation house when he noticed the slave who was whipped, bent over a cotton plant. In fact all the slaves was still picking the sharp, white bulbs as if nothing had just happened to one of their own. The one who was whipped kept on picking, too, like he weren't bleeding half to death, his raw skin exposed to the hot sun, his shirt almost gone.

Van swung his leg around the back of the saddle and dismounted. He noticed all of them tense black backs stiffen up as he walked towards them. Not one of them stopped their work when Mr. Van approached the man whose wounds were already forming blisters. Mr. Van knelt on one knee next to the man.

"Son," Mr. Van said, "please stop what you are doing and look at me."

"Yessir." The slave's hands fell by his side, one holding the burlap sack half-filled with cotton. He turned his head towards the plantation owner, but cast his eyes down at the dirt like slaves was supposed to do.

"Look at me," Mr. Van said soft-like. The man kept his head down but lifted his eyelashes just enough to see Mr. Van's tie, knotted at his collar. He reached out with two fingers and lifted the slave man's chin until they could look each other eye-to-eye. The man tried to lower his gaze, but Mr. Van lifted his chin higher.

"What's your name, Son?"

"I be called, Tom, sir."

"Tom, I'm Gordon Van, Master Shelton's son, and I recently inherited this plantation from my father." The other slaves kept on picking cotton, but they ears was opened to what Mr. Van said to Tom. "I'm sorry about what just happened. Buckley was out of line. It won't happen again. If it does, I invite you to come to my house and inform me. I want to know if my men do not follow my new rules."

"Yessir." Tom tried to cast his eyes down again but Mr. Van lifted his chin higher still.

"You have a wife, Tom?"

"Yessir, Mr. Van, sir."

"Where is she?"

"That's my Harriet over there, sir." Tom pointed at a young woman on the other side of the row. She was still picking, her kerchief-wrapped head bent to her knees. She didn't look up.

"Tom, I want you and Harriet to stop picking cotton and go back to your cabin where she can clean those wounds. I'll send one of my house girls with some salve and gauze; we don't want you infected. And don't come back to the fields today, you hear?"

"Yes, sir." Tom said. "Thank you, sir, but we got our limit to pick today. We can't go taking no time out the fields."

"You do as I say, let me worry about your limits, okay?"

"I mean no disrespect, sir, but I scared to do that, sir."

"The only person you need to fear on this plantation is me, do you understand? And I say go home and get those cuts tended to." Van took his hand from Tom's chin and put it under his sweaty arm pit. The stench of body sweat mixed with dust-turned-to-mud that ran down the slave's face was almost unbearable to the white man, but he hid his disgust. As Van stood, he lifted Tom to his feet, their faces inches apart, Tom's eyes cast towards the dirt under his worn-out shoes. With his arm *still under Tom's, the plantation owner turned towards the field workers and made an announcement.*

"Things will be different here. It is my intention to see that all of you are well fed, have rest time, and are not punished with violence. You have my word." With that, Van handed Tom to Harriet and instructed her to give him a bath in the tub near the cistern before she took him to their cabin.

"Lizzie will bring you supplies, Harriet," he said. "Your job is to take care of your man." He turned, mounted his horse, and galloped towards the house.

The five hired hands were gathered near the back porch of the house when Van rode up. Some smoked, some spit tobacco, they all talked and laughed. They acted like they didn't notice Mr. Van arrive. He stayed on his horse and cleared his throat. All but the youngest ignored him.

"Wait here," Van said as he dismounted. He went through the back door of the house and called for Lizzie. A few minutes later, he stormed back down the steps, two at a time, and in three strides was standing in front of the men. They were chatting, laughing, spitting, and ignoring Mr. Van, all except one.

"What's your name, Son," Mr. Van asked the young man whose attention he had.

"William, sir. William Henley," the boy said.

"How old are you, William Henley?"

"I'm twenty-two, sir," he said. The other hands listened but were chattering among themselves as if Van wasn't there.

"How long have you worked here, Son?" Mr. Van asked.

"Two years, sir."

"And what do you do here?"

"Whatever Mr. Buckley tells me to do, sir."

"And what sorts of things does Mr. Buckley tell you to do, William Henley?"

"Well, sir, I ride the fields to see which slaves are picking and who is sloughing off. I keep track of sacks that look to be near full so I can send a wagon to pick up the full sacks and give the niggers empty ones. I count heads to make sure all the slaves are working like they should and see to it they only take ten minutes for dinner and get two scoops of water every day, one mid morning and one mid afternoon."

"Sounds like you stay busy, William."

"Yes, sir, Mr. Van," he said.

"If you do all of that, William, tell me this: What does Mr. Buckley do?"

"Why, I don't rightly know, sir." William looked confused. "I just take my orders and do as I'm tole. I don't stay around to see what the others do."

"Thank you for your honesty, Son," Van said. "Now if you will humor me a moment." Van turned towards the four other hands who were now interested in the conversation, but didn't look at Van. They shuffled their boots in the dirt, spit tobacco, lit cigarettes, and generally tried to look busy.

"Buckley!" Van said. Buckley ignored Van. "Buckley, I'm talking to you!" Buckley was half-turned away from Van. He looked over his shoulder at the plantation owner but didn't turn his body.

"You're fired, Buckley," Van said. "Get on your horse and get off my property. NOW! And take these three no-accounts with you!"

"You can't do that!" Buckley yelled.

"I just did," Mr. Van said. "Now leave, all of you. Get off my plantation and don't come back." The men shuffled their feet in the dirt and waited for Buckley to tell them what to do.

"Don't look at Buckley, you idiots. I'm the boss. He's nothing. He's fired and so are the rest of you. GET OUT! NOW!"

Mr. Van held the whip Buckley used on Tom. He lashed it out and it made a loud snap in the air.

"The next time I swing this thing it will hit one of you," Van said. "Now, get off my property!" Buckley reached for his pistol, but Van was too quick for him. He cracked the whip and caught Buckley's wrist, pulling it way from his body so hard that Buckley fell on his face in the dirt. His gun flew towards Van, who grabbed the gun and pointed it at Buckley in one motion.

"Someone's deaf!" Van shouted. "I said, 'GET OFF MY PLANTATION!' The next hit will be from a bullet, not a whip."

The three hands ran towards their horses. No one tried to help Buckley out of the dirt. Van stood over him until he got on all-fours and tried to stand up.

"I should kick the shit out of you right now, you disrespectful piece of crap. Get up and get out. And before you ask, the answer is 'No!' Someone pulls a gun on me, it becomes my gun." Van turned towards William and said, "Son, I want you to get on your horse, ride it around to the front of the house where you can tie him up to the hitching post and sit in one of those rockers on the porch until I get there. I'm going to escort Mr. Buckley off my property."

"Yes, sir, Mr. Van, sir." William mounted his pony and walked the horse around, out of sight.

Van remounted the sorrel while Buckley untied his horse from the post. Reins in hand, he guided the mare down the long, tree-lined drive to South Jefferson Street Extension. Without a word, Buckley mounted his horse and galloped towards Jean Ville.

When Van returned to the front of the plantation house, William's stiff frame sat in a rocker that could have been a straight-backed chair for all the rocking it was doing. Mr. Van held back a chuckle, hitched his Sorrel loosely to the post and mounted the twenty steps, two at a time.

"Come inside, Son," Van said. He opened the front door and William followed him into a huge hall, about sixteen to eighteen feet wide that ran the entire length of the house. The ceilings were high and the curved staircase climbed up to a railed landing with more high

ceilings; the result was an entrance that reached at least thirty feet in the air. The plantation hand glanced down the long hall and could see out towards the fields through the glass on the back door at the end. Several huge doors about twelve feet high flanked both sides of the hall and obviously led to grand rooms. William tried not to gasp.

Mr. Van led William through the first door on the left and into a large room with a huge mahogany desk in the center, a lush sofa against the wall and two wing-backed chairs that encircled a low iron-and-glass table atop a thick rug. Two tall, wine-colored leather chairs sat in front of the desk and a massive brown one was behind it. Van rang a bell, then pointed to one of the wine-colored chairs that faced the desk and tole William to take a seat, while Mr. Van strode around to the back of the desk and sat in what was, obviously, his throne.

"Will you have coffee or tea, or something stronger, William?" Van asked when Lizzie entered the study.

"Nothing for me, thank you, sir," William said. Lizzie was out of breath, smoothing her dark hair that she wore in a bun at the nape of her neck.

"Did you get Tom and Harriet taken care of, Lizzie?"

"Yes, sir. I just got back."

"Thank you. Now, would you please bring us a pot of coffee, two cups, and some biscuits or cakes from the kitchen?"

"Yes, sir." The pretty, young house girl left the room as quietly as she entered it.

"I think I'm a good judge of character, William." Van wasted no time getting to the point. William was confused, but he sat at attention.

"I've only been back a month or so and I was not prepared for this plantation and all that goes with it. I spent most of my young life at boarding schools up north and in Europe after my mother died. I didn't pay much attention to the business side of things here at Shadowland. Who knew my dad would die in his fifties?" Van looked out of the front window and scratched his freshly shaved chin. You could tell he was *thinking about what had led him to this point in his life. He looked back at William.*

"I have a lot more to learn, but I did go to college and can do the math. We have fifteen slaves and five hired hands. That seems like overkill to me. Three slaves for every hand. It's my opinion that we could operate this business with one overseer and one livestock hand. What do you think, William?"

"Well, I don't know, sir," William was caught off-guard, and Mr. Van noticed the young man's discomfort.

"What does an overseer do here?" Van asked.

"He tells someone like me what to do."

"Right, but does he do anything himself, or does he just tell someone else to do it for him?" Van asked. William stammered. "Let me ask it this way: when you come to work in the morning, do you report to Buckley and ask him what you should do that day, is it different every day? Or do you show up and do the same thing you did the day before?"

"Well, sir," William said. "At first he tole me what to do, then, when I'd ask, he'd say, 'You know what to do. Do I have to tell you every day?'"

"What did the other hands do?" Van asked.

"Not sure, sir," William said. "They whittled handles, braided ropes, and attached leather strips to make whips. They went to town for supplies. They rode through the fields sometimes to use their whips on the slaves; there was a contest about who could draw first blood, and that determined the best whip."

"Who tends the livestock? Feeds and waters, milks the cows, walks and brushes the horses, keeps the barn clean, keeps the tack oiled and ready for use?"

"Why, I think George does all that, sir," William said.

"George? Who's George?"

"George is one of the slaves. He's real good with the stock, so he takes care of pretty much everything in the barn."

"A slave cares for my livestock?" Van asked.

"Yes, sir, as far as I know," William said

"Where can I find George?"

"I'm sure he's in the barn, sir."

Lizzie came in with a tray of coffee and some cakes and set it on the table in front of the sofa. Mr. Van took his watch out his pocket.

"What do you say we go to the barn and meet George, William?"

"Yes, sir."

Mr. Van's strides were long and determined. The two men, one following the other, approached the barn, about 200 yards from the cookhouse—a stone building behind the main house with a huge chimney and double iron doors on the front.

They found George setting buckets of oats in the horse stalls. Finely oiled tack hung from the rack on the wall before the first stall. On the other wall were five horizontal poles on notched hangers; each held a folded blanket. Saddles were neatly arranged on a stack of saddle racks someone had crafted from wood and iron. Fresh hay covered the floors of all eight stalls and the air smelled of leather and oil and fresh hay. Between the stalls was a hallway of sorts that ran from the front to the back of the barn. It had a dirt floor that had recently been swept and leveled, with no ruts, mud, or dung anywhere.

"Are you George?" Van asked the man, who froze with a bucket in each hand.

"Yes, sir," he said. He looked at his feet. He was so dark-skinned that the whites of his eyes gleamed in the semi-dark barn. He wore a short-brimmed straw hat pulled down to the top of his large ears, fanned out from the pressure of the too-big hat.

"I'm Gordon Van, the new plantation owner. I'm sure you heard that my father died and his son inherited the place."

"Yes, sir," George said. He continued to stare at the dirt floor.

"Put those buckets down, George, and look at me," Van said. George set the buckets on the dirt, took off his hat, and stood as straight as he

was able; a small hunch in his upper back kept him bent forward a few inches. His feet shuffled softly in the dirt and his head revealed a bald spot in its infancy, surrounded by short, nappy hair.

"Please look at me, George." George lifted his eyes to reveal black pupils with yellowish irises. His nose was wide, almost as wide as his mouth, which showed huge, pouty, red lips. A shhhhsh-ing sound emerged softly from somewhere between the two over-sized facial orifices as he tried to hide his fear. He was almost chinless and his wide neck was non-existent where it connected his head to his shoulders. He was short, maybe five and-a-half feet, but he stood tall and proud and his demeanor was pleasant, almost amusing.

"I understand you take care of the livestock on this plantation, is that right, George?"

"Yes, sir. I try, sir, but if I'm not doing something right, I can do better, sir."

"Oh, you're doing fine." Van said. "I have a few questions for you, George." George stared over Van's shoulder and stood still. Fear mounted and red splotches appeared on his short neck.

"Tell me George, what did Buckley and his hands do around here?"

"I'm not sure, sir."

"Did you see those men every day?"

"Yessir."

"Did they talk to you, give you orders? Tell me what your experience with them was like, George."

"Well, sir," George stammered. "They come in every morning and tell me to tend they's horses, wash them down, feed and water 'em and have 'em ready to ride if they need."

"What else, George?"

"Well, sir, I don't know what else."

"The men are gone, so don't worry about what they might do to you. I fired them; all but William, here, and I need to make a decision about him. Can you help me, George?"

"I'll help you anyways I can, sir."

"Then tell me what the men did to you, said to you, tole you to do—everything. William, come here." William walked to Van's side and stood still. George looked from one to the other.

"Would you feel more comfortable talking about Buckley and his men if William was not here, George?"

"No, sir. Mr. William, he a good man. He never whip me or yell at me or nothing like that. It's just that he has to do what Mr. Buckley say."

"Not anymore, George. William has to do what I say. And if he tells you to do something that doesn't sound like it comes from me, you need to tell me."

"I don't know what you mean, sir." George looked confused.

"Let me be clear. I still have a lot to learn about this plantation, but I've discovered some things I want to change now. First of all, no one will whip my slaves. No one will mistreat them, curse them, call them names, or make them work beyond their capabilities. Do you understand that, George?"

"Yes, sir, Mr. Van, sir."

"So if William, or any other white man or woman on this plantation does any of those things, you know they are against my orders, right?"

"Well, Mr. Van, I guess so, sir."

"There's no guessing, George. Now, tell me what I would NOT tell someone to do to you."

"Beat or curse me or call me 'Nigger' or 'Boy', or tell me to do something that's not my job, sir."

"That's right. Do you know what the word 'demeaning' means?"

"No, sir."

"It means when someone does something to make you look and feel low, such as, if someone ordered you to eat dirt, or crawl on all-fours, or pushed your head under water and held it until you choked. It also *means when someone points a gun at you or threatens you with a whip. Do you understand, George?"*

"Yes, sir, Mr. Van," George stammered. "I guess so, sir."

"Take you shirt off, George."

"Sir?"

"Just take your shirt off," Van said. "This is not meant to demean you; I want to look at your back."

George pulled his shirt over his head. Two long red scars ran across his chest in a big "X."

"Turn around, George." His back was layered with scars; the freshest ones still bulged and oozed pus and a watery red liquid. "You can put your shirt back on." George slipped back into the stained, off-white shirt.

"William, where do we store clothing for our slaves?"

"I think it's here in the tack room, right, George?" William asked.

"Yes, sir, Mr. William. I can show you if you want," George said.

He moved towards the door in the back of the barn next to the last stall on the right. The two white men followed him. George opened the door and they all went in. It was a big room with deep shelves and hooks on the sidewalls that held bridles, ropes, horseshoes, stirrups, and spare leather parts, all neat and clean. On the shelves were boxes, stacks of blankets, and lots of stuff like tobacco, cigarette papers, pipes, bottles of whiskey, jerky, all sorts of food, drinks and smokes.

George grabbed a wooden bench and dragged it to the shelves. He climbed on it, pulled a box off the upper shelf, and let it fall in his arms. He stepped off the bench and placed the box where his feet had been.

"They's in here." George patted the box.

Van reached into his front, right pocket and pulled out a switchblade knife. He cut through the tape on top of the box and ripped it open. A folded stack of thin, off-white muslin was crammed into the cardboard container. Van lifted the first piece of muslin out of the box and let it fall from its folds. It had a drawstring around the neck and long, loose sleeves that, along with the bottom of the shirt, were not hemmed. Van put the shirt on the bench and shuffled through the box until he found a pair of pants, also un-hemmed, also with a drawstring around the waist.

"What do we give the women to wear?" Van asked. He stared into the box and directed his question at no one.

"The men and women all get the same clothes, twice a year," William said.

"I see the women in skirts in the fields," Van said. "Where do they get skirts?" He turned to look at the two men who faced him. Neither answered. "George?"

"Well, sir. My wife, Audrey, she use what she can find to make her skirt. Sometime we find an old shirt your daddy throw in the trash. Sometime the Missus throw away some curtains to get new ones or a sheet or blanket and Bessie and Maureen divides it up with the womens."

"We need to change some things; lots of things. I'm going to need your help, George, to talk to the others and tell them about the new rules. You are going to help William learn where to order clothing and other items the slaves need. No, not slaves. We'll call them workers, until I can come up with a better term." Van turned and looked directly into George's bright eyes.

"Tomorrow I want to tour the Quarters and the fields. George, you will come with me and William and show us the Quarters. William will take me on a tour of the fields. I'll see you in the morning, George." Van turned around. "Come with me, William." William hurried to follow Van.

"Next stop, the cookhouse," Van said to William. "Then back to my study. Just stay with me, Son."

"Yes, sir."

Van and William entered the cookhouse where Van interrogated Bessie about meals for the slaves, what she fed them, how often, how much, and how she felt about their meals. He tole her that there was no reason to prepare separate meals. Whatever she cooked for the workers she could feed him.

The two men went in the back door of the plantation house and Mr. Van stopped Maureen in the hall to ask her about other provisions for the workers, fabrics for the women, linens for their beds, and other household needs, especially for the women and children. When Van and William entered the study, they sat across from each other in the wing-backed chairs, the tray of refreshments on the table between them. Van felt the pot; it was still hot. He poured them each a cup of coffee that they both doctored with cream and sugar, then they attacked the cakes. It had been a long day and the sun was about to disappear behind the trees.

"Today has been a real eye-opener for me, William. I have a lot more to learn but I need to make decisions along the way and not wait until I know everything to change things. How much do I pay you?"

"I make $25 a month, sir."

"I'm going to double that. I want you to be my right-hand man. How does that sound, son?"

"That sounds real good, Mr. Van. You tell me what you want me to do. I follow orders real good!"

"Let's begin with philosophy." William's mouth fell open; he was out of his league. Philosophy?

"It's a big word, but it has a simple meaning," Van said. "We have to believe the same things, or you have to learn to believe what I do. The most important thing I believe is that we are all God's children, white, black, poor, rich, and we all deserve a decent life. Just because my life was handed to me doesn't mean I don't have to work hard to keep it, build it, make it better. Just like you have to work hard to make your life better. Slaves are no different in that way."

"And if you can't believe that, William, believe this: if we don't treat our slaves in a humane fashion—feed them well, clothe them properly, give them time to rest with plenty of water for hydration, they

will get sick and even die. Then what do we have? Do you understand what I'm trying to tell you, William?"

"Yes, sir, Mr. Van," William said. Silence filled the air until he added, "No disrespect, sir, and I don't mean to talk out of turn, but I never whipped a slave. Mr. Buckley ordered me to do it many times but he would ride off and expect that I'd carry out his orders. I didn't do it, sir. I couldn't."

"Explain that to me, William. Why couldn't you whip a slave?"

"Well, sir, I believe the Bible. It says to treat the least of men like we would treat Jesus. Slaves are the least of men, ain't that right, sir?"

"That's close enough, William." A silence hovered above the men as they both considered the words that hung between them. "We both have lots to learn and we'll learn it together. You and I will turn this place around and make a profit; and when we do, you'll get a bonus."

William didn't respond, he simply stared at his boss and wondered what was coming next. He was probably thinking about that raise, double salary, and not having to answer to Buckley any longer.

"What say we have something a little stronger, William?" Mr. Van walked to the back of his desk, pulled out the bottom drawer, and produced a bottle of fine bourbon whiskey. He lifted two crystal glasses from the drawer and set it all on the desk. After he poured the brown liquid in the glasses, he walked back to the tray of refreshments and handed one to William.

Mr. Van sat back down in the facing chair, the men lifted their glasses, nodded, and turned them up so the bourbon slid down their throats in one fiery gulp.

The story of Mr. Van gave me hope that there might be someone, somewhere, who would help Rodney, even though I knew the South was full of people like Buckley and his men.

I stopped at the post office on Utopia on my way home from work every afternoon during my first week at Shilling Publishing.

Each day the box was empty, until Friday, when I saw a letter through the three-inch section of smoky glass, "204" stamped in white across it. I tried to insert my key in the hole above the glass and fumbled around until it finally slid in and I turned it to the left. The latch gave way and I pulled the door opened with my key. I took out the white envelope with my name and address scrawled across the front. No return address, just a sticker that said the letter had been forwarded from my address on campus.

The postmark was eight days prior. My hands shook as I closed the door to my mailbox and walked to the tall table in the corner where customers addressed and stamped letters and packages. People came in and out of the main door, bringing with them gusts of hot air and the smell of gasoline and dirty socks. I couldn't get the letter opened and ended up tearing the envelope in three pieces. I unfolded four sheets of ruled pages, torn from a composition book, written on front and back.

I stuffed the letter and torn envelope in my purse and rushed out of the post office and almost ran the rest of the way to my apartment, six long blocks. I flopped into my big, overstuffed chair in the corner of the living room and dug the letter out of my purse. I sat with my elbows on my knees, bent forward, Rodney's handwriting almost touching my eyes, to make sure I read every word.

～ Chapter Five ～

Jackson

Jun 17, 2974

Dear Susie,

Where do I start? First, let me say I love you more than anything and I'm praying you will wait for me. I'll be there as soon as I can, but I'm not sure how long that will be.

The people who followed me and my dad to Jackson must have been surprised when I jumped from the car, because they drove up the road a ways before they found a place to turn around. I relied on the cover of darkness for protection until I could lose them.

I was wearing jeans and a white T-shirt, too easy to spot, so I ran across the road and backtracked to a deep ditch in a stand of pine trees, hoping the change of direction would put more time between me and the posse, which is what I called them in my mind. I slid into the ditch, pulled black sweat pants and a long sleeved black T-shirt from my duffle bag and changed clothes, then pulled my black baseball cap low over my eyes. I figured these men would not be tricked easily but I know I can pass for white if I cover my head.

I crept through the trees and jogged to the back of a small shopping strip and made my way to the back of the last store then crossed the street as casually as possible and weaved in and out of small businesses, an open lot, and a warehouse until I reached the train station. I hid behind a big pine tree and counted the men who staked out the parking area. I could make out five of them, spread out, stooped low on the sides of cars and pickup trucks, and peeking around trees. They didn't wear white sheets and dunce hats, but I knew their faces: Toussaint Parish Sheriff Guidry, one of his deputies, and three businessmen from Jean Ville.

Darren Bordelon, who owns the Five and Dime, was chewing tobacco behind a line of tree. I don't know if you remember him, a short squatty man built like a stump, real mean, and ready to fight with whites or coloreds. Always itching for a reason to use his hairy fists on someone's jaw. He'll join any group, the Klan, the White Camellias, or the Dixie Gang when Guidry calls for warriors to seek racial justice. He'll wear any uniform, sheet, or mask and jump in the back of a pickup with his hunting rifle, so it didn't surprise me to see him there.

The Moreau brothers who own the Mobil station on the other side of town hate my dad because he's colored and has a competing gas station. Those two might not join just any vigilante group, but they would certainly agree to ride with the Klan against the Thibault family. None of the Moreaus get along with each other until they have a common cause against some poor Negro who they think has wronged the whites.

Jack Moreau is tall and thin as a reed. From the back, his narrow butt and long thin torso are the opposite of his frontal view, which seems to belong to a different person: a pot belly that hangs over the big, silver cowboy buckle and a huge, wide chest. His brother, Eric, is shorter by a few inches and has no neck. His round shaved head looks like a large ping pong ball sitting on a board, and his squared shoulders give way to short, dangling arms.

The most dangerous of the five men, by far, is Sheriff Guidry. I've never seen his head because it's always covered by a white, felt cowboy hat with a red band around the base and a small feather on one side. I wonder if he sleeps in that hat. Guidry is a big man, not simply in height—you know, he's probably six-feet-five if he's an inch—but also in girth. I'll bet he weighs at least 300 pounds and he always wears starched Levis with sharp creases down the front of the legs and a stiff, white long-sleeved shirt with snaps up the front and on both breast pockets. The pointed toes of his alligator boots peek out from under his jeans that would probably brush the ground in the back if the heels on his boots weren't two inches high. He wasn't wearing his badge that night, I guess because this was personal business, but at home his bright silver "Sheriff" star is always pinned above his left pocket.

I played football against Deputy Keith Rousseau. He was a defensive lineman who sacked me more times than I can count. It was personal for Keith, taking down a colored quarterback in front of an audience. He's a big, hulking, Cajun boy with a beer belly and long brown, shaggy hair that hangs over his eyes. He grins on one side of his mouth and some of his teeth are missing. He's a mean one and he hates coloreds, especially me...

I watched the five of them for a while and wondered how many more there were on this mission. I could almost smell their excitement and perspiration. I wondered who I had not spotted, since they usually travel in pairs. They outnumbered me like a pack of dogs against one rabbit, and had probably planned this attack as thoroughly as a general against the Viet Cong.

How did they know my dad would take me to Jackson? Did they follow me? And if they followed, how did all these men get here ahead of us and take their positions?

I knew none of that mattered; all that mattered was that I outsmart them and stay alive.

I circled around the station and crossed the track, grateful for the tall weeds and the lack of Mississippi pride that would keep the grass down and the trees pruned. One of the few states lower than Louisiana in education, racial progress, and economy is Mississippi. Alabama and Arkansas could probably go toe-to-toe with both states on the racial issue.

I am desperate to get out of the South.

The weeds and bushes on the backside of the tracks provided cover as I worked my way north for about a quarter mile. The train pulled into the station, people got off and got on, and the whistle blew to indicate it was ready to depart for Memphis. When half of the train passed me, I jumped onto the step between two cars and held the side rail until I got my bearings, then I boarded.

Tucker Thevenot was sitting near the window on the right, about halfway down. He's a nasty man from Toussaint Parish who people say does perverted things to children, even his own. He's blond with a thin goatee and mustache that makes his face look dirty. He looked at me as I walked down the aisle as casually and nonchalant as I could with my head down and my cap pulled low to hide my eyes.

I pretended to look for a seat and a place to stash my bags. Just before I reached the back of the car I spotted Antoine Borrel on the last row, sitting near the aisle. You remember Antoine, he was in your graduating class, I think. He's a customer at the Esso station and I've had many conversations with Antoine about football and other sports, both local and national. His dad's a carpenter and they've never treated me like I'm colored so it shocked me that Borrel was part of this witch hunt. I continued down the aisle and stepped out of the back door and into the next car, marked "Colored."

I felt a sense of urgency and went through door that joined the colored car to the caboose. As soon as I emerged between the two cars, the train slowed in a curve and I jumped. I stayed still and quiet in a ravine for ten or fifteen minutes to make sure no one had followed me. A line of trees that ran parallel to the tracks was set back about six yards and I used them for cover as I made my way south to the small town of Richland, about five miles out of Jackson.

I dropped into a convenience store, bought a Coke and asked the colored clerk for directions to the Greyhound bus station. It was only three blocks away. The guys on the train hadn't followed so I felt safe, until I got to the bus station and spotted two familiar faces outside the entrance. Oh, God, I thought, now it's really personal. Your brother James and his friend Earl, "Big Earl" Daigrepont were waiting. James had a pistol tucked inside his belt.

"What?" I screamed and put the letter in my lap. "James? My brother, James was after Rodney with a gun? Oh, God! This is personal." I felt sweat gather in my neck and scalp and had an eerie feeling my dad was behind this whole stakeout that Rodney called a *posse.*

I picked the letter up and read on…

James started running towards me yelling at Big Earl to cut me off. You know, your brother was a running back in high school and he's still tall, slim, wide-shouldered and fast. Didn't he finish LSU Law School last year? Anyway, James is in great shape and he gained on me. I threw my duffle bag at him as if it was a football and it hit him in the face. My loafers and the two books inside the duffle made it heavy and it stopped him for a minute, but it didn't knock him down. He kept coming, but now I had a lead.

Big Earl is a huge, scary-looking fellow with beady eyes and a shaved head, bigger than a beach ball. He isn't fast, just big—very big and strong.

I zigzagged through the area using some of the buildings for protection in an effort to lose James and Earl. I made my way back to the convenience store, since I knew the layout. I ran through the front door, past the colored clerk who barely looked up from the girlie magazine he had on the counter, towards the back hall, past the restrooms, and through a door with a sign that said "Employees only." I peeked out the back door into the parking lot to make sure no one was waiting, then stepped out and started running.

I tripped and fell on the concrete and looked up to see Big Earl standing over me, laughing. Before Earl could grab me, I kicked him hard in the ankle and caught him off-guard. He tripped and stumbled but didn't fall, but it gave me time to get to my feet and I kicked Earl in the crotch as hard as I could. Earl screamed and bent over, holding himself in agony. James rounded the corner and saw that Earl was hurt, which stopped him long enough to check on his friend; then James took off running after me.

I didn't wait around to see what happened with Earl and James. I had a lead and was out of sight. My only hope was that James would be confused about which direction I went, so I doubled back to the last place I thought James would look—the convenience store. I ran in the front door, down the back hall, and hid in the stockroom. Once I stopped and sat behind a stack of boxes I felt fatigue seep through my bones. I hadn't stopped for days, since I was kidnapped, shot, jailed, and picked up by my dad.

I know James is smart, so I needed a plan if I was going to outsmart him. I tried to think, but it was difficult; I was too tired and afraid that my exhaustion would cause me to make a mistake, one that could cost me my life. So I decided to rest, then think.

The clerk came to the back to see where I had gone. I asked the young guy, who seemed laid back and agreeable, to cover for me and allow me to rest up in his stock room.

"This ain't my store, man. You can stay long as you want."

"Please, can you cover if any of those white men come looking for me?"

"One already come in and axed were you here, I tole him I don't see you since the time you ran through."

"Thanks, man; I appreciate that."

"What you think, I not take care of a brother. I just soon kill them white boys as look at them, if I thought I could get away with it." He was younger than me by a few years and much smaller—short, in fact, and very thin. He had a wad of tobacco in his cheek and talked slowly. His baseball cap said "Mustangs," and was pushed back on his forehead

73

so you could see his hairline and brought attention to his wide-set eyes, big as walnuts with pupils as dark as ink wells. He picked up a box, put it on his shoulder, and left the storeroom. I began to relax.

I wondered how many Klan members were after me. James and Earl and the guys who were staking out the train station—oh, and the ones on the train to Memphis. So far I'd counted nine. They seemed to anticipate places I would be before I got there, something that confused me, still does, because even I didn't know I would go to the bus station in Richland. Did they have men positioned at every transportation hub in every town and city between Baton Rouge and Memphis, and all the way to Illinois?

I questioned why I was so important. Then I remembered that I am trying to marry the daughter of a senator, the former mayor of Jean Ville, and that he's the type who had to save face.

I figured the men trailing me would expect me to keep moving and probably head north, so I decided to do the opposite. While the posse staked out all the modes of transportation I might take to go north, I took a nap in the convenience store in Richland. At about three-thirty in the morning the clerk, Devon—he later told me he pronounced it Dah-VON—came into the storeroom and pulled on the waist of his jeans to hike them up over his flat butt.

"Hey, man. They gonna start making deliveries around four," he said. "You'd better scoot." I woke with a start and was disoriented for a few minutes. I shook my head and opened and closed my eyes a few times, trying to focus.

"Are they gone?" I stood, stretched, and looked side-to-side as if waiting for someone to jump out from behind one of the boxes where I'd been hiding.

"Yep. Haven't seen any of them since midnight. Doesn't mean they won't be back after they get rested up," Devon said. I was still disoriented and tried to think of my next move when he surprised me.

"Look, man. I have an old pickup out behind the store. Why don't you lay low in the cab and I'll take you where you want to go when I get off at five."

"Yeah. Uhm, thanks. I'll take you up on that." I said. I went out the back door and got into the rusted Chevy pickup. The door squealed when I opened it and I looked around the mud-dark night to see if I'd awakened a nemesis. Unsure, but without options, I climbed into the cab and folded myself in half on the bench seat. I must have fallen asleep again because I was startled by the squeal of metal when Devon climbed into the cab.

"You musta been pretty tired," Devon said. "You done nothing but sleep since I saw you last night."

"Yeah. I've been on the run. Didn't have much rest till now. Thanks, man."

"No problem."

I had been thinking about where to go since I'd stashed myself in the storeroom. I asked Devon if he could take me to Pearl and he said, no problem, it was only about five or ten miles away.

I knew about a faction of the National Urban League that had a chapter in Pearl, Mississippi. One of their organizers had been to Jean Ville to try to start a league chapter a few years back. I remembered him because a friend I played football with at Adams High School got a scholarship to play for Mississippi State. He had settled in Pearl. We'd kept in touch and my friend, I don't want to tell you his name in case someone gets hold of this letter, got a job coaching at a middle school in Pearl. I had asked the Deacon representative, Jason, if he knew my friend and Jason said he did and told me that my friend was a member of the League in Pearl.

"You know anyone in the League?" I asked Devon.

"Sure. I go to meetings."

"Do you know (I said his name to Devon)? We went to high school together."

"Sure. Everyone in Pearl knows him. He coaches over at the colored middle school. Straight-up guy." Just as the sun began to peek over the horizon, I showed up at my old friend's back door. The look on my face must have alarmed him because he opened the door and ushered me into his kitchen without a word. Devon waved at us from his truck and backed out onto the side street, tucked in a cul-de-sac, and backed up to the woods.

And that's where I am now, with my friend.

He called a few members of the League to meet with us on Friday, to come up with a plan. My friend says all League members' phones are tapped so I can't call you.

Susie, I'm worried about you. The guys here believe there could be people watching you, staking you out in case I show up. Please be careful. I'm glad all I have is a post office box for your address. I hope no one knows your physical address.

I miss you more than anything. I don't know what's going to happen but trust me when I say I'm doing everything I can to get to New York so we can be married.

Forever yours,

Rod

The meeting must have taken place last Friday, I thought as I turned the pages over and started reading the letter again from the beginning. At least he's alive. If anything happened to him or to anyone in his family, it would be all my fault.

I needed to start looking over my shoulder because I was probably being followed and watched. It felt spooky.

∽ Chapter Six ∽

∽

Burton

THE BEGINNING OF MY third week at Shilling Publishing I was sitting at my desk when I heard a familiar voice say my name at the reception desk. I hurried into the ladies' room. About fifteen minutes passed and one of my co-workers came in.

"Your dad's here, Susie. He said he came all the way from Louisiana to see his little girl." Harriet Goldie worked at the desk next to mine. We shared a cubicle and had become fast friends during my first two weeks at Shilling. Harriet was a dark-haired Jewish girl with a big nose and bright, brown eyes. She was short and a bit stocky, but attractive in her own way, and always well dressed. She gave me suggestions on where to find a nice sweater on sale or which lipstick by Revlon would go best with a green dress. And she made me laugh. I needed to laugh.

"Oh, God, Harriet, you have to help me," I begged her.

"What's wrong?" she asked. "You're trembling."

"He'll kill me," I told her.

"You can't mean it. He's out there charming everyone. He's the nicest guy. I wish he was my dad." She searched my face for clues that I had gone off the deep end or was flat-out lying.

"No, you don't." I clouded over as I thought of what he had done to me, how often he'd beaten me, once almost to death. I thought about what he might do to me if he had the chance, now.

Tears welled up in my eyes and I fought to hold them back. I had to keep my wits about me.

"Look," Harriet said. "I'll go tell him you're in the ladies' room and that you'll be out in a minute." She walked to the door and started to pull it open. I pushed it shut with my back and faced her.

"You have to believe me, Harriett. *He will kill me.* That's why he's here. He tried to kill me the last time I went home, but I ran away."

"You're exaggerating," she said, but I saw something change in how she looked at me. We stared at each other.

"Okay," Harriet said. "Let's say I believe you and want to help you. What do you want me to do?"

"Can you tell him I went home sick?" I begged her.

"That would have to come from Mr. Mobley," she said.

"Okay, then; can you just divert his attention long enough for me to go down the stairs and get out of this building? I can lose myself in the street crowd."

"We're twenty-two stories up, Susie," she reminded me.

"It's down. I can do it. Please help me."

"Will he go to your home?" she asked.

"He doesn't know where I live." I told her that I'd moved and didn't leave a forwarding address. I still didn't know how he found out where I worked.

"Please, Harriet. You've got to do it." She stared at me, and something in her expression made me believe she might help me. "I need my purse. My subway tokens and apartment keys are in it." Just then, someone tried to get in the ladies' room and began to knock on the door. I went into a stall and stood on the toilet and bent forward so my feet couldn't be seen under the door or my head above the stall. I prayed I could trust Harriet.

"Is she in here?" I heard Shelia, another co-worker, ask.

"Nope," Harriet said. "I've looked in every stall. Let's go look in the break room." I heard them leave and stayed where I was, hoping against hope that Harriet would come through for me. A couple of minutes went by and I heard the door open and saw my purse slide under the stall door. Then the door to the ladies room closed. I slipped out of the bathroom, turned the corner, and headed for the stairwell.

I wondered how my dad found out where I worked. I'd only had the job two weeks, and Merrick had promised not to tell anyone but Rodney. If Daddy could get someone to tell him about my job, he could get someone to tell him where I lived. I couldn't remember whether I'd used my current or old address when I applied for the job.

As I ran down the stairs and onto the subway, I thought about how my dad would be charming Mr. Mobley into looking up my current address. I got on the subway and when it stopped at my station, I remained on it and got off closer to St. John's campus. I went to a pay phone in the coffee shop that Merrick and I frequented and called him.

"Merrick, it's me."

"Susie, you sound flustered. Are you okay?"

"Did you tell my dad where I work?"

"What? I've never met your dad. What are you talking about? Where are you?"

"I'm at the coffee shop. I'm scared."

"I'll be right there."

I didn't wait for Merrick. I was too close to campus, where my dad might find me. I got back on the subway and went into the city. Without thinking about where to go, I wandered into the New York City Library and felt safe, hidden in the massive building among the herds of people and racks of books. I stayed until it closed at nine o'clock, got on the subway, and went directly to my apartment. No one was there. I let myself in, double-bolted the door, sat in my chair and cried.

I didn't go to work the next day. At around noon I called Harriet and she said my dad had been there again looking for me. The following day, he returned to the publishing house. I asked Harriet whether Mr. Mobley gave him my home address. Harriet didn't know but said the two men were in Mobley's office for a long time the second day.

I was afraid to go back to work so I began to look for another job in Soho and Greenwich Village. I was a ball of nerves and knew I would give a bad impression in interviews, but I couldn't help myself. I called Harriet and she told me my dad hadn't come back Thursday, but I was still afraid to return to work. When I didn't show up on Monday or Tuesday of the following week, Mr. Mobley called Merrick and asked him to have me call him.

Merrick showed up at my apartment to give me the message from Mr. Mobley and reprimanded me because I refused to give anyone, even Merrick, my phone number.

Mr. Mobley and I met at a coffee house near Shilling.

I didn't want to tell him about my dad because it was a reflection on me, but Mr. Mobley seemed to know. He told me that my dad had tried charm, persuasion, and finally threats to coerce Mobley into showing him my application.

"There was something about him, Susie, that didn't sit right with me," Mr. Mobley said. "I wondered why a father wouldn't know where his daughter lived, why he had to obtain her address that way. Something seemed off. When you didn't return to work I realized my instincts might not be so crazy. I talked to some of your co-workers; most of them were clueless, but I could tell Harriet knew something. She didn't want to tell me, but I convinced her I was on your side."

"I'm sorry, Mr. Mobley. I never wanted to cause you or the

publishing house trouble. I love my job, but I can't go back now that he knows I work there."

"I've thought about that. I want you to come back. You are smart and talented and you have intuition. You're going to move up quickly in our company." He told me he would protect me, and if my dad showed up everyone would know to keep him busy until I could get away. He said he would keep my file at his house and falsify the one he kept in his office, in case my dad was able to convince someone else to show it to him.

Mobley talked me into returning, but I lived in fear for a long time.

I felt the August heat through my bones when I picked up my mail at the post office after work. I was still reluctant to give out my apartment address, especially after my dad's visit. I threw the mail on the kitchen counter when I got home and went to the bedroom to shed my work clothes and put on an old pair of jeans and a T-shirt.

I flopped into my pillowed chair, put my feet on the ottoman, and flipped through the bills, flyers, and junk mail. Then, suddenly, I recognized Rodney's handwriting on an envelope. The postmark said it had been mailed six days before and was forwarded from the post office at the university. I wish I could write back to him and give him my new address and phone number, but I didn't know where he was. I tore the envelope open and began to read the letter written about a week after the first one I'd received.

July 22, 1974
Dear Susie,
There's so much to tell you, I'm not sure where to begin.
When I got to my friend's house and told him our story, he felt I should lay low for a week and he'd put out feelers to see if any of the men from Jean Ville were still hanging around. He has lots of friends and

people who could tell him if there were any unusual white men in Jackson.

During the rest of the week several young men came and went, bringing information about the activities of the white guys from Jean Ville. Every day the number in the posse was fewer until, by the end of the week, it appeared they were gone, although no one was really sure. My friend invited a few members of the League to his house the beginning of the second week to help us formulate a plan.

The League members are sure their phones are tapped, so they all agreed I shouldn't make any calls. They keep promising to take me to a pay phone in the next county so I can call you and my family, only that hasn't happened because no one feels the danger is over.

The members that showed up included one white guy and three other Negroes, besides me and my friend.

Steven is a light-skinned colored man about thirty years old with an easy disposition and a quick smile. He has two small children and recently finished college in accounting by going to night school and working as a mechanic during the day. He got involved with the League because of the abuse he and his friends and family suffered at the hands of white supremacists when they tried to integrate the schools in 1971. Two of his friends were shot and dumped in a bayou, found four months later half eaten by gators. Of course I thought about Jeffrey and continued to wonder whether he'd survive the beating and lynching he'd received. I think about him all the time and was too choked up to respond to Steven, so I just squeezed his shoulder.

Tobias and Mickey came in together. Toby is medium brown, tall, thin, and quiet. He has huge wide-set eyes that make me feel like he's looking at several people at the same time. He wore overalls with one strap falling around his knee, a sleeveless T-shirt and sneakers, no socks. His hair is a big afro, standing about six-inches from his head like a fuzzy black ball. We shook hands but he didn't say anything.

Mickey is short, squatty and has a smile plastered to his face as if, when he sleeps at night, it might still be there. When he talks his wide, white teeth show, and his huge lips spread across the bottom of his face, clown-like. He's friendly and talkative, and whistles when words with s's and th's come from his lips.

"How you doing?" he asked me when we shook hands. "You from around here?"

"No, Louisiana," I told him.

"Whatcha doing in these parts?"

"Running from a posse from Toussaint Parish that seems to know my every move."

"Why they after you?"

"Long story."

"I got time."

We were interrupted by Reggie Johnson, the only white guy in the group. He has reddish hair and fair skin and a keeps a three-day beard that's neatly trimmed. His green eyes remind me of a cat, but a friendly one.

"Reggie," he said when he shook my hand.

"Pleased," I said and stared at him as if I couldn't figure out why he was there.

"I know, you're wondering what a white guy is doing in this group. I guess no one warned you. I married a colored girl, so I'm a member of the club, whether I like it or not."

"Oh." I was surprised that anyone in the South was married to someone of the other race. He had lots of questions, but Steven, who seemed to be in charge, asked everyone to sit and we all found places on the sofa and in chairs in the small living room.

"So it seems we have a problem, right?" Steven asked and looked directly at me. I was caught off-guard and stammered a bit.

"Thanks for coming, guys." My friend saved me from my tied-up tongue. "This is Rodney Thibault. We grew up together in Louisiana,

went to high school, played football. He's a good guy. He's in real trouble. Maybe he should explain."

I told them about you and how I was trying to get to New York so we could get married. I told them about Jeffrey and that I didn't know whether he was still alive.

"Last time I talked to my dad, Jeffrey was in a coma. They weren't sure he'd make it. I'm frantic to find out about my brother."

"We can't risk a phone call. We'll all be discovered." Steven looked around the room and his eyes rested on Reggie. "I think one of us needs to make a trip down to Jean Ville."

"I guess I'm the most logical one, huh?" Reggie said.

"Yep. It's got to be you, whitey." They all laughed.

"Okay. I'll go in the next couple days. Let's say we come back together next Friday."

"That's another week," I said. "Susie will be a basket case. She hasn't heard from me except for one letter I was able to get off to her more than a week ago."

"Listen up, Rod," my friend said. "This is not just for your safety, but for hers, too. Trust me. They'll be stalking her to find you. Does anyone know where she is?"

I told them I wasn't sure whether your parents had your address. I'm not sure if you're still at your apartment on campus since you've graduated. I told them I don't even know where you live and they said that was probably best.

"When they can't find you they'll try to find her and wait for you to show up."

"Damn. I don't want anything to happen to her."

"Let's hope they are still on your trail and haven't had to resort to looking for you in New York."

I told them that your dad would kill you if he finds you, but I don't think they took me literally. Reggie said he'd need some contacts in Jean Ville and I gave him Dr. Switzer's name and, of course, my dad's. I *asked Reggie to find out about Jeffrey and to ask my dad to call you and tell you I'm alive, in case you aren't getting my letters.*

I'll write you when Reggie gets back with news. I hope you are getting my letters and I wish like hell you could write me back, but I can't risk sending you the address.

Yours forever,
Rod

~ Chapter Seven ~

Home

THE NEXT WEEK I stopped at the post office and noticed an envelope that felt thick, as though it had something in it other than a letter. It was a long, white envelope with familiar handwriting, addressed to me in a beautiful cursive hand and forwarded from my address on campus.

I was afraid to open the envelope because I knew, from experience, what was in it.

Every August I received an envelope with pictures of the little girl I'd given birth to on August 21, 1969. She'd be five, I thought, and I put the unopened envelope on the side table near the lamp. I also received Christmas pictures every January.

I remembered the initial picture after the baby's first Christmas: a chubby, mostly bald, four-month old lying on a quilt on the floor with a silent, toothless laugh. The following August there was a picture of a toddler standing up, holding on to the sofa table, pride lighting her face, plus another shot of her taking a step. She wore a red dress with smocking across the bodice and a big bow in back. Her hair was a little longer than in the bald picture and looked light brown. Loose curls fell over her forehead.

I didn't open the envelopes that came the following years. I put them in my bottom dresser drawer under my pajamas, along with the first two that I'd opened. I put the new, unopened envelope with the others and tried not to think about the small stack that was growing.

There was a letter from Rodney in the stack. It had been written ten days before and looked as though it had been forwarded twice, first to the wrong address then finally to my PO box on Utopia Parkway.

July 29, 1974
Dear Susie,
Reggie got back from Jean Ville with good news and not-so-good news.

It was after eleven o'clock on Friday when we all got together. Everyone looked tired.

Reggie said that Jeffrey is out of his coma, but not out of the woods. He's still in the hospital and Dr. Switzer is taking care of him. Reggie got to see Jeffrey and he asked Reggie to deliver a message to me: "Tell my brother this is not his fault. He needs to follow his dreams. We all do." That's what he said. I know what he means because we've talked about it a lot. As Negroes, we have to work doubly hard to achieve our dreams. I think what he was trying to say is don't let my race dictate my life.

The fear and uncertainty I'd been able to keep at a distance for almost a month seemed to shroud me like a thick, dark cloak. The other men sat around and waited for me to pull myself together. It took a few minutes, but I got hold of my emotions.

The bad news is that they are keeping two men in Jackson at all times, Reggie told me. He had a stubble on his face that had collected over the past week while he'd been in Louisiana and I felt responsible that he'd been away from his family that long. He said the word on the street in Jean Ville is that the "posse" your dad recruited to keep me from getting to you thinks I'm still in Mississippi. They watch the train and bus stations and have guys who live in Jackson working with them. Reggie said he thinks they have you staked out, too, and since I haven't shown up there, it confirms their belief that I haven't gotten out of the South.

Most importantly, Dr. Switzer told Reggie that your dad and mom are planning a trip to New York to visit you. Do they know where to find you?

This is important, Susie. Reggie said that Dr. Switzer thinks that if I go to New York, the Klan, or the posse, or whatever you want to call these bigots, will hurt my sisters or my mother. In fact, he suggested that they could be molested, among other atrocities. Dr. David told Reggie that I have another choice: go back home.

I know; it doesn't make sense. It would be walking into a trap. But Dr. David believes that if I go home and pretend I've been on vacation or off at school, it will be as though you and I never had plans to run away together. He said your dad would have egg on his face and the Klan would not only call off the massacre, but they'd probably never believe your father again.

I'd never considered going back home and I didn't understand how that could solve anything, other than have me walk right into a trap. But Reggie explained that Dr. David said that if I showed up in Jean Ville with my colored girlfriend and pretended the two of us had been away together, "Two birds, one stone is how the doctor put it," Reggie told me.

Frankly, Susie, I've never considered what the Klan might do to the rest of my family. I know your dad is evil. I witnessed what he did to you. But to hurt my mother or molest my sisters? I just can't wrap my mind around that.

Dr. Switzer told Reggie that's what would happen if I make it to New York and we get married. I suppose that's something we should think about. Reggie said I should think hard and long about what I'm giving up by marrying you.

I asked him: "So you're telling me that if I go back to Jean Ville without Susie, all of this will go away? Susie's dad will get off her trail, the Klan will let go of Jeffrey and my family. Everything will die down?"

Reggie said that was his opinion and Dr. David's. The other guys looked at me and shook their heads.

I asked Reggie what he would do if he were me.

Reggie walked over to where I was sitting and stood in front of me, his hands deep in his pockets, and said this to me: "My family won't see me. They are paralyzed with fear about what will happen to them. They live each day as if it's their last, waiting for the Klan to attack, or waiting for word that I've been killed. I miss them. I love my wife, but I'm not sure I'd make the same decision, knowing what I know now. I was young and impetuous and thought, 'to hell with people who don't understand.' But really, they are the ones who understood. Now, I'm living with the consequences."

I wanted to choke him, to tell him he couldn't understand how much we love each other and deserve to be together.

"I'm just saying think about it, Rodney." Reggie was compassionate, yet firm. "In a few years, after all of the excitement of being with her every day has worn off, will you miss your family? How will you feel knowing you can never go back home? Never see Jean Ville again, or your brother? And how will you feel if your brother dies? Or if they string up your dad again or do God knows what to your sisters and mother?"

His last biting message had to do with you. He said, if none of the things they could do to my family scares me, what if they hurt you, molest you, even kill you. I could never live with myself if something happened to you.

It's a lot to think about. What do you think we should do?

Steven said he tried to call you from his work to bring you up to date and so you could let us know if you are safe and whether you are receiving my letters, but your phone has been disconnected. I don't know how to reach you. Marianne told Reggie that she talked to you but that you called her and wouldn't give her your new phone number. Why do you have a new phone number, have you moved? Stupid me, I'm acting like you can answer my questions.

It looks like neither of us can find the other.
And I can't leave this house, unless I go back home to Jean Ville.
I'm not sure what to do.
I love you. I miss you.
Forever yours,
Rod

I called Marianne as soon as I finished reading Rodney's letter.

"I thought you knew." She sounded surprised and caught her breath. "Maybe you should sit down."

"What is it? Is he okay?"

"He's home."

"What?" I sat down hard in one of my kitchen chairs.

"He's been back almost four days."

"Is Annette with him?"

"Yes. I'm sorry."

"Is he going to marry her?"

"He's not sure. He wants you safe. He wants his family safe."

When she hung up I held onto the receiver until the dial tone turned to a squawking sound and brought me to my senses. I couldn't cry. I was out of tears. I had to find some way to move through life without Rodney.

It was over.

I slumped into my chair and crumpled Rodney's letter. Hearing the crackle of the page gave me a start and I threw it, like a baseball, across the room. *He could have told me himself,* I thought. Then, once again, I remembered he didn't know how to reach me other than letters that took almost two weeks to get here.

On the one hand I wanted him to fight for me—then again, I didn't want him killed. I'd rather not have him than live in a world where he no longer existed. I thought about calling Rodney or writing to him, but that would be all wrong. I had to let him go.

*

Some days I'd have talks with myself, dress in something that made me feel sexy or pretty or professional, whatever my mood dictated that day. I'd make myself walk with a lilt and a swagger. I'd arrive at the office with donuts for everyone and go to lunch with some of the girls. Other days I'd wrap myself in an old sweater, slump my shoulders, put my head down and forge through the crowds, get to work, and not speak to a soul.

I felt schizophrenic and I knew the people I worked with wondered from day to day, which Susie would show up. But I couldn't help myself.

A week after I found out Rodney had moved home I got a letter from Marianne.

July 7, 1974
Dear Susie,

How's your new career in publishing? I'm loving my job at the hospital. I was promoted to night supervisor and, other than the crazy hours, it's great. Mom is doing good. She only works until about three o'clock every day now so she has more time at home. She misses Granddaddy. We all do. We miss you too. When do you think you'll come for a visit?

Rodney took a job with the Toussaint Parish District Attorney. He's getting married next May. I thought you'd like to know. He seems happy.

I hope you're happy too. Tell me all about your love life. Mine is great. You'd love Lucy, she's a real character.

Gotta run. Sure do miss you.

Love,
Mari

After I read Marianne's letter, an invisible force walked me to my bedroom and made me open the bottom drawer of my dresser and dig out the stack of white envelopes with the cursive handwriting written across the fronts. My legs wouldn't move so I sat cross-legged in the middle of the floor with the drawer still pulled opened, and put the stack in my lap.

Before I realized what I was doing, all of the pictures of the baby—my baby—were lined up, beginning with her at four months old; then at one year; then one year, four months; then two years; two years, four months; three years old; then three years, four months and the latest on her fourth birthday, wearing a pink dress, white shoes that buckled on the sides, white lace-trimmed socks, and a pink bow in her shoulder-length, curly brown hair. She had huge, almond-shaped eyes that laughed at the camera. She was beautiful, like Rodney.

I wondered who sent the pictures. Was it Emalene Franklin? Would she send pictures of her child to the biological mother? I felt so totally alone without Rodney but somehow the pictures of the child we had made together gave me a ray of happiness.

I examined each picture until I had the little girl's growth memorized. I also looked for hints that I might be a welcomed visitor, if I could find her.

I finally put the empty envelopes back in my bottom drawer. The pictures, however, I lined up in chronological order on the bulletin board over my desk and pinned each one with a stickpin. As I sat at my desk and stared at Rodney's baby, I thought about Catfish. I wondered what he'd tell me to do.

Then I remembered a story he'd told me about a child being wretched away from his mother. The thought to somehow get Rodney's child back began to germinate inside me without my knowledge, while my consciousness considered the injustice of dislocating a child from her family. If I could only meet her, see her in person. Would that be enough?

Catfish told me that changes ran rampant the first year Mr. Gordon Van took over Shadowland. I could hear Catfish's deep, throaty drawl with a hint of laughter in every sentence. I picked up my pen and began to write his words on the ruled sheets of paper on my desk.

Samuel

1855

In the beginning the slaves was uneasy and thought it might be a trap 'cause it seemed too good to be true, yes indeed. They lined up at the cookhouse and got theyselves three hearty meals every day and could ask for more if they was still hungry when they bowls was empty. They could go to the barn for new work clothes when theirs wore out and George made sure everyone had at least two sets, so they had something to wear when they washed.

The womens had several bolts of fabric to choose from to make theyselves skirts and such, and George would cut any length they wanted. There was real sheets and pillow slips for their new straw mattresses and pillows, big iron kettles for each family for days, like Sundays, when they cooked they own meals. Bessie gave out corn meal, flour, sugar, coffee grounds, and such as they needed and she kept a tally to make sure no one took too much—but that was not one of Mr. Van's rules, it was Bessie's rule and it kept everyone in check.

I could still hear Catfish chuckle when he made a comment like that. "The biggest change for the slaves was the work hours," he told me.

Before Mr. Gordon come back, everyone worked from sun-up to sundown with no breaks. Now they only worked ten hours a day and had three breaks, fifteen minutes in the morning and afternoon when they was given as much water to drink as they wanted and thirty minutes for dinner at one o'clock. At first George say some of them drank water and ate so much dinner so much they got sick. Hah!

At six o'clock Mr. William rang the bell for supper and they got all the time they wanted to eat 'cause after they ate, they didn't have to go back in the fields. They had time to sit in the quarter, sing hymns, visit neighbors, care for their children, and rest.

And wonder of wonders, they didn't work on Sundays. They could have they own church service or walk to the Bethel Baptist Church about four miles across town.

Best of all, no one saw a whip.

About six months after Mr. Gordon came to Shadowland, he and William was up in town to pick up some seeds and twine for straw bales when he heard a commotion in the town square. Mr. Gordon tells the story about my granddaddy different than what I heard direct from Granddaddy. Maureen said William told her what happened.

Mr. Gordon paid his bill and left William to see that the supplies were loaded in the flatbed wagon and walked out of the Feed & Seed in the bright sunlight. The excitement in front of the courthouse was a slave auction. Mr. Gordon didn't like the way slave owners and buyers put them poor black folks on risers, wrists and ankles chained, a metal ring around they necks, with one end of another chain hooked to it, the other end held by the owner. Mr. Van thought it was cruel.

When he needed a field worker, which is what he called his slaves, he asked around and found out about plantation owners who had some to sell. He'd visit the owners and meet the worker, then decide whether the worker would meet his needs.

On this particular day, Mr. Van wasn't in the market for a new field worker but he started walking towards the auction block when he saw a boy about ten years old take his place on the stand. The owner jerked the boy's collar so hard it scraped the boy's neck raw.

"What do I hear for this big, strapping boy?" the auctioneer barked. The boy wasn't big or strapping. He was just a little squirt of a thing and *didn't look as if he'd ever done a day's work in a field. Mr. Van said he blocked out the sounds of cheers, jeers, and screams from the men and women spectators but couldn't ignore the spit and clods of dirt flung at the boy. The boy was scared. It was obvious he had cried for hours, probably torn from his mother at a plantation far away by a ruthless owner who saw an opportunity for quick income and one less mouth to feed.*

The bidding started at ten dollars. "Do I hear fifteen, fifteen, anyone bid fifteen?" the auctioneer asked. Without a thought, Van raised his hand, "Fifteen," he shouted. Half the crowd turned to look towards him where he stood in back of the crowd.

"Fifteen from Mr. Gordon Van, do I hear twenty? Twenty dollars for this strong young body?" No one responded. The auctioneer repeated the bid at twenty dollars. Still no response. Mr. Van say he was surprised because a boy like that should go for $100, for sure.

"Sold to Mr. Gordon Van of Shadowland Plantation in Jean Ville!" Mr. Van pulled his billfold from the inside pocket of his jacket and peeled off fifteen dollars, walked to the block and handed the money to the man who sat behind a small table on the side. The owner, from Alexandria, approached to sign a bill of sale that transferred ownership of ten-year-old Samuel Harrison Massey to Mr. Gordon Van.

"You got a deal, Van," the owner said. Mr. Van ignored him, signed his name to the two identical documents, watched the seller do the same, picked up his copy off the table, folded it and stuck it in the pocket with his billfold.

"I said you stole that nigger, Van," the owner taunted. Van ignored him. The man jerked on the chain and the boy fell off the block on his side, his arm jammed between his body and the ground.

"You can unlock the chains now," Mr. Van said to the owner.

"I deliver him to your wagon, that's part of the deal."

"Not necessary," Mr. Van said. "Just unlock the chains and I'll get him to the wagon."

"You crazy, man," the owner said. "He a nigger slave. He'll run off as soon as the chains is off. Where's your wagon?"

"Follow me." Mr. Van told William he wanted to help the boy off the ground but the crowd watched the exchange with great interest. He would have to make it up to the boy later. The owner practically dragged the boy through the dust, the youngster scrambled to keep up, tripped, fell, stood and fell again over and over until they reached Mr. Van's wagon in front of the feed store. William stood next to the wagon that was loaded with supplies. There was enough room near the rear edge of the wagon for the boy. Van heaved him onto the flatbed where the boy sat up straight, his neck bleeding and oozing, his wrists and ankles blistered from the restraints.

"You have some chains to put on this boy when I take these off?" the owner asked.

"Sure," Mr. Van said. "Just release him, take your chains and go. He's my responsibility now. Leave us be." The owner used a key to unlock the ankles, wrists and, finally, the neck ring. He gathered his chains and strolled off, shaking his head.

"Get me a bucket of water and a ladle, William," Mr. Van didn't take his eyes off the boy, who kept his gaze downward towards his bare, bleeding feet. Gordon Van was in temporary shock. William said the boy's wounds, cuts, blisters, and infected mosquito bites were beyond Mr. Van's understanding. The child's only clothing was a pair of drawstring pants cut off at the knees; no shirt, no shoes, no hat to shield his nappy head from the blaring sun.

"How can a human being treat another like this?" he asked William, who had no answer.

William handed Mr. Van the bucket of water and Mr. Van dipped the ladle in the bucket then held it under the boy's mouth.

"Drink," he said. The boy tried to sip politely but, after a couple of slurps, he gulped the water in one breath. Mr. Van continued to fill the ladle and the boy continued to gulp the contents. When he finally had his *fill, Mr. Van placed the bucket next to the boy, removed his white pocket handkerchief from the outside pocket of his jacket, dipped it deep into the bucket and brought it up, dripping with water. He placed the wet rag on the boy's head and allowed the water to drip down his face. He dipped the handkerchief again, wrung it slightly and gently wiped the boy's face. He repeated the process on the boy's neck, then the scrapes on his knees and elbows, and finally, he held the bucket so the boy could place his feet, one at a time, in the water while Van reached in with the cloth—now stained red and brown—and washed the boy's feet.*

A crowd gathered and watched the process with combined interest and confusion. William tried to lure them away, but the crowd grew. When Mr. Van had completed his tasks, he handed the bucket to William and asked him to rinse and refill it with clean water. He removed his straw hat and placed it on the boy's head. The frizzy hair helped it to fit snugly. When William returned, Mr. Van placed the bucket beside the boy and handed the ladle to him. He reached in William's front pocket and removed a bandana, which he wet and loosely wrapped around the boy's blistered neck.

No words were exchanged during this ceremonial process. The boy's eyes were opened wide with fear and sadness, Mr. Van's with remorse and pity. The smell of horses, straw, and dampness filled the air while the auctioneer's barks could be heard above the snorts of horses, murmurs of the crowds, and wagon wheels that came and went on Main Street.

Gordon Van ignored it all. He climbed on the wagon bench and motioned for William to join him. The boy sat on the back of the wagon; his feet dangled off the edge and he held the bucket close to him to keep it from falling out. He wouldn't try to escape. Where would he go? All those people knew he was a slave, bought and paid for. One of them would catch him, probably beat him, and return him to his owner. He was brought into this town blindfolded so he didn't know how to get back to his Mama, and it was a long, long way. It had taken them all day to get here.

The trip to Mr. Van's plantation took about twenty minutes. He instructed William to lead the horses straight to the barn where Mr. Van jumped off the bench to find George. William went to the back of the wagon and lifted the boy to the ground.

"Follow me," William said. The boy followed close behind the overseer. They went in the barn as Mr. Van and George were walking towards them.

"Son," Mr. Van said to the boy. "This is George. He takes care of the livestock. He's going to get you cleaned up, bandaged and fed, then he'll show you where you will stay. For now your job will be to help George. He's your boss, you understand?"

"This nigger my boss?" the boy blurted. The three men laughed. It was the first words the boy had spoken in his high-pitched, squeaky voice.

"Yes, son, George is your boss. William here is George's boss. I'm everyone's boss. Now, what's your name?"

"Samuel, sir," he said. "Samuel Harrison Massey."

"Pleased to meet you, Samuel Harrison Massey. That's a big name. What do you like to be called?"

"At Kent House they call me, 'Li'l Nigga' but I likes 'Samuel', sir."

"Then 'Samuel', it is. George, take care of this one. He's going to grow up to be a fine young man. He has quite a future ahead of him here. You explain the rules." He turned to Samuel, "And if you have questions no one else can answer, you come see me up at the house, you hear?"

"Yes, sir!" Samuel said. His confusion complicated the sadness and pain he carried, but somehow he felt safe, even safer than he had felt with his Mama. But he missed his Mama every day and hated the men who had taken him away from her.

"That little squirt turned out to be my granddaddy," Catfish told me. "And he tole me so many stories I don't know I have time in my life to share them with you, Missy."

He called me 'missy' from the time I was seven, even though he knew my name. I put my pen down and thought about the gentle man who taught me what real love felt like. And it had all started when I gave him a turtle. That was a story I should write at another time.

I looked at the pictures of Emalene and Joe Franklin's daughter. My daughter. Rodney's daughter.

What would I have named her if I'd been able to keep her? I thought back to why I gave her up: I was eighteen, pregnant by a colored boy, 2000 miles from home, trying to get through college, no job, no way to care for a baby. If I'd gone home with a child, half-Negro, I'd be killed and maybe the child would be, too. I couldn't raise her alone in New York. I had no job, no income.

My choices were abortion or adoption. I could never take the life of an unborn child, so I went to Catholic Charities and asked whether I could interview mixed-race couples who wanted a newborn. Emalene and Joe Franklin stood out among the couples I met. Joe, a white college professor, and Emma, a beautiful, brown attorney, couldn't have children of their own and wanted a baby more than anything.

The nurses cut the baby's cord and took her away. I knew that the Franklins were waiting for my baby in the hall. I'm not sure how long she remained in the nursery before they took her home but I never went to the window to see her. I never looked at my little girl. I never held her because I was afraid if I did, I would never be able to let her go.

Now I was twenty-two years old, had a master's degree, and a good job. Could I possibly get her back? Or would I be just as cruel as the people who took Samuel away from his mother and sold him to Mr. Gordon Van?

*

Marianne called me at work about a month after I'd talked to her about Rodney getting married. I rarely got phone calls at Shilling, so I was nervous when I picked up the phone.

"Hi, it's me," she said.

"I gave you my home phone number." I whispered because we weren't supposed to take personal calls at the office. "Why are you calling me at work?"

"This can't wait." Marianne whispered, too. "It's about Rodney, and I know you don't want to know about him, but I think you need to know this."

I rubbed my eyes with my thumb and forefinger then tried to spread out the wrinkles on my forehead. I felt a massive headache coming on.

"He's been drafted." Marianne sounded upset.

"What?"

"In the army. I guess they waited until he finished college and law school. Something about a college deferment and a lottery. His name came up and they sent him a letter. He reported to the recruitment office and, sure enough, he's in the army."

"Oh." That's all I could muster from my aching head and pounding heart. "When?"

"He left yesterday."

"Where is he?"

"Basic training first, then probably Vietnam."

"Oh, God! I thought the war was over."

"The US still has troops there and an embassy staff," Marianne said.

I was sitting at my desk. I put the phone down, dangled my head between my legs, and took deep breaths. I could hear Marianne through the receiver on my desk above me, "Susie, you still there? Susie?" She eventually hung up. I got through the day and called her back when I got home that evening. She was at work. I dialed the nurses' station at the hospital and she answered on the first ring.

"It's me," I said in a whisper. "What about his wedding?"

"It's been postponed, indefinitely."

"Oh."

Marianne told me that Annette wanted to get married before Rodney left for the army but he refused. "He said he's not ready." Mari said she thought it was his way of saying that it was over with Annette. She told me that Rodney confided in her that he didn't think he loved Annette enough to spend the rest of his life with her. I didn't want to know those details but I couldn't talk, so I had to listen while she continued. "I think he gets to come home after his training, before they ship him overseas."

"Is there a chance he'll go somewhere else? Not Vietnam?"

"If he was white, maybe. With his degrees you'd think they'd cut him some slack, but I understand the army has a plan to protect the intelligent whiteys and put the dumbasses and coloreds on the front lines. I don't hold out much hope."

"Maybe the war will end."

"Maybe." Marianne also told me that my dad's campaign for re-election to his Senate seat didn't look good. She said the white people were backing his opponent, Mr. Jack Roy, and that the coloreds wouldn't vote for my dad because of what happened to Jeffrey. "They know your dad was behind it and after Rodney came back they believe your dad tricked everyone." I got some sort of sick pleasure knowing that my dad might lose. He hated to lose. "And Sheriff Guidry is up for reelection, too. He's got competition this time, a guy named Desiré."

"Dolby Desiré?"

"Yep. That's him. A progressive, they say. The coloreds are for him because he says he'll take down all the 'whites only' signs."

"That's the kiss of death," I said, thinking about how the white people in Jean Ville wanted to keep the Negroes *in their place.* "Your people need to register to vote. There aren't enough Negro voters in Toussaint Parish to unseat Guidry."

"We're working on that. Me and Lucy and a group of young people are spearheading a 'get out and register' campaign that seems to be working. And there's a group of Democrats—whites who believe in integration—who are behind Desiré. Things could really change around here if your dad and Guidry both lose. They've had the Klan busy all these years."

When I hung up I was distraught. I felt so alone, deserted.

~ Chapter Eight ~

Lilly Franklin

I HIT A DEAD end at Catholic Charities. They said I'd signed a form that gave up all rights to know who the adopted couple was or where they lived. I had met them and knew their names, so I had a lot more to go on than most birth mothers looking for a child they gave away.

I searched phone books, law firms, university staff lists but couldn't find anyone named Joseph or Emalene Franklin.

I tried to reach Dr. Josh Ryan. I left messages at the hospital switchboard, which was the only place I knew to find him.

I had met Josh Ryan when I was eighteen and arrived in the emergency room by ambulance after fainting in my dorm at Sarah Lawrence. He was assigned to be my doctor, a handsome young obstetrical resident who took an interest in me. When he told me I was pregnant I was shocked. Once I recovered from dehydration and was on medication to keep me from throwing up everything I put in my body, Josh discharged me, then drove me back to the college himself. After that day, he started calling me and taking me to lunch or dinner to make sure I was eating properly and taking care of myself.

For the next seven and one half months, Josh Ryan stood by me and when I went into labor he was my friend, my coach, and my doctor. He delivered my baby girl and met Emalene and Joe when they came to take my baby home with them. That was the last time I had seen Josh. He walked out of my life and I figured it was because he realized that my child's father was a Negro when he saw that Emalene and Joe were a mixed-race couple. I had surmised that Josh Ryan couldn't stomach that fact.

Since he'd delivered my baby I thought he might know where I could find her, but he didn't return my phone calls and I was at my wits' end.

I sat on a bench in Utopia Park with Rodney's letter in my lap, contemplating how I would answer it.

August 13, 1974
Dear Susie,

I guess you've heard that I was drafted. I'm at Fort Benning, Georgia, and expect to have a couple weeks leave before they ship me to Vietnam. I want to see you. Please say you want me to come to New York next month.

I love you.
Yours forever,
Rod

It was late spring and the first day in months it had been warm enough to venture outdoors on a Saturday. I took a book by Ernest Gaines, *The Autobiography of Miss Jane Pittman*, that had been published a couple of years before. Gaines was one of my favorite authors. His stories were set in a place called, Bayonne, which was actually New Roads, Louisiana, in Pointe Coupée Parish, just over the Atchafalaya River from Toussaint Parish. I'd driven along False River, the oxbow lake where children played and old men fished, every time I drove from Jean Ville to Baton Rouge on Highway 1. I could picture the slave cabins and the plantation homes that bordered the beautiful waters that had once been part of the

Mississippi River that re-routed itself through the centuries.

I felt someone sit on the other end of the bench, but didn't look up. I was trying to concentrate on the story of Jane Pittman who begins as a young slave girl and advances to one hundred years old by the end of the book. My mind wandered to Rodney's letter that I'd stuck in the back of the book.

"Do you have the time?" a male voice asked.

I looked from my book to see the profile of a handsome man, dressed in green scrubs and a white lab coat, at the end of the bench.

"Uh, yes. It's almost three o'clock." I looked down at my book but something about the man made me look back up. He was watching a bird pecking at something on the ground. The man had a small bag of popcorn and was throwing pieces on the sidewalk in front of the bench. Several more birds began to gather.

"Are those seagulls?" I asked without realizing the words came out of my mouth.

"They're called great black-backed gulls." He didn't look up. He kept scattering the popcorn and now about ten birds that looked a lot like the seagulls I used to chase on the Mississippi Gulf Coast as a child had gathered and were pecking at the white specks on the ground. I watched without thinking. It was mesmerizing.

"They look like seagulls," I said.

"They are smaller, fatter, and notice how the feathers on their backs are black. Seagulls are white and grey." I watched the birds and I watched the man. He looked sad. His shoulders were slumped and he hadn't shaved in a couple of days.

"Are you a doctor?"

"Yes." He was busy with the birds and lost in his own thoughts. I decided it would be more polite to go back to my book and not intrude on his private time. I began to read. I turned a page and was learning how Jane got her name when the man on the bench abruptly stood up. The bench shook a bit and I noticed his shoes in front of me, almost touching the toes of mine.

I put my book in my lap and my eyes followed the pants legs up and traveled to the drawstring, then the green V-neck shirt that was semi-tucked into the pants. His hands were in the pockets of his lab coat. I think I was afraid to look at his face, but I wasn't afraid of him. Something about this man made me feel safe.

When I finally lifted my chin and saw the wavy brown hair with a touch of grey at the temples and the large green eyes staring at me, I realized I knew him.

"Josh?"

"Yep. In all my glory." I stood up and we hugged. He held me a little longer than was probably normal, but it felt good. He put his hands on my shoulders and stepped back, staring at me as if trying to read my mind. "Let me look at you, Susie Burton. It's been a long time. You are still the most beautiful girl I know." He grinned at me.

"You look good, Josh," I said. "Tired, but good. How have you been?"

"Do you have time for a cup of coffee?"

"Now?"

"You busy right now? I just got off a 48-hour surgery emergency. Eleven patients involved in a school bus accident. We lost three children and the driver, but were able to save the rest. I could actually use a drink. What do you say?"

"It's too early for a drink, but I'll sit with you while you have one."

"Follow me." He took my hand and sort of pulled me out of the park, down the sidewalk and into an Irish Pub about three blocks away. We didn't talk while we walked. It was as though we were on a mission.

We sat in a booth in the back of the pub, near a window where we could watch people walk by. Josh ordered a beer and I got a cup of tea.

"I've been trying to reach you, Josh." I stirred my tea and dipped the bag in repeatedly.

"I know. Busy." He looked up at me and his frown started to disappear. "Actually, I've avoided you, because… well. I didn't want to see you again and find out I still feel something."

"Josh…" I didn't know what to say. I knew what it felt like to care about someone you couldn't have, so my heart broke for him.

"Tell me about yourself, Susie." He was staring at me as though trying to recognize something he'd lost.

"Nothing to tell. I graduated from Sarah Lawrence, went to graduate school at St. John's, finished last May, and I'm working in the publishing industry."

"You attached?"

"What kind of question is that?"

"It's not like we don't know each other well enough to be blunt."

"Josh, we haven't seen each other in, what? Four or five years?"

"How old is your little girl now?" That stopped me dead. I put my cup down with a clink and stared at the brown liquid. "Is that a taboo subject? I was there, remember?"

"Actually, that's what I've been calling you about. Do you know where she is?"

"Why do you care now?"

"I just do. I've grown up. I'd like to meet her."

"She's happy. She has great parents, a wonderful life. Do you really want to waltz in and disrupt her? Are you that selfish?" His look told me he disapproved but I didn't care. I had to meet my little girl, Rodney's baby. I just had to.

"Susie, I've kept up with you ever since your daughter was born. When I saw what you did—gave your child away—I knew you must love that guy in Louisiana more than you could ever love me. I realized I couldn't compete with him, so I walked out. I was right, wasn't I?"

"Hmmmm. I don't know what to say. You've caught me off guard." We were quiet for a long time. I was thinking about when Josh walked out, and how I'd thought he left because he realized my baby was mixed-race. Was he saying something different?

He nursed his beer, barely drinking, just playing with it, running his thumb around the rim of the glass, moving the mug around in the moisture that gathered under it. I watched for a while. I wanted to get up and leave. I didn't want to answer questions or face Josh and his displeasure, but I needed to find my child.

Josh had been my rock throughout my pregnancy and never pressed me to tell him about the father. He didn't try to have sex with me. He didn't judge me for being unmarried and pregnant. He just doted on me for over seven months, then walked out of my hospital room and never called me again.

"What about you, Josh? What have you been up to? Married? Children?"

"I've had a couple relationships. Nothing to write home about. They weren't you."

"Josh. Please."

"What? You don't want to hear that I've never gotten over you?"

"You walked out. Not me."

"Yep. That's right. I knew I couldn't have you, that you would never love me. You belonged to someone else."

"I'm sorry. I really am."

"Okay. So we've seen each other again. Now we can move forward. Is that what you're saying?"

"What I'm saying... What I'm asking, is... can you help me find my daughter?"

"I'll see what I can do. Call me in a few days." He put a piece of paper on the table, slid out of the booth, and walked away. I watched him stop to put money on the bar, then he marched past the front windows and took long strides down the sidewalk. He didn't look at me; he just stared ahead, walking quickly, almost running. I sat in the booth for a long time. Finally, I put the piece of paper in my pocket, picked up my book and purse and left.

That night in my apartment, I took the paper out of my pocket, looked at it, and dialed.

"Josh, I'm sorry. Look, I'm healing from something."

"I know."

"What do you know?"

"I know you're sad. I'm sad, too. I'll try to set something up for you to meet Lilly." He hung up. His voice was still kind and thoughtful but he was abrupt in a way that didn't suit him.

I called him back.

"Lilly? Is that her name?" I whispered when he answered.

"Meet me at Marco's tomorrow night? Say seven?" He asked, a bit more docile than before.

"Okay." I held the phone, but he hung up again.

The Italian restaurant had been one of our favorites. I'd lost weight the first few months of my pregnancy so Josh would take me out to eat something he called "substantial." He'd order a pizza and eat the entire thing, less the one piece he'd make sure I consumed, except for the outer crust which I didn't like. He'd eat that. He had been fun and funny and he was about the most handsome white man I'd ever known. He was almost six-four with thick, wavy, dark brown hair that he wore a bit long, cut over his ears but hanging past his collar where it flipped up.

It was comfortable being with Josh before, but there was a wall between us now; a barrier of untold stories.

"Have you seen her?" I was in the restaurant near Utopia Park chewing my pizza and he was sitting across from me.

"Who?"

"My daughter."

"Yes."

"Well?"

"I'll give you the address. Her parents have agreed to let you meet her." He pushed a piece of paper across the table.

"Oh, Josh. How can I thank you?" I stood up and slipped into the booth on his side and hugged him. He didn't hug me back.

"I guess that's all you wanted. If you want to see me again, you have my number." He couldn't get out of the booth because I had him trapped. I kept my arms around his waist and my head on his chest. His heart was racing in my ear. I didn't let go and eventually he put his arms around me. The top of my head began to feel wet and I looked up to see huge tears rolling down his face. He shut his eyes so he didn't have to look at me.

*

I stood on the front stoop of an attached craftsman-style home in a row of two-story brick residences in the Laurelton area of New York City, called Springfield Gardens. Leaves blew off the trees like snowflakes and there was a sweet, pungent zing in the air as though it were about to rain. I pulled my coat tighter around me and lifted the collar to ward off the biting wind as I pressed the white button next to the door.

I heard the doorknob jiggle and a second later the white, wooden door with an oval glass swung open and there was Emalene Franklin with a smile on her face. She wore a brown-plaid shirtwaist dress with a skinny, gold belt and looked as beautiful as I remembered her from the day she and Joe came to take my baby girl home with them.

Behind Emalene's skirt, I could see the top of a small head with curly, reddish-brown hair. The little girl peeked shyly around her mother's side and I winked at her. She smiled and wrapped herself in Emalene's dress. I stood like a statue, not knowing what to expect, when Emalene reached for me with both hands and folded me into her arms, as a mother would her wayward child.

I was speechless. Maybe it was the anticipation, the fear of not knowing what to expect, the loss of Rodney and our dreams for the future. Maybe it all came on me at once because I melted into Emalene's arms. She stroked my back and said, "We are so happy to know you, Susie."

Emalene put one arm over my shoulder and ushered me into the warm living room with a fire blazing in the fireplace. We sat on the sofa and the little girl climbed on her mother's lap.

"Lilly," Emalene said. "This is Susie."

Lilly stared at me and the sides of her mouth started to lift. Her eyes were amber with green specks and she looked so much like Rodney that I wanted to grab and squeeze her. When she finally broke into a smile, the dimples in both her cheeks were so deep it was difficult to see the bottoms.

"Hi," she said. She slid off her mother's lap and stood directly in front of me. Then she held her skirt out on both sides and curtsied. I burst out laughing. She was the most adorable child I'd ever laid eyes on and I was instantly in love.

I reached out to shake hands with her and was reminded of the time Catfish shook my little hand. I wondered if Lilly looked at my pink hand and saw the difference in color, although it was not as dramatic a difference as Catfish's. Her hand was light brown, as though she'd spent all her time in the sun. My skin was so fair that next to anyone else's there was a contrast. I folded her tiny hand in both of mine and stared at her. We both smiled broadly and I felt goose bumps on my arms.

I saw Rodney in Lilly, but some of myself, too. She was precocious and soon took me by the hand and led me to her room to show me her baby dolls and stuffed animals. Emalene left us alone to spend an hour playing tea party with her dolls at a small table with four pint-sized chairs set in the center of her pink, blue, and white bedroom that smelled of lavender and pine. I couldn't remember ever having had so much fun.

Later, as Emalene and I sat in the kitchen with real cups of tea after Lilly went down for her nap, we talked about why I'd waited more than four years to visit.

"So many reasons, Emma," I said. "I was afraid I'd fall in love with her, which I have. I was afraid she'd love me. Or that she wouldn't. I was afraid I'd want her. I knew it wasn't fair to disrupt her life or yours and Joe's."

"We want you in Lilly's life," she said. I looked at her with the strangest feelings. How could they welcome me in this way knowing that, as Lilly's birth mother, I might try to take her away? How could Emalene not be jealous of my love for this precious child she had raised from birth?

"I'm surprised you allowed me to come."

"What surprises you, Susie?" She looked at me with the kindest stare. Her eyes were dark brown and her skin was about the color of Tootsie's—"like pecans," as Tootsie would say. "When you have a child, you want everyone to love her. There could never be too many people who love Lilly. The more people who love and nurture her, the richer her life will be."

"But aren't you afraid she might love someone... uh, uh... love me, more than she loves you?"

"That's a selfish love. It's not the kind of love you have for your child. The kind of love you have for your child is total and giving.

We want what's best for her, not what's best for us."

I'd never known such unselfish love. Even Rodney had his loyalties that superseded his love for me. And my parents, well, I'm not sure what you'd call their kind of love.

I was equally perplexed and intrigued by Emalene. She was special, and I realized how blessed I was to have chosen her to be Lilly's mom. Even at eighteen, I must have had some sort of instinct. I held on to that positive thought about myself because I didn't have much else I liked about me at that time.

We talked for hours. She said that they'd always told Lilly she was adopted, "We use the word *chosen*," she said, and that they celebrated her adoption day and birthday on the same day every year, August 21. "Because we did adopt her the day she was born. That was so generous of you, Susie,"

"Rodney." I didn't know how to say it. "That's his name. Lilly's, ummm, you know…"

"Biological dad?"

"Yes."

"You're still in love with him, huh?"

"Uh-huh." I nodded because I couldn't talk.

"Do you want to tell me what happened?"

"Well. I guess you realize he's, ummm…"

"A Negro? I figured as much."

"He and I. Well. We just couldn't…"

"In the South?"

"Uh-huh."

"Why didn't he come up here so the two of you could be together?"

"We tried. They almost killed his brother. Before that, his dad."

"Oh, Susie. I'm so sorry. I've read about prejudice in the South. It's hard to believe."

"Believe."

"How long has it been since the two of you gave up on being together?"

"Not quite a year, I guess."

"I can't imagine that kind of hatred," she said. "The kind that keeps two people from loving each other." She was quiet for a while, and I knew she was thinking about how she and Joe could have been kept apart had they grown up in a different place. She put her arm over my shoulder and pulled me to her, and when I put my head on her chest I felt comforted in the way Tootsie had made me feel when I was a little girl.

I told Emalene about Rodney. I described his gentleness. I told her how gorgeous he was and how much we loved each other. I told her how much Lilly resembled him, and Emma said she saw a lot of me in Lilly.

Lilly came stumbling into the kitchen, rubbing her eyes with the backs of her hands. She ran into Emalene's lap, which I thought was my cue to leave, but when I rose from the sofa, she ran to me and wrapped her little arms around my legs.

"Please don't go, Susie." She looked up at me with those amber eyes, her thick eyelashes touched her eyebrows and a soft furrow crossed her forehead. Her loose curls were tossed around her head like she'd slept upside down. She looked so much like Rodney in that moment.

"Looks like you're staying for dinner," Emalene said. "Now, you two run off and play while I put something in the oven." She disappeared and Lilly took my hand and led me back to her room.

We got into a routine. Every Wednesday afternoon I'd get off early, pick Lilly up at school, and take her for an outing. On nice days we'd go to the park or the zoo. On dreary days we'd take the subway downtown and go to the library. She loved the books, the smells, the quiet whispers we spoke in.

Lilly was smart beyond her four years and inquisitive, like a sponge soaking up everything around her—the sounds, the way people walked, the different languages she overheard when we sat in cafés, and I introduced her to hot chocolate with espresso. Emalene scolded me when Lilly couldn't sleep on Wednesday nights, but I knew it was more than caffeine that kept her awake. It was her little brain running overtime. I'd stay for dinner and put Lilly to bed on those nights, reading books to her and telling her stories—Catfish's stories.

My love for Lilly and hers for me salved the open wounds left by losing Rodney. I didn't answer his letters that begged me to see him. I knew it was fruitless and would leave me miserable and unable to recover. I needed to move on with my life, without Rodney.

It wasn't simply the love I shared with Lilly that filled the huge gap Rodney left in my life. Emalene was like a big sister and mother. Joe was the gentle, kind, big brother that James had never been. I'd found a family to substitute for Catfish, Tootsie, and Marianne, who had been my adopted family in Jean Ville.

Once I settled into a new, contented life I was able to focus on my Catfish stories. In the evenings, I wrote. It was as though my hand glided across the page, the ink from my blue ballpoint pen making words as quickly as my mind could relay them to my fingers. I could visualize Catfish telling me the stories in his deep, soft, Afro-Cajun drawl, eyes twinkling, feet hitting the floor of the porch as his rocker went back and forth.

I had wanted to write the stories as though Catfish were talking to me, because that was how they could be told with truth and integrity. I'd heard him tell stories for years before he died and his voice echoed in my head when I thought of his tales.

He had told me how things changed at Shadowland Plantation after Mr. Van got married. I had thought I would be married by now, to Rodney, so the story of falling in love and getting married had a certain ring to it for me.

"After a few years running the plantation, Mr. Gordon Van knew it was time to marry," Catfish told me.

I sat there with my pen in my hand and closed my eyes. In my mind, I pictured Catfish rocking on his porch, staring at the corn field with a thoughtful grimace across his face.

Changes at Shadowland
1860
Mr. Van was almost forty years old and while he learned the business of growing cotton, corn, and sugar cane, and rebuilt the plantation, he looked for the perfect match. He wanted love, desire, beauty, intelligence—someone who could give him smart, handsome children. And he needed a lady who could entertain—he owed lots of people who'd invited him to they houses.

He had his eyes on a beauty at Evergreen's Oakwold Plantation, about fifteen or twenty miles southwest of Jean Ville. There were a couple of drawbacks: she was young, about twenty years his junior, and she had a serious suitor, the son of a plantation owner on Big Bend with about 2000 acres. Mr. Van was no competition with only 900 acres, but he was not the son, he was the Man. Maybe that counted for something.

Her name was Marguerite Annabelle Pearce and her father was a solicitor who farmed about 1000 acres of sugar cane and another 500 in cotton and corn. He was in politics and spent lots of time in Baton Rouge with Governor Moore, also an attorney and plantation owner. Mr. Van supported Moore for Governor in the 1859 election and attended his inauguration in January, 1860, where he met Pearce. A few weeks later, Van received an invitation to Pearce's daughter's début, an event that occurred later in her life than customary because she wanted to finish college before she got presented.

Mr. Van found out about Miss Marguerite's age and college education at the party. They was lots of eligible young ladies who seemed to take an interest in him even though he was near the age of some of those girls' fathers. He told Maureen he danced with all of them womens who was there but, for some reason, he couldn't take his eyes off Marguerite Pearce.

He said he axed himself what was it about her, but couldn't put his finger on it until he danced the last dance of the night with her. He told Maureen he liked the way Marguerite felt in his arms, the grace with which she followed his lead, how she held her head back, a little tilted to the side so she could look at him or look away without turning her neck. He liked her laugh; it wasn't giddy and nervous like some of the other girls.

But it was her intelligence he admired most; somehow she seemed more mature than her twenty-one years. Besides her beauty, "her long, dark hair pinned up on the sides with the back flowing in curls to her waist, the large dark eyes framed by thick black eyelashes that curled up towards perfectly-shaped eyebrows, wide pink lips that turned up on the sides while the bottom one pooched out in a permanent pout, and a perfectly straight nose that hinted at a pug," he told Maureen.

Mr. Van said that Marguerite seemed worldly; she'd traveled abroad. She'd got herself a bachelor's degree in history and English from Newcomb College in New Orleans, where she graduated with honors. Mr. Van said he had never met a woman with a college degree since he'd been back in the United States.

He wondered how serious she was about Gerard Laborde from Big Bend.

The dance ended and so did the party. Mr. Van waited until the crowd thinned and when he reached the Pearce family who stood at the door to say their good nights, he took both of Marguerite's hands in his, looked her in the eye and said, "I'd like to see you again. May I ask your father for that occasion?" She seemed surprised and paused a moment before she responded.

"Yes, Mr. Van," she said. She looked directly into his eyes. She didn't blink. "I'd like that."

"It's Gordon, Miss Pearce. Not, Mister Van, okay? Don't make me feel old," he laughed. She couldn't hold back the smile that broke through. He told Maureen that Miss Marguerite's smile captured his heart. Mr. Van could be real charming when he wanted to really turn it on. That charm probably came through his blue eyes and wide grin and caught that girl off guard.

"Okay, Gordon," she said. He later learned that she was enchanted, too. When Mr. Van shook hands with Mr. Pearce he asked whether he would be welcomed as a suitor for Marguerite.

"I understand there may already be someone of interest, but if there are no commitments, I'd like to throw my hat in the ring," Mr. Van said.

"If my daughter has no reservations, I have none," Pearce said.

"Thank you, sir," Van said. "I should like to call on Wednesday late afternoon if that suits your schedule." Pearce looked at his wife who stood next to him and had overheard the conversation. She nodded gently.

"That will be fine, Van," Pearce said. They shook hands and Gordon Van walked through the front door, then turned back to see Marguerite watching him leave. He winked at her. She blushed and turned away. Van said he laughed as he entered his coach. "Let's go home, George." He shut the door, leaned back, and slept a shallow sleep on the ride to Jean Ville.

The courtship was sweet and quick. Mr. Van called on Marguerite every week for three months, then asked for her hand. He was smitten and it showed when he was at Shadowland. He whistled and hummed all day and Maureen said she'd catch him daydreaming. The slaves all got a big kick out of that.

The wedding was the social event of the year, held over at the newly built Sacred Heart Catholic Church in Moreauville, which had replaced St. Paul's in Hydropolis. It was a mini-cathedral and had been filled with flowers and candles for the wedding. It was the first wedding held at Sacred Heart, one of two Catholic churches in Toussaint Parish. The other one was in Mansura, five miles south of Jean Ville, only three miles from Shadowland, but it was too small for the wedding, so the Peace family and friends traveled eighteen miles from Evergreen to the magnificent church in Moreauville.

Mr. William was there, and he told George that the pews were stuffed with friends and family and the bridesmaids dressed in pink gowns that Mrs. Pearce called "dusty rose." Mr. William got a big kick out of that. He said the bride walked through an archway of lilies and hydrangeas and was like a fairy queen in her white, lace gown that dusted the new aisle.

Maureen and Mr. William helped Mr. Van plan the honeymoon in New Orleans, which included a riverboat cruise to South Padre Island, Texas, with a side trip to Galveston. Two weeks later, the bride and groom took a train to Mansura from New Orleans where George met them with the buggy. George said that Mr. Van and Miss Marguerite, now Mrs. Van, kissed and touched each other constantly on the long trip home, as if they knew that once life began for real, they could never recapture their innocent love and affection. Maureen told my granny about a time just after the Vans got home from their honeymoon.

Mr. Van rang his bell after he met with Mr. William one evening and asked Lizzie to fetch Mrs. Van and said that lady "glided into the study, a vision in a pale-pink gown with a plunging neckline that revealed the tops of her ample bosoms." Lizzie would laugh when she'd talk about Mrs. Van but she was scared to death of that woman. She said Mr. Gordon shut the door and reached for his wife. Lizzie listened at the door in the hall and could tell that he pulled his wife down on the sofa and they went at it. They was newlyweds, after all.

Lizzie said she heard the latch flip on the door to the hall where she was crouched with her ear against the jam and that Mr. Van and the Missus was panting and laughing.

"Our first night in our home, Mrs. Van," Lizzie heard Mr. Gordon say. Lizzie said they was making out in there and she could hear the whole thing. She heard Mr. Van say he never wanted a woman so bad as he wanted Miss Marguerite. And that the Missus just laughed at him. He said he could do this all day and night. Lizzie heard him say that the Missus was his muse, whatever that is, and that he was her prisoner. He told her he liked it that way. Then it was quiet for a while and Lizzie was about to walk away when they both screamed out, then they screams was muffled like they had put they hands over each other's mouths. Next thing, Lizzie say, they was laughing. She heard the Missus say she needed to get herself straightened up 'cause he messed her legs and such.

"We're newly married," Mr. Gordon said. "We are expected to have these moments."

"I can't face anyone with my thighs stuck together and my petticoats wet with your... well, you know." They both laughed. "And, I hope this is not because we are newly married. I hope it will happen until we are old and grey."

"It will, my love," Mr. Gordon said, and Lizzie said she could tell they was kissing again.

"You are asking for trouble, Mr. Van," Miss Marguerite said, breathless.

"I hope so, Mrs. Van," he said, and it started over again.

Finally she heard Mr. Van axe the Missus what was for dinner and she said, no idea. Lizzie ran down the hall to the kitchen and told Miss Bessie that she thought the Vans was about to come to the dining room so Bessie got dinner hot and ready, but it was another hour and Bessie had to reheat that dinner two more times. She was fiery mad at Lizzie for not getting it right.

"Now Mrs. Van," Catfish would say and shake his head side-to-side. "She was something else, turned this plantation upside down for a while. She took on the job of redecorating the plantation house while Mr. Gordon operated the business side.

"Everyone on the plantation knew Mr. Gordon Van was taken by his wife," Catfish said. "And when I say 'taken' I mean he was ate up with her. He was head over heels. He would agree to anything she wanted, and she wanted a lot."

I thought about how we would sit on Catfish's back porch and he would tell me these stories, then nod off with his straw hat pulled down over his eyes, his feet pushing softly on the floor to move his rocker back and forth ever so slowly. I missed Catfish. I had Emalene, Joe, and Lilly, but no one could ever replace Catfish.

Or Rodney.

Part Two: 1975

∽ Chapter Nine ∽

∾

Vietnam

AFTER RODNEY WAS DRAFTED into the army, I read every newspaper article about the conflict in Vietnam with deep interest. The war itself had ended on January 23, 1973 with the signing of the Paris Peace Accords, which called for a complete ceasefire and US troop withdrawal, taking place four days later. All US POWs were released and North Vietnam was allowed to retain the territories it had captured. President Thieu of South Vietnam was not happy with the agreement because he still had his own rebels, the Viet Cong, to contend with. As an enticement to sign the accord, President Nixon offered Thieu US airpower to enforce the peace terms and some army troops remained in the country.

The US elected Richard Nixon based on his campaign promise to end the war, but it dragged on for another four years. Between 1969 and 1973, more than 20,000 US soldiers were killed while a peace accord was negotiated at a snail's pace. Finally, at its end, everyone breathed a sigh of relief as their fathers, husbands, and sons came home. There was a feeling that the end of the war was the beginning of a new world, and a new era of the country.

Christmas Eve 1974 was on a Tuesday, and Mr. Mobley let us off early that day. I went home to gather my gifts for Lilly, Emalene, and Joe, who had invited me to spend the night at their house so I could be with them when Lilly got up to see what Santa brought her the next morning. When I walked in the door of my apartment, the phone was ringing. I dropped my purse and keys on the table in the foyer and picked up the receiver on the kitchen wall.

"Hello!" I was breathless and unfocused.

"Susie, it's Rod." I couldn't talk. "Please don't hang up." The last time I'd heard his voice was in May, and he was the last person I thought would be calling me on Christmas Eve. "Are you there?" I opened my mouth but no sounds came out. "I hear you breathing so you must still be on the line." I slid to the floor and held the receiver so tight that my fingers began to tingle.

"Uh, yes. I'm here."

"I know it's a shock hearing from me. It took an Act of Congress to get your phone number from Marianne. Please don't be mad at her. I needed to be the one to tell you something important."

"Uh. Okay."

"Are you listening?"

"Yes. I'm here."

"I'm being shipped out… to Vietnam."

"Vietnam? I thought the war was over."

Rodney explained that he was being assigned to the embassy in Saigon, that there were still thousands of Americans and tens of thousands of Vietnamese sympathizers trying to fend off the North Vietnamese Army. He said they needed JAG personnel, which were lawyers in the Army who could decide the fate of defectors. He said that these military lawyers also try court-martials, advise commanders on military justice procedures, and deal with other legal problems.

"It's Christmas," I said.

"They don't care. There's a war going on over there and even though we pulled our troops out last year, we are still hoping to keep Ho Chi Minh and the communists out of South Vietnam. I learned a lot in training but I still have a lot more to learn." He was talking as though we'd been in touch all these months, like we talked every day and he was keeping me updated. I inhaled deeply and tried not to be angry. I settled for hearing his voice but knew that I now would have to spend more months trying to forget him all over again.

"I was hoping we could write to each other while I'm over there, Susie." He had a catch in his throat and he hesitated, gulped, and tried to speak but couldn't seem to push the words out. The silence between us was deafening, but I held onto it because, well, he was on the other end of the line and I could hear him breathing, and that mattered.

I felt alive for the first time in months.

"Okay, Rod." I couldn't say anything else. "We can."

"Will you send me your address?"

"I guess so, if you want me to."

"Susie…"

"Please don't say it, Rod. It will only make things harder."

"Okay. But you know."

"I'll write. And I'll pray for you."

"Thanks. I don't deserve it after what I've done to you."

"Please don't go there. We always knew…"

"Yeah. I guess." We didn't say goodbye. We didn't talk anymore. We just listened to each other breathe for the longest time and finally, I hung up because the urge to cry was so strong I couldn't hold back the tears any longer. I sat on the kitchen floor and sobbed. I'm not sure how long I sat there before the phone started ringing. I thought it was Rodney calling back so when I picked up the receiver I didn't say "Hello."

"Susie, are you there?" It was Emalene. "Susie?"

"Yes. I'm here, Emma."

"We're so worried about you. Are you still coming tonight?"

"What time is it?"

"Eleven."

"Oh, God. I'm so sorry. Something came up. I mean, something happened. Is it too late?"

"You can still come. Lilly is asleep but I know she would be glad to see you in the morning."

"I'm so sorry, Emma."

"Are you okay?"

"No, probably not, but I'll pull myself together."

Christmas morning was magical. Emalene and Joe's living room was awash in Christmas smells, sounds, and colors. They'd put the Christmas tree up the previous weekend and I'd helped them decorate it. Under the thick, fir branches were piles of beautifully wrapped gifts, mine among them. Next to the sofa was a new tricycle, a stuffed Winnie the Pooh about two feet high, and a miniature kitchen, complete with refrigerator, stove, sink, and cabinets. Lilly jumped up and down, clapped her hands, and ran from her mom to her dad, then to me, and hugged us. I sat on the floor near the tricycle and watched her move from toy to toy, draped in delight and surprise. It was a full hour before she settled down enough that we could open the gifts under the tree.

"We wanted to open these last night, Susie. We waited for you," Joe said. I could tell he was perturbed with me and I felt bad for ruining their plans, especially since they bent all their traditions to include me.

"I'm so sorry, Joe. I don't know what to say."

"It's okay," he said, but I could tell it wasn't okay. I had no excuse for forgetting Christmas Eve with this family who treated me like one of their own. I'd been selfish and had forgotten about everyone but me.

I watched Lilly tear paper off boxes and wondered how I had failed to put her first. I would have been a terrible mother, I thought in that moment. I was so grateful for Emalene and Joe, who had stood in for me and Rodney. We were two selfish people who couldn't see past our love for each other.

I opened a set of pink pajamas, a tube of Revlon lipstick in a mauve shade, a new wallet, and a large barrette for my hair. Emma and Joe seemed pleased with the new pressure cooker that was advertised as a time-saver for working families, the black leather belt Emma told me Joe needed, and the pair of fake pearl earrings for Emma. I knew about the little kitchen for Lilly so I'd bought her sets of pots and pans and dishes, and declared we'd have lots of choices when we played tea party. I also bought her a frilly nightgown and mittens with a matching knit cap that had a small beak, all in pink, of course.

Eventually, we sat at the table and Joe carved a golden turkey while Emma piled on mashed potatoes, dressing, and brussels sprouts. I thought of the dirty rice, pork roast, sweet potatoes, and green bean casserole my Mom would be serving and almost got nostalgic, before I remembered I missed only the food and my siblings.

Lilly took a nap, and Joe picked up paper and boxes and burned everything in a barrel in the backyard while Emalene and I cleaned the kitchen and put the leftover food away.

"You want to tell me what happened?"

"What do you mean?" I couldn't look at her. I was wiping off the table.

"It's not like you to forget something as special as Christmas Eve. And I think I know you well enough to tell that you're preoccupied today."

"I'm so sorry, Emma. I was selfish. I didn't mean to forget. I let my emotions control me."

"What happened, Susie?"

"Rodney called."

"Humph. Well, then…"

"I know. That's what I'm trying to say. I shouldn't have let it get to me. I couldn't stop crying and I lost track of time; of everything."

"Anything you want to tell me about the conversation?"

"He's being shipped out."

"Shipped out?"

"Vietnam."

"Oh, Susie. I'm so sorry."

"I told him I'd write to him."

"Of course."

"I'm still sorry I got all tied up in my emotions and let the time slip. I feel like I ruined Christmas for everyone."

"We adjusted. It's fine."

"Yeah. I guess." But I knew it wasn't fine. I didn't feel any better about what I'd done.

*

Fighting in Vietnam continued in defiance of the peace agreement, so President Thieu publicly stated that the Paris Accord was no longer in effect. The situation worsened after the beginning of 1975. President Richard Nixon resigned due to the Watergate scandal. Then came the passage of the Foreign Assistance Act of 1974 by Congress, which cut off all military aid to Saigon, the capital of South Vietnam. This opened the door for North Vietnam to attack, and Phuoc Long Province fell quickly, compelling the North to storm through the South and threaten Saigon.

It was in this atmosphere that Rodney found himself in the middle of Saigon, with Ho Chi Minh, the communist president of North Vietnam, pressing down from the North and the Viet Cong leading the rebels from the South.

Feb 1, 1975
Dear Susie,

I've been attached to the embassy in Saigon. It looks like we might be coming home before the year is out. At least I hope so. It's hot and rainy here, but I'm in a building with electricity and running water. That's something. I can't tell you anything about what we do every day. It's top secret.

My dad says Jeffrey is doing well. He's been recuperating at home and is even shooting some hoops with the neighborhood gang. Dad says he improves every day. We are all hoping he will be normal when his recovery is complete. I know he wants to return to Southern University and finish law school.

I've been thinking about us a lot since I've been here. I miss you more than anything. There has to be a way for us. I love you. You must still love me. Please give me some hope that, when I return from this godforsaken place, you'll give me another chance.

I hope you are doing well in New York, loving your job, making lots of friends. I want you to be happy. That would make me happy.

I look forward to your letters.

Yours, forever,

Rod

I didn't know how to respond. There had been some positive changes in south Louisiana with the election of a new sheriff, but not enough change that a black man could marry a white woman and get away with it. I felt Rodney must have lost his mind on another continent and had forgotten about the danger to his family, and the fact that he had chosen their safety over our love.

February 13, 1975

Dear Rod,

Thank you for your newsy letter. I enjoy hearing from you.

I crumpled that letter up and threw it in the trashcan and started over.

Dear Rod,

Top secret sounds intriguing. I'm happy Jeffrey is doing well. I am well and like my job in publishing. I continue to work on the Catfish stories and hope to find a publisher this year.

I'm not sure about hope or happiness; I gave up on both when I lost you.

Always,

S

February 21, 1975

Dear Susie,

Surely you haven't given up on us. I haven't. I never will. Once this war is over and I'm back stateside, I'm coming to see you. I know we can make it work. We still love each other and that's all that counts.

I miss you every day.

Yours forever,

Rod

March 1, 1975

Dear Rodney,

I'm sorry I can't bring myself to believe your promises that things have changed enough for a colored guy and a white girl to be married, or to even have any kind of relationship. Love is not everything. If we've learned nothing over the past nine years, it's that.

I hope you are safe and that you are able to get back to the US soon.

Always,

Susie

March 18, 1975

Dear Susie,

This war will end and I will show up on your doorstep. We can't be kept apart.

Yours forever,

Rod

April 1, 1975

Dear Rod,

There's more than a war keeping us apart. When you get home, you'll come to your senses and realize that.

Always,

Susie

In April, I read in the newspaper that a helicopter operation to transport more than 2,000 orphans and others out of Vietnam had been successful, but that one of the helicopters crashed killing 155 people. I panicked, wondering if Rodney was on that chopper. A few days later, the news reported that more than 100,000 Vietnamese refugees had been evacuated to US ships in the South China Sea. Surely they'd send Rodney home if everyone was leaving the country.

I didn't receive any letters from Rodney for several weeks, then, the second week of May, there were three in my mailbox. He said he was on a ship called the *USS Blue Ridge* and that he'd been one of the last to get out of Saigon. He had evacuated with the Ambassador, Graham Martin, who was technically the field officer in charge after the US ground troops were gone.

"Brave man, that Martin," Rodney said in his letter. "He was one of the last to evacuate and only did so under orders from President Ford. The pilot of the helicopter, Gerry Berry, had the orders written in grease pencil on his kneepads. It was surreal."

Rodney said it was five o'clock in the morning when they boarded the last helicopter to leave Saigon. "We left more than four hundred people, Vietnamese and South Koreans, in the embassy. We don't know what will happen to them. Ambassador Martin is bereft with grief and was pleading with the helicopter pilots to return to the embassy to pick up the few hundred remaining hopefuls waiting to be evacuated.

"I don't know whether they'll send me back to the States or somewhere else while they wrap this thing up. I technically still have another year to serve."

His letters all ended with this:

I want to see you when I get home. Say you'll let me come to New York for a visit. I miss you.
Yours forever,
Rod

I wrote to him to say how happy I was that he made it out of Vietnam alive. And I was happy. But I couldn't let myself get pulled back into hope. Hope was a useless emotion.

May 15, 1975
Dear Susie,
I'm stationed at Fort Riley, Kansas, where, of all things, they are training troops to fight in Vietnam. I wonder about the Army sometimes.
I wonder about you, too. I've put off taking the two weeks leave I've accumulated. I want to come to New York to see you if you will tell me what dates will work.
I miss you and love you. I hope you still love me.
Yours forever,
Rod

I was in the park with Rodney's letter on my lap trying to decide how to respond when Josh appeared out of nowhere. I hadn't seen or talked to him since he gave me Lilly's address.

"Hi." He sat next to me, but far enough away that we weren't touching.

"Are you stalking me?" I looked at him and he was staring at the letter opened on my lap. I quickly folded it and put it in my pocket.

"Still holding on to that guy from Louisiana?"

"No. And answer me—did you follow me here?"

"I come here often to feed the gulls. I've seen you here a number of times and didn't speak to you. So, no. I'm not stalking you or following you." We sat silently for several minutes and Josh started to feed the black-backed gulls. He stood and scattered popcorn on the concrete and they gathered around the white kernels near his feet.

I watched, mesmerized for a while. He returned to the bench and put both his arms on the back, one of his hands grazing my shoulder.

"Would you go to dinner with me sometime?" He didn't look at me, just spoke to the breeze that was blowing the leaves softly against the sky.

"I guess so." I remembered how safe I always felt with Josh, with no pressure.

"You don't have to be so enthusiastic." He was laughing, and that made me laugh, too. We made a date for the following Saturday evening and he left the park.

When I got home, I re-read Rodney's letter that ended with:

I want to come to New York to see you if you will tell me what dates will work.
Yours forever,
Rod

I sat at my desk and tried to put into words what I was feeling.

May 25, 1975
Dear Rod,
I can't see you again. The last time was too painful. It's still painful,
losing you. I can't to do it again. This has been a pattern—you saying we
can make it work, then something happens to blow our world apart. One
thing maturity has taught me is to learn from the past; it repeats itself.
Use your leave to visit your family. Start a new life. It will never
work out for us.
I'm trying to move on. Please let me…
Always,
S

Having Josh back in my life helped me to move on from
Rodney, to be brave and smart, not to let him come back then leave
me again.

A door opened just a crack in my heart and I began to be honest
with Josh. I told him about Rodney going to Vietnam and wanting
to come to see me.

"Are you going to see him?" Josh was stirring cream into his
coffee a few days later when we met near the hospital where he
worked.

"No." I explained why our relationship had ended, how the Ku
Klux Klan and my dad did everything they could to keep Rodney
and me apart. I told Josh how Rodney and I were able to see each
other when I was at LSU when I was a freshman, and Rodney was at
Southern University, both colleges in Baton Rouge. I told Josh that
my dad sensed something was going on and sent me to Sarah
Lawrence after my first semester.

"Rodney and I didn't see each other for a long time, almost two years, then he showed up in New York the fall of my junior year." I spoke softly as if by whispering my words would go unheard.

"Does he know about Lilly?"

"No. Of course not."

"You never told him?" Josh looked at me like I was lying, but I just shook my head side to side.

"It happened when he was here in New York that fall. I had just turned eighteen. He was twenty. We didn't see each other again until after college graduation, another three years."

"Why didn't you tell him?"

"It's too complicated." We didn't talk any more that day, but Josh didn't run away after he heard my story. It didn't bother him that Rodney was colored. He glazed over that.

A month or so later, we were at a restaurant near the park and he asked about my dad. Our conversation became very strained because I was evasive about my relationship with my father.

"I don't know what to tell you. He's very controlling and he was determined that I not be involved with a Negro."

"He found out about Rodney?"

"I don't know what he knew, but he found out I went to the Quarters to see Catfish, and he beat me."

"Beat you? How bad?"

"Bad." It took a number of conversations over several months before I was able to tell Josh everything about how my dad beat me, sometimes so badly I had to be hospitalized. And that once, I'd almost died. Those stories came out in spurts. I would start to tell him about a time Daddy barged into my room in the middle of the night, then I couldn't say any more. A few weeks later, we'd pick up on a story like that and I'd go a little further. I thought that once Josh found out how I was raised, abused, beaten, he'd desert me. I felt like that would be more than he could stomach.

"I didn't leave you when you were pregnant by some unnamed guy. I didn't leave you when I discovered he was colored. Why would I leave you now?"

"Everyone leaves at some point."

"Not this person. Not Josh Ryan." He reached across the table and took both of my hands and looked directly into my eyes. His pupils were small and the green surrounding them was almost emerald when the light from the pendant lamp above the table bounced off them. A soft, brown curl fell on his forehead above his left eyebrow and gave him a rakish look. I thought, *if I'd let myself, I could fall for this guy,* but I couldn't take the chance of being hurt again. "I'm in this for the long haul," he said in his most sincere voice.

"Even after you know all the gory details of my life?"

"Even after all that. And more. Try me."

"You walked out on me once."

"You were in love with someone else. I couldn't compete."

"How do you know I'm not still in love with him?" I think I was asking myself that question, too.

"I think I know. The question is, do you know?"

"I'm not sure. It's been a long time."

"And you've changed, right? Grown?"

"Yes, I think so. I don't know whether the person I am today would still love the person he is."

"Maybe you should find out."

"How?"

"See him."

That made me stop to think. How long had it been since I'd seen Rodney? More than a year; May 1974. And before that it had been three years. Should I write to Rodney and agree to see him, or should I continue to try to forget him, to let myself fall for Josh Ryan?

That question was answered for me when I wrote to Rodney and told him he could come to New York at Thanksgiving. He wrote back to say he was sorry, but he had taken his leave and gone to Jean Ville. It would be another six months before he could take an extended vacation.

"Why don't you come to Kansas? You can stay in a hotel and I can see you in the evenings," he wrote.

I tore up his letter and threw it in the trashcan. I didn't write back.

～Chapter Ten ～

～

Josh

JOSH AND I SAW each other once or twice a week and talked on the phone almost every day. I'd forgotten how comfortable and easy it was to be with him.

I told Emma that I was seeing a man named Josh Ryan, and asked her if it would be all right if Lilly met him. I explained how he had been with me during my pregnancy and had been the doctor who delivered Lilly.

"Oh, he's that good-looking white doctor with the longish hair who came into the waiting room to tell us that the baby was a healthy girl. Of course I remember him."

"I didn't know he did that. But, yes, he's the one."

"Sure. You can introduce Lilly to Josh."

Josh met Lilly and me in the park one Wednesday afternoon. He was dressed in jeans and an aqua polo shirt with a black windbreaker over the top. It was windy and his hair blew over his collar. The waves fell on his forehead, making him look like a little boy. He bent to kiss me on the cheek then got down on one knee so he could be eye-level with Lilly. She threw her arms around his neck and said, "Uncle Josh!" I watched the exchange with utter disbelief.

They played chase for a while and Josh handed her a bag of popcorn so she could feed the black-backed gulls. While Lilly was occupied, Josh sat next to me. I turned with a jerk.

"You and Lilly know each other? All this time we've talked about her and you never told me. What?"

"Emma, Joe, and I thought we'd keep it under wraps until you suggested we meet. How do you think I've kept up with you?"

"You know Emalene and Joe?"

"After Lilly was born we kept in touch. I'd lost you but I didn't want to lose the baby, too. I felt like I had nurtured her in the womb and was like a surrogate father."

"I feel betrayed. Lied to."

"No one has lied to you. Yes, there were things we didn't tell you—that Emalene, Joe, Lilly, and I have been friends for almost five years. After all, you are the one who refused to respond to the pictures I sent you. Then, six months ago you just decided to waltz into their lives and now you are angry with me, with Emma and Joe?"

"So this is a set-up?" I felt the same way I'd felt years before when I discovered that my dad had been fooling around with Tootsie since before I was born and that nobody—not Tootsie, not Catfish, not even Marianne—had told me. When I shared my feelings about that situation with Rodney, he told me that no one meant to betray me; it was about them protecting themselves and had nothing to do with me personally.

"I don't want to think about him," Marianne had said. That's when I realized why she was so light-skinned and had wavy hair and hazel eyes. Her dad was white. Her dad was my dad. I had felt betrayed because everyone in the Quarters knew about the affair between Tootsie and my dad, and kept it from me.

I wondered whether this was similar, whether I was taking it as a personal affront when it had nothing to do with me.

I sat and sulked while Josh and Lilly laughed and played. Every now and then Lilly would grab my hand and try to get me to join in their fun, but I'd say, "I'm tired right now. You go on and play with *Uncle* Josh."

The three of us got burgers and fries at McDonald's—Lilly's favorite place—then she and I rode the bus to Springfield Gardens. Joe put Lilly to bed while Emma and I had a cup of tea in the kitchen.

"You didn't tell me about Josh," I said.

"What was there to tell? He started coming around soon after we brought Lilly home. He's been a dear friend all these years."

"Why didn't you tell me?"

"You never asked."

"Emma. That's not fair. You told Josh where to find me."

"After I realized it was over between you and Rodney, I mentioned to Josh that I felt you might need a friend. He took it from there."

"I feel betrayed. By you. By Josh. By Joe. I'm hurt."

"I'm really sorry you're hurt. None of us meant for that to happen. We didn't know what to expect from you, really. For four years Josh sent you pictures of Lilly and none of us heard from you. Then you showed up six months ago. We decided to trust you. Trust that you won't walk out on Lilly. Trust that you are sincere. But Josh... well he has been with us day in and day out since Lilly was born. I'm not sure how we are supposed to divide our loyalties."

I didn't spend the night with Lilly that Wednesday like I had from time to time. I wanted to be alone, to think.

The next morning, after very little sleep, I called Josh. "Are you working today?"

"I'm off all weekend."

"Can we talk?"

Josh picked me up and we went to a café close to my apartment.

"She's something," he said after we sat across from each other in a booth. The smell of frying onions and burgers filled the air and we didn't say much while we waited for the waitress to bring our drinks.

"Yes, she is, isn't she?"

"I can tell you're smitten."

"Does it show?" I laughed, knowing Josh could see right through me and was teasing me. I watched him sip his beer and it hit me, suddenly, how much I'd come to rely on having him in my life again. I thought about how easy it was with Joe and Emma, who were now like family to me, and how Josh fit right in. I'd had a long talk with myself about not being defensive and making everything about me.

"Josh, I want to feel good about your relationship with the Franklins and the fact that none of you told me. Can you help me?"

"Susie, after I knew I'd lost you I held on to the next best thing—your child. And I fell in love with Lilly. Then there's Emalene and Joe, two of the most special people I know, and easy to love. We rarely talked about you, except when we would choose which pictures of Lilly to send you.

Josh said that the day we met in the park and I asked him to help me find Lilly, he'd gone to see the Franklins and that they were delighted I wanted to know her.

"You showed up and they loved you. I had to coordinate when I would be there around your visits because we didn't want to complicate things between you and Lilly." Josh said he would ask Emma and Joe about me and how after Rodney returned from Vietnam and it was obvious our relationship was over, Emma told Josh I might need a friend.

"A friend?"

"Well, it was no secret I'd never gotten over you. I'd brought a couple of girls to meet Emma and Joe, but those relationships weren't going anywhere, and they knew it. Think of it this way: Emma and Joe love us both and want us to love each other."

"You make it sound benevolent."

"Maybe it is benevolence. They are the most sincere folks I know." Josh and I sat in that booth and talked until the lights blinked and we realized we were the last people in the restaurant and the staff wanted to go home. We didn't talk as he drove me home, but we held hands on the console.

I felt a wave of maturity wash over me. Perhaps I could begin to see things from other people's perspectives and not stay stuck in my own feelings. Was that a sign of growing up? I was almost twenty-four years old; it was about time.

When Josh walked me to the door of my apartment I was thinking about how I needed to protect myself from being hurt again.

"What's wrong?" He put his hand over mine as I inserted the key in the doorknob. "Talk to me."

"Nothing's wrong." I didn't turn around as I tried to unlock the door. He put his hand over my wrist and tugged me towards him. I turned and faced him, my eyes level with his collar.

"What's changed all of a sudden? Everything was fine and now you're in retreat mode. Did I say something?"

"No. In fact, the opposite."

"Make sense. Talk to me." He took my other hand, and pulled me closer, into his personal space. I tried to step back. "Please don't pull away. Tell me what you're feeling."

"You won't understand."

"Try me." I didn't say anything. I stared at our hands, his wrapped over mine, and I could feel tears gather behind my eyelids. Josh's scent caught in my throat, spice and Dove soap and minty freshness. I thought about the first time Catfish shook my hand and

I looked down and noticed how brown his hands were. When he let go and I saw that his palms were pink. I was startled.

Josh's hands were long, like Catfish's. I stared at them and felt the warmth that went from his palms into my hands and had goose bumps up my arms.

"I can't do this." I looked up at him.

"Do what?"

"Fall in love with you."

"Then don't. I'm not asking you for anything. We can take it as slow as you want. I'm in no hurry." He pulled me a little closer. I don't know what I was thinking. Part of me was glad he was patient and kind; the other part wanted him to grab me and force me to give in to him. "Although I'd like to kiss you and hold you every time we're together," he whispered and chuckled as if it were a joke.

I was aware of the sound of car engines as they pulled into the parking lot and the clop-clop-clop of shoes on the pavement, but what I felt was the warmth from Josh's chest penetrate the air between us, even though our bodies weren't quite touching.

"Why don't you?" I couldn't believe those words slipped out of me. I looked up with a jerk, surprised at what came out of my mouth. "I didn't mean..." Josh was laughing hard now, tears running down his cheeks. Whew, I thought. He didn't take me seriously.

"What do you mean?" He was trying to control his laughter and I had a grin inching across my face, which was close to his. I could smell the beer on his breath and see the glint in his eye. He was smirking, trying not to break out into an all-out smile.

"What's so funny?"

"You," he said. I wanted to laugh but I didn't get the joke. Our lips were so close I could feel the heat from his, but he didn't move in or try to kiss me. "You're quite a fighter," he said and I tasted his words while I watched his mouth move. Something happened inside me. I moved my face closer to his and our lips touched. He closed his eyes but didn't move his mouth. It was the ultimate in self-control.

I kissed him. He didn't pull away, but he didn't kiss me back. I moved my lips on his and sucked in a little, then I felt his arm move around my back and he began to respond; softly, gently. He pulled away and looked at me as though he could see inside me.

"I like the way you taste," he whispered. "I always wondered."

"You said we could take it slow. Right?"

"Are you afraid of me?"

"No, I'm afraid of me. When I fall, I fall hard."

"Yes, I know that about you. That's something I hold on to." Josh turned to leave and I unlocked the doorknob.

"Want to come in?" I said it over my shoulder in a whisper, hoping he didn't hear me.

"I'd better not."

"Will you kiss me goodnight?" I turned around, my back against the door as I looked directly into his eyes. There was an unusual energy between us as we looked at each other. I realized I'd never locked gazes with Josh before. I'd avoided such an intimate connection, but now it was here and it was real, and I was mesmerized by him.

"Only if it's your idea." He kissed me deeply, no tongue, but with every fiber of his being, and my knees got weak. I almost fell, but he tightened his arms around me and I hung onto his neck to keep from sliding to the ground. "Good?" His breath was warm in my ear when he pulled his lips away but not his arms.

"Yes. Too good." I didn't open my eyes. My head rested against his cheek and I could feel him breathing, even and steady.

"Never too good," he said as he put his hands on my waist and put some distance between us. My hands slipped from his neck to his shoulders and I looked at him with what I guess was longing.

"Goodnight. I'll call you soon," he said, and pecked me on the forehead, leaving me a bit confused. I watched him walk to his car with that confident saunter that was at once provocative and cute, and knew I was in trouble.

Josh Ryan was some kind of man.

I got ready for bed and tried to read but couldn't concentrate. I tried to sleep, but that didn't work either, so I got up and sat at my desk, opened the composition book where I wrote Catfish's stories, and began to think about the story he told me about Mr. Henry Van, Gordon and Marguerite's son. It was Maureen, the housekeeper who would tell the cook, Bessie, about what went on in the big house and Bessie, who lived in the Quarters, would pass the stories around. As I wrote what I remembered, I could hear Catfish talking in his slow Cajun drawl, stopping to laugh his belly laugh now and then. He'd look at me sideways to make sure I was listening, bend forward in his rocker, and stamp one foot on the floor of the porch over and over as his back lifted with each howl. Hearty as gumbo, I thought when I'd hear him laugh like that.

The story of a new baby made me think of Lilly and how I felt when she was born, and I cringed to think I was like Marguerite Van.

A Baby
1860
Maureen said Miss Marguerite wanted to spend her first year at Van Plantation redecorating and staffing the house properly. It had been a man's domain for too long, she said often. Her mother came for a visit six weeks after the wedding and stayed a month. She brought the wedding gifts that Maureen and Lizzie unpacked, washed, and stored—stuff like bone china, sterling silver, Baccarat crystal, whatever that is, silk linens, and other things Mrs. Pearce said would make the home more posh.

Mrs. Pearce brought Miss Marguerite's personal maid, Ellie, to live at the plantation. Ellie was a slight young thing, not even as old as Miss Marguerite. She was dark skinned, almost as dark as ole George, with the whitest eyes you ever did see. And she was meek. She didn't say three words at a time and she stuttered when she tried to talk. That made Mrs. Van awful mad and she'd say, "Spit it out, Ellie. Stop that stuttering and say what you need to say." That Mrs. Van, now she was something.

The ladies ordered drapery fabrics, furnishings, and new gas light fixtures. Mrs. Van had talked Mr. Gordon into bringing gas lighting to the house and she wanted to install fixtures in every room with chandeliers in the dining room, parlor, and study, and other fancy lights all around, even outside on the porch.

After Miss Marguerite's mother went back to Oakwold, Miss Marguerite got sick. She couldn't hold down solid food, stayed in bed all day and refused to sleep with her husband, whose bedroom joined her chambers through a short hall with a pan closet on either side. Pan closets was small rooms with toilets where the waste went into a catch basin underneath. The housekeepers emptied it just like they emptied chamber pots. Course we had outhouses, still do.

Mr. Van, he thought his wife was sick 'cause she was missing her mama and would get better when she got busy again, but she wouldn't get out the bed.

Maureen said she could tell both Mr. and Mrs. Van's beds been slept in when she cleaned in the mornings and she said that Miss Marguerite's door was still locked between the two rooms when she brought Mr. Gordon's breakfast. Mr. Van was building a water storage tank in the attic so he could install new washdown closets, toilets with water tanks over them pipes to carry the waste out of the house and into the pond way back in the field. He thought that would make the new missus happy and get her to stop yearning for her mama and Oakwold. Poor Mr. Van was beside hisself, wanting to fix things so the missus would get back to loving him and being his wife.

Meanwhile Mrs. Van depended on Ellie and Lizzie to keep her chamber pots nearby, empty them, and return with them clean. Lizzie said that Mrs. Van was vomiting regular-like.

Mr. Gordon sat by her bed and held her hand in the evenings and tried to spoon feed her clear broth, which she threw up every time. Afraid she would die of dehydration, Mr. Gordon went to town to ask Dr. Tarleton to visit the plantation and see about his wife. The doctor came every week and talk to Mrs. Van about forcing herself to hold down water and broth if she wanted to live. Lizzie said his urgings were helpful 'cause Mrs. Van started to keep liquids from coming back up. Solid foods, now that was another thing. They wouldn't stay down for nothing, Lizzie said. After about a month Dr. Tarleton did some exams and said he thought Mrs. Van was with child.

Mr. Gordon was elated. Miss Marguerite was mad. She was angry with her husband for making her pregnant, angry with the baby for making her sick, angry with Ellie and Lizzie for breathing. Maureen said Miss Marguerite did not want a baby. Not yet! She had things to do, parties to host, a house to decorate, a new wardrobe to assemble. Now she had to wait an entire social season to stay home and hide her sins.

It was another month before the nausea and tiredness finally passed and Mrs. Van was able to go downstairs for dinner in the evenings, but she couldn't hide her displeasure from Mr. Van.

"I'm not ready to be a mother," she told him every night when they sat beneath the new gas chandelier and ate off bone china. "I need more time to accomplish things before I have to care for a child."

Mr. Van was hurt. At forty, he was ready for children. He wanted a house full of them. He tried to hide his delight from his wife, but she knew he was happy about the baby. This was the first wedge to lodge between the lovebirds. The honeymoon was definitely over!

Henry Van was born in December, 1860. From the beginning, the missus refused to feed him, said it would make her breasts fall. Josie had birthed another girl about a month before, and Maureen sent Anna Lee to fetch her to the house. Ellie brought baby Henry from the nursery and Josie nursed him until he was content. Every day, four times a day, Josie would nurse her little girl on one side then Henry on the other. Maureen said Josie had plenty of milk and it seemed to multiply the more she nursed. Henry cried at night for the first week, hungry but unfed, then Lizzie would take him to the kitchen around five o'clock in the morning where Josie would fill his little tummy.

The boy thrived but his mother barely noticed. Ellie, Maureen, and Lizzie tended the missus and the baby, and Maureen's daughter by Mr. Shelton, Anna Lee, who was six-years-old, played with him and was his friend and babysitter. Before long, she would rock him to sleep, stay in his room at night, and take him downstairs in the mornings to be fed. Mrs. Van got busy decorating the house and planning parties and kept Maureen, Lizzie, and Ellie so busy that Anna Lee fell into the role of nanny.

Maureen said a second wedge grew between Mr. Gordon and Miss Marguerite when she refused to sleep with him. She told him she didn't want to get pregnant again, so she slept in her room, he in his, and she locked the adjoining door at night. Mr. Gordon tried to question her at dinner, and that was about the only time he saw her, but she wouldn't discuss it except to say "I don't want another baby right now."

Mr. Van was frustrated and one day, right in the middle of the morning, he went to Mrs. Van's chambers to speak to her. Maureen was in the hall and saw him raise his fist to knock on the tall, oak door when he heard a commotion inside. Maureen said there was a slap, then another, then Miss Marguerite's voice bellowed through the closed door.

"Don't touch that, Lizzie. I told you not to go near my dressing table."

"Sorry, Ma'am," Lizzie said. "I wanted to dust it for you." Another slap.

"Don't speak to me unless I ask you a question! I've told you this a hundred times. Are you simple-minded? Get out!"

"Ellie, where are you girl?" Van heard his wife scream and stood in the hallway, dumbfounded. "Get in here and brush my hair, you lazy bitch. I'll show you what happens when you slough off!" Another slap. Then another. Lizzie opened the door to leave and ran right into Mr. Van, who walked around her and into the room, unnoticed. He stood and watched his beautiful, cultured wife yell obscenities and strike Ellie over and over. Lizzie and Maureen watched from the hall through the open doorway as Mr. Van walked up behind Miss Marguerite and, when she reached her arm up to hit Ellie again, he grabbed her wrist.

Mrs. Van look shocked. She turned around to see her husband glaring down at her. While staring directly into his wife's eyes he said, "Ellie, go to my study. Take Lizzie with you. I will meet you there momentarily."

"What are you doing in my chambers?" Mrs. Van spit as she barked at her husband.

"Listen to me, Marguerite, and listen well. I will not repeat myself. We do not *mistreat our workers. Do you understand?"*

"I did not mistreat anyone. Slaves have to be kept in line or they will be lazy. I will not allow my slaves that pleasure."

"On this plantation they are not slaves. They are housekeepers, field workers, staff. We do not *mistreat them. Do you understand?"*

"No, I do not understand!" she said. Lizzie and Ellie stood in the hall next to Maureen and cowered.

"Then I shall explain." Mr. Van sounded as if he spoke through clenched teeth.

"Release my arm. You're hurting me." He grabbed her other wrist and held them both, tight, in the air above her head.

"First of all, these are not your workers, they are mine. This is my plantation, my home, my rules. I have spent the past five years working hard to change rules, policies, and business practices so that this plantation can be profitable again. I will not allow you, or anyone else, to undermine my efforts."

"But..." Mrs. Van said.

"No buts. Let me finish. Secondly, you will either adopt my beliefs and policies or you will return to Oakwold. You are no longer a wife to me. You are certainly not a mother to Henry. I have no use for you but to admire your beauty, so it would not hurt me to send you home where you can beat human beings and lord your whiteness over them. Now, do you understand?"

Tears ran down her face and she tried to pull away from her husband, but he held her wrists in his big hands and refused to release them. A silence filled the air that only her sniffles passed through. She nodded.

"Say it, Marguerite. Say you understand."

"I understand," she said, her eyes downcast.

"Look at me and say it!" Mr. Van yelled. Lizzie said she had never seen him angry since the time he fired Buckley. Mrs. Van looked into his eyes. "Look, Gordon. My daddy whips his slaves and my mother slaps hers. That's how I was taught. Who says you're right?"

"I say. And this is my plantation. What they do at Oakwold is none of my business but what anyone does on my property is very much my business. Do you understand?"

"I understand," she said. Lizzie and Ellie ran down the stairs and into the study just as they saw Mr. Van release Mrs. Van's wrists and turn sharply to leave her room, pulling the door shut behind him with a thud. They could hear his footsteps descend the staircase in a hurry, then he walked into the study and slammed the door.

Maureen was still standing in the upstairs hall when Mrs. Van removed her shoes and, in stocking feet, crept down the stairs and stood in the entrance hall next to the door to her husband's study. She could not hear much through the heavy door but she thought she heard him say, "Now, you go back and do your best, but if she strikes you again, I want to know about it. Do you understand?" Mrs. Van was leaning against the study door when it opened and the two women walked out.

They cast their eyes down as if they didn't see her, but Mr. Van saw his wife standing there.

"Eavesdropping?" he said.

"No," she said. "I came to apologize."

"In your stocking feet? You had shoes on when I left you minutes ago." Shame reddened her face and tears streamed down her cheeks. She turned and ran back up the stairs, through her chamber door and slammed it shut. Mr. Van strolled out of the study and down the hall towards the kitchen.

"Maureen," he called out.

"Yes, sir," Maureen had come downstairs behind Mrs. Van and she entered the hall from the dining room where she had begun setting the table for dinner.

"Will you see to it that Mrs. Van has dinner brought to her room tonight? I will have my dinner in the nursery."

"Yes, sir," Maureen said. She stared at Mr. Van's back with a confused look as he turned and strolled back down the hall towards his study. He bypassed the door and climbed the stairs instead. She watched as he turned left at the top of the stairs and walked around to the west side of the house where the nursery was located. She heard murmurs, then Anna Lee came down the staircase and walked toward her. They went into the kitchen together to prepare trays. Neither mentioned the incident, nor did Ellie, nor Lizzie, not until they were all in the Quarters that night and the women got together to gossip.

Maureen said that, from that day on, except for occasions when there were guests, dinner was served on trays, one in Mrs. Van's chambers, the other in the nursery for Mr. Van.

I remembered when Catfish first told me that story; I was appalled that any woman could be like Marguerite. I couldn't understand how she could not want her baby. Now, as I wrote the story from memory, I thought about how I had done the same thing—given my baby away because I wasn't ready to be a mother.

Selfish women do selfish things, and revisiting the story of Marguerite made me look honestly at myself and my own failings.

I put my pen down and thought about how the people who knew me—Emma, Josh, Joe—and who knew what I had done, were the ones who seemed to love me and accept me with all my faults and sins. How could I be so lucky?

~ Chapter Eleven ~

Emalene

M Y MOTHER WROTE TO me in October 1975. It was a shock to see her handwriting across the beige envelope and the personalized fold-over card inside. I hoped it was a birthday card, since my twenty-fourth was in one week. Somehow, though, I knew my mother wouldn't remember my birthday. She never did.

October 15, 1975
Susannah,
Your father is ill. He would like to see you. You should make plans to come to Jean Ville soon. Abigail misses you.
Mother

Abigail was, of course, my fifteen-year-old sister. We called her Sissy. Was she the only one who missed me?

The letter was in the mail at my apartment, not my post office box. I read it on the bus trip out to Springfield Gardens Friday evening; Joe had asked me to visit. I wondered how my mother got my mailing address. Marianne was the only person who had it and she was sworn to silence.

I felt a cold chill up my spine. Someone must have followed me, stalking, watching. *Well,* I thought. *They didn't see me doing anything wrong. No Rodney. Just going about my life.*

I was almost at the bus stop near Joe and Emalene's home when I stopped feeling creepy and started thinking about why Joe would have called me—he never did.

When Joe answered the door I knew something was wrong.

"Susie," he said. "Thanks for coming out."

"What is it, Joe? You've got me worried." I stood on the porch, daylight ending rapidly, and he was inside the door, holding the knob. He didn't invite me in.

"I'm sorry. I should have explained on the phone. Emalene is not feeling well. We thought it would be best if you'd take Lilly for the weekend."

"Uh. Okay. I'll get her things together. But, can I see Emma?"

"Hmmmm. Let me ask her." Joe walked into the house and left me on the porch, the door ajar. I let myself in and found Lilly in her room playing tea party with her dolls. She ran into my arms and hugged me around my legs and I bent to hug her neck. When we finally parted, I noticed big tears running down her cheeks.

"What's wrong Lil?" I got on my knees and held onto her waist. She let the tears run down her face, unfettered. Lilly's room smelled of baby powder and lilac, and when I kissed her cheek I tasted the salt from her tears.

"Mommy is sick."

"I know but the doctor will make her well."

"You promise?"

"I'm sure of it." I didn't want to promise. I didn't know what was wrong with Emalene but it must be serious for Joe to call and ask me to take Lilly. She'd never spent the night with me and we were both excited. I put some of her clothes in a pink duffle bag and we talked about tea parties and baby dolls. Lilly asked if she could bring her baby doll and, of course, I said yes.

Joe came into Lilly's room and said I could see Emalene, and he stayed with Lilly while I walked down the dark hall to the master bedroom. I hadn't been in Joe and Emma's boudoir and I felt a bit embarrassed when I walked through the opened door.

Emma was sitting in a chair in the corner of the room, wearing a blue, fleece robe and fuzzy slippers, her feet propped on an ottoman. She looked as beautiful as ever and I never would have known she was ill if Joe hadn't told me.

She moved her feet over and pointed to the ottoman. I sat facing her, my hands folded in my lap, unsure what to say.

"Susie, how fortunate you came over today. Joe tells me Lilly is going to your place for a sleepover. Will she stay with you all weekend?"

"Do you want her to?"

"It's up to you, sweetheart. Where's Josh?"

"He's on call at the hospital all weekend," I'm sure Emalene noticed the confusion on my face. "Of course I want her. But... what's... I mean..."

"We're not sure. I've been run down, probably working too hard," Emma took both my hands in hers and stared at me. She looked fine, except for dark circles under her eyes. She smiled, and asked, "How are you?"

I hesitated, then said, "Can I talk to you about something? I was unsure I should mention my mother's note at a time like this.

"I'm okay, Susie. Nothing that a little rest won't cure."

I told her about my mother writing to say my dad was ill and I needed to go to Jean Ville.

"I want to help you and Joe, but I'm not sure whether my dad is dying or just sick." I searched Emalene's face for some sort of clue as to how she felt about me dumping this on her.

"You have to go. Don't worry about Lilly. We'll be fine."

"I need to call Marianne and see if she can find out what's going on with Dad, how sick he really is." I laid my head on Emma's lap and she stroked my hair. "I'm afraid."

"What are you afraid of?"

"Everything. Jean Ville. Rodney. My dad. Things are just starting to feel right with Josh and I'm afraid if I see Rodney again. Well..." We didn't talk any more.

Lilly and I were both tired when we got to my apartment and I heated soup and made sandwiches for dinner. I put sheets and a blanket on the pull-out sofa and read to Lilly until her eyelids were heavy, then I got ready for bed and called Josh. He was at the hospital and couldn't talk, but promised to call me when things slowed down. Josh had changed his specialty from obstetrics to surgery and was very busy when he worked weekends.

I got in my bed, and before I fell asleep I heard little feet shuffling down the hall. Soon, I saw Lilly's brown curls bobbing through my doorway and I pulled my covers back so she could climb in next to me. We slept close and I think we both drew comfort and strength from each other.

On Saturday, we went to McDonald's, then to the park where she chased the gulls. I felt guilty for not buying popcorn for her to feed the birds, but she seemed happy just being there. I took her home Sunday afternoon.

Emalene was in the den, dressed in jeans and a T-shirt and looked better than she had on Friday evening. Joe picked up his little girl and hugged her, then Lilly ran into Emalene's lap.

"We had fun at Susie's apartment," Lilly told her mom. I watched them and wondered why I didn't feel jealous; then I remembered what Emma had taught me: "When you love your child, there can't be too many other people who love her. It takes a village, and the stronger the love in the village, the stronger your child will be."

I kissed Lilly goodbye and she hugged me extra long, as though she was afraid for me to leave. I got on one knee and looked her in the eye. "I'll be back this week and if you want to come stay at my apartment, I can take you to school in the mornings and pick you up at the after-school program. How does that sound?

"Good," she said. "If it's okay with Mama and Daddy."

"Well, we'll see what they say. They'll call me if they want you to come stay with me."

*

I called Marianne when I got home and she told me that Tootsie said my dad was very sick.

"What's wrong with him?" I was sitting at the table in my kitchen, the coiled phone cord stretched to its maximum length.

"They don't know for sure. I think he just came back from a big medical center in New Orleans. My mama says he might die."

"Oh, God. Maybe I need to go to Jean Ville. It's just that, I have a friend who's sick and she's asked me to help with her little girl."

"You can bring the little girl. Just come for a long weekend."

"Hmmm. I'd have to talk to her parents about that."

"You can stay with me." Marianne told me that she had moved into Catfish's cabin and had a sofa bed in the sitting room. "I have lots of room."

"I'll think about it and let you know."

I picked Lilly up at school on Wednesday and when I took her home I told Emma about my dad.

"Marianne says it's serious. He could die." I was standing at the foot of Emalene's bed, folding clothes. She was propped up on pillows with her legs stretched out in front of her. I was worried about her because, again, she looked tired. "I'm not sure what to do."

"He's your father, Susie. You only get one. You don't get to choose your parents, God does that for you. In the same breath, you must protect yourself."

"What are you saying?"

"You should go see your father. I just don't think you should stay in the house with him. Do you have friends or relatives you can stay with?"

"There are a couple of places, I guess. But I shouldn't go to Louisiana and leave you. Joe will need help with Lilly until you are feeling better." I had written my mother a short note that said it was impossible for me to come at this time but she should keep me informed.

Emalene looked spent, so I kissed her on the forehead and slipped out of her bedroom. I found Joe and Lilly in the kitchen and asked if Lilly needed to go home with me.

"Not tonight, Susie, thanks. Maybe next week. I know Emma would like to have her home this weekend. Can we leave it open?"

"Of course. Just let me know if you need me. I can keep her all of next week and take her to and from school."

"That might be an option."

I didn't hear from Josh that night. I called him from work on Friday and asked him to meet me for dinner. He said he was off all weekend.

"Of course I'll meet you. This sounds serious—you've never asked me for a date." He laughed, but I could tell he was concerned. We met at a sushi place and sat in a corner booth. He slid in across from me and immediately reached for my hands across the table. I slipped my fingers into his palms.

The waitress brought our drinks and Josh sat back in the booth. I leaned on the table, my chin in my hands, my glass of wine beside me.

"First we need to talk about Emma." My voice was quivering and he knew I was upset.

"Please don't be mad at me. I tried for months to convince her to tell you that she wasn't well." Josh took a sip of his beer and stared at the foam for a few seconds.

"What's wrong with her?"

"Didn't she tell you?" He put his glass mug on the table and wiped the moisture with a paper napkin.

"She says she's tired, overworked; yet I see something more in her eyes." Warm tears gathered in my lower eyelids but I held them in check.

"Oh, well, she has a doctor's appointment this week and is probably waiting for a definitive diagnosis."

"This sounds more serious than I imagined." I reached for his hand and he looked at me with a compassionate expression.

"You'll have to wait until Emma tells you. It's her story to tell, not mine."

"Josh. Help me out here. I don't want to be blindsided. You know how much I love Emalene." I squeezed his hands and he slid out of his side of the booth and into mine. He put his arm over my shoulder and I leaned my head on his chest.

"I think she's afraid you'll disappear if things get, uh, well... complicated."

"What kind of person does she think I am?"

"I can't speak for Joe and Emma, but as for me, I can't imagine loving someone this much if she wasn't the best person in the world." He put his fingers under my chin and lifted my face so that we could look at each other. I could smell toothpaste on his breath and see a few strands of white hair at his temples.

"Wait, now *you're* complicating things. What's this about love?" I sat back hard and created some distance between us. He still had his arm over my shoulder.

"You're right, that's a conversation for another time. Let me answer your question in a better way. I think you are wonderful and trustworthy. I believe you've been hurt deeply, and that because of what your father did to you, you have a difficult time trusting people, especially men."

"Well, my mother was no nurturer, either," I whispered. "But I've trusted Emma... until now. I feel like she, all of you, are keeping something from me." I opened my purse and pulled out a wad of tissue and blew my nose.

"Okay, so you don't trust anyone. I don't blame you. No one blames you. We only ask for a chance to prove that we are trustworthy. Now there I go speaking for others. Let me rephrase that. I, Josh Ryan! I want a chance to prove that you can trust me. And I don't care how long it takes. I'm not going to leave you, desert you, choose someone over you." His facial expression was so sincere I was sucked in for a minute.

He was right. I didn't trust anyone, which meant I was always on my guard. I'd been that way with Rodney too. It took years before I admitted I loved him. Then, once I finally did, he left me.

Josh and I sat in silence for a while. He watched me but I didn't feel conspicuous since his feelings seemed honest and true.

"I have to go to Louisiana." I looked up and watched Josh wrap his hands around the half-full beer mug. His brow lowered over his eyes and two lines appeared across his forehead, which always happened when he was worried.

"What gives?" he asked. I told him about my dad's illness, or at least what I knew.

"Let me go with you. We can stay in a hotel. I'll protect you."

"To begin with there are no hotels in Jean Ville." I tried to laugh but it wasn't really funny. "Anyway, there's too much to protect me from. I think I need to go back and face the music, alone."

"Are you more afraid of your dad or of Rodney?"

"I'm not sure. Rodney is still in the army, so I don't know whether I'll see him. My dad is very sick, so he can't..."

"But he can intimidate you."

"Let me think about it. I'm going to offer to take Lilly with me."

We took sips of our drinks and our food came. The waitress put our plates on the table and engaged in a little small talk with Josh. I wasn't listening.

*

When Josh took me home, he agreed to come inside for a minute. It was the first time he'd been in my apartment. He looked around and made nice comments about my choice of furnishings and art, said I had good taste, and that he didn't know what I might think about his place.

"Where do you live, Josh?"

"I thought you'd never ask." He was still standing between the kitchen and living room. I was ashamed that we'd spent most of our time talking about me.

"Sit down, Josh." I took his hand and led him to my favorite chair—the comfy seat with an ottoman. I went to the kitchen and poured a beer into a mug and chardonnay into a wine glass, then took the drinks into the living room, and sat on the sofa catty-cornered to Josh. He sat forward with his elbows on his knees and rolled the mug between his two hands as if he were playing a game. He was pensive; far away.

"Where do you live, Josh?"

"I have a brownstone in Brooklyn Heights." He said it as if embarrassed, and he didn't look up. I gasped. "It's not that fancy so don't get ideas that I have a lot of money." He laughed. I hadn't thought about Josh Ryan as wealthy, in fact I never thought about what he might or might not have, but you had to be somewhat affluent to own a brownstone in Brooklyn Heights.

"How long have you lived there?"

"Hmmmm. Since I started my residency about five years ago, I guess. Before that I had a condo in Manhattan because it was closer to the med school." Dang, I thought. I don't know anything about this guy.

"When will you invite me over?"

"When you tell me we don't have to go slow any more. I'm waiting on you, Susie." He was bent forward and his chin almost touched his chest. He lifted his eyelashes and looked from his beer mug to me.

"Maybe when I get back from Louisiana?"

"Maybe." He rolled his mug and stared at the untouched liquid. I put my glass of wine on the coffee table and took his beer from his hands and set it down next to mine. I got up and sat on the ottoman facing Josh. My knees were between his opened legs and he was still bent forward. I put one hand on each of his cheeks and pulled him to me.

We kissed. It was almost sterile at first, and he didn't touch me. Then I slid onto his lap and he folded his arms around me. He whispered into my mouth as our lips came together.

"Careful. I'm not promising you I can stop again. It took everything I had not to grab you and carry you to bed the last time you kissed me."

"You said we could take it slow."

"This isn't slow. You're sitting in my lap. Your arms are around my neck and I taste your breath. Tell me you want this or I need to go."

"Do I have to declare now? Can we try to take it slow, see if there's chemistry, make sure it's what we want?" My words were muffled by his lips on mine, but he heard me. He kissed me and with his face pressing on mine I fell backwards against the armrest, my legs draped over his in our sitting position. His tongue touched the inside of my lips ever so slightly and I met it with my tongue. I opened my eyes and he was staring at me.

"Is there?" he asked blowing the words into my mouth. "Chemistry?"

"Yes." I breathed into his voice. There was a sound like wind whirling and the smell of evergreen and musk. I inhaled deeply and sighed. "Chemistry. Yes." We kissed a little longer then I pulled away. "But slow, okay?"

"Okay." He sat up straight. I got off his lap and returned to my seat on the sofa. "I'd better go. I have an early morning."

He kissed me goodnight at the door, then walked off and didn't turn back for a last look.

*

It was still early when Josh left. I took a shower, dressed for bed, and felt wide awake so I sat at my desk and thought about Catfish telling me about the trouble in the Vans' marriage. He would talk like he'd been there himself, even though most of these stories were handed down by his grandmother and other older people in the Quarters.

When I wrote the stories, I had to write the way he spoke, with that distinct drawl; it was the only way the stories jumped off the pages.

"Maureen told everyone in the Quarters that Mr. Van doted on that little boy, Mr. Henry," I could hear Catfish say. "Probably because Henry would be his only child, since his wife wouldn't sleep with him no more 'cause she didn't want no more children." Catfish would swing back and forth in his rocker as he relayed the saga Maureen told his granny that was passed down through the family in the Quarters.

Lil Henry
1860-1938
Before little Mr. Henry started to walk, Mr. Van was taking the boy

with him to the fields. That big ole man be putting that boy in the saddle between those long legs, holding the baby round the waist with one arm. When the Missus wasn't busy, she took to her chambers and read books. She'd come downstairs during the day when Mr. Van was in the fields or in town and, sometimes, when he was in his study. Maureen said she busied herself with dinner menus, lists, and trips to town for personal supplies and was still decorating that house. Didn't look like it would have needed too many decorations to me, but I guess that's what a woman does when she's got nothing else to do.

Maureen said that Mrs. Van had carpenters in the house most of the time. First she had them wall off Mr. Van's old room and made it a guest room Then she went and had that wall taken down to enlarge the space for her new Queen Anne desk and other furnishings that made it a woman's suite with an office. What kind of woman needs an office, I ask you? But then, that was Mrs. Van.

Mr. Gordon got him some men to remodel the nursery while Mrs. Van was pregnant. After the two had that fight about Mrs. Van slapping Lizzie and Ellie, Mr. Van went to living in the room attached to the nursery on the west side, which was the front of the house. Soon he had carpenters up there every day and he wouldn't let no one go near. He had moved his bed into the nursery and slept near little Henry's bed. It took about a month and when Maureen and Lizzie went up to clean and dust they saw the changes.

The entire front of the upstairs was a huge set of rooms. There was a grand entrance with double doors that led into a foyer. To the right was Mr. Henry's nursery. To the left was Mr. Van's bedroom and closet, with a big desk set under the front windows. Between the two rooms was a hall with a big bathroom on one side and a smaller one on the other. In the big one was a huge copper tub and a washdown closet that we now call a flush toilet. In the smaller bathroom was another washdown and a sink.

Maureen said it was really something to see. Mr. Van's bed was high up off the floor so he had the men build three steps at the foot so Mr. Henry could climb in with his daddy if he got scared at night. Maureen said most mornings when she brought breakfast up, little Henry was in Mr. Van's bed, sometimes sound asleep, and Mr. Van would be sitting in his wing-backed chair near the window, reading the newspaper.

Maureen said Mrs. Van got herself a new washdown water closet and tub installed in the hall that joined her bedroom to her new office. She got them carpenters to make two guest rooms across the hall, on the north side of the house that faced towards town. They put a water closet in between—even though they was never no guests come to Shadowland. Mrs. Van didn't even invite her mother to come stay, because Maureen said, the Missus didn't want her mama to know about her new marriage arrangement.

At Christmas time, Mrs. Van went to Oakwold for a visit and she didn't take Mr. Henry. Maureen said she don't know if she wanted him or not but Mr. Gordon and little Henry had their first St. Nicholas together at Shadowland Plantation. All the workers were invited to come up to the big house and have food and drinks on Christmas Eve.

Now, from what I hear, that was quite a celebration and all the slaves, I mean workers, dressed in their best and cleanest clothes and the way they tell it, they was eggnog and cakes and all sorts of food. And they was bags of fruits and nuts for each of them to take home. And Mr. Van gave ever man five dollars and all the womens and children each a crisp dollar bill. My granddaddy was a teenager then and, through the years, he'd tell about that Christmas like it was the best, most magical night of his life.

Things didn't get no better between Mr. Van and the Missus and eventually, she'd go visit her people in Evergreen and stay a month or more. Maureen said everything ran much better when the Missus wasn't around. When Mr. Henry was about four, Mrs. Van went to Oakwold for Christmas as usual, and didn't come back. That summer, Mr. Van got papers from a lawyer that he signed and sent back. About a year later we found out Mrs. Van married that man she'd been cadoodling with before she met Mr. Van. I don't know did they ever have kids. I don't think that woman was fit to raise no kids.

Anyway, Mr. Van got little Henry and, far as I know, that boy didn't ever see his mama again. Didn't matter none 'cause he had lots of mamas: Anna Lee, Maureen, and Lizzie, for sure. Ellie went to Oakwold with Mrs. Van and when the missus didn't come back, Ellie didn't come back neither.

I put my pen down and yawned. I wondered about divorce. It was a scandal in those days, and it was something that I'd been raised to believe was a mortal sin. I didn't want to get married if I thought it might end in divorce. But then, I wasn't considering marriage, not since Rodney left me practically standing at the altar.

It was almost three in the morning, but it was Saturday so I could sleep in. I crawled in my bed and slept like a rock.

*

When the phone started ringing, I thought I was dreaming, and I turned over and pulled my pillow over my head. But the ringing continued, and finally I turned and looked at the clock—nine o'clock.

I jumped from my bed and ran to the kitchen. By the time I got to the phone, the caller had given up. I went to the bathroom to brush my teeth and it started ringing again.

"Hello?"

"Susie, it's Joe. Can you come out to the house?"

"Well, uhm. Sure, Joe. When?"

"How about now?"

I dressed quickly, put my hair in a ponytail and almost ran to the bus stop.

Emma was sitting in the living room. She looked pale and drawn, but was smiling. I was out of breath and scared, my heart pounding and tears stinging the backs of my eyelids. I stood there and looked at her. I couldn't speak.

"I'm sorry Joe upset you." Emma reached out for me and took my hand. "I tried to call you back to tell you to take your time, but there was no answer. Guess you'd already left." I sat on the sofa with a plop. My purse was in my lap and I hugged it as though it could protect me from whatever news I was about to hear.

"Well?"

"Joe and I were wondering whether you'd like to take Lilly with you to Louisiana. It would help us out. It looks like I'm going into the hospital for a few days."

"What's wrong?"

"They want to run some tests." She put her arm around me and I practically fell into her lap.

"I don't have to go to Louisiana, Emma. I can stay here with Lilly, or keep her at my apartment."

"You need to go see your dad. Remember, you only..."

"Get one. I know." We didn't talk for a while. I was thinking about my options. Emma was waiting for me to tell her what I was going to do so she could make plans to go to the hospital. It was all too much.

"Look. I'll take Lilly home with me for the weekend. I have to talk to Mr. Mobley on Monday and it will take a few days to make travel arrangements. You do what you need to do and I'll take care of Lilly. Just don't worry."

"Okay. But I'm not going in the hospital unless you promise me you will go to see your dad. I could never forgive myself if you didn't get to see him, and he, well you know..."

"Died?"

"Well, yes, and all because you stayed here for me. Put my mind at ease, Susie. Please."

"Okay, okay. We'll go. But you have to know how worried I am about you."

"I'm not going anywhere but to the hospital. I'll be here when you get back."

"Promise?"

"Promise."

~ Chapter Twelve ~

Louisiana

MARIANNE WAS WAITING FOR us when our plane landed in Baton Rouge the following Thursday. I walked into baggage claim holding Lilly's hand and saw Marianne's expression go from surprise to resignation in a matter of seconds. I wanted to laugh at her reaction but there was too much turf to cover.

"Lilly, this is my best friend, Marianne. Marianne, Lilly."

"Well, hello Lilly. It's a pleasure." Marianne looked up at me with a big question mark on her face and I shrugged, coyly, and grinned.

"Hi," Lilly curtsied and Marianne got to her knees and grabbed Lilly in a big bear hug.

"You are way too cute, Miss Lilly." Marianne let go of Lilly and held her at arms' length, eye-to-eye.

"Thank you, ma'am." Lilly curtsied again and smiled.

"Oh, my God, Susie, where did you find this precious child?" Marianne looked up at me.

"Lilly's parents let her come with me since we'll only be here a few days. I hope it's okay?" I was grinning.

"It's great. My sisters and cousins will love you, Lilly." Marianne looked at Lilly.

"If you're Susie's friend, does that mean you're my friend, too?" Lilly wrapped her arms around Marianne's neck as if they were old friends and I laughed at how innocent and loving she was at five years old.

"Aren't you precocious? Of course it does." Marianne hugged Lilly again and looked at me over her curly brown locks. I shrugged and smiled, proud of Lilly for being so grown-up, yet innocent at the same time.

"What's pre-coh-shuss?" She pulled away and looked at Marianne.

"It means wonderful." Marianne was still on one knee and Lilly hugged her again, then came back to my side and put one arm around my leg.

"I like our friend," Lilly looked up at me and I winked at her.

"I knew you would. Now let's go get our luggage." I reached out to hug Marianne and Lilly ran off to the baggage carousel that had just begun to turn and spit suitcases onto the conveyor belt. She was mesmerized and forgot Marianne and I were there.

"Where's Lucy?" I was pulling my bag off the carousel and Lilly was watching the luggage go round and round in amazement.

"She's working. You'll meet her tonight."

"Thanks for driving all the way to Baton Rouge to get us. We could have taken the bus to Jean Ville."

"No problem. I wanted time with you, but I guess our conversation will have to wait."

"Lilly will fall asleep in the car. She's exhausted. She was too excited to sleep on the plane."

"What gives?" Marianne looked at me, then at Lilly. "I mean?"

"I'm friends with her parents and her mother is sick. I'm helping out." I tried to avoid Marianne's inquisitive look and ignored the way she stared at Lilly as if trying to figure out where she'd seen that face before. We walked to the parking lot, Marianne with my bag, me holding Lilly's hand in one of mine, her duffle in my other. I pulled her stuffed Pooh out of the duffle and handed it to her when I laid her down on the back seat of Marianne's Datsun.

"Is this new?" I was admiring the gold, four-door car that looked like a miniature station wagon.

"About a year, I guess."

"Fancy."

"Yeah. I'm doing okay." She was about to open her car door and our eyes met over the top of the little sedan.

"I'm so proud of you, Mari."

"Thanks, Susie-Q. I'm proud of you, too." We got in our separate doors and soon were headed north on Highway 190. Lilly went right to sleep and Marianne and I whispered on and off for the next two hours. I told her about Emalene's undiagnosed illness and explained how worried I was, and how Emma and Joe had become family and helped fill the hole left by Rodney. I told her that I spent lots of time with Lilly and I really loved her. We also talked about my job.

"At first I was bored," I pulled down the visor hoping there was a mirror so I could apply some lipstick, but nope. I flipped it back up and turned slightly towards Marianne. "The publishing company where I work mostly publishes textbooks, but several months ago I convinced my boss, Mr. Mobley, to take on a memoir written by a new author, Phillip Agee. It's about the CIA and called *Inside the Company.* I think it will do well, and if it does, maybe Shilling will agree to publish similar books"

I told Marianne that I was mostly relegated to line-editing textbooks, but with memoirs and nonfiction written more descriptively, almost like novels, my boss had pretty much given me free rein to find books that we should consider and bring them to him. I acted like an in-house agent, reading manuscripts and interviewing authors to determine whether the books they submitted were a good fit for our publishing house. He then had to take them to a committee that made the ultimate decision.

"I think Shilling will publish *The Catfish Stories*." I tried not to act as excited as I was.

"So you waited all this time to tell me the best news of all. That's wonderful. When?" Marianne tried to look at me a couple of times but was driving and paying attention to the highway.

"I don't know. I'm afraid if I talk about it, it won't happen. I'm crossing all my fingers and toes." I was laughing.

"Please let me know. I'll come to New York for your book launch."

"Would you, really? You've never come to visit me."

"Well, this will be a momentous occasion I wouldn't miss." She smiled and I knew she was genuinely proud of me, also proud her grandfather's stories would finally be in print. She drove in silence for a while.

"What about your love life. It's been over a year since… Rodney." Marianne stared out the front windshield and I looked at her profile. She was so beautiful. Her burgundy hair was wavy and full, although she'd cut it to shoulder length. She had a small nose and big eyes that were almost violet in color, a combination of green and hazel, with a bit of blue. The only features that tied her to the Negro race were her full lips and deep forehead. Her hair was curly, but not frizzy, and her eyes were set a bit far apart—the shape of almonds, almost oriental.

The fact that my dad had fathered her still boggled my mind, and I knew she didn't want to accept it. She hated him more than anything or anybody because he had taken advantage of her mother at such an early age and never acknowledged Marianne as his child.

"More like a year and a half," I quipped and tried to laugh, but it came across as a weak joke. "I've been seeing someone, but it's not serious. I mean we've only kissed a couple times."

"What's his name?"

"Josh. Josh Ryan. He's a doctor. I knew him years ago, then we lost touch. He's friends with Lilly's parents, Emma and Joe, and it's comfortable."

"I'm glad, Susie. You need to move on. Rodney... well."

"Please, can we not talk about him?" She didn't say anything else, but I knew she had something important to tell me that I wasn't ready to hear. "Tell me about you. And Lucy."

"It's still hard to be, well, you know..."

"Gay?"

"Yeah. It's hard to have a relationship with someone who is your gender, especially in such a small town. Most people think we are best friends. And we are. It's just that I get lots of questions about why I'm not dating anyone and when will I settle down and have kids and stuff like that."

"I'm sorry it's so hard. Have the two of you thought about moving to a city?"

"We talk about it but I can't leave Mama."

We drove in silence until we crossed the Atchafalaya River from Pointe Coupée into Toussaint Parish. I inhaled deeply and when I exhaled I inadvertently let out a moan.

"What's wrong?" Marianne reached over and patted my leg.

"Lots of emotions." I thought about the last time I crossed the river, going the other way, thinking my entire life was ahead of me and that I'd spend it married to Rodney. I also thought about how close I was to Jean Ville and, although I was eager to see my siblings, I was afraid to face my dad. The last time I saw him, he had beat me. Now I was going to see him on his sick bed.

"Your dad? I hear he's not doing very well."

"What do you know about his condition?"

"Maybe my mama should tell you what she knows. She's at their house every day and helps take care of him. It's ironic, isn't it?" She let the last words come out as a whisper. I would never learn to accept what I considered a love triangle—Mama and Tootsie, Daddy and Tootsie, Mama and Daddy. Then there was me, and James and Will and Robby and Sissy and Albert; finally, there was Marianne. We Burton kids had two Mamas—Tootsie and Anne Burton. I guess Daddy liked them both.

Marianne didn't seem angry about my dad, like she had when I would mention him in the past. I was surprised.

"Have you accepted it?" I was really asking whether she had accepted that my dad was her dad.

"I've had to accept a lot of things. I've decided to accept that he is my biological. That's as far as I'll ever go with that bastard."

"Don't blame you."

"I hope he dies." Marianne gasped at her own statement. "I'm sorry. I didn't mean to say that out loud."

"It's okay. I get it. I won't miss him, either. He's a mean, angry person." We both sat with that thought and I knew we'd never need to discuss him again. We'd said it all; there was nothing more and it was a waste of time and energy to talk about him.

"I haven't heard from Rodney since he survived the fall of Saigon and was at an army base in Kansas." I spoke softly as though I were afraid to talk about him. "We wrote to each other when he was in Vietnam, then a little when he got back. I think I'm the one who quit. No use."

"He came home on leave. He looked good, but he's changed." Marianne told me that Rodney seemed sad and preoccupied. She said he wouldn't talk about anything that happened in Vietnam but he said, "It wasn't good. None of it was good."

Marianne said Rodney talked about staying in the army after his time was up. He said it would be a good life now that the war was over. She told me that he was done with Annette and he'd met a woman in the army, also a lawyer, whom he was seeing. Marianne said, "She's colored. His parents approve."

"Oh." I wanted to be happy for Rodney. You want those you love to be happy, don't you? I was trying, but it was so hard to picture him with someone else. Marianne and I were quiet for a while.

"You want to tell me about Lilly?" Marianne whispered. I turned to check on Lilly and she was still sound asleep.

"What's there to tell? Her parents are my friends. Her mom is sick."

"You think I don't see the resemblance?"

"Mari, please don't go there."

"Susie. Others will see it, too. I can't believe you never told me."

"Look. I just met her, less than a year ago, after…"

"Mama will see it right away," Marianne said.

"Do you think she'll say anything? She is Lilly Franklin, daughter of Joe and Emalene Franklin. That's the whole story."

"Does he know?" She ignored what I said.

"Who?"

"Susie. It's me, Mari. Come on."

"No. And I don't want him to know. Please. Can you respect that? She's not our child. She's Lilly Frank…"

"I know, daughter of Joe and Emalene Franklin…" Her voice had a quirk in it. I wanted to explain why I didn't want Rodney to know about Lilly, but I wasn't sure of the reasons myself.

"He's my cousin you know. Family."

"What am I? Minced meat?" We laughed but were both thinking that we were sisters, and that's closer than cousins. "Really, Mari, there's nothing to tell. Lilly Franklin!" Then we got serious again.

"Emalene is a very special person who believes her child will be more secure and develop a strong sense of self if she is loved by lots of people. She says the more people who love your child, the better your child's life will be and the more likely she is to be and do anything she sets her mind to."

"Wow. I never thought about it that way." Marianne seemed truly enchanted by Emalene's philosophy.

"I know. That's what I mean. Emalene Franklin is special." I explained how I'd become a part of Emalene and Joe's family. "I was so lonely after Rodney... well, uhm... after it was over. Emma and Joe took me in and helped fill that void."

"Why didn't you tell Rodney about Lilly?" Marianne was still not convinced, and I couldn't explain that Lilly's life was better without the drama and complexities of the forbidden love between me and Rodney.

"Nothing to tell. She belongs to Emalene and Joe." We were quiet for a while, then I said, "Rodney chose his family's safety over me. And rightly so!"

"Things have changed a lot around here, Susie."

"How so?"

"To start with, Sheriff Desiré changed all the rules. There's no separate seating for coloreds and whites. That means we all sit together at the movies, restaurants, buses, trains, everywhere. The bank has one line and both colors stand in it together! The sheriff insists that school integration laws are followed so black and white kids go to school together. Of course, lots of families send their kids to St. Alphonse's Catholic School. I know of Baptists who send their kids to the Catholic school just to keep them from us dirty black people." Marianne laughed and slapped the steering wheel.

"Black people?"

"Oh, yes. It's the new term we are supposed to call ourselves. It's taking me some time getting used to it, but it came about with the Black Panthers movement. We are supposed to refer to ourselves as African Americans, not Negroes." Marianne laughed at her own statement but I didn't know whether to laugh with her.

"You don't say? How do you feel about that?"

"The new rules or the new titles?"

"All of the above."

"It's all good. We're making progress. A few months ago, a black man right here in Toussaint Parish was found innocent by an all-white jury. Now that's progress."

"I'll say. Next thing you'll tell me is that there are mixed-race marriages."

"Not yet. That might never happen in Jean Ville."

We pulled up in the Quarters and I sat in the car and took it all in. The sugar cane was blowing in the wind, the pecan trees budding and full of soon-to-be nuts, the old red barn had been repaired and painted, Catfish's garden was overgrown with weeds and the little fence was falling in. All the cabins were still in their places and about a dozen children were running and playing in the dusty backyard.

The five little cabins were once slave cabins on Shadowland plantation owned by the Vans, all in a row, their back porches almost touching each other, facing a dirt yard with a fire pit in the center and cane fields beyond that. There were three new cabins facing the old ones, the dusty yard and fire pit between the two rows.

I came of age in the old falling-down barn set a few hundred feet in the backyard, and in the cane fields and pecan groves that stretched as far as you could see. Those fields were a special place for me, Mari, and Rod to take long walks, talk about personal things, and feel shielded from the cruel world that judged relationships like ours so harshly. It was there ours became the closest of friendships.

"Not much has changed here, has it?"

"Not much, except for the additional cabins built for my married cousins." Marianne winked at me and got out the car. I reached behind me and touched Lilly's leg. She was stirring and I knew she'd be waking soon. I didn't want her to wake up in the car alone so I sat and watched her, turned around in my seat as far as I could. Marianne was busy getting our bags out of the back of the car and I could hear the screeches and chatter of the kids. A rubber ball hit the windshield and I jumped.

"Hey, don't hit my car with your balls!" Marianne started chasing a little boy about five years old and he was giggling as he ran away from her. She grabbed him and turned him upside down, dangling him by his legs. He squealed with laughter and happiness.

Lilly sat up in the back seat of the car, grinned like a Cheshire cat, and reached for the door handle. She was ready to join the fun.

I took her by the hand and led her through the pecan trees to the barn, showing her around the yard littered with cockleburs that looked like Spartan balls. She was mesmerized by the hundreds of pecans on the ground and I found an old bucket in the barn to gather some of the nuts. We walked through the grove, Lilly swinging a bucket, the pecans crunching under our feet.

Within minutes, a parade of curious kids was following us and helping to fill the bucket with nuts off the ground. I knew most of Marianne's nieces and nephews and began introducing everyone to Lilly. Lilly let go of my hand and wandered away from me with the children. They were all laughing and some were showing her how to distinguish pecans that were ripe enough to be picked.

I lost complete control and watched the kids gather nuts, play ring-around-the-rosie, and weave in and out of the sheets and towels hanging on the clothesline, laughing and shouting at each other. My fear of Lilly feeling uneasy in a strange place was dispelled as she ran through the dirt and followed the other children in the yard, passing the bucket around, nuts falling from it into the thick St. Augustine grass.

I climbed the three little steps onto Catfish's porch. His rocker was in the same place, and the green Naugahyde chair with the torn seat was still next to it. I sat in the rocker and watched the children just like I had when I visited Catfish through the years. Marianne came out and sat next to me.

"Do you have a phone?" I was watching the kids run and giggle.

"Yep. In the kitchen."

"I'd like to call Joe and tell him we got here safe and sound. Do you mind?"

"You gonna call Josh, too?"

"I'll pay for the calls."

"Don't worry about it. Go ahead."

I called the hospital and asked for Emalene's room. Joe answered the phone. I told him we'd made it, that we were in Jean Ville, and that Lilly had already made a bunch of friends and was having a ball. He didn't seem interested in what I was saying. He handed the phone to Josh who happened to be in the room checking on Emma.

"Hi. You okay?" He seemed chipper but I could tell there was something wrong.

"What is it, Josh? How's Emma?"

"She can tell you when the two of you talk." I could hear him breathing into the phone.

"How are you, Josh?"

"I miss you." He whispered and sighed. I could picture him rubbing his forehead with his thumb and forefinger as though trying to spread out the frown lines.

"I'll be home in a few days."

"Have you seen your dad, yet?"

"No. I'll go there soon. It's only a few blocks away and Marianne will watch Lilly. She's running and playing with Marianne's cousins, having a ball."

"That's good. Keep her busy so she doesn't get homesick."

"I'll try."

"Susie..."

"Huh?"

"I... well... bye."

"Kiss Emma for me. Goodbye, Josh."

I sat in Catfish's rocker on the porch and Marianne sat in the straight-backed chair. We didn't talk for a long time, just watched the kids. I was lost in the memories of the first time Rodney kissed me in that old barn and the last time we met there when he was skittish because the Klan had threatened his family again. We should have known a mixed-race relationship wouldn't work in a small town in the Deep South. It wasn't just the Klan that kept us apart. My dad was determined it would never happen. I guess he won, after all.

"I probably need to go see my dad."

"You want to use my car? I'll stay here with Lilly."

"No, I'll walk. I used to do it all the time." We both giggled when we remembered all the times I would sneak off to the Quarters to visit Catfish and Marianne and, hopefully, meet up with Rodney. I remembered how invincible I felt, until my dad found out and beat me within an inch of my life. Still, Rodney and I continued to try to make it work.

We must have been crazy.

*

I walked up South Jefferson Street towards the big antebellum house on the corner of Marshall Road and stopped in front of a ranch-style house—the Burton family home where I had lived until I was about ten or eleven. The low-slung roof had been replaced, and the white siding was painted blue, but the big ditch and the dogwood trees were still there.

A horn scared me out of my thoughts and I turned to see my childhood friend, Callie leaning out the window of a new Cutlass Supreme.

"Hi, stranger. When'd you get to town?" Callie grew up across the street from me and we'd been like sisters in elementary school. We'd walked to and from school together every day and spent lots of nights at each other's houses. I hadn't seen her since I went off to college, eight years before.

"Callie! Hi. You look great! What have you been up to?" I looked in the back seat and saw a baby strapped in an infant carrier. "Is this your baby?"

"Yep, John and I have two of these little monsters. Where you going?"

"To my parents' house. I just flew in from New York."

"Hop in and I'll take you the rest of the way." We talked nonstop for the three-block drive and sat in my parents' driveway for fifteen minutes catching up. Callie didn't ask why I was walking up South Jefferson or where I was staying while I was in Jean Ville. I guess she took it for granted I would stay at my parents' house and that I was taking a walk around the block.

"Will you come to dinner while you're here?"

"I need to see about my dad before I make any plans. Can I call you?"

"Sure. Here's my phone number. We live a few blocks towards town in the old Tucker home."

"I'll call you." We hugged and I got out of the car and waved until she was out of sight. I think I was trying to postpone my entrance into my former home. I walked to the back of the house, intending to go in through the back door. Two of my brothers were playing basketball near the carport and Will ran up to me. We hugged, then I pulled away.

"How's Dad?"

"Not good. I'm glad you're here."

"What's wrong with him, Will?" I was only a year older than Will and we'd been very close growing up. My older brother, James, had been a tyrant and had also tried to kill Rodney in Jackson a couple of years before. He was lingering near the basketball goal as though he didn't know what to say to me. I approached him, and before he could say anything, I hugged him. He hugged me back and when he pulled away there was moisture in his eyes. "You worried about Daddy, James?"

"I guess. He looks bad."

"Do you two want to come with me to see him?"

"Sure," Will said, and he took my hand and practically pulled me up the back steps. James followed close behind. When we walked into the kitchen, Robby, who was number four, about three years younger than Will, was getting something out of the fridge. He was surprised to see me and hugged me extra tight. "You're so tall, Rob. What happened?"

"I grew. I'm almost twenty-one, you know."

"Where's Sissy?""

"She's in Dad's room," Robby said. "Come on. He'll be glad to see you. He's asked about you a hundred times."

I watched my three brothers walk with confidence into my parents' bedroom while I held back, feeling scared and insecure. Will grabbed my hand and pulled me.

I barely recognized Daddy. His skin was grayish-yellow and his hair white. My once big-chested, broad-shouldered dad looked like he'd lost fifty pounds, yet under the sheets I could see his stomach protruding a foot in the air.

He hadn't shaved in a few days and the uneven growth on his face was white and made his nose look huge. His eyes were closed. Sissy was sitting on the far side of the room next to Daddy's bed and when she saw me she jumped up and ran into my arms. We hugged and I noticed that she was taller, although not as tall as me. When had she grown up? She took my hand and drew me towards Daddy's bed.

"Daddy, guess who's here?" She spoke in a voice just above a whisper. "It's Susie." Daddy opened his eyes a slit and looked at me. His hand, thick and hairy, came out from under the covers and he reached for me. I was afraid to take it; afraid he'd jerk me towards him and hit me, so I stiffened my arm and held back.

"Come closer, Susie." His voice was a hoarse whisper. "Let me look at my beautiful daughter." I took a step towards the bed but didn't loosen my elbow. His grip was weak and when I realized I was probably stronger than he was, I relaxed and moved closer. He patted the mattress near his hip and I sat on one side of my butt, the other hanging off the edge of the bed. "You're still beautiful."

"Hi Daddy. How are you?"

"Better now that you're here." He attempted a smile but it looked more like a smirk.

"I wanted to see you." I didn't know what to say and I wasn't making sense. I sat there for a while and he held onto my hand while I kept my arm stiff and tried not to fall off the bed. I noticed bruises on the top of his hand and his forearm. There was also a big bruise, like a hickey, on his neck. He closed his eyes and seemed to drift off so I got up and moved towards Sissy and the boys.

"What's the doctor say?" I looked from James to Robby to Will to Sissy. "And where's Mama?"

"Dr. Switzer comes twice a day. The doctors in New Orleans said it's cirrhosis."

"Liver disease? How advanced?"

"It's pretty bad."

"Can it be cured?"

"They feel as though he's had it for years. The question is whether there is permanent damage to his liver. They say we have to wait and see if his liver will repair itself or continue to deteriorate."

"He's getting a shot every week and takes medication that can help repair the liver, but he's really sick." James was standing in front of me and it was the first time I'd ever seen him show any emotion.

"And he's confused and sometimes slurs his speech," Sissy said.

"Mama?" I looked at my siblings with a big question across my forehead.

"Mama took Albert and went to visit Aunt Betty. She said she couldn't take it." Albert was the baby of the family, born when I was in college. He was ten and I wondered what Mama was doing about Albert going to school.

"Mama left Daddy and went to Houston?"

"Yep. That's why we need you here." Sissy looked from me to James and back to me.

"Wait. I'm not staying. I can't stay. I have a job, responsibilities. I just came to see Daddy in case…"

"In case he's going to die? And you don't want to feel guilty if that happens?" James stormed out of the room. I followed him and cornered him in the kitchen.

"What do you care? He beat you, too."

"That's in the past. He needs us now. Can't you forgive and forget?" James walked out the back door and left in his old Chevy pickup truck. I went down the hall to the front door and sat on the porch swing. After a few minutes, Sissy and Will came out and sat in the rockers. We didn't talk for a few minutes but I couldn't stop thinking that Mama left Daddy, sick in bed, and went to Houston.

"I'm not staying. I can't. Sorry." I sat with one leg across the swing, the other dangling over the side, and pushed myself slowly back and forth.

"How long can you stay?" Sissy was staring at Dr. Switzer's house across the street.

"My plane returns to New York Monday. I can't just walk out on my job. And I'm helping a family out right now. The mother is sick and I'm keeping their daughter." I didn't mention that Lilly was with me in Jean Ville.

"I think Mama is depending on you staying here with Daddy until he gets well. You're the oldest daughter."

"He's Mama's responsibility, not mine. Sorry, you guys. I'm not staying." I got off the swing and walked down the thirteen steps to the front yard, down the sidewalk to the blacktop, and turned right. I kept walking until I reached the Quarters fifteen minutes later. No one followed me.

I couldn't believe what I'd just encountered—my siblings expected me to leave New York and come to Jean Ville to take care of a father who had abused me my entire life, all because my mother gave up on him. Well, he was her responsibility, not mine. As far as I was concerned, they could put him in a nursing home.

I was indignant when I walked up on Catfish's porch and plopped into the rocker. Lilly ran up the little steps, hugged me, then ran back into the yard to play with her cousins. *Oh. Her cousins,* I thought.

It hit me that Lilly was actually with her biological family. Marianne and I were half-sisters, so Marianne's nieces and cousins were related to my daughter. In fact, Rodney's Uncle Bo was married to Marianne's Aunt Jesse, so their children were related to Lilly, too.

Catfish's house, now Marianne's, was on the end of the row in the Quarters, closest to Gravier Road. Next was Tootsie's, then Sam's, Catfish's oldest son, and his family, then Bo and Jesse's cabin. The last house belonged to the second brother, Tom. Tom and Sam's kids were starting to have kids of their own and some of them lived in the three new cabins facing the five originals.

Marianne walked out of the house with a pitcher of sweet tea and three glasses.

"Lucy's on the way over. How'd it go at your dad's?"

"Did you know my mother skipped out?"

"Mama told me. She's been gone over a week now, I think."

"They want me to leave my life and move back here to take care of him."

"Oh, my. Well?"

"I'm not going to do it."

"Don't blame you." Lucy must have parked in front of the house because she walked around to the back and climbed the little steps to the porch. She pecked Marianne on the top of her head and shook my hand.

"I've heard a lot about you." She sat on the floor of the porch with her legs dangling over the edge. She was a bit masculine, but pretty, with short, brown hair that had been ironed straight and hung over one eyebrow. Her skin tone was copper and she had dark eyes and brows and wore a small gold stud in the side of her nose. Lucy was thin and lanky, almost athletic, and spoke in a husky voice. Her dry wit was magnetic. She laughed a lot and was fun to be around. I soon forgot about the dysfunction at the antebellum house on the corner of Marshall and Jefferson Streets.

Marianne fired up the charcoal grill and laid out a couple of chickens, then she opened a bottle of wine and poured some into three jelly glasses. The three of us watched the children and laughed while evening fell around us and the chickens cooked. I called to Lilly and she came in, tired and dirty. I washed her up at the kitchen sink, dressed her in the pink pajamas we'd packed, and fed her a bowl of cereal. She was too tired to eat a meal. She fell fast asleep on the pull-out sofa in the next room.

Marianne's little cabin had three rooms, in shotgun fashion, which meant each room had a door into the next. "No halls," Catfish had told me. "That's a waste of space. Plantation owners called them 'shotgun houses' 'cause they said you could shoot your gun through the front door and kill a chicken in the backyard." Catfish laughed when he told me that, several times.

The room on the rear of the house, off the porch, was the kitchen. It had a stove, a sink with a faucet with running water, and a small refrigerator, which was new because Catfish had an old-fashioned icebox. There was a round table with four chairs and an old pine cabinet that held dishes and glasses. The middle room was the sitting room and Marianne had installed a black-and-white television across from the small sofa. There was also an old rocking chair.

The last room, on the front of the house, was a bedroom. I hadn't been in it since after Catfish's funeral. At the time it had a small bed, a dresser and a rod across one corner where he hung his clothes. A picture of Jesus had been over the bed. I wondered what Marianne had done to change the room, but didn't ask. I'd see it later.

The three of us polished off two bottles of wine and one of the chickens, and laughed until we were all exhausted. I asked about the bathroom and they looked at each other funny.

"You still have an outhouse?" I looked from Marianne to Lucy.

"We're just pulling your leg. I built a bathroom with running water, even hot, on the front porch. Just go through the bedroom."

I checked on Lilly as I walked through the sitting room. She was sound asleep. I opened the door to the bedroom and it no longer looked like the one I remembered. A large bed sat under the windows on the right and a big dresser with a huge mirror was across from it. On the far wall, next to the front door, was an armoire that I figured held Marianne's clothes. Nice, navy draperies hung from the two windows and there was a bedside table with a lamp on each side of the bed.

I opened the front door and, instead of a porch, there was a modern bathroom, complete with tub, toilet, and sink. I was impressed.

When I returned to the kitchen, I walked in on Marianne and Lucy kissing and turned around and closed the door between that room and the sitting room. I went into the bathroom, took a hot bath, dressed in my pajamas, and crawled into bed with Lilly. I was asleep before my eyes were totally shut.

~Chapter Thirteen ~

~

Stay or Go?

I HEARD VOICES, AND when I opened my eyes, rays of sunshine made fingers of light like a prism on the wall. Lilly was snuggled up against me, so I propped a pillow under her back and crept out of bed. I walked through Marianne's bedroom to the bathroom, put on my jeans and a T-shirt, and tiptoed into the kitchen. Tootsie was sitting at the table having coffee with Marianne.

"Did you ever go to bed last night?" I joked with Mari as I hugged Tootsie. "It's so good to see you, Toot."

"You, too, honey-chile. How you been? You looking good."

"Doing fine. How about you?" Tootsie told me about each of her other four daughters and her two baby granddaughters. She lit up when she described how Betsy's older daughter, Celeste, was going to be a beauty and so smart. The baby, Leah, was six months old and just beginning to sit up. I loved the way Tootsie talked, her animated gestures, how her eyes got big as peaches when she discussed something that excited her, like her grandbabies.

"Are you going to work today?" I twisted a strand of red hair that had fallen over my eye and tucked it behind my ear, then I got up and poured a cup of coffee and returned to the table.

"It's Saturday and I don't work weekends, but I be heading out to your daddy's house in a few minutes. I need to check on him and make sure they got something to feed him over the weekend."

"What's going on over there?"

"Hard to say. Your Mama, she done left. Left me and Sissy to take care of him. And he sick, too."

"Look, Toot. My siblings ganged up on me yesterday. They expect me to leave my job, my friends, my life in New York and move back here to take care of him. I'm not doing it."

"I don't blame you none, honey-chile. He not your responsibility."

"He's not yours, either."

"Well, somebody got to do it."

"So Sissy stays with him at night and you take care of him in the daytime while she's at school?"

"She don't complain but I know she need help. Your brothers help out on weekends, but she there most of the time." I thought about how unfair it was to expect a fifteen-year-old to take care of a sick man, but I couldn't get sucked into feeling guilty and giving up my life.

"How are you getting there this morning?" I looked from Tootsie to Marianne.

"Mari gonna take me."

"I can't leave Lilly," I said. "I'll be down there later when someone is here to watch her."

"Who's Lilly?" Tootsie looked at Marianne who shrugged her shoulders and looked at me. I was surprised she hadn't told her mother.

"Lilly is the daughter of my friends, Joe and Emalene. She's five. Emma is in the hospital. I had already agreed to keep Lilly before I found out about Daddy, so I brought her with me."

"Oh. I'll be back by noon and be happy to watch her so you can go see your Daddy," Tootsie said.

"I'm not working this weekend. I'll watch Lilly," Marianne said. "You two take my car."

"We can walk," I said.

"I ain't walking," Tootsie raised her eyebrows and looked at me over the top of her coffee, her chin down, her eyelashes up. Marianne and I both laughed at the face she made.

Lilly stumbled into the kitchen rubbing her eyes and climbed into my lap. She laid her head on my chest and wrapped her little arms around my neck.

"Hi, sleepyhead." I rubbed her back and she leaned back to look at me.

"Are we still in Jean Ville?" She smiled and her breath smelled like sour milk.

"Yes. Still at Marianne's house. This is Tootsie, Marianne's mama." I turned her around in my lap so she was facing the table. Tootsie's eyes got big, her eyebrows lifted, and she looked at me with a sheepish grin.

"Hi, Lilly."

"Tootsie? Is that your real name?" Lilly scooted off my lap and was standing on the wood floor, facing Tootsie.

"Well, my real name is Theresa, but everyone calls me Tootsie." She took both of Lilly's hands in hers and pulled her closer.

"I like the name Tootsie. It feels good in my mouth, like sucking on a lollipop." Lilly was serious but Tootsie burst out laughing and soon we were all hysterical, with Lilly sitting in Tootsie's lap sipping from Tootsie's coffee cup. I could tell that Lilly and Tootsie would be a great pair. I just worried Tootsie would ask questions I was not ready to answer.

*

I stayed with Daddy all day Saturday so Sissy could get out with her friends and take a break. I actually felt sorry for him. He looked so vulnerable and was dependent on me for everything. He couldn't get up to use the bathroom, so I had to handle a urinal. James and Will came over and helped him to the toilet once, and I wondered how

Sissy and Tootsie handled that part when the boys weren't around. Daddy was a big, heavy man, even in his weakened condition.

I tried to be as attentive and patient as I could, but Daddy was a difficult and demanding patient. First he wanted to be turned, then to sit up, then he decided that didn't work and needed to lie down. He'd ask for a drink of water then say it didn't taste right and could I get him a soda. Then he'd say maybe lemonade. I tried to feed him Jell-O but he didn't like lime, so I made a batch of cherry which took a while to set and he got impatient waiting for it. I fed him soup and he said he didn't eat canned soup, he liked homemade. I drew the line there. The way he was acting, I knew he wouldn't eat it if I went to the trouble.

He awoke from a nap about mid-afternoon and I was sitting in the corner, reading.

"Hi." He whispered and coughed a couple of times. "Hi, pretty girl. You still here?" He started to move around in the bed and I got up to help him.

"Do you need something, Daddy?" I pulled the covers up and straightened them across his chest, under his arms.

"No. I'm just glad you're here." He patted the bed beside him and moved over a bit to give me room to sit.

"What can I do to make you more comfortable?" I sat on the edge of the bed, my butt touching his hip through the covers.

"I'm okay for now. I just want to visit with you a bit." He opened his eyes fully and I could see that the whites were yellow. He was pale and his lips were chapped and parched. There was some petroleum jelly on the bedside table so I put my pinky finger in it and spread a little on his lips.

"You want some water?" I picked up his glass and held the straw to his lips and he drank a few sips.

"Thanks. Look, Susie. I know we've had a tough go, but I want you to know that I love you." One solitary tear ran out the corner of his eye and down into his thinning hair.

"I know, Daddy. You don't have to talk about it." I was shocked to hear him talk this way and thought, *he must believe he's dying.*

"I always knew you were special and I think I was afraid you wouldn't reach your potential. That you would make a bad decision that could ruin your future." He looked at the ceiling and folded his hands together on his chest as if praying.

"Oh." I was so shocked at his statement that I didn't know what to say.

"I just want you to know. It was because I love you." He closed his eyes and began to breathe deeply, as if drifting off to sleep. I took that as my cue that the conversation was over. I left the bedroom and went to the kitchen to freshen his glass of water and leaned on the counter to catch my breath, which is when I realized I'd been holding it, afraid of what Daddy would say and startled at what he actually did say.

Robby still lived at my parents' house when he was home from college, so he was there when Will and James came over Saturday afternoon. That evening we sat at the kitchen table and opened a bottle of wine. James was drinking beer and was irritated. We discussed the different options available if Mama didn't come home. I kept thinking of what Daddy had said to me that afternoon, but I didn't share it with my brothers.

James said he was going to Houston to bring Mama home, that it was ridiculous that she would run out on the family at a time like this. We came up with some ideas for how to handle the situation once I returned to New York.

It almost took permission from the Queen, but I was able to get a week off from work and Joe agreed to let Lilly miss a week of kindergarten. Emma would be in the hospital all week, so if we went home I'd be keeping Lilly anyway.

"If it's permanent liver damage, it's serious." Josh said when we finally talked on the phone about my dad Sunday night. "He's probably had it for years and now the liver is diseased. Since he's been a heavy drinker, I'd say he has five years; maybe more if he doesn't drink again."

"What kind of care will he need?"

"If I were to guess, I'd say he has a virus in his weakened liver that's making him acutely ill and once the virus has cleared up—if it clears up and doesn't end up destroying his liver—he'll feel better. He will have fatigue and swelling, probably some abdominal discomfort, and he needs to limit salt and eat a balanced diet, not high in fat. And mild exercise, such as walking or swimming, once he's over the virus. But, Susie, he'll be a sick man the rest of his life, however long that is."

"Okay." I didn't say anything for a while. "Josh?"

"Yes."

"I... well... I..."

"You miss me?" He started laughing. I laughed, too.

"Yeah. You got it."

"I know, Susie. Hang in there. And, if you want me to come to Louisiana, if you need me..."

"I'm okay. We'll talk again soon." When we hung up I sat by the phone and tried to hold onto Josh's voice and feel his presence. I DID need him, but I would never ask him to come to Jean Ville.

*

I walked back to the Quarters from my dad's house on Monday, just as the sun turned orange on the horizon and sent rays of red, yellow, and white halos over the tops of the moss-draped oak trees. I thought how none of my brothers asked me where I was staying.

Marianne was home, pulling stuff out of the fridge to start dinner.

"Let me go get burgers so you don't have to cook tonight, Mari."
I put my purse on the table and hugged her.

"That would be great. I had a long day." She started to put
everything back and asked if I'd like a glass of wine.

"I'll have one when I get back. Can I use your car?"

"Sure." She took her keys from her purse and handed them to
me.

"Where's Lilly?"

"She's next door. Mama's fixing macaroni and cheese for her and
Tom's daughter, Anna, and Sam's, Chrissy." She took a bottle of
wine from the fridge and started to wrestle with the cork.

"They must be around Lilly's age, right?"

"Yes, and the three of them are thick as underbrush." Marianne
laughed and sat at the table.

*

The Burger Barn was owned by Mr. Joffrion, the dad of one of my
friends, who stopped me when I walked in to order hamburgers for
dinner.

"Susie Burton. Well how the heck are you? Long time, no see."
He came around the counter and hugged me.

"I'm fine, Mr. Joffrion. Just in for a visit."

"Where you living now?"

"I'm still in New York. How's Cindy?"

"Oh, she's fine. Has three children now. They live just down the
street from me and Beverly." He had his hands on my shoulders and
was looking at me like he was trying to figure me out.

"That's just great, Mr. Joffrion." I took a step back and looked
up at the menu written on a huge blackboard mounted on the wall
behind the counter. He moved back to his spot behind the cash
register.

"I'll have three cheeseburgers with fries, please."

"Gotcha. Want that to go or to eat here?" He started laughing at his own foolish question, as if I would eat all three burgers. I laughed, too. He wrote my order on a little pad, ripped it off, and hung it on a string under the blackboard, using a clothes hanger to attach it. His back was to me and he was talking to the cook through the opening when I heard the cowbell sound on the door.

I turned towards the door and froze. There was Rodney standing in the opened doorway, the handle still in his hand, also suspended in time, not moving. I think my mouth was open but no sound came out, nor could I hear a sound around me. It was as though everything and everyone had become petrified and only Rodney and I were in this space where I could hear him breathe and smell the aftershave on his skin, starch in his dress shirt, and toothpaste on his breath.

A smile crept across his face, slowly, and his eyes lit up. His feet sounded like bullets as they padded across the wood-planked floor when he walked towards me. I couldn't breathe or move or hear him speak, although I saw his lips move and knew he was saying my name.

He took both my hands in his and I looked at our four sets of fingers, twenty of them, entwined in the space between us. When I looked up he was glaring at me with a huge grin.

He was still gorgeous. He was dressed in green slacks with sharp creases, a tan, long-sleeved cotton shirt starched stiff, and a brown tie loosened at the neck, the first two buttons of his shirt unfastened, obviously his army uniform.

"You are still the most beautiful girl I've ever seen," he said. "And I've been all over the world. I've seen lots of girls."

"Oh." That's all I could say. It took a few moments before I came to my senses and looked past him at Mr. Joffrion, who had turned back around and was watching us. I tried to detach from Rodney's hands but he didn't seem to notice we were being glared at.

"When did you get in town? How long will you be here?" He was whispering and I couldn't answer. I was drawn into his aura and felt it bathe me in a glow that reminded me of the time we ran into each other at the Cow Palace when I was fifteen. That encounter had been the reason the Klan tried to lynch his dad and burned their house to the ground.

That thought brought me back to the present and I pulled away from him, placing my hands in the pockets of my denim jacket.

"You want to take a walk?" Rodney was looking at me, and I looked over Mr. Joffrion's head at the menu.

"Here? You're kidding, of course." I whispered over my shoulder, not looking at him.

"Where are you staying?" He was standing behind me as if in line and whispered into my ear.

"Marianne," I said as softly as I could. "I've already ordered." I said louder and moved aside so he could face Mr. Joffrion and place his order. I didn't listen to their exchange and soon my order was ready. I paid and left without saying another word to anyone.

I rushed into Marianne's house.

"Where's Lilly?" I was frantic that Rodney would follow me back to the Quarters and see her.

"She's still with Mama."

"Can you make sure she stays there? I think Rodney is on his way over here."

"Sure." Marianne walked out the backdoor and I heard the door to Tootsie's cabin slam. She was back in the kitchen a few minutes later and I was still standing there with the paper bag of burgers in my hand. Marianne took them from me as soon as we heard a car engine pull into the Quarters. I met Rodney outside at the bottom of the steps to keep him from going into the house.

We walked towards the old red barn. He held my hand and the familiar goose bumps crawled up my arms and down my spine telling me this man still had an effect on me.

The big sliding doors that were once on both sides of the barn had been removed years before and the windows, which had never had glass or screens, provided cross ventilation. We didn't talk as we headed towards the red building that had recently been painted, although it must not have been scraped first because there were bubbles in sections that indicated it would start peeling again soon.

It was breezy and I could smell the mushroomy odor of pecans and a whiff of the camellia bush in Catfish's old garden. Under it all was the familiar smell of Rodney—something I detected only on him, something like a mixture of mint, orange, and lilac. It was hard to describe, but if I were deaf and blind and he walked into my room, I'd know it was Rodney.

"Want to go inside?" He stopped in front of the barn, pulled my hand to his mouth and kissed the top of it. I rubbed my free hand along the sleeve of my jacket trying to calm the goose bumps underneath. "You cold?"

"No, I'm okay. I haven't been inside in years, have you?"

"Not since... you." The last time we'd been in that barn was a month after he'd come to New York. I was eighteen and we'd made love for the first time before he left the city. Six weeks later I'd discovered I was pregnant.

Before I found out I was expecting a baby, I had come home for Christmas and we'd met, but something was wrong. We didn't stay in the barn long. We didn't kiss or make love. He had been skittish and non-communicative and I kept asking him whether something had happened to change things between us, to which he'd said "Nothing." We were at an impasse and, eventually, he left and I sat in the hayloft and cried.

The next day we'd met in Baton Rouge and he told me that there had been new threats against his family. "Leave the white girl alone," the Klan had written in black paint across the Thibaults' new house. We'd spent the night together in Baton Rouge and he put me on a plane back to New York the next day. We didn't see each other again until after we'd both graduated from college almost three years later. I'd gone to Jean Ville for the summer while I made last-ditch attempts to get a full scholarship to graduate school, which I finally did, at St. John's.

Before I flew back to New York that August, I'd called Rodney. He was living in Baton Rouge, working at the clerk of court's office, waiting to start law school that fall. He met me at the airport and we spent the night in a motel on Airline Highway. It was bittersweet because we both knew our relationship was doomed. The only way it could work would be if Rodney moved to New York where mixed-race marriages were acceptable, but that wasn't an option because he was determined to go to law school for another three years. We'd said goodbye again the next morning when I left for New York.

The barn was cooling off from the day's heat when we stepped inside the opening where the double doors had once hung. It still smelled of horse manure and wet straw, even though there had not been livestock on the place since before Catfish died. Rodney led the way up the ladder into the hayloft. It was obvious people had been up there—piles of hay were scattered about and imprints of feet and bodies were everywhere.

"I guess the kids come up here." He spread some straw out for a place to sit under the window. I joined him and we sat with our backs against the wall. My arm was against his and even though he wore long sleeves I could feel his body heat penetrate my skin. The wind blew through the window above us and cooled off the loft. It was getting dark outside, and through the far window I could see violet rays glowing brightly behind the gathering clouds and I smelled moisture in the air.

"It's going to rain tonight," I said without thinking. He lifted my hand and kissed my fingertips, then put our hands on his knee.

He had long, strong fingers and my hand felt lost under his. I felt tingles inside and tried to hide my physical reaction.

"How are you?" We said it at the same time, then we laughed. "You first." We said that together, too. "Hmmmm," I said.

"Tell me about your life, Rod." He told me that he was having a hard time forgetting the atrocities of the war. "They think JAG officers don't see action, but I could tell you stories that would make your hair curl." He said he was getting better, but still had a ways to go to get rid of the nightmares and depression that plagued him.

He told me about Maria, a girl he met in Vietnam, the only woman JAG officer there. "She has the same nightmares. I guess that's what we have most in common—an understanding of..." He looked up at the rafters and I could tell he was thinking about something awful.

"At least you're telling me yourself this time. About Maria, I mean."

"Susie. I didn't have a phone number. I didn't know if my letters from Jackson ever got to you. It was as though you'd disappeared."

"I had to move and I didn't give my address to anyone because of my dad. He came to New York looking for me."

"Oh. I didn't know."

"Water under the bridge." We were silent for a while.

"I wanted to come to New York to see you when I got back from Vietnam, but you wouldn't answer my requests." He didn't look at me, just stared straight ahead out the window. I supposed he was watching the same sunset and accumulating rain clouds.

"I invited you up last Thanksgiving."

"I couldn't go, but I asked you to come to Kansas and you never responded."

"I didn't want to see you, Rodney. I don't want to see you now, either." I could feel the anger bubbling up in my throat. I pulled my hand away and tried to scoot over to create some distance and get out of his energy field.

"Why? I don't understand."

"That's because you are not the one who waited in Union Station for more than twenty-four hours watching people get off the trains from Chicago."

"I was in the emergency room, then jail, then escaping to Jackson."

"I know. I'm sorry, but I didn't know then, and I waited and waited. I pictured you every way a dead man could be, then I pictured you with Annette. Then I found out you brought Annette back to Jean Ville and were engaged."

"Susie..."

"And I had to find all of this out from other people. You didn't have the decency to tell me yourself." I scooted to the top of the ladder and started down. He caught up with me when I was almost at Marianne's porch.

"Wait. Please." He grabbed my arm and stopped me. He was standing behind me and I could feel his breath on my neck. "Please." I twisted around and faced him. He kissed me, long, hard, and passionately and, although I tried not to respond, I felt myself melt into his arms and return his kiss.

Finally, I came to my senses, broke out of his embrace, and ran up the steps and into the house. I closed the door to the sitting room and threw myself on the sofa bed. I could hear Marianne and Rodney talking on the porch. She refused to let him in the house to talk to me.

That night in bed with Lilly, I couldn't sleep. I went to the kitchen and had a cup of hot tea to calm my nerves.

I was still in love with Rodney, but it was hopeless. There had been changes—integration, a sheriff who enforced laws, but people still did not accept mixed-race relationships and, from what I'd heard, the Klan was still active; just a bit more discreet. I saw it written on Mr. Joffrion's face. They might go after the Thibault family tonight because of my encounter with Rodney at the Burger Barn.

I tossed and turned all night wondering what I'd do if he tried to see me again.

Rodney called the next day. I told Marianne to tell him I was unavailable. He called every afternoon for three days, but I didn't talk to him. He drove to Marianne's house Wednesday night, but when I saw his car pull up I grabbed Lilly's hand and we went to Tootsie's cabin next door.

Tootsie and I visited in her sitting room and Lilly watched the little TV in Tootsie's bedroom with Chrissy. I cried and told Tootsie I was miserable because I still loved Rodney and wanted to be with him, but it would never work and I was afraid of what they'd do to his family. She nodded in agreement.

"Yeah, chile. They's not much has changed underneath. They still got those who would get revenge on the Thibaults if you try to be with Rodney." Tootsie sympathized with me but gave me no hope.

He didn't stay very long at Marianne's house that evening and she never told me about their conversation, but he quit calling. I moped all week. Everything upset me—when I looked at my pitiful, sick dad, when I talked to my mother on the phone and she acted like he was my problem, when James yelled at me and called me selfish, when Lilly scraped her knee and wanted her mama. All those times, though, I knew I was angry because I'd lost Rodney and our dream, again.

It was really over, and I'd have to learn to live with that reality.

*

My brothers and I decided I should ask Tootsie if she would move into the house to take care of Dad and Sissy. Sissy needed stability and supervision so she could be a regular high schooler. Tootsie said yes without thinking twice, as though she had been waiting for the chance to live in my mother's house and take care of Daddy.

"Are you sure?" We were sitting in her kitchen. Lilly was playing in the yard and it was almost dark. The smell of gumbo on Tootsie's stove was comforting and familiar, and my mouth watered as I thought about the thick, hearty soup of sausage and chicken and shrimp over rice.

"It would be easier for me than going back and forth." She got up and stirred the tall, silver pot and lifted the lid on the rice. Steam shot up towards the low ceiling and she put the top back on. "Looking good!"

"What about your family?"

"They not going anywheres. I can come down here any time. Your daddy needs me and he been good to me all these years." She was so matter-of-fact that it made me feel better about her taking care of Daddy.

I visited him every day and we didn't argue because I refused to engage when he prodded me with hateful questions about my love life, why I chose to live so far away, and the fact that I visited so seldom.

He was sitting in his recliner on Friday when I went to tell him good-bye. His skin was not as yellowed and he smiled a crooked smile when I walked into his bedroom.

"You're looking better. Out of bed for a change." I tucked his afghan around his legs and pulled up the one sock that was slipping off his foot. I sat in the chair facing him and we chatted as if we had a relationship. He asked about my job and I talked about New York and even told him a little about Josh.

"He's a surgeon."

"About time you met someone who deserves you." We both laughed.

"Have you heard from Mama?" I was helping him back to his bed.

"Yes, she called last night to check on me. I don't think she's coming back until I'm well." He sat on the edge of the bed and looked at me with a sad expression.

"I'm sorry, Daddy. I guess she can't handle seeing you sick like this."

"I guess. I'm thankful Tootsie agreed to stay with me until I'm on my feet." He lay back in the bed and I pulled his afghan up to his chest.

"Me, too. She's very patient and kind and will take good care of you." I wanted to add, "She always has taken care of you, hasn't she," but I decided to leave it alone. *I really must be growing up,* I thought again.

James came in just as I was leaving to go back to the Quarters. "I need to talk to you." He turned and marched down the hall to the front porch. I followed and he sat in one of the rockers facing the street, I sat on the swing facing him.

"I just got back from Houston. Mama's not coming back. Ever."

"I don't believe you. Daddy talked to her last night."

"I think she has a boyfriend."

"At her age?"

"What? She's in her forties. That's not old."

"Oh, so you're taking up for her?" I wasn't looking at him but I could feel him staring at the side of my face. He had always been mean to me, and we'd never gotten along, but I felt bad for him. He was the oldest and I guess he felt responsible for the family falling apart.

"Look," he said. "You don't know everything." He stopped rocking, stood up, and faced me on the swing. I looked up at him.

He was tall and handsome, sandy blond hair, blue eyes, broad shoulders. He began to talk, slowly at first, and softly. He told me that Daddy had beat Mama when we were growing up. He said that I didn't know about it because I was so embroiled in my own struggles to survive. He said Daddy broke Mama's nose once and that he would slap her across the face if she said something he didn't like.

"I had to pull him off her more than once." James looked over my head and stared into space as if remembering something awful. "He would hit her so hard she'd pass out on the floor and he'd be on top of her, slapping her, telling her to get up. I'd have to pull him off and help her to bed, put cold compresses on her head and try to revive her. It was awful.

"She's had enough. She said after all he's done to her she's not going to take care of him." The sad look on James's face made me hurt for him for the first time.

My mother and I never had a good relationship but I thought it was because she was jealous of me; I didn't know she was being abused, too.

"What about Albert?"

"Mama said she's going to send Albert back here once Daddy is back on his feet," James sat down hard in the rocker. "She said he needs his father and that she's tired of raising kids, she's ready to have a life of her own." He looked up at the ceiling of the porch as though pondering a far-off thought. He whispered, "I'll help with Albert. Will and Robby will pitch in." He rocked quietly for a while.

"Look, Susie, you need to go back to New York." He stopped rocking and turned his body towards me. "There's nothing for you here. With Tootsie's help, we'll handle things." It was like James was giving me permission to have a life. Somehow that meant a lot to me.

I stood and hugged him and he hugged me back. I walked back to the Quarters and felt like everything around me was crumbling—my family, Rodney, my dreams. But I also felt I'd renewed my relationship with Sissy, Marianne, and Tootsie, and I was starting a new one with James. As for my dad, that would take some work.

∾ Chapter Fourteen ∾

∾

Custody

MARIANNE TOOK LILLY AND me to the Baton Rouge airport Saturday morning. Marianne carried Lilly into the terminal, her little arms wrapped around Mari's neck.

"I want you to come with us," Lilly cried into Mari's shoulder.

"I can't leave my mama, and you need to go back to your mama." Marianne tried to reason with Lilly, but she was inconsolable.

"When will I see you again?" Lilly was whining and holding onto Mari.

"You'll be back. And I'll come to New York to see you."

"Promise?"

"I promise." I was secretly excited about going home, but Lilly and I were still sad to leave Marianne.

Marianne put Lilly down, and we both cried when we said goodbye, but we were secretly excited about going home.

I expected to get a cab to my apartment, but Josh was waiting in baggage claim when we came down the escalator. Lilly started jumping up and down, yelling, "Uncle Josh! Uncle Josh!" She sprang into his arms and he winked at me over her shoulder. He finally put her down so she could run to the baggage carousel. He wrapped both arms around me and pulled me to him. He kissed me hard.

"I missed you!" He looked at me with a longing I hadn't seen in a very long time. I wanted to respond but I couldn't. Rodney had broken my heart again, and I felt distant and unsure of how I felt about Josh.

"Josh, a lot has happened. I think I'll need some time." I pulled away from him, but he kept holding one of my hands.

"You think?" He laughed, pulled me by my hand, and we caught up with Lilly. He acted like he didn't hear me.

By the time we pulled up at my apartment, it was after eight o'clock and Lilly was sound asleep in the back seat of the car. Josh carried her up the stairs and put her on my bed. I pulled off her socks and jeans and tucked her in.

"You're a natural at that." Josh had been standing at the foot of the bed watching.

"At what?"

"Mothering." He took my hand and led me to the living room. He pulled me to him and wrapped his arms around me.

"Want something to drink?" I pulled away without looking him in the eye and went to the kitchen, got him a beer, and poured myself a glass of chardonnay. He sat in the chair, and I sat on the sofa.

"Well, tell me about it."

"I saw him."

"Rodney?"

"Uh, huh?" I took a long sip of my wine and tried not to look at Josh but I could feel his stare boring a hole through me.

"So?"

"It's over between us. He has someone else." I didn't look at him, and I felt tears gather under my eyelids.

"What does that mean?"

"I'm not sure, but I'm very hurt and sad."

"I'm sorry, Susie. I hate to see you hurting, but take all the time you need. I told you I'm in no rush. I'm not going away." He talked in a whisper as if he wasn't sure he meant it, but I couldn't deal with his feelings, I was too wrapped up in my own.

"Can we talk about Emalene?" I asked. I'd been thinking about her the entire time. I'd talked to Joe several times but he never let me speak to her.

"She's better and will probably go home from the hospital this week."

"What did they find?" I was standing in the living room in front of the chair where he was sitting.

"I'll let her tell you." He stood up and took me into his arms. I realized it felt good that Josh could help me forget Rodney, but I would never use Josh or be dishonest with him. I snuggled into his embrace and wrapped my arms around his waist. We stood there for a long time.

*

When I called Emalene on Sunday, Joe answered and asked me to keep Lilly until Wednesday. He said Emma was asleep and he'd have her call me back, but she never did, and I figured Joe didn't tell her.

I picked Lilly up at her after-school program when I got off work on Wednesday and we rode the bus out to Springfield Gardens. She was jumping up and down, and I was holding her pink duffle bag packed with clean clothes on one shoulder and her school backpack on the other when Joe opened the front door. Lilly jumped into his arms and he picked her up, hugged her, and put her down. She took off running down the hall towards the master bedroom. Joe turned and walked into the house and left me standing on the porch. He never said hello, thank you, come inside, nothing.

I let myself in and went to Lilly's room to put her things away, then I found Joe in the kitchen. He was sitting at the table with a half-empty bottle of bourbon in front of him and a large shot glass. He filled the glass and downed it. Then he poured another shot.

"You okay?"

"This glass is too small." He got up and found a tumbler in the cabinet next to the refrigerator. He sat back down and poured the glass half-full of bourbon.

"Joe? Are you okay?"

"NO! I'm NOT OKAY! Stop asking." He downed half the liquid in the glass and put his head on the table. I walked out and went to Emalene's bedroom. Lilly was in bed with her and they were sitting with their backs propped against the headboard. Emma was as beautiful as ever but very thin. I hugged her, and we chatted for a few minutes. I wanted to know what the doctors found, but she didn't want to talk in front of Lilly.

"Do you want me to pick Lilly up at school tomorrow?"

"I think I'll keep her home with me the rest of the week." She hugged Lilly, and the two of them snuggled under the covers and giggled. I was happy Lilly was back with her mother. They were good together. I marveled that I wasn't jealous of their relationship and I hoped it was because Emalene's goodness was rubbing off on me.

I let myself out of the house without saying anything to Joe. When I got home I was worried; too wired to sleep. I poured myself a glass of wine and called Josh.

"Please tell me what's wrong with Emma." I sat at my kitchen table, one hand holding the phone, the other holding my aching head. "She can't talk to me with Lilly around and I don't know how to get her alone."

"Can I call you back in just a minute?" He sounded like I might have disturbed him and I was taken aback. He'd always been so available to me. We hung up, and I drank my wine and poured myself another glass. I rarely drank more than one, so I knew I was in a bad place.

He called back about thirty minutes later.

"Emma said you should go to see her tomorrow. I'll be there, and I'll take Lilly for a walk or something." Josh was speaking slowly and softly, and it scared me.

"Why can't you tell me now?"

"Emma wants to tell you herself." He took a deep breath and sighed.

"Josh. You're scaring me. This sounds serious." I rubbed my forehead as if to push the thoughts in and out.

"Just go to see her tomorrow afternoon. I'll see you there." He hung up, and I listened to the dial tone for several long seconds thinking about Emma and wondering what was wrong with her that was so secretive. I had to wait another day to find out.

*

"How long have you known?" I was sitting on the ottoman facing her in her over-stuffed chair.

"I had surgery two years ago, and radiation. We thought it was gone. But..."

"Oh, Emma!" I put my head in her lap, and she stroked my hair and said something like, "There, there. It'll be fine." But I knew it wouldn't. What would I do without Emalene and Joe? And what would happen to Lilly? "Did Josh know two years ago?"

"Of course. He helped me when I was first diagnosed. He lined me up with the best breast surgeon in New York and got me in with a leading research oncologist. I don't know how I would have handled the medical part of this without Josh."

"But he didn't tell me."

"I don't think he felt it was his story to tell. I'm telling you now. The surgery two years ago was to remove the tumor. Two weeks ago, after you and Lilly left for Louisiana, I had a double mastectomy."

"Emma, how serious is this?"

"Serious but treatable. I'm going to start chemotherapy on

Monday. I might need your help with Lilly if it makes me sick. I don't want Joe to miss too much work, yet."

"Anything. I'll do anything you need." We didn't talk for the longest time. I just let her stroke my hair, and I inhaled her scent of lilac mixed with something like lemons. Finally, I lifted my head and looked at her. It was hard for me to believe she was sick.

Later Josh drove me home, and I asked him about Emma's prognosis.

"I don't know, Susie. Cancer is such a difficult disease to predict. Two years ago we removed the tumor and she had a series of radiation treatments. We thought she was healed, and in many cases, that's all it takes. With this recurrence, radiation will not work; the only option is chemo." He was driving slowly and looked at me out the corner of his eye.

"She looks thin and pale, doesn't she? I'm worried."

"Yeah. Me too." We drove into my parking lot, and he stopped the car but left the engine running. I looked at him, and he smiled and winked. I wanted to be mad at him for not telling me about Emma's cancer. I wanted to stay mad at all of them for keeping secrets. But, somehow, in the face of the seriousness of things that were happening, none of that seemed to matter.

Again, I thought how much I had grown over the past year.

*

The next month was a blur of putting one foot in front of the other, trying to move on from Rodney, but feeling stuck. I was also concerned about my family's problems—Mama gone, Daddy sick. And worse, Emalene had cancer.

Lilly was the bright spot in my life. I lived for Wednesdays and Saturdays when we would be together. During most of the week I'd go to work, come home, read, work on my Catfish stories and go to bed. On Wednesdays, I'd pick Lilly up at school and she'd spend the night at my apartment. I'd take her to school Thursday mornings and watch her curls bounce as she ran into the building, waving her hand over her shoulder saying, "I love you, Susie."

On Saturdays, I would restock my fridge and pantry, wash my clothes, vacuum, and try to stay busy until about three o'clock when I'd head back to Springfield Gardens.

Every week Emma looked a little better and seemed a bit more chipper. The chemo treatments were hard on her, and the doctors had to reduce the amount and frequency. When she was having treatments, she was lethargic and stayed in bed a lot. And she was thin, but was always in good spirits and happy to see me when I arrived.

As soon as I walked in the door, Joe would walk out without a word. I'd stay until he returned, unless it was after ten at night, which it often was, in which case I'd spend the night with Lilly in her double bed, then have to hustle to get to work in the morning.

I started going to mass on Sundays at the chapel on the campus of St. John's. It was familiar, and I had missed my Catholic roots. I prayed a lot during those long, sad months. I prayed for Rodney. I prayed that I would heal and that God would show me what I should do with my life without Rodney in it.

I enjoyed my job and the people I worked with. It was a great diversion from my personal life. I was becoming a star at work, well respected and moving up in the ranks.

Josh called every night. Sometimes I just didn't answer the phone. When I did answer, he mostly carried on a one-sided conversation, and we'd hang up. But he never ridiculed me or made me feel guilty for the distance I put between us. He was there for me if I needed him, but he didn't crowd me while I felt my way through the murkiness of my life.

It got cold, it snowed, and merchants began displaying Christmas decorations. On Thanksgiving, I went to Emalene and

Joe's for dinner. When I rang the doorbell that afternoon, Lilly came running into my arms and pulled me into the house by my hand.

"Guess who's here!" She was excited, and I laughed at her giddiness, followed her into the kitchen, and watched her jump into Josh's arms. "It's Uncle Josh!" She hugged his neck and scampered down to the floor.

Josh was standing in the middle of the kitchen wearing one of Emalene's aprons, with an oven mitt on his hand. He had flour on one of his cheeks and a sheepish grin on his face.

"Joe's not here, and I somehow got roped into cooking a turkey, under the direction of Maestro Emma!" He was laughing. I started laughing, too, at the sight of Josh, the grin on his face, the mess in the kitchen—the entire scene was comical. I wanted to kiss him, but instead, I joined the party.

Emalene sat at the table, giggling. She was instructing him on how to make Thanksgiving dinner yet he'd never stirred a pot in his life. Soon I had on an apron, and Josh and I were both taking direction from Emma, all of us laughing and cutting up like children. We opened a bottle of wine and sat at the table while the dressing-stuffed turkey baked and the potatoes boiled.

"Where's Joe?"

"Not sure," Emma said and looked at Josh as though he could explain.

"We aren't sweeping things under the table. The one thing Emalene needs is honesty and for everyone to act like she's Emma, not Cancer!"

"Okay, but what does that have to do with Joe?"

"Joe hasn't been coming home much lately," Emalene said.

"Oh?"

"He can't handle this. I need him, but I understand how he could feel overwhelmed and need time to figure things out."

"Reminds me of my mother. She ran out on my dad when he got sick." I didn't mean to blurt out my own problems. I hadn't discussed my situation with Emma because she'd been sick. I hadn't told Josh much either.

"Oh, Susie, I'm sorry. You never told me what happened in Louisiana. You've been so sad since you returned, but you and I haven't really had time to talk about it."

"It's nothing. It's just I was thinking how some people can't deal with a change like chronic illness when it's someone they love. I mean I wonder…" I couldn't finish my thought about how some people couldn't watch their loved one waste away and die.

We were all quiet. I had ruined the festive spirit, but Lilly ran into the room and started dancing and asking for music. Josh got up and put a Christmas record on the stereo, and he and Lilly danced to "Santa Claus is Coming to Town." Emma and I watched them and smiled, but we were both lost in our own losses—she'd lost Joe, I'd lost Rodney.

We'd just sat down to dinner when Joe stumbled in, drunk. Josh practically carried him to the bedroom and, I guess, got him in bed where he passed out cold. Emalene proceeded with Thanksgiving as though nothing had happened and I watched as she made everything appear wonderful for Lilly. I thought for the umpteenth time what a wonderful mother Emalene was and how lucky I was to have chosen her.

Neither Josh nor I wanted to leave Emma and Lilly in the house with Joe, but Emalene insisted they would be fine. I had originally thought I'd spend the night, but no longer felt it was a good idea, so I offered to take Lilly home with me. Emalene said, "No, it's Thanksgiving, I'd rather have her with me. You're welcome to stay with us, Susie," but I declined.

Josh offered to drive me home. When I hesitated, he said, "It's just a ride, so you don't have to take the bus so far this late at night."

We didn't talk in the car. When he pulled up at my apartment, I said thank you and opened the door. He didn't try to stop me, but before I got fully out of the car, I turned around and looked at him.

"I'm really sorry about how I'm acting, Josh. I can't help myself."

"I'm the last person you need to explain yourself to. You've had a lot of losses—your dad, your parents' marriage, Emma, Joe, Rodney. Take all the time you need to grieve. When you get tired of carrying all of this alone, I'm here, available, and willing to walk with you through this tunnel." He stared at me, and I wondered how anyone could love me so unconditionally when I was so flawed. Mostly I wondered why I couldn't love Josh Ryan, who was probably perfect for me.

Time can move slowly sometimes; other times it speeds by, and you wonder how so much could happen in such a short span.

We got into a new routine after Christmas. I'd pick Lilly up at school on Monday afternoons and keep her at my apartment all week, then take her home on Friday afternoon. Joe would show up on Saturdays, and I'd go home and spend the rest of the weekend at my apartment.

One Friday in March when I took Lilly home, Emalene was on the floor in the kitchen, out cold. I called an ambulance, then called Josh, who said he would find Joe. Lilly was beside herself, crying, screaming, wanting to get in the ambulance with her mother, so the two of us got in the back with the paramedic and sped off to the hospital.

Josh was in the Emergency Room when we arrived. Lilly jumped into his arms, and I fell against him. He hugged us both and led us to a private waiting room, then left to see about Emalene. A pretty young nurse came in and asked if we needed anything and even though we said, "No," she brought us sodas and crackers. An hour later, Josh came back and sat down at the round table in the center of the room. Lilly sat on his lap, and I was across from them.

"Joe's with her now. It's not good. We did some X-rays and a CT scan, and the cancer has spread. She fainted because she hasn't had anything to eat all week and is dehydrated. We have to make some kind of arrangements for care since Joe doesn't go home much, and that means Emalene is alone most of the week." He looked so sad and helpless. I reached across the table and took his hand. Lilly was hanging onto his neck, and I wished I could be in her place. I needed to hang on to someone.

Joe moved out of the house, and I moved in to help care for Emalene. She told me that Joe was disgusted with her since her mastectomy and didn't want to be married to her anymore. It was the saddest thing I'd ever heard, and it made me see my problems as minute in comparison.

I prepared dinner at night and made sure Emma ate and kept up her fluid intake; I'd fix leftover plates for the next day for Emma and the sitter Joe had hired to help out. In the morning I'd take Lilly to school and go to work.

The doctors decided Emalene could no longer tolerate the chemotherapy, even in the lower doses they'd been administering.

"No more? Ever? What does that mean?" I was sitting on the sofa in Emma's living room. Josh had come over to check on Emma and have dinner with us.

"Cancer is a strange bird. This one could be slow-growing, and she could have lots of years. Or it could be fast, and we could lose her in a matter of months. Without treatment, we know it will grow; how fast, we don't know." Josh was honest and I could tell he was sad. I was, too. He moved to the sofa and put his arms around me. I laid my head on his chest, and we cried quietly together for our friend, and for ourselves.

Finally, I got hold of myself and sat up straight. He still had his arm over my shoulder, and he held my hand in my lap.

"How's Joe?" He squeezed my shoulder, and I could feel his breath on my hair, so I knew he was looking at me.

"I hardly know Joe anymore. He's retreated into himself and doesn't communicate at all." I sat there like a zombie, unable to put all the pieces together.

On Sunday Josh took Lilly and me to the park and to Marco's for pizza. I was distant and quiet, absorbed in all the feelings of loss, and too depressed to see the person right in front of me offering the kind of devotion and love I needed most.

*

Joe came home some nights to see Lilly, which gave me a little time to myself. He didn't speak to me, and I wondered whether he spoke to Emma when they were alone.

We turned the storage room into a small bedroom for me, although I usually slept with Lilly. I had a single bed and a small table that served as a desk, and the space was private enough—a place to write and think.

Emma rarely got out of bed. She was thin and weak and could barely make it to the bathroom without help. Yet she was always positive and light-hearted, insisting Lilly and I play cards or dominoes with her, or pile in the bed and watch TV and eat popcorn together.

Josh came over two or three evenings a week and had dinner with us. He'd examine Emma and check on her medications. Joe sometimes came to visit Lilly on Saturdays, or Josh would relieve me so I could go to my apartment to water my plants, pick up my mail, and get the things I needed. Those once-a-week visits to my place seemed to keep me grounded in my life, disrupted and crazy as it was.

When I was home on Saturdays I called to check on Daddy, who was slowly getting better, yet, as Josh explained, he'd never be totally healthy again. When I talked to him, he sounded happy to hear from me and would ask me about my life, my job, my writing. At the end of every conversation, he'd say, "I love you, pretty girl." His new attitude towards me kept me off-balance.

Mama didn't go home. James went to visit her in Houston again and said she was living with some old, rich man. He brought Albert back to Jean Ville to live with Daddy because everyone thought it was a better situation. Tootsie moved into James's old bedroom in the back of the house and did a great job of loving Sissy and Albert and raising them into beautiful, caring young people, something Mama probably would have failed at.

*

One June morning I awoke to a peculiar smell outside the window of Lilly's bedroom. I slipped out of bed and walked barefoot across the hall to the bathroom. I thought I heard a cat crying under the floorboards and, other than that faint sound, there was an eerie silence in the house. I brushed my teeth and went to the kitchen to start the coffee pot when I felt cold chills run up my spine and the taste in my mouth turned from toothpaste-mint to lemon-sour in a millisecond.

I tiptoed into Emalene's bedroom as if I were expecting to encounter a burglar. Emma was propped on her pillows just as I had left her the night before and seemed to be sleeping peacefully, but something was not right, I could feel it in my soul.

I crept to the side of her bed, still expecting someone to jump out from behind a curtain or door and surprise me, yet it was so quiet I could have heard an intruder breathing had he been in the room with us. That's when I knew what was wrong.

No one was breathing. Not even me. I gasped and tried not to scream because I didn't want to scare Lilly. I scrambled onto

Emalene's bed and lay my ear on her chest—no movement, no sound.

Suddenly the eerie silence was broken by the sound of a train running through my head, its whistle blowing, its coal engines churning, its iron wheels chugging. It was so loud and all encompassing that I couldn't think or feel or reason. The noise reverberated in my skull as if someone was throwing metal balls inside my head and they were pinging back and forth across my brain. I heard a scream, "Noooooooooooooo!" The silence outside my head broke wide open, and I knew that scream came from my own throat, from deep inside my chest.

"Noooooooooooooo!!" Emmmmmmmaaaaaaa!"

Lilly came running into the room in her pajamas and jumped onto the bed. We were both hovering over Emalene. I pumped her chest and Lilly tried to breathe into Emma's mouth as though we were performing CPR in tandem. I'm not sure how long we bounced on Emalene's bed trying to revive her or how long the train railed through my head and the smell of rotting leaves surrounded us, but at some point, Emma took a breath, and her eyelids fluttered. She gasped and started to cough.

I sat back on my heels, grabbed Lilly and rocked her in my lap while we cried and watched Emma breathe. I got two cold, wet rags from the bathroom and put one across Emma's forehead, the other on her neck. She was sitting half-way up in bed and looked pale. She had a blank stare in her eyes that scared me. I kept trying to get her to talk, but she would look at me as though she didn't understand what I was saying.

I called an ambulance then dialed Josh's home phone. He answered on the first ring.

"It's Emma. She's stopped breathing. We brought her back with CPR, but her breathing is labored and shallow. She doesn't look right. I called for an ambulance."

"I'll be right over." When he walked into the bedroom, Lilly was lying next to Emma, hugging her. Emma's arms lay limp by her side but her eyes were opened, and she was breathing. I sat beside them, holding Emma's hand and rubbing Lilly's back, too stunned to cry any more.

Josh put his hands on my shoulders and pulled a little to get me to move so he could check on Emma. He put his stethoscope on her chest and moved it around, felt her neck with his fingers. She grinned at him, the first expression of real life she'd shown since I'd found her.

"Emma, the ambulance in on its way. We're going to take you to the hospital to see what's causing this breathing problem."

"Okay." It was good to hear Emma speak. Lilly crawled over Emma and into my lap.

We didn't go with Josh and Emma to the hospital because Josh said children weren't allowed on the floors, and that he'd keep us posted.

"The cancer is in one of the lobes in Emma's left lung," Josh told me on the phone. "Right now she's too weak for surgery so she's going to the rehab floor where they will help build her strength."

"How long will she be in the hospital?"

"That's something we have to discuss. I'm going to find Joe, and the three of us need to meet to talk about a long term-plan for Emma."

*

On Wednesday while Lilly was at school, Joe, Josh, and I met at a restaurant close to Shilling Publishing. Josh said that Emma would never be well again, and if she survived lung surgery and more chemo, she would need to be in a long-term care center.

"She can't stay at home anymore," Josh said. "Even with full-time care, she's too sick and frail."

"What's her long-term prognosis?" Joe pushed his food around his plate and never took a bite.

"I'm not sure how long she went without breathing before Susie brought her back, but indications are that she's lost some brain function. That complicates her physical problems."

"What are you saying, Josh?" I tried to keep my voice steady and concentrate. Josh was blunt. He told us that Emma would have surgery in two weeks to remove the lung cancer, then would recover in a rehab unit for a couple of weeks before being moved to a nursing home.

He said he didn't expect she would ever be normal again, even if she survived the cancer.

Joe didn't ask any questions, just stared at Josh as if he didn't understand the explanation. Eventually, he stood up and walked out of the restaurant.

The next day I went to visit Emma at the hospital. She didn't know me, although she smiled and we chatted. I talked about Lilly, but Emma didn't seem to understand who I was talking about. I was glad there was a rule about children not visiting patients in the hospital because Lilly would be devastated if Emma didn't know her.

"Her neurologist said that it's possible some of her brain function will return." Josh and I were in his car, parked in front of Lilly's school on Friday afternoon, waiting for her to come out. Mr. Mobley often let us off early on Fridays and Josh had the weekend off, so we'd planned to take Lilly to Coney Island.

"As for her memory, I think that's one of the last functions to return." He was turned in his seat so he could look at me, his left arm over the steering wheel, hand dangling over the dashboard.

"So will she ever know Lilly?"

"I am not sure. It's very sad. She didn't know Joe when he went to see her, either." Josh put his right arm on the back of my seat and pinched my shoulder lightly. "I'm sorry, Susie. I know it was hard for you."

Emma survived lung surgery and went back to rehab. She was moved to a nursing home five weeks after I'd found her not breathing. Finally, Lilly could visit her.

"She might not know you, sweetheart," I tried to explain to Lilly that her mother looked different. She wore a turban because they'd shaved her hair. She was very thin, and her skin was splotched with red hives. I went to see her twice a week, and she began to know me as a regular visitor, but she didn't remember me from before she was hospitalized.

"She will know me. Mamas always know their little girls." Lilly was skipping down the sidewalk in her new white shoes and lace-trimmed socks. Josh was waiting in his BMW convertible at the curb. He got out of the car and came around to open the doors for us. Lilly slid into the back seat, I got in the front.

"Uncle Josh needs to explain, Lilly." I turned to Josh, anguish across my face. "I've tried to tell Lilly that her mother might not know her but she doesn't believe me."

"Let's not borrow trouble." He turned in his seat so he could see Lilly who was sitting behind me. "But I don't want you to get hysterical if your mom can't remember you, Lil."

"What's hysterical?"

"Crying and screaming. If you do any of that, the people who run the facility won't let you come back. Do you understand what I'm saying?"

"I guess so. But why would I scream and cry?"

"Let's just say that your mom looks different. She acts differently. You might not know her, and she might not know you." Josh reached behind my seat and patted Lilly's leg.

When we entered Emma's bright corner room with lots of windows, she was sitting up in bed. Lilly ran in the door yelling,

"Mama," and jumped up into Emma's bed. Emma cringed and grabbed her chest, afraid Lilly would hug her and hurt her incision, still sore from surgery.

She looked over Lilly's brown curls at Josh and me; we were as surprised by Lilly's actions as Emma was. Lilly hugged Emma and slid under the covers next to her. Emma put her arm under Lilly's neck and her little head lay softly on Emma's shoulder.

We went to visit Emma every Saturday, and Emma learned to talk to Lilly about dolls and school and other things, in a generic way, but Lilly began to notice that her mother didn't remember her or her childhood. Joe continued to come home to the house in Springfield Gardens every Saturday and spent the night with Lilly so I could go to my apartment for a break. I never asked him where he lived during the week; in fact, we didn't talk much. The fourth Saturday after Emma had been moved to the nursing home, Lilly didn't want to go visit her.

"Let's do something else today, Susie. Maybe we can go somewhere with Uncle Josh." She refused to wear the pink dress I'd laid out on the bed for the visit with her mama and, instead, slipped into a pair of shorts and a T-shirt that didn't match. I wanted to laugh, but I held back and gently suggested we change her shirt to another, cleaner one.

"Josh is on call this weekend. Maybe you and I can go to the library?" I pulled the blinds open on her window and saw that it was drizzling outside.

"Okay." She seemed cheerful, even though this would be a day with only me.

After that, I insisted that we visit Emma at least once a month, but nothing changed in the way she responded to me, or Lilly. She was pleasant and distant, as though visiting with strangers. I knew Lilly was hurt and confused and I tried to keep her busy and make her feel loved.

Lilly became my whole world, and I wouldn't have traded that for anything. In fact, I realized I was no longer depressed and rarely thought about Rodney or worried about my dad and mom or any of the losses in my life.

I guess you could say I'd moved on. Finally.

*

One Saturday, Josh came over and took us to the park. It was a beautiful day and the black-backed gulls were out in force. Josh had his ever-present bag of popcorn and Lilly helped him feed the birds. Soon she was chasing one that took off with more than his share, and Josh and I sat on the bench to watch.

"I saw Joe this week." He was staring at one of the gulls, but I knew he didn't see the bird, or the concrete, or the trees. He was sad and thoughtful. "He wants me to talk to you about Lilly."

"What about Lilly?"

"He wants to move back in to the house and for you to move out."

"Just me? Or me and Lilly?"

"Just you."

"I'm not leaving her. She needs me. She can come to live with me. I'll get a bigger place and Joe can move back in to their house."

"Joe has a girlfriend, a student. Seems he's been seeing her for a while, maybe before Emalene got sick. He says he's going to marry this girl."

"What about Lilly?"

"He has this vision of a happy little family." Josh looked up at Lilly who was running around in a circle chasing one of the gulls. "She needs her daddy."

"I'm her mother. I should have rights."

"You are her biological mother, but Joe and Emalene adopted her and have legal rights. You have none. They raised her from birth. Can you really take her from the only father she's ever known?"

"Joe has been an absent father for over a year while I've taken care of her. I'll get a lawyer. I'll fight for her."

"You should think about it first. Think about Lilly and think about yourself. It's a big responsibility that I'm not sure you're ready for."

"What do you think I've been doing this past year?" I was angry. I'd been there for Lilly, for Emalene, even for Joe when he was home. I'd taken on the world, and no one seemed to think anything of it.

I knew what he meant, though. I was sad and often despondent. It was time for me to get a grip, quit feeling sorry for myself, and move on with my life.

"Please don't be mad at me. I just want you to think about it before you decide." He put his arm on my shoulder. I resisted at first but eventually scooted closer, telling myself it was so we could hear each other without raising our voices.

"What's to think about? Lilly is my daughter. I would never desert her." I figured Josh was thinking that I had deserted her once, but that was a different Susie Burton. I'd grown up. I was ready to be her mother.

That evening I packed Lilly's things and took her to my apartment. I told her it would be better for us to be away from the house that held so much sadness, and she seemed to understand. In reality, I wanted her with me while I fought for her.

I went to see an attorney Mr. Mobley told me about who handled custody cases. The lawyer got a judge to sign an injunction giving custody of Lilly to me, pending a hearing, which would be held the following month.

I called Joe every day for a week and left messages, but he never answered the phone or called me back. Finally, Josh went to see Joe at the university where he taught.

"He said they served him with papers and it made him think." Josh was sitting in my den that evening after I put Lilly to bed. "He doesn't want a court battle. He said maybe the two of you can share custody, like a divorced couple, where he could have her every other weekend. Something like that."

"I like that idea. Lilly needs her daddy. I don't want him out of her life." I was whispering in case Lilly was not yet asleep in the bedroom of my little apartment. "But we need to talk about it. I've tried to call him every day, and he doesn't call me back."

All the details had to be worked out with lawyers, and I stood firm on having legal custody of Lilly. I agreed that Joe could take her for weekend visits and could come to see her during the week if he wanted to.

At first, Joe was diligent about his visitation schedule, but after a couple months he would call and say something had come up and would reschedule. I made sure Lilly talked to him on the phone on weekends when he didn't pick her up, and we went out to the house in Springfield Gardens every couple weeks to get some of her things and let her revisit her home.

Sometimes Joe was there, but most times not.

Part Three: 1976-1983

~ Chapter Fifteen ~

Engaged

LILLY AND I, WITH Josh's help, went on an apartment search and found a roomy two-bedroom with lots of windows. It was in a secure building with a doorman and elevators, and had a courtyard out back with a fenced playground. Joe had agreed to help pay the additional rent, as child support of sorts; he wanted Lilly to live in a nice neighborhood.

Neither of us were totally ready to let go of the past, so we had Lilly's bedroom furniture and Emalene's dining room table, chairs, and hutch moved to our new place along with all my things. We shopped together to select some new stuff that tied everything together and made us feel like we were stepping towards the future, even if they were baby steps.

We began to laugh again. Lilly shared her sadness with me, told me how much she missed her parents, and I listened and tried to be her rock, while all the time I missed them, too.

We were unpacking boxes in the kitchen of our new apartment when Josh arrived with pizza. It was nearing the end of August and Lilly would be starting first grade the following week. She was excited but nervous. It would be a new school in a new area, but it was a beautiful part of Queens, and we weren't far from the nursing home where we visited Emma every Saturday and attended mass on Sundays.

Josh put Lilly to bed while I cleaned up the kitchen. He walked up behind me and put his arms around me, bent his head and kissed my neck through my hair. It was the first time he'd really touched me in that way in a year, and it surprised me because I had been distant and unapproachable. I turned inside his arms and faced him.

"What are you doing?"

"Letting you know how I feel. You don't have to feel it, too; just let me feel it for a moment." He put his chin on the top of my head as he spoke and I slowly raised my arms and put them around his neck. I bent back to look at him. One fat tear rolled down the right side of his face. I used my thumb to smear it off.

I can't say exactly when I knew I was in love with Josh Ryan. I felt like he had always been part of my life, and Lilly's. He still called me every day as he had for two years, and no matter how I responded to him, he was always the same Josh—solid, dependable, loving, non-judging.

I didn't really get *over* Rodney; I merely grew accustomed to living without him. It was a gradual thing.

"I think I'm ready for you to feel it. Maybe I'm ready to feel it, too." I tightened my grip on his neck and he bent to kiss me. It was a gentle, sweet, loving kiss and I felt it down to my toes. When he pulled away to look at me, I had my eyes closed.

"We can take it slow." He whispered, but I heard a question in his statement.

"Not too slow." I opened my eyes, and the way he was looking at me gave me chills down my arms and back. He kissed me again, and I felt his tongue lick the inside of my lips. He tasted minty and warm, and I could feel a wetness start to gather between my legs. It was the first time I'd been sexually aroused by anyone other than Rodney, and it took me by surprise. Josh rubbed my back with one hand, and the other found its way to the top of my butt. He started to kiss my ear and neck, and I lost myself in the way he felt and tasted and smelled. My nipples got hard and rubbed against his chest.

"Hmmmmm. This is too good. Tell me I should stop." He was putting bird kisses on my shoulders and neck.

"Tell me you love me, Josh. Tell me you want me, not just now, not just tonight." I had my mouth against his ear when I said it. He put his hands on my shoulders and pushed me away a few inches but held onto me.

"I have loved you since the first day I saw you in that hospital bed, young, pregnant, and scared. I loved you while you chased a dream. I loved you while you ignored me and grieved. I've watched you mature, and I've loved you more with each growth spurt. I couldn't love you more if you grew wings and a halo. I want you forever, but only if and when you can love me, too; when you can forget the past and want a future with me."

"I think I've loved you for a long time, I just didn't know what real, mature love was. I compared it to teenage love, first love, love for the person you have a child by. I've come to realize I can't compare what I feel for you with anything I've ever felt before."

When Josh made love to me that night, I didn't think of Rodney. I didn't think of anything but Josh and how I wanted to be close to him, how I wanted us to merge, to become one.

After that first time, we fell so deeply in love we couldn't stay away from each other. We'd meet for lunch during the week, and he'd come for dinner almost every night.

About a month after I moved into my new place, Joe took Lilly for an overnight stay. I'd spent countless hours trying to prepare her for the visit because Joe's girlfriend would be with them. I tried to tell her the things Emalene would have said, "He's your daddy, you only get one. Forgive him. He loves you the best he can. Try not to expect him to give you more than he has to give." We met Joe at the university, and I watched them drive off in his new Volvo. I hadn't met his girlfriend and was glad he would spend some time with Lilly alone before he introduced them.

I took the subway to the hospital, then Josh and I drove to Brooklyn Heights for my first visit to his house. I wasn't prepared for the beauty of the neighborhood or the lavishness of his brownstone. The furnishings were gorgeous and he admitted an interior designer had done the place for him.

He had a housekeeper. Imagine! A housekeeper! Her name was Ruby, and she came every afternoon, cleaned his house, did his laundry, and prepared dinner if he was going to be home that night. She had set the dining room table with candles, silver, and bone china, and the smells coming out of the kitchen told me that something special was in the oven. There was a silver champagne chiller with a bottle of Dom Perignon on ice, and two Baccarat flutes beside it. I thought how Catfish would have said "whatever that is" and laughed from deep in his belly.

"Let me show you around," Josh acted like he didn't notice my mouth agape or the way I was admiring the beautiful tapestries, Aubusson rugs, priceless art, and exquisite furniture. I'd known Josh for seven years, and it never occurred to me that he was wealthy and lived like royalty. He was so normal, down-to-earth, non-assuming.

He showed me the two gorgeous guest rooms, each with an ensuite bath. We stepped into his master bedroom and I gasped. It must have been 1000 square feet and had a spa bathroom at least half that size. His walk-in closets were the size of my bedrooms, and his backyard was like a small park. He held my hand as he described each room and some of the art. He stopped in the hall to show me pictures of his late dad, his mother and her husband, and his sister and her two children who lived in Ohio. There were a number of medals and commendations on the walls, but he didn't want to talk about them, so we moved on. When we returned to the dining room, Ruby was putting hors d'oeuvres on the table, and Josh introduced us.

"I finally get to meet the lady who stole my man's heart." She was a delightful Russian woman with a big bust and ample hips who wore a black uniform with a starched, white apron. She was bubbly and obviously loved Josh like a mother hen. "Don't you go breaking his heart, now."

"I won't, Ruby." She bent and whispered in my ear, loud enough that Josh could hear.

"You're the first lady he's ever brought home. I been waiting a long time to fix dinner for a woman." She laughed, and it was contagious. Josh and I both joined her and she poked him in the ribs.

"Ruby, you want a glass of champagne?"

"Oh, no, Dr. Ryan. I'm going home to my man. We like vodka." She laughed again and left the room. Josh popped the cork on the champagne and poured both glasses. He handed me one and toasted.

"To you, Susie." He winked at me, and I melted. I put my glass down and reached for him. He pulled me to him and kissed me hard, then he handed me my glass, took my other hand, and led me to the sofa. There was a huge fireplace surrounded by granite, but it was too warm for a fire. Porcelain lamps on side tables provided just enough light and atmosphere as we sat down with our glasses of champagne.

"Please, Josh, tell me more about yourself. Tell me all the things I don't know about Josh Ryan."

"I'm afraid if I tell you everything you won't love me."

"If you can love me with all my warts…?" I looked at him sideways and he laughed.

"I told you my dad was a doctor. What I didn't tell you is that his dad was an oil baron of sorts, owned property in Texas and

Arizona, where they struck oil when my dad was a kid. He grew up wealthy. My mother was the daughter of a railroad tycoon here in New York. They met when my dad was in medical school at Columbia. I grew up in a house three times the size of this one, and we had a home on the coast of Maine where we spent summers."

"Why aren't you a snot?"

"I've worked at that. My dad would never let us take things for granted. He told us that we were just lucky, that it was by the grace of God and undeserved luck that we were born into privilege and that we should never think we were better than anyone else. 'the luck of the draw', he called it, and he never took it for granted. When he died, I was determined to be the man he'd always wanted me to be." Josh told me lots of things that weekend; things I should have asked him all along, but I had always been too caught up in myself.

He told me he had recently been accepted into a fellowship program in plastic surgery. I didn't know he'd spent the past two years in a plastic surgery residency program after his three years as general surgery resident. He said he'd had lots of offers for fellowships outside of New York, but he'd waited until he got one in the city. "I'm not leaving you and Lilly. No career is worth that sacrifice."

"Josh, surely you aren't staying in New York for us."

"Yes, Ma'am. You can't run me off. Ever." He told me that his dream was to operate on children with cleft lips and pallets, especially in second and third-world countries where most kids didn't have doctors or money for the operation.

"Lots of those children are ostracized by their entire society, thought to be deformed. Even kids with cleft lips who live in the States are bullied and marginalized. I want to help them." The more he talked, the more I loved him. I forgot that I'd ever been with another man.

Josh was my beginning and my end; I didn't want anything else, not even memories.

I'd call Marianne, and she would tease me about "gushing" over Josh. She told me Rodney was married and living in California, and that he and his wife were still hoping to be shipped overseas. I meant it when I said I was happy for him. I believed we had been childhood sweethearts and that after we grew up, none of the things that made us love each other existed anymore because we'd become different people.

One evening, Josh told Lilly and me that he wanted to take us out somewhere special that weekend, that we should get all dressed up for a night out in Manhattan. I took Lilly shopping and bought her the prettiest red dress and black patent leather shoes, and white socks trimmed in lace. I put a red bow in her hair, and when I think back to that night, I realize she looked like the character in *Annie*, with her reddish-brown curly hair, big, bright eyes, and that red dress with the white cuffs and black belt.

Our doorbell rang, and I buzzed Josh up on the elevator. He oohed and ahhed when he saw us. I wore a black sheath with a plunging neckline and tiny straps. It reached past my knees, and I had on black heels with sling-back straps, my toes showing. My hair was loose and fell almost to my waist, and I'd pulled one side back with a tortoiseshell comb.

Josh wore a simple black tuxedo and bowtie and was the most handsome man I'd ever seen, his dark wavy hair brushed away from his face, flipping out over his collar, and a few loose curls springing out on his forehead. His green, almost emerald eyes shone as bright as a flashlight when he looked at us standing there in the foyer.

When we got downstairs, the doorman ushered us to a waiting limousine and opened the door for Lilly and me to slide in. Josh went around and entered from the street side. Lilly sat between us and couldn't keep her hands off all the buttons and the bar with decanters and crystal glasses. Josh poured a 7-Up into a champagne flute for Lilly and real champagne for me. He had two fingers of bourbon in a highball glass. Lilly chatted nonstop, but I was so dumbfounded I couldn't find words until we were several blocks away from my building.

"What's the occasion? This is extreme, isn't it?"

"Not too extreme for tonight, no," He winked at Lilly and she beamed as though she was in on some secret and I was the only one who didn't know. We went to a Broadway play, *The Wiz*, an unusual hit for its all-black cast. Lilly fell asleep after Act 1, which Josh said was just as well since the Wicked Witch in Act 2 would have frightened her and, he said, "She needs a nap if she is going to be awake for dinner at Sardi's," where he had reservations after the show.

Lilly woke up when we walked out of the theatre into the fresh air. Josh was carrying her, and her head was on his shoulder. She rubbed her eyes and asked, "What happened?"

"In the play?" Josh pushed her hair off her face and handed me the bow that was dangling by a few loose strands.

"Yes, to Dorothy? And the Lion and Scarecrow and Tin Man."

"Oh, Dorothy went back to Kansas, and her friends all got what they wanted and stayed in Oz to make the city a great place."

"Oh! Can we go see it again one day?"

"Sure sweetheart," Josh winked at me and put Lilly down on the sidewalk so she could climb into the limo. Arriving at Sardi's in a limo was not unusual, but it certainly made the doorman pay attention and suggest that the maître d' seat us at a table near a window so we could people-watch. Lilly acted like a little lady, put her napkin on her lap, and sat up straight in her chair. We talked about the play and her school and Josh's work and the book with the Catfish stories I was almost finished writing.

After dinner, the waiter brought a small coconut cake, alight with sparklers, and set it in front of me.

"You have the wrong table. It's not my birthday." I looked at Josh, whose smile was larger than life. Lilly's ladylike demeanor disappeared, and she sat on her knees in her chair and started bouncing up and down, clapping. It seemed everyone in the restaurant stopped talking and were all looking at us. Before I could gather my wits about me, Josh was on one knee between my chair and Lilly's. He opened a black velvet box and the largest diamond I'd ever seen sent rays up to the chandelier over our table. Lilly continued bouncing and clapping. My hand automatically went to my mouth to muffle a screech I felt was about to escape.

"Will you marry me? Both of you?" He stared at me with those emerald eyes and thick eyelashes, a plea on his face, and a smile on his lips. We hadn't discussed marriage, so I was caught off-guard. I looked at this man and knew I wanted to spend the rest of my life with him; I wanted to grow old with him.

"Lilly, what do you think?" I winked at Lilly and she said, "Yes! Say yes, Susie!" Josh was looking from Lilly to me. When his eyes locked on mine I nodded my head and mouthed, "Yes," and he took the ring from the box and slid it on my finger. The restaurant erupted in applause and flashbulbs went off as though we were celebrities. I bent at the waist and put my hands on Josh's cheeks and kissed him on the lips. His mouth was warm and moist, and I wanted to lock onto it and not let go, but Lilly was climbing on his back, and he reached around and put her on his knee between us. Then he pulled out another, smaller box and opened it. Inside was a little gold ring with a solitary ruby in a simple setting, perfect for a six-year-old girl. Lilly was so excited when Josh slipped the ring on her finger that she couldn't keep still. She ran around the table flashing her hand in the air so everyone could see the red stone.

Josh corralled her and we had a group hug that lasted until Lilly said, "Let's eat the cake!" We laughed, as did everyone in the restaurant who then went back to their meals and conversations while our waiter cut the cake and poured champagne into our flutes.

It was a magical night that ended with Josh spending the night at our apartment, although he had to sleep on the couch since Lilly slept with me and her little bed was much too small for his six-foot-three-inch length. He whispered in my ear that we'd have to work on sleeping arrangements once we were married, and we both laughed. He kissed me goodnight, pecked Lilly on the cheek and, as excited as we all were, we must have been exhausted because everyone fell sound asleep.

Over the next few months, Josh and I talked about where we would live and decided on his place as a temporary home until we could find something that was more family-oriented. Josh wanted me to stop working and write full-time, but I wasn't ready to give up my independence just yet. Although we wanted to get married right away, Lilly would have to change schools again, so we decided to wait until summer so she could have time to settle down in our new home and start second grade in the fall.

*

Meanwhile, I was working hard on *The Catfish Stories* and wanted to make progress on the book that Mr. Mobley said Shilling might be willing to publish. I took out my composition book one evening and thought about the story of Anna Lee, because it was a love story, and a story of the redemption of colored people through education.

I thought about how Catfish sounded when he told me stories, especially when he talked about Anna Lee, who was his grandmother and the person he said did the most for the people in the Quarters. His voice would raise an octave, and he'd rock a little faster when he talked about her. I can still hear the excitement in his voice as he told the story about how his granddaddy ended up married to the woman everyone called Annie.

"It started with the end of the Civil War which was also the end of slavery," Catfish said.

Anna Lee
1865

Mr. Van called a meeting in the Quarters and sat in a circle with all the workers and their children. That's when he told them they were free. They could go anywhere they wanted, or they could stay at Shadowland and work for him.

"You will have everything you have now: a house to live in, clothing, meals, and my protection. In addition, I'll pay you five dollars every month, and you can do whatever you want with that money." Mr. Van told the workers he appreciated all they'd done to help him turn the place around and that now it made a profit. He wanted everyone to stay if they wanted to. Most of the people stayed, but some, like Big Bugger, left.

"Turned out Maureen's daughter, Anna Lee, was real smart and the preacher and his wife, Mr. and Mrs. Harris up at the Bethel Baptist where all my people still go to church every Sunday, took a liking to her and they started teaching her to read the Bible. Annie would stay after church on Sundays when the other folks had finished their picnics and set back to walking home, and Mr. and Mrs. Harris would give Annie some lessons. Soon they was teaching her how to add numbers and about history and other stuff. Maureen would clean up the Harrises' house and the church while she waited for Annie to finish her lessons, and they would come on back to the Quarters just before dark.

Every Sunday night the people in the Quarters would have a hoedown. The men would play the harmonica and the banjo, mostly homemade instruments. They'd have someone with a tee-fer, or a petit fer—that's a Cajun triangle made from the iron tines of a hay rake. Kids would pound on washtubs and use spoons on the bottoms of pots. If someone showed up with an accordion or a fiddle, we'd really have a hoedown.

They'd get the music churning, and soon they'd be dancing and singing. Everyone would put something in a big pot of water that sat on a fire in the middle of the yard and, soon, they'd have gumbo or stew of some sort.

Well, after a few years Miss Maureen wanted to come back with the others for the hoedown, 'cause the Harrises was keeping Annie later, sometimes 'til after dark, teaching her all sorts of lessons. Annie was about ten or eleven at the time, and Miss Maureen axed Samuel, who ended up being my granddaddy, would he stay back and walk Annie home. He was about fifteen or sixteen, and at first he resented the job of waiting for Anna Lee while the others went back to the Quarters, but soon he was learning to read, too. He and Anna Lee became friends. Samuel had never had a friend, and the two talked easily while they walked the hour-and-a-half back to the Quarters alone on Sunday evenings.

Samuel and Annie learned to read and write and do some arithmetic, and they both learned the Bible front to back. They also learned about each other as they talked about everything: their dreams, their hopes, their desires, their futures.

"I never thought I'd be a free man," Samuel told her when he was about eighteen. "At first I thought about going north. They say black men are treated like white men up there."

"You have a job here on the plantation. Don't Mr. Van pay you?"

"Yeah, and he gives me a place to stay."

"When you came to Shadowland I was about five. You didn't come to church with us for those first years."

"On the plantation I come from, slaves weren't allowed to leave the property to go to church. We had our own service in the Quarters."

"What was it like there, at Kent House? Do you remember much?"

"Oh, I remember a lot," he said. "Most of it I want to forget, except I don't ever want to forget my mama. It's been eight years since I seen her, but it seems like yesterday. I can still smell her when I get near a wisteria vine, and I can picture her singing at our Sunday services. She had a beautiful voice."

"It must be hard, not having your mama."

"I had to grow up real fast," Samuel answered. "What took me a long time to understand was that Mr. Van was not like Mr. Kent and his men. When I come here, I don't know I can go to a church on Sunday, that you could leave the plantation to have a service. I was too scared to try; that's why I didn't go with ya'll 'til after the war."

"Yes, we sure are blessed," she said. "Mr. Van's a good man."

So my granny and granddaddy learned to read and write and do numbers. That started something that turned my people upside down.

First thing to happen is, after a few years of walking Annie home after dark, my granddaddy axed would she marry him. He knew she was all kinds of special. They waited 'til she was of age, fifteen or so, and my granddaddy went up to the big house and knocked on the back door. Lizzie, the house girl, came through the kitchen and pushed that screen door open and saw my granddaddy standing there with the red sun setting behind him, his hat in his hands, a clean shirt, and suspenders holding up his baggy pants.

"What you want, boy?" Miss Lizzie asked. She weren't much older than my granddaddy, but she thought she was better 'cause she work up at the house. Anyway, my granddaddy say he wanted to talk to Mr. Van.

"Now why you think a busy man like Mistah Van want to come talk to the likes of you?"

"He told me if I ever needed to tell him something to just come up to the house. So here I am. I'd appreciate it if you would fetch him, Miss Lizzie." My granddaddy was charming, and he won over Miss Lizzie. Soon Mr. Van was standing outside at the bottom of the steps in his backyard, facing Samuel.

"Mr. Van, sir. I come to axe can I marry Anna Lee."

"Well, son, this is a surprise. How old are you now?"

"I think I'm about twenty, that's if I was ten when I come here, sir."

"And how old is Annie? About fifteen?"

"Yessir."

"She's a fine one. She practically raised my Henry. He loves her like a big sister." Samuel said he could tell Mr. Van was talking to hisself, kind of thinking out loud, so Samuel just stood and waited. *"Does she want to marry you, Samuel?"*

"Yessir, she say she do."

"Well, the two of you come by here tomorrow after supper, and we can talk together. That sound okay to you?"

"Yessir. Thank you."

"Samuel. I understand that the Harrises have been teaching you to read and write along with Annie. Is that right?"

"Yessir."

"Then you need to start talking like you're educated. I'm sure the Harrises taught you better than to say, 'I come to axe can I,' and 'she do.'"

"Yessir. I've come here to ask you if I can marry Anna Lee. She says she does want to marry me."

"Good job, son. I'll see you both tomorrow."

The next evening Mr. Van sat with Samuel and Annie at the iron table under the massive oak tree in the backyard of the plantation house. He had Lizzie bring out a pitcher of lemonade and sent for Maureen to join them. Mr. Van asked Annie if she loved Samuel and she didn't know how to respond.

"You are supposed to love the man you marry, Annie."

"Yes, sir. I guess I love Samuel. I hadn't thought about it."

"Do you want to spend the rest of your life with him?" She looked at Samuel and blushed. He winked at her and her smile lit up her entire face. Maureen was watching and started to cry.

"How do you feel about this marriage, Maureen? Annie is your little girl. Do you approve?" Maureen looked from Samuel to Annie and back to Mr. Van.

"Yes, sir. I think they good for each other. And I'll have my girl right here close by."

"If they have your blessing, they have mine." The young couple looked at each other and were embarrassed. Mr. Van told them they could have the empty one-room cabin at the end of the row that Bugger used to live in before the war ended and he headed north. It was small and needed work, but it would be theirs, and they were happy about that.

The following Sunday at the Bethel Baptist, Preacher Harris pronounced Samuel and Anna Lee man and wife, and they started their life together. The other workers would laugh at them because they would make love all night and be so tired in the morning they had to drag themselves out of bed and push through the day's work; then they'd come back together in the evenings unable to wait until after supper to pull each other's clothes off and feel their skins touch. The others could hear them through the thin-sheeted walls and would tease them the next day.

It was two years later when they had they first child, my daddy. They named him Samuel, Junior and called him Sammy. Maybe two or three years later, Simon come along, and the next year, Jacob.

The cotton field was where Anna Lee liked to be, working with Samuel. She said his skin glistened in the sun and reminded her of chocolate, sweet and desirable. The little boys would play and run in the fields, take they naps under a big oak tree and pretend they was helping out. When Annie had been about ten, she'd taught little Henry, who was four or five at the time, how to sound out his words. She taught him his ABCs and how to tie his shoes. After she started having kids of her own, she took to teaching them to read and write. That's when she got the idea that maybe she could teach the other children in the Quarters.

So she went up to the big house to see Mr. Van. By now, Mr. Henry was about twenty and was in college over in Baton Rouge, but he was home for vacation when Annie went there. Mr. Henry had a soft spot for Annie because she had helped raise him and he said the reason he was so smart was because she started teaching him how to read as soon as he could talk. Annie axed Mr. Van could she use the barn in the evenings when it was nobody in there. He wasn't too keen on the idea, but Mr. Henry, well, he took up for Annie and next thing you know they had a chalkboard on wheels they kept in the tack room that George would roll out into the breezeway for her, and she set about making a school when she got out the fields in the evenings.

Next thing you know, they was up at the Bethel Baptist one Sunday, and the preacher and his wife had been hearing about Annie teaching the children at Shadowland. They told her they was getting old and tired and would she start teaching the children who stayed after church on Sundays. One thing led to another, and before long the mamas and daddies was asking Annie if she would teach they children on the weekdays when the grownups was in the fields and the children didn't have nothing to do.

By this time the war had been over nearly fifteen years and Sammy was about five or so. Annie wasn't making nothing working in the fields 'cause Mr. Van, he just paid the men to work, so she went up to the big house to talk to him. She said beings as they was free and that she was working in the fields for nothing, she wanted to start teaching school in the daytime. Mr. Van said she didn't work for free, that she had a house to live in and clothes to wear and food for her family. She say she know all that, but Samuel would get that stuff if he weren't married to her and she made a case for teaching. Mr. Van said he'd think about it and when Mr. Henry came home for Christmas, why he talked his daddy into giving Annie her way.

"That's how the first Negro school got started in these parts," Catfish told me. "Before that, the coloreds couldn't read or write and had to sign they names with an X, but my granny changed all that, she shore did. And my daddy was smart, why he was something. And he saw to it that all his children learned."

I asked Catfish whether he could read and write and he said, "shore nuff." I was puzzled because of the way he spoke—his dialect, and lack of grammar—but he explained that it was the way his people talked and, "hit don't have no bearing whatsoever on how smart we are."

I remember laughing when he told me that, and I started bringing him books from the library to read when he was sitting on his porch in the afternoons doing nothing. Later we'd discuss what he thought about the plot and the characters. Turned out the joke was on me—Catfish was pretty smart and a voracious reader.

I thought about Catfish and how much he'd taught me about life, about love, about how to be kind. Through him, I learned not to judge or discriminate. I knew he'd be proud of the woman I was becoming.

~ Chapter Sixteen ~

Jean Ville

IN APRIL, JOSH, LILLY, and I flew to New Orleans and rented a car to drive to Jean Ville. We drove up the back drive at my dad's house and the place looked deserted. I felt uneasy, afraid of what I'd find inside. We didn't knock, just walked in the back door as you would naturally do at your parents' house. There was no one in the kitchen, and it was eerily quiet. I started calling out, "Anybody home?" "Dad, are you here?"

Before I could stop her, Lilly went running through the kitchen and into the hall, which spanned the distance between the front and back doors, about 60 to 70 feet, and it was at least 18 feet wide. She gasped when she saw the expanse, then she ran out the front door and onto the porch. Josh was hot on her trail and grabbed her just before the door slammed shut behind her.

"Don't run in the house, Lilly," he said. "You know the rules. Especially in someone else's house." They were standing in the opened doorway, Josh holding Lilly's hand, her arm outstretched as though trying to get away from him.

It smelled like alcohol and dust in the house, stale and musty. Josh and Lilly said something to someone on the porch, and I followed them out the door. Daddy was sitting in a rocker wearing old khaki slacks, an oversized grey T-shirt, and flip-flops. He was unshaven and smelled like he hadn't bathed in days.

"Well. Who do we have here?" He was staring at Lilly, who by now, was acting shy, peeking around Josh's pant leg.

"I'm Lilly." She walked around Josh, still holding his pants in one fist.

"And I'm Josh. Joshua Ryan. Pleased to meet you, Mr. Burton. Sorry for the intrusion." Josh reached out to shake hands, but Daddy couldn't take his eyes off Lilly. She cowered on the side of Josh and I stood in the opened doorway and watched, frozen.

"Who's Lilly?" Daddy had a scowl on his face and was trying to peer around Josh to get a better look at her.

"Lilly Franklin. Her mother is very sick, and Susie has been caring for her." Josh didn't mention that I had custody and I was glad.

"Come here, Lilly. Let me look at you." Daddy reached out his hand, and I wanted to grab Lilly and run back through the house to the car with her, afraid of what he might do to my little girl. After all, I wasn't much older than she when he started beating me.

Lilly let go of Josh's slacks and walked slowly around to the front of Josh, leaning back against him, both her arms behind her back. Josh put his hands on her shoulders in a protective manner.

"Well, aren't you a pretty little thing." Daddy was staring at her as though he couldn't quite put his finger on something and I was worried he might see a resemblance to Rodney or me in Lilly.

"Hi Daddy, how are you feeling." I walked quickly from the door, around Josh and Lilly, and stood blocking them from Daddy while I bent to kiss him on the forehead. "You look much better than you did the last time I was here." I must have distracted him for a minute.

"Hi, pretty girl. It's good to see you." He reached up and pulled me into a platonic embrace, and as I kissed both his cheeks, I could smell whiskey on his breath.

Lilly ran down the steps into the front yard and was trying to climb on the tire swing hanging from the old oak tree beside the walkway. Daddy gave Josh a limp handshake and watched Lilly.

"Who is she, Susie?" He tilted his head back and pointed his chin at Lilly. Josh and I looked at each other, and I could tell Josh was taken aback by Daddy's tone and demeanor.

"Her name is Lilly. Lilly Franklin." Josh was standing behind me, and he moved around and sat on the swing. I sat next to him. We all watched Lilly on the tire swing for a while, not speaking.

Josh went down the steps two at a time and began to push Lilly on the swing.

"What's with the child?" Daddy didn't look at me.

"Well, as Josh said, her mother is very ill and she's my best friend. I've been helping with Lilly for a couple of years while Emalene has been fighting cancer and a form of dementia brought on by lack of oxygen to the brain."

I pushed myself back and forth slowly on the swing with my feet. "Lilly's dad, Joe, well, he hasn't taken his wife's disability very well and sort of ran out on them. So Lilly has been staying with me." I watched Josh push Lilly on the swing, and she squealed and laughed aloud.

I told Daddy that Josh and I were engaged and that we might get custody of Lilly. I was trying to lay the groundwork for what would happen, so he didn't jump to conclusions. He seemed to accept what I told him.

Josh and Lilly joined us on the porch and we visited for about an hour. Daddy was civil, which a stretch since I couldn't remember a time when he'd treated me with anything close to decency.

"Let me look at you, little Lilly." Daddy reached one of his hands towards the swing and Lilly jumped off and stood in front of him. "Aren't you a pretty little thing. Are you colored?"

"What's colored mean?" She looked at me and Josh, who were both shocked into silence for a few seconds.

"It means that you…" he started to say, but I interrupted.

"Dad. Stop." I jumped off the swing and picked Lilly up. She wiggled out of my arms and climbed on Daddy's lap and kissed him on the cheek. He was so shocked he didn't respond and she slid down before he could comment. Lilly ran down the steps into the yard and got back on the tire swing. "Dad. We don't talk about race in New York."

"Well, is she? A Negro?"

"Her mother is colored, her dad is white. Emalene is a lawyer and Joe is a college professor. Please don't say anything to Lilly about race, okay." I stared at him with contempt but he merely shrugged his shoulders and said, okay.

I considered it a victory when we left and there had been no harsh words. Daddy and Josh had a friendly conversation about medicine, Daddy's condition, New York and, when he tried to steer the conversation back toward Lilly, Josh was able to divert it.

I gave Josh directions to the Quarters, only a few blocks down South Jefferson. I didn't look to see if Daddy was still on the porch when we rode in front of the house.

Marianne met our car before it came to a stop and was beaming from ear to ear. Behind her, Tootsie was waiting with her arms opened wide for a hug. We were barely out of the car before they were all over Josh, gushing over his good looks, then Marianne had Lilly on her back riding the horsey around the car. We all sat on Marianne's porch, and Tootsie brought out sweet tea and cupcakes, Lilly's favorite. Tootsie hadn't forgotten. I could see the tension leave Josh, replaced with laughter and a feeling of belonging.

That night, Lilly wanted to stay with Marianne and play with the kids in the Quarters, so Josh and I were alone at the Hotel Bentley in Alexandria, about thirty miles from Jean Ville. We talked about the difference in the two families—one home that was huge, lavish, and beautiful, furnished to the hilt, but lonely and sickly; the other home small, quaint, and simple, but filled with love and acceptance. I was glad we had come to Louisiana so Josh could understand how Catfish and his family were my true family growing up, and why I didn't come to visit my dad very often.

The next day we were back in the Quarters, and I went for a short visit with my dad. He was up and around but looked pale. The way he acted, you'd swear he loved me like any dad loves his daughter.

Sissy and I sat in the kitchen, drank tea and laughed.

"Dad said you brought a handsome man and a little girl home with you." She was curious but not probing.

"You need to come to the Quarters to meet Josh. You'll love him. You'll love Lilly, too." I stirred my tea and didn't look at Sissy.

"Dad said she's the daughter of your friend."

"My best friend, Emalene Franklin, who is very sick; actually, she's in a nursing home."

"That's so sad." She changed the subject and told me she'd come to the Quarters the next day to meet the two people I was so in love with.

Marianne was at work when I returned to the Quarters, so I sat with Tootsie on her porch and watched Josh walk with Lilly through the rows of sugar cane. Tootsie sat in a rocker, shelling peas, a big silver bowl between her legs. She told me she didn't spend the night at Daddy's house anymore.

"He too mean." She shook her head as though remembering something gruesome. "When he start to get around again, he took to slapping me and yelling and cussing. I don't have to take that no more."

"No you don't, Toot," I said. I patted her hand and rubbed my thumb over her wrist. I couldn't help but think what my mother must have endured all those years and felt less judgmental about her leaving. I considered what Emalene would have said, "You have no idea what goes on in someone's life or what you would do in their place. It's not your job to judge them; it's your place to love them."

"Do you miss Catfish?" I didn't look at Tootsie when I asked.

"Every day." Her nimble fingers deftly pulled a string on the side of a pea pod. When she bent it in half, it cracked open, and five or six peas that looked like green pearls fell into the bowl.

"I was thinking the other day about some of the stories Catfish tole me," Tootsie said. "Did he ever tell you about his daddy, Sammy?"

"He told me a couple of stories about Sammy when he was a boy." I watched her rhythmically shell the peas, thinking how she wasn't aware she was doing it, the process was so natural. "He told me about his granddaddy and the Vans, about George and Maureen and Anna Lee. He told me about the school Anna Lee started and how that changed things for colored people around here."

"Sure did. She was quite a woman, according to everyone knew her. Now, she would be my great-grandmother, Catfish's grandmother," Tootsie put her index finger beside her mouth and tapped her face rapidly as though she were pushing the thoughts out. I listened to her distinct southern drawl mixed with her own bent on the English language and got lost in her story and the telling:

Sammy; by Tootsie
1875-1931
Anna Lee died when Daddy was in his twenties, so he knew her pretty good, but I never did. His daddy, Sammy, now that was a character. Sammy was born in 1875, I remember that date 'cause it's on his headstone over in the cemetery and I read it when I go visit Catfish's grave. He was my granddaddy but we always call him 'sammy,' not 'Granddaddy'.

When Sammy was about three or four—Mr. Van, he was probably in his fifties I'd say—the two met. Sammy was with his daddy in the barn while Samuel was milking ole Daisy. It was early, before daylight and Mr. Van walked in calling for George to saddle his horse. The way my daddy tole it, Sammy just marched right up to that tall, white man, stuck his arm out and said, "My name Sammy. I'm pleased to make your acquaintance."

From that day Mr. Van, he took a liking to Sammy. Mr. Van would let Sammy climb up behind that man's saddle on his sorrel horse, named Bud, and ride with him in the fields. When the boy was about eight or nine, Mr. Van's mare had a foal, and he gave the pony to Sammy. He tole the boy he was in charge of that animal, that he had to take good care of it because it would be his best friend did he do a good job.

Well, Sammy, he would wash that horse down every evening and brush him 'til he glowed. And he'd comb the mane and tail and he'd feed that horse apples and pears and would sit there and crack pecans and feed the nut meat to the horse. He named that horse Jonesie, because he said the young thoroughbred, 'he looks like a Jonesie.' Mr. Van taught Sammy to ride that horse and sometimes the two of them would ride they horses in the fields together to check and see how the crops was growing.

One day they rode to town together. Mr. Van was in the Feed and Seed, and Sammy was standing outside watching the horses 'cause coloreds weren't allowed inside the stores in those days. Three white men came up on Sammy and one of them slapped Jonesie on the rump and yelled, and that horse razed up with his front legs in the air and almost tromped on Sammy. He had to let go the horse's bridle to keep it from coming down on him. Jonesie took off galloping fast as he could through the streets of Jean Ville, around the courthouse square and somewheres Sammy couldn't see.

Now, Sammy couldn't go after Jonesie 'cause he was responsible for Mr. Van's horse, Bud, so he stayed there outside the feed store and held onto Bud's lead rope, even while it was around the hitching post.

Those white men was laughing and spitting tobacco at Sammy's feet, and one of them started to slapping him upside the head; first one side, then the other. Sammy didn't do nothing 'cause he know he'd get in big trouble did he go against a white man. The man's slaps was getting harder and harder and then he hit Sammy's nose and it started to bleed. Then one of the other men whacked Sammy in his face and cut his cheek near his eye. Sammy tried to put his head down, and the men was slapping him on the head, calling him nappy head and Brillo pad and such.

Mr. Van walked out the store and saw the men beating on Sammy and Sammy just a'hanging on to Mr. Van's horse and taking the licking.

"What the hell?" Mr. Van stormed over to the men and pushed the one who was hitting on Sammy and he fell on the ground on his butt. The other two went to jump on Mr. Van, but he was too quick and pulled out his gun on them. "You might be safe hitting this boy here, but you try something with me and it won't go so well. I suggest you three haul ass if you know what's good for you."

"You gonna protect this nigga?" The man on the ground was yelling out.

"You three better get going, NOW." Mr. Van clicked back the hammer on that gun and the men started to back off. "You okay, Sammy?"

"Yes, sir. But they run Jonesie off."

"Don't worry about that horse. He knows where he lives. I'll bet he beats us home." Mr. Van got on his horse and reached an arm out for Sammy, who pulled hisself up and straddled behind the saddle, holding Mr. Van around the waist like he done many times when he was a boy.

They trotted home and, sure nuff, there was Jonesie waiting outside the barn. Sammy slid off Mr. Van's sorrel and ran up to that thoroughbred and it started licking Sammy and nudging him under his chin, like he was pushing him into the barn. Sammy got a bucket of water and the horse drank down half of it. Then Sammy poured the rest over his own head, washing the blood and dirt away.

He learned that day if you take good care of your horse, he'll come on home if he gets loose. From that day, Sammy never had to worry if Jonesie was inside the fence or roaming out in the field, that horse would be at the barn when Sammy got there.

Sammy used to ride Jonesie to church on Sunday, and he could leave that horse tied loose on the post and the animal would wait all day in the hot sun for Sammy to ride it home.

Now, Sammy, he had his eye on a girl at the church name of Mary. Mary was about twelve or so when Sammy started flirting with her, but she don't know nothing about flirt, so she would just play chase and pickup sticks and jacks and such with the other girls. When Mary turned fourteen or fifteen, and Sammy was helping his granny teach them children, 'cause he was about nineteen or twenty and could read and write good as anyone, well, Mary had learned about flirt and started to flirt with Sammy. He saw she might be old enough, so he axe her did she want to go for a walk. Starting that day, every Sunday after church and lessons, Sammy and Mary would walk Jonesie down to the Indian park and go sit on the banks of Old River and talk. Least that's what they say they was doing.

Tootsie had her chin down, her face turned to the bowl in her lap, but she lifted her dark eyes and looked at me out the tops of her lids, the whites of her eyes huge at the bottom of those inkwell pupils. Her look said, "I don't believe they was just talking." I laughed at her, and she went on:

Wasn't long that Sammy axed his daddy could he marry Mary and his daddy say you need to talk to Mary's daddy and if he say okay, you need to see about what Mr. Van says, 'cause if you bring someone to live here on his property, he need to approve that.

Sammy talked to Mr. Williams after church the next Sunday and he said it would be okay if Mary came here to live at Shadowland and marry my granddaddy. That evening after he got back from the Bethel Baptist, it was almost dark and Sammy went over to the big house. He'd been there with his daddy a few times to bring messages from the fields or to meet Mr. Van for a horse ride, but he'd never been there on personal business. Sammy was still in his Sunday clothes, his white shirt clean and his baggy black pants cinched at the waist with a belt made it look like a drawstring gathered up like a skirt 'cause he was so skinny and his pants was way too big.

He knocked on the back door and Bessie stuck her head out the cookhouse and axed what he was doing there at suppertime. Sammy said he'd wait 'til the Vans was finished eating, but he needed to talk to The Man. Bessie went inside the house, and Sammy thought she would tell Mr. Van the boy waiting. Well, an hour passed, and Bessie didn't come back. Then another hour. It was real dark by now, and the crickets was chirping and the frogs was croaking, and the mosquitoes was biting, but Sammy just sat on the back step of that house and waited. He must have fell asleep, 'cause next thing he knew the toe of a boot attached to a long leg was pushing on his side.

Sammy jumped up and was staring at Mr. Van, all dressed and holding his hat in his hand.

"What are you doing sleeping on my back steps Sammy?" The Man asked.

"I'm waiting to talk to you, sir."

"How long you been waiting?"

"Oh, since about six, I guess."

"Six at night or six in the morning?"

"At night. I came here after church, Mr. Van."

"Well, it's Monday morning, son. I guess you waited all night." Mr. Van started laughing and Sammy thought he was pulling his leg, but shore nuff, that boy had spent the night waiting to talk to Mr. Van and

Bessie never did tell The Man Sammy was there. I guess he'd still be waiting if Mr. Van hadn't been leaving early that morning to go to Baton Rouge for a meeting.

Tootsie was laughing so hard it made me laugh too, just watching her. She rocked back and forth, lifting her feet high off the floor, and when she'd rock forward, she'd push herself back hard and lean back until she was almost parallel to the ground. I was afraid the rocker would tip over backwards, but it never did, and she just kept pushing off hard and laughing at the thought of her grandfather spending the night on Mr. Van's back steps, determined to ask whether he could marry Mary Williams.

I thought about how, when two people love each other, like Sammy and Mary Williams did, nothing should keep them apart. I also thought about the cruelty towards black folks that dated back to when they first arrived on American soil. Would it ever end?

Tootsie didn't finish the story because Lilly came on the porch and Marianne got back from the grocery store, then Josh started the coals for the steaks she'd bought. I went with Mari into her house to put some potatoes in the oven and make a salad. Tootsie got Lilly and her two friends inside, gave them a bath, and dressed them for bed.

The three girls, all brown-skinned and pink-cheeked from running and playing, ate bowls of cereal and climbed in the bed in Marianne's sitting room, snuggled up and fell asleep. I'd never seen Lilly so happy, tired, and playful since before Emalene went into the nursing home. I was grateful that my little girl could have this carefree time.

*

Sissy came over the next day and was completely taken with Josh, and he with her. They got into comical banter, and it was the first time I'd seen the comedic Josh. Sissy brought it out in him and they became fast friends.

The three of us talked about how Daddy seemed to have changed, and even Sissy noticed.

"I think he got scared when he almost died." She was sitting on the steps of Marianne's porch and I was sitting next to her.

"He almost acts like he likes me; as if we never had problems."

"I think he realizes that he's lost Mama and Tootsie, and he needs you and me. Maybe he's trying to change." Sissy looked at me as if she wanted me to believe her; I wanted to try, but I just didn't know how to forget a lifetime of abuse. I wondered what Emalene would say about forgiveness if she were still herself.

"Forgiveness is a gift you give yourself because un-forgiveness only hurts the person harboring it." That's what Emalene Franklin would say.

I wanted to give myself the gift of forgiveness.

~Chapter Seventeen ~

≈

'til Death

I MARRIED JOSHUA DAVID Ryan, MD, in a private ceremony in the chapel at St. John's with the campus priest officiating. Lilly was our bridesmaid and Joe stood up for Josh. He didn't bring his girlfriend and acted like the old Joe. He was happy for us.

It took some doing, but I was able to convince Marianne and Sissy to fly up for the occasion and they arrived on Thursday night. It was the first time my sisters had spent significant time together, and the two of them immediately connected the way Marianne and I had when we met at twelve years old.

Lilly and Josh came with me to meet them at the airport. Sissy kept making comments about his dreamy eyes and thick eyelashes and Marianne said she wished she was straight so she could steal him from me. It was lighthearted fun that continued when we stopped for pizza at Marco's, and Marianne commented that Negroes don't eat pizza, they eat chitlins.

Josh stayed with Lilly Friday night and we three sisters took the subway into Manhattan, a real excursion for Sissy and Marianne. We had dinner at the famed Delmonico's, with its fine napery and crystal and a large selection of dinner items on the menu. The girls were giddy and wanted to visit the Waldorf Astoria they had heard so much about, so after dinner, we took a cab to Park Avenue and 49th Street where we climbed the stairs to the double front doors that were opened for us by a red-coated uniformed man with a top hat and white gloves.

Sissy giggled, and Marianne punched her in the side. Watching my colored and white sisters cut up like school girls who really liked each other was good for my heart. Two people I loved seemed to love each other. We splurged for a cab all the way back to Brooklyn Heights and got into a serious conversation in the back seat.

"Did Marianne tell you about Daddy and Tootsie?" I was sitting between the two girls and turned to look at Sissy.

"She didn't have to. It was obvious after Tootsie moved in with us for that year." Sissy looked from me to the window and stared at the passing lampposts as though remembering something unpleasant.

"I mean, did she tell you about...?"

"No, I didn't tell her." Marianne barked at me, and I knew she didn't want me to breach the subject, so I dropped it. The next morning I had the chance to speak with Sissy alone when we were in the kitchen making coffee and Marianne was in the shower. It was my wedding day, and I was excited, but I had something important on my mind and didn't know when I'd have the chance to talk to Sissy about it again.

"Marianne doesn't want to hear about this, but you need to know that Daddy is..."

"I figured it out the first time I met her. I'm not stupid." Sissy poured herself a cup of coffee and was stirring cream and sugar into the lightening liquid.

"Then you realize we are all..." I couldn't complete the sentence. The word *sister* seemed sacred and it stuck in my throat.

"Yes. At first I was pretty upset about it, mostly because no one told me. I was angry with you, with Daddy, with Tootsie. I felt betrayed. Now, I'm just happy to have another sister. And she is in Jean Ville where I can see her. I need a big sister, especially since

Mama left." She turned and walked out of the kitchen with her coffee, the smell of her shampoo and roasted beans filled the air.

The little chapel at St. John's was filled to overflowing with my friends from the publishing house, former college classmates, young people I'd taught as a graduate student, even Merrick and his wife. It was the first time I'd met Mrs. Harper. She was a lovely person and, yes, I felt guilty, but it was my wedding day and I was in love with Josh Ryan.

Josh's partners and their wives were there and lots of doctors, nurses, and orderlies from the hospital. His sister, her husband Doug and their two teenagers came in from Cincinnati and, along with Marianne and Sissy, comprised our family sections at the noon wedding. In all, there were close to one hundred people at the church, which shocked me because I didn't think we had that many friends in New York.

Lilly and I walked up the short aisle together, each holding a bouquet of white lilies. I didn't think of having my dad give me away, because I was giving myself to Josh. He stood next to Father George, Joe by his side.

Josh looked happy, handsome, and high-browed in his tuxedo with white morning jacket, a boyish grin across his face that lifted his eyes and made them squint a bit. A few loose curls threatened to spring onto his forehead at any moment.

My hand was sweating when I put it in his cool palm, and he grinned at me, acknowledging my nervousness. The pure masculine essence of spice that was so specific to Joshua Ryan filled the air.

Lilly was almost giddy with excitement, and when he bent to kiss her on the cheek, I heard him say, "You look beautiful, and today you will be my little girl and have two daddies." She beamed and hugged his neck then dutifully stood next to me. When Josh and I recited our vows our eyes were locked and I could tell he loved me in his soul, and that I could trust him to never leave me. His kiss was gentle and authentic, then he put his hand in the small of my back, took Lilly's hand, and we walked out of the chapel into the beautiful June sunshine, and God smiled on our marriage and the start of our little family that we hoped would grow.

The reception was at the Stratton, a popular boulevard spot and one of the most distinguished restaurants in Queens. I floated on the dance floor when Josh held me and we swayed to "All You Need Is Love." While we were dancing, he whispered, "I'd rather dance to 'Hey Jude' because it's more than six minutes long and this song is only a little over three. I want to hold you like this forever."

"Only for the rest of your life, husband," I whispered. He squeezed me, and I thought I could never be happier than I was in that moment, on that elevated dance floor, the music of the Beatles in my ears and Josh's piquant of zesty scents filling my senses. He danced with Lilly, as did Joe, and she had the time of her life. Josh said we were creating a monster, meaning she would want this kind of entertainment regularly, but Lilly was a simple girl with simple tastes who just happened to fit in and enjoy any moment in time.

Joe kept Lilly at his bachelor apartment while Josh and I honeymooned. Joe's relationship with his girlfriend hadn't worked out, and he had sold the house in Springfield Gardens and was enjoying the single life. I was happy Lilly would have her dad all to herself while Josh and I went to Italy and took a cruise from Venice to Rome.

We landed in Venice, and I was astonished when a boat picked us up at the airport to take us to our hotel, which was on one of the canals. It was like walking a gangplank when we got off the boat and climbed to the sidewalk where a doorman met us and took our luggage. The first night, we took a gondola ride through several of the main canals where we saw marketplaces and locals walking on the narrow sidewalks that lined the waters that weaved in and out of neighborhoods. Fire boats and police boats whizzed by as if they were cars on streets.

On the third day, we boarded a cruise ship called the Royal Princess that left Venice and took us to ports along the Adriatic Sea on the east side of Italy. We visited Split and Dubrovnik in Yugoslavia where we climbed hundreds of steps up to ancient castles on the side of cliffs that hung over the sea.

From there we went to Corfu on the Greek Isles and joined ten people in a canoe that took us through the Blue Grotto on the Megisti Island. The man who rowed the boat told us about how the tides could come up suddenly, and we might have to swim out of the small entrance into the cave where the top was black and the bottom of the water clear blue. It was a magical experience I'll never forget.

We rounded the boot of Italy into the Tyrrhenian Sea and stopped at Marsala where I bought beautiful lace that I didn't know what I'd do with once I got it home. It was handmade, and I felt one day it would be meaningful. Our last stop was Naples, and we traveled to Mount Vesuvius and were wowed by all the frescos in the Duomo di San Gennaro Cathedral.

The ten-day cruise ended near Rome, where Josh and I spent three days. On the first day, we toured Vatican City and attended Mass at St. Peter's Basilica and sat with our heads bent backward to view Michelangelo's 16th-century paintings on the ceiling of the Sistine Chapel. The next day we went to the Coliseum with its ancient Roman gladiator arena, then to the Pantheon temple built in the first century. It housed Renaissance tombs, including Raphael's, who was the artist who painted the large Madonna at the Vatican.

We swore we would return to tour all of the museums and other places we didn't have time for and left Italy in love with the Italian people and each other.

*

When we got home from our honeymoon, all of my and Lilly's things had been moved to Josh's house.

Josh, Lilly, and I were gloriously in love, and Lilly blossomed in our little family. Joe came over once a week or so for dinner and took Lilly overnight a couple times a month. We decided legal custody was the best way to handle things and were frank with Lilly. She was angry, at first, and said I was trying to steal her from her parents, but Josh, always the peacemaker and arbitrator, eventually convinced her that we all loved her and that now she had four parents, wasn't she the lucky one?

Lilly was sad that she didn't see Joe every day, but as he healed from losing Emma and the break-up with his girlfriend, he returned to his old self and was much more available to Lilly, which made us all happy. Sometimes he took Lilly to visit Emalene, and they would talk about how hard it was for both of them that she didn't really know them. Joe was almost as much a part of our lives during our first year of marriage as Lilly.

We wanted children right away. I was almost twenty-five, Josh was thirty-four, and we made love every chance we got. We would comment that, of course, it was because we were trying to make a baby, but, really, we couldn't keep our hands off each other when we were alone. Every month when my period came we were disappointed, but we just tried harder.

Josh completed his plastics fellowship and went to work with a large plastic surgery practice in Manhattan. We'd been married two years when he announced that he was going to Guatemala with *Operation Smile* to perform surgery on children with cleft lips and pallets. We had never been apart, and he suggested I go with him. Joe couldn't keep Lilly for two entire weeks, and I didn't want to take that much time from work, so I stayed home.

The trips to different countries for *Operation Smile* became annual events and Josh loved the experiences. He'd come home with story after story and envelopes of pictures of children who'd been transformed by the operation. The best part was when he'd return to those countries the following years to see the recovered children. He said their lives were turned around and they and their families were happy and grateful.

*

We were six years into our marriage and still, no babies. I decided to quit working and try to finish my book. Maybe I'd be more relaxed and would get pregnant. In addition, Lilly was almost a teenager and needed more of my attention, so there seemed to be more reasons than not to quit my job and stay home.

She freaked out when she started her period, and I was glad I was there to guide her and teach her how to handle girl-things. She had a short-term boyfriend who broke her heart, and we worked through that turmoil with grace. She swore off boys after that—she said none of them were smart enough, anyway.

Lilly had quite a brain. Josh helped her with science and math, I helped her with English and history, and she excelled in all of her classes. Josh and I met with her teachers each semester and beamed with pride when they told us what a good student Lilly was and how kind she was to the other pupils. She was in a private school that was mostly white, but it didn't seem to affect Lilly, her teachers, or her friends that she was colored.

She had lots of friends, played the flute in the band, and had a beautiful singing voice, so she joined the chorus. After I quit working, I felt like a taxi service taking my little girl, who was growing into a beautiful pre-teen, to after-school practices, sessions, try-outs, rehearsals, and meetings. She spent a few hours every week tutoring younger students who were struggling with academics, and she volunteered with the literacy council to teach English and reading to immigrants.

Josh and I were proud of Lilly, but we wanted more children; some of our own. We discussed adopting; after all, we looked at Lilly as an example of how beautiful adoption could work out.

"Maybe we should think about adopting one of the *Operation Smile* children." Josh was sitting next to me on the sofa and we were looking at pictures of children who would have surgery that summer. He said we might think about one of the children he operated on in Haiti or Mexico.

Although we talked about it every year, we didn't pursue it with fervor until 1981, the summer Josh went to Peru with *Operation Smile*.

He was excited about the patients on his list, having received pictures and medical records in advance. One of his patients would be a baby boy named Hernando whose mother had died during childbirth.

Josh showed me the picture of this one-year-old child who he thought might be the right one for us.

"He's adorable." I held a picture of a brown-skinned boy with dark, straight hair and the largest brown eyes I'd ever seen. His crooked smile showed a few baby teeth above which was the cleft lip that deformed the bottom of his nose and upper lip.

"His name is Hernando." Josh read his profile and talked about the possibility of bringing him back to the States. "If things look positive once I meet him and talk to the people who run the orphanage, you should plan to meet me in Peru."

I was excited about Hernando and made Josh promise to do everything he could to bring the boy home with him.

Josh called me when he arrived in Peru for his mission, and again midway through the two weeks, as he'd always done. The day before his two weeks was up he always called to confirm his flight information with me because Lilly and I made a ritual of meeting him at the airport when he arrived back in New York.

When he called, I asked if he'd seen Hernando and he said he had, and asked if I would fly to Peru and meet the boy?

"That will only delay things, Josh. Just bring him home with you. I know I'll love him," I told him over the phone.

"He lives in a remote village. I'll have to find transportation back there, which will delay me coming home." Josh asked me again to go to Peru to meet him but I refused to leave Lilly and begged him to go get Hernando. He said he'd try and would be home the following Friday.

I thought I'd written the date wrong on my calendar when I didn't hear from Josh the next Friday. I waited all day Saturday and still had no phone call but thought he was making arrangements for me to join him, or maybe the adoption process was underway. I was excited about Hernando.

On Sunday morning the doorbell rang. Lilly and I were alone, because Ruby didn't come in on weekends so I slipped on my robe and slippers and went to the foyer. I pressed the button on the monitor and saw two strangers, men dressed in suits and ties, standing on the stoop. I pressed the intercom and asked who they were and what they wanted.

"We're with *Operation Smile*. We have news for you about Dr. Joshua Ryan." The taller man had taken off his hat and leaned into the intercom. I thought maybe Josh had sent them with travel arrangements for me to meet him in Peru, but something sinister crept up my spine.

"Give me a minute." I went to the phone and called the security guard our association had on staff and asked him to come to my front door and check the credentials of the people on my stoop. I watched the monitor as Officer Jesup approached the men. They took out their wallets and Jesup examined several cards, then he looked into the monitor and nodded. I pressed the button.

"You can let them in, Mrs. Ryan. I'll come in with them." I pressed the door release and heard the click. When the door opened I smelled stale cigarette smoke that lingered on one of their jackets and I backed away as if their aura was contagious. By now Lilly, in her pajamas and robe, was standing next to me and we had our arms around each other.

"Mrs. Ryan. There's been an accident." The shorter man was talking but I no longer heard the words coming from his mouth about how Josh had taken a helicopter from a remote village in Peru with a little boy named Hernando.

"It crashed into a mountain before it reached the Lima airport." The taller man's lips were moving but nothing reached my buzzing ears.

It was as though a silent movie was playing in front of me in slow motion—lips moving, hands in the air, but no sound. Lilly screamed and buried her head in my chest, and I stood straight and tall and stared at the three men as though they were not there. There was no air in the room, as if someone had suctioned all life out.

In that dead silence, I could taste ashes and salt. Everything went black, and I fell to the bottom of a deep well where I was hollering and the sound of my screams was bouncing off the sides of the bricks inside the hole. My feet were in about a foot of water and something was crawling up my back. I started to swat at the creature, but it stuck to me and I fell and became drenched in the liquid that had turned red and coated me. I felt like I was breathing blood through my nose and that my lungs were filling with the thick substance.

When I stood up in the well, I was all alone, except for the feeling of something tightening around my waist. At first I thought the strange being was climbing up my body and would squeeze my chest and I would stop breathing; instead, I felt hands pulling on me and saw Lilly attached to me as if I was her life raft and could save her, even though I, myself, was drowning.

Somehow the two of us made it to the sofa where we spent the rest of the day.

I don't remember eating or drinking or going to the bathroom or talking. I only remember Lilly's arms around me, and how her tears drenched my nightgown and made it stick to me. I didn't cry. I couldn't feel anything but guilt. It was all my fault.

If I hadn't insisted that Josh bring Hernando home, they would both still be alive.

Joe came over that evening, but he was as bereft as we were. We all sat and stared at shadows in the living room.

Ruby came in the next morning and sat with Lilly and me all day, crying, sniffling, rubbing her eyes. My friends from Shilling Publications came and went. People from my church brought food and drinks. Joe hung around, left, and came back often. The priest from St. John's was there almost daily, I think.

Ruby walked around with red-rimmed eyes and Lilly would sit in the club chair in the corner of my bedroom and watch me. Mostly I stayed in my bed and stared at the ceiling. I might have slept in spurts but I can't say I remember sleeping or waking or crying or screaming or laughing, but later people told me I did all of that.

I vaguely remember the florist arriving with a huge bouquet of white lilies. I asked Ruby why they weren't brought to the funeral home and she said the delivery man said the instructions were specific—deliver them to the home. Every day or so, the doorbell rang and there was a long white box with one long-stemmed white lily to add to the bouquet. When some of the original ones started turning brown and dropping petals, Ruby would remove them. She added the new ones and the entire house was filled with a wonderful, fresh aroma.

It was the only thing I noticed over the next month.

They finally brought Josh's body home a week after I got the news. We held a funeral mass at St. John's. I remember wearing black and hanging onto Lilly. We sat in the first row and watched the priest go through the rituals of Mass and Communion. Marianne and Sissy appeared as if out of nowhere and sat on either side of Lilly and me, Sissy holding my hand, Marianne rubbing Lilly's back,

I remember the cemetery and the hole in the ground where Josh's brass-rimmed coffin rested on green straps. I remember smelling freshly cut grass and newly turned earth, and watching earthworms churn up the soil that was piled a few yards from the green tent with a row of cloth-draped chairs underneath.

I know Joe was there because he rode with Lilly, Sissy, Marianne, and me in a black car to and from the church and the cemetery, and back to our house in Brooklyn Heights—the house Josh and I were supposed to sell when we found something more family oriented, the house where Josh and I would start our family of at least four children with curly hair and green eyes and thick eyelashes.

The house with a vase overflowing with white, long-stemmed lilies that came from some nameless person every few days.

Sissy and Marianne went home, but returned about four weeks after the funeral. I was still in bed staring at the ceiling. They got me in the shower, made me put on decent clothes, not the sweats and T-shirts I'd been wearing for a month, and took Lilly and me to an Italian restaurant. It was the first time I'd been out of the house in a month, except for the funeral. They made me eat a slice of pizza and were very kind, but firm with me.

"You have to get a grip. Look at Lilly. She's hurting too. She needs you," Lilly had not left me, not even to spend a weekend with Joe. Marianne was holding both of my hands on the table. I finally started to cry. We got in a cab and went back to the house in Brooklyn Heights, and I cried all the way home. When we walked inside, and I looked around, I saw and felt and smelled Josh in every wall and door and lamp and rug and picture. I became hysterical.

It was as though someone had opened a dam and all the pain, disbelief, shock, and loss flooded out of me at once. I'd stand in Josh's closet and wrap his clothes around me, inhale his scent, then wipe my tears on one of his suits. Lilly, Sissy, and Marianne took turns consoling me while my hysteria went on for two days and I finally ran out of tears.

At breakfast that Wednesday we all sat in the kitchen. Ruby, still red-eyed, was frying bacon and we had cups of coffee in front of us.

"Okay, Susie. We need to talk about your future—yours and Lilly's." Marianne had her arm around Lilly and Sissy was holding one of my hands. "You have to move on. You can't stay mired in this muck and grief. Josh would not want that." For the first time in over a month, I heard words come out of someone's mouth. And I listened.

Josh's lawyer came to meet with me that afternoon. We went into Josh's study and I asked Mr. Milton to sit behind the desk in Josh's chair. I sat in one of the French chairs in front of the desk, Lilly sat in the other. He told us that Josh left a will, and that almost everything was bequeathed to me—the Brooklyn Heights home we lived in, the condo in Manhattan I'd never seen that had been leased for years, his partnership in the plastic surgery practice, thousands of acres of land in Texas and Arizona where I'd never been, and money he'd inherited that had been in an investment account since his dad died. He also left a trust fund for Lilly that would be worth a fortune in the coming years. In addition, he left an endowment for *Operation Smile.*

"He set up a living trust for you about five years ago, Mrs. Ryan, in case something like this happened. He didn't want his money tied up where you couldn't get to it until the succession was completed."

"What does that mean?"

"It means you have a good deal of cash readily available while the will is probated and the properties are transferred to you. Lilly's trust fund is simple—she gets the first distribution at eighteen, then annual payments until she's twenty-five, when she'll get another lump sum. She will continue to receive annual disbursements as well as generous withdrawals every five years for life. Until then, if you need money for her care, you can draw on her trust since you are the trustee."

I thought about what Mr. Milton said—"He set it up five years ago in case something like this happened." Did Josh know he would die young? Why would a thirty-something year old think to set up something this complicated, *in case?*

When Mr. Milton left, I leaned against the inside of the front door and stared at Lilly who was standing almost toe-to-toe with me. We were both overwhelmed. Josh's generosity was astounding; what's more, I had not been aware that Josh had so much money and property. He worked hard and was down-to-earth, so normal, not at all like a privileged kid who had inherited a fortune.

Mr. Milton left a file with the names of the investment people who handled Josh's money, the titles for the properties, the lease, and a lot of other papers I didn't care about. Lilly and I were sitting in the den holding hands and whispering things we remembered about Josh. She was crying softly and I rubbed her back to soothe her pain.

Marianne and Sissy came in and sat across from us.

"Our flights back to Louisiana are scheduled for tomorrow," Marianne said. "We're worried about leaving you two here alone." I took a deep breath and squeezed Lilly's hand. She turned to me with a frightened look and a big tear ran down her face. I couldn't imagine what we would do without my two sisters, Lilly's aunts, who loved us so well.

"Come home with us for a couple weeks. It would be good for you and for Lilly." Sissy got up and squeezed onto the sofa next to me and put her arm on my shoulder. She was my baby sister, nine years my junior, but now she was taking care of me.

"Look, you don't have to stay at the house with Daddy. You can stay in the Quarters with Marianne and Tootsie and I'll come over every day." Sissy squeezed my shoulder, and I looked at Lilly and saw her pain, and my heart broke for my daughter.

"What do you think, Lilly?" I reached my arm over her shoulder and she fell into my lap and hugged me around the waist. When she finished crying and pulling strength from me, she sat up.

"I'd like to go to Jean Ville and be with Tootsie, Marianne, and the families in the Quarters. It would be good to get out of this house for a while." She meant where Josh's ghost was in every corner and cubbyhole, and that if we were going to heal, we had to get away from the source of the pain, even if temporarily. *Out of the mouths of babes...*

*

Lilly was right; being in the Quarters in Jean Ville was good medicine for our spirits. The Massey family had become a massive crew of nieces and nephews and first and second cousins; kids of every age from birth to twenty-one, as well as adults, lived in the now eight cabins. Catfish's four children—Sam, Tom, Tootsie, and Jesse lived in the original row of former slave cabins where they had raised their children and Marianne lived in the fifth, which had been Catfish's house. The three newer cabins, facing the old row, had siding and roofing tiles, unlike the wooden structures with tin roofs and wood planks for exterior walls.

Tom and Gloria's youngest, Anna, was almost thirteen, a few months older than Lilly. The oldest of the Massey clan, Sam, had a married daughter named LaVergne who lived in one of the newer cabins and had a twelve-year-old named Christine who everyone called Chrissy. The three girls—Lilly, Anna, and Chrissy—had been friends since our first visit to Jean Ville when they were five. They had also been pen pals through the years and occasionally I let Lilly call them long distance.

It was like balm for my soul to watch Lilly and her dearest friends. Of course, they were actually her cousins, but I hadn't explained that to her yet. They played and stole off to the barn where I knew they shared secrets and talked about boys, school, books, and probably coming-of-age feelings like Marianne and I had done when we were twelve and thirteen. It was a slow and quiet environment, and so different from the city life Lilly and I had been living.

The second day we were in the Quarters in Jean Ville, a van from the only florist shop in town pulled up and parked in front of Marianne's cabin. I watched a young man walk up the steps of the house and give her a long white box. After he walked away she came onto the porch and put the box in my lap.

"It's for you."

"Who's it from?"

"Don't know. Same thing happened at your house in New York just about every day when I was there."

"What do you mean?"

"Every day or so someone delivered a box like this and there was one, long-stemmed white lily inside. Ruby would add it to the already full vase on your dining room table."

"Oh, I think I remember someone telling me about that. They smelled wonderful." I walked into the kitchen holding the box like someone would hold a baby—arms extended, elbows locked at my sides, the box resting across my hands like a miniature white coffin.

"Aren't you going to open it?"

"Would you do it for me?" I handed the box to Marianne and went out the door, letting the screen door slam behind me. I'm not sure what I was thinking but that box felt like a hot potato that I needed to drop. Later that day, I noticed the white lily in a large Mason jar in the middle of Marianne's kitchen table. I ignored it.

The next day I saw the florist's van pull into the Quarters and a young man got out with another long white box. I went into the bathroom, took a long bath, and came out an hour later. Marianne had gone to work and there were two lilies in the jar on the table. It was hard to ignore the fragrance that filled the small house. Every day a new lily arrived, the bouquet grew, and the house smelled like a rose garden.

It didn't escape me that I was the only white person among the clan of African Americans and that they saw me as different; yet, I loved them and felt more at home with this family than anywhere else or with anyone else. And Lilly was one of them, literally. I began to consider how and when I would tell her the truth. Joe and I had talked about it and he felt she should know at some point.

"You're her birth mother. You'll know when the time is right and you'll have the perfect words." Joe had reassured me, but I didn't feel like such a competent mother. I wasn't afraid to tell her I was her mother. I was afraid of the questions she would have about her biological father and I wasn't ready to answer those. Emalene would know exactly what to say. So would Josh.

A wave of grief washed over me and I cried for the next hour. It was like that—I'd be doing fine, and then a wave would hit me and knock me down a deep, dark hole. I'd feel like I was being washed up in a tsunami of grief and couldn't breathe, like the day I discovered Emalene wasn't breathing and the day the men came to tell me about Josh.

I felt guilty about Josh's death since I had pressured him to bring Hernando home to me. Had he not taken that helicopter to the boy's village, he would have flown home with the other doctors and would still be with me. My guilt was complicated by the way I started to question whether I'd really loved him the way I thought I did—the way I'd once loved Rodney.

As months passed, I noticed that the time between grief and guilt tsunamis was longer and the depth of the hole more shallow, but the waves kept coming, and for the first year, it felt almost murderous at times.

*

I sat on Tootsie's porch that evening, drinking sweet tea and watched Lilly and the girls jump rope. Tootsie was mending something, pulling a needle through fabric.

She had taught me to sew when I was a little girl and I'd become pretty good at it. I'd bought a used Singer sewing machine in New York and made baby doll clothes for Lilly when she was younger. We'd go to the fabric shop and choose materials, buttons, lace and other items and go back to my apartment and make dresses, aprons, and bonnets, even shoes for her dolls. Tootsie had taught me most of the important things I had learned growing up, and I looked at her tenderly, with gratitude.

"I love you, Toot. You've been such a good mother to me."

"I love you, Susie. You were easy to raise." She laughed and rocked and pulled that needle and thread through the fabric.

"Who taught you to sew?"

"My Mama. She was something, now; could do anything—pick cotton, hoe a row, ride a horse, strap a buggy together, cook any meal you yearned for, sew up clothes and curtains that looked store-bought. And she could gossip, too. I loved to sit right here and listen to her tell stories about those people who lived in the plantation house before my time, even before her time.

"I remember Mama telling the story about Mr. Henry Van." Tootsie stared at the darkening sky and sighed. "Now he was Mr. Gordon's only chile and Mr. Henry's mama done run off so it was just them two men in that big house. I guess you could say Maureen, Lizzie, Bessie, and even Anna Lee, was that boy's mama.

The Hoodoo: by Tootsie
1860-1935

Now, Mr. Henry, he was in college, then he went off to Europe and some other places. He came back to the plantation when he was about thirty and Sammy was somewhere in the teenage years, about fifteen or sixteen, I believe. And they took a liking to each other. You see, Sammy, he was extra smart. He started going to his mama's school when he could barely walk. He could read anything—the newspaper, the Bible, books. And he could write like you wouldn't believe, almost like an artist.

So Mr. Van and Mr. Henry would rely on Sammy to write up some things for them, bills of sale, contracts, and such. I think Mr. Henry respected that Sammy was smart and it gave him someone he could talk to about books and history and such as that.

Now me, I didn't get past eighth grade. You know I was pregnant with Marianne when I was fourteen or so. And, anyway, my mama, maybe being from Mississippi, thought learning was a waste of time for girls.

Anyways, after Mr. Gordon died, Mr. Henry took over the crops and such and my granddaddy Sammy worked for him doing everything, and Mr. Henry let Sammy sharecrop. Sammy, he invented a new kind of way to grow corn that made more corn on each stalk, and the people from LSU came here to see what he'd done and start to teach what Sammy done about growing good crops over at the college to they students. It was like he had a green hand when he planted corn and cane, and even cotton. His crops was always bigger and better than anyone's.

I know Catfish tole you about when Mr. Gordon died how he left these cabins and an acre land they's on to my granddaddy and them, and that's how we got to own our own place. And Mr. Henry, well he gave my granddaddy, Sammy, fifty acres of land through the years and now we got all this property here on Gravier Road and Jefferson Extension.

And my granddaddy, he would teach all Mr. Henry's workers how to make the crops big and full, and they'd have more corn than they could use and more cotton than they could pick and more pecans—why, they was pecans big as pine cones all over the grounds. That made Mr. Henry a rich man and my granddaddy, he was successful, too, and left all that to my daddy and us. It's all up at the Confederate Bank, I guess. We never spent the money. My daddy said it was for emergencies.

Mr. Henry, he married a girl from Baton Rouge name of Catherine, and she come to live here and they had them a little girl with white hair and the bluest eyes, Catfish said. That little girl named Angela was same age as Catfish and he thought she was beautiful but he said her skin so white it glowed and made him think of the haunt.

Miss Catherine, she won't let Angela play with Catfish or the others in the Quarters, and Catfish say Angela used to watch the kids play in the Quarters through the fence Miss Catherine made the workers build to separate the whites from the coloreds. They said Mr. Henry got so mad he took a shovel and tried to break down the fence one night.

Miss Catherine got real sick when Angela was little and they sent for the doctor but he didn't know what to do and he tried everything, bleeding her, medicines, steam, but she just got worse. And she wouldn't let no coloreds go around her or her daughter, but when she got so delirious on fever that she didn't know who was in there, Mr. Henry got Maureen and Bessie up in Miss Catherine's room and they put the healing mojo on her with herbs and some medicines they make from the earth.

And it was like a miracle after a couple days that Miss Catherine start to get better. And when her fever was gone and she saw Maureen in her room she start to screaming for Mr. Henry to come get that nigress out her room 'cause she think Maureen has the witchcraft in her and she trying to make Miss Catherine have a fit.

Mr. Henry got up in that room and calmed his wife down and start to tell her that it was Maureen and Bessie what got her well, and she don't believe him and they got in a big argument. Then little Angela go and climb in her mama's bed and tell her mama that her daddy tell the truth and how she so grateful that Maureen and them save her mama's life and all.

Catfish say things changed around here after that.

Tootsie pointed to the end of the row where the field spread out towards the plantation house with the barn midway between where a fence separated the properties. I silently followed her direction with my eyes.

Well, soon after Miss Catherine start to get well, that fence came down and Angela would run and play with Catfish and the other kids here in the Quarters. Course it would happen that Angela and Sam, that was Catfish oldest brother, named after they daddy, and them, got to be friends. They was just children then. Angela was about seven and Sam, he was maybe nine or ten. But when they got to be teenagers they was starting to like each other more like boyfriend and girlfriend and that was too much for Miss Catherine.

Next thing you know, Angela got shipped off to boarding school somewhere near Lafayette. They say Sam was so upset when Miss Angela left that he registered for the draft and went in the Army during the First War. They call it the first war but it weren't the first, 'cause the war of the states that some call the Civil War, now that was the first one and it happened right here.

So, Sam, he got shipped over to France, but he didn't make it to battle 'cause he died from the Spanish flu on a ship somewhere in the ocean. They say Sammy was angry and blamed Miss Catherine for his son's death, but Miss Catherine don't care one hoot or holler, you hear. She just went about her business and Maureen say Miss Catherine was glad Sam died 'cause she didn't have to worry her daughter would have a colored baby. I don't know what happened to Angela Van. No one ever talked about her after Sam died.

When he died, that made Catfish the oldest son and he had to learn to grow crops like his daddy and them. But Catfish, he didn't like farming. He liked to draw and fish and hunt and chase girls.

When Mr. Henry died in '38, Catfish was in his thirties, I guess. He and my mama were married by then and I was a baby. Well, Miss Catherine, she didn't want nothing to do with staying on at Shadowland—it wasn't a plantation no more, no way—so she put everything up for sale. They sold off the land part and parcel and you can see all these houses done gone up all along Jefferson Extension since then. Why that road was just a driveway back then, now they's houses on both sides and they done paved it.

Then Miss Catherine Van sold off the big old house to some people didn't take care of it and it looked all broken down for years. A new doctor came to town and bought it and they got it all fixed up and it looks good as new.

"I hear that doctor's wife got all the new appliances and stuff and that she big society in Jean Ville." Tootsie rocked back and forth and stared at the plantation house. "They young and have some young children I see playing in the yard sometime, but I never met them. They put up a fence where the old one was, so our children don't mix.

"Just when you think things is changing, they go back to the same."

"What y'all talking about?" Marianne walked up the steps onto Tootsie's porch and sat on the edge, dangling her legs off the side, her feet scraping the dust.

"Tootsie's telling me stories about Catfish and the Vans." I rocked hard in the chair and patted my feet on the wood slats. Tootsie stared at that field and the barn and the fence and rocked in her chair, the needle not moving, the thread blowing slightly in the breeze.

Her stories were not so different from Catfish's, but her telling—now that was something special.

⟿ Chapter Eighteen ⟿

Gravier Road

SISSY INSISTED ON TALKING on our way back to Jean Ville from a shopping trip in Alexandria. It was hot and humid, and we had the air conditioner on full blast, so that the whishing noise coupled with the clack-clack-clack of the tires on the concrete highway made it hard to have a conversation. The air was thick like it gets in Louisiana when it's about to rain. She asked about Lilly.

"What about her?" My hands gripped tighter around the steering wheel.

"Tell me about her parents. How did you and Josh end up with her?"

"It's complicated." I rolled the window down a few inches to release the pressure I was feeling, but all that accomplished was a whiff from a paper mill that smelled like sewage and the extreme moist heat so familiar to south Louisiana. We were about fifteen minutes from the Quarters and I stepped on the gas, wanting to cut the conversation short.

"You realize she looks a lot like you, huh?"

"No she doesn't. She's not even white."

"Duh!" Sissy rolled her eyes and reminded me of Mama, the way she'd make that face behind Daddy's back when he talked about how colored people were just like white people. Mama knew all along that

Daddy was a hypocrite, but we thought Mama was the one who was prejudiced.

"Her mother, Emalene, is black and her dad, Joe, is white. Emma was, is… was my dear friend, as close as Marianne, but older, more like a sister-mother type. She's in a nursing home and has dementia. She doesn't even know Lilly or me anymore. It's very sad."

I told Sissy about Joe being a college professor and how he went off the deep end when Emma had a double mastectomy, and took up with a young girl, one of his students. I explained how I helped out the year Emma and Joe fought the cancer, and that after Emma quit breathing and we brought her back, it damaged her brain.

"Too long without oxygen, they say." I wanted to keep the conversation about the Franklins. "Joe needed me to help, so I said yes and kept Lilly because she'd basically lost both her parents and, well, I love her."

"She obviously loves you too."

"I came into her life when she was four. When you get down to it, I've been her surrogate mother longer than Emma was her actual mother."

"Lilly told me she was adopted."

"She told you that? She's never talked to me about it. Emma and Joe told her from the beginning that she was chosen."

"Chosen, that's a nice way of saying it."

"Emalene Franklin had nice ways of saying all sorts of things." Sissy wouldn't give up the conversation no matter how I explained the way I'd come to have custody of Lilly. I tried changing the subject, but she kept bringing it up.

"Why are you pushing this, Sissy?" It started to rain and I turned on the windshield wipers.

"Because. She looks like you, except she's obviously part colored."

"They use the term black now, and African American."

"Okay. But Susie, there were rumors about you when you were a teenager. You know that, right?"

"I don't care about rumors."

"About you and a *black* guy. Ray Thibault's son."

"Rumors are just that—rumors." The rain came down harder, and I had to concentrate on the slick roads. I didn't want to have this conversation.

"Well, I happen to believe them. I remember when I was little, maybe eight or nine, you were sitting in a car in Dr. Switzer's driveway and a tall, colored boy, maybe he was a Mulatto 'cause he was light-skinned, he was yelling at Daddy from across the street. Then y'all drove off—you and the boy. I was on the porch with Mama."

"Hmmm."

"Marianne told me that he's divorced."

"Who?"

"Rodney Thibault."

"She didn't tell me that and, anyway, it doesn't matter. History."

We drove for several miles without talking and I was thinking about Rodney, Josh, and Daddy; all the thoughts were rushing in and out of my brain.

"He told me he was sorry." I drove slowly in the pouring rain.

"Who?"

"Daddy. He told me he was afraid I wouldn't fulfill my potential." I thought about Daddy and how hard it must have been for him to admit he had handled things badly.

"He said that to you?"

"Yes. I feel like I need to try with Daddy. To forgive him."

Sissy didn't comment.

Lilly was waiting outside in the rain when we drove up. She threw herself into my arms and started crying. I hugged her so tightly that she gasped. We were drenched by the time we walked into

Marianne's kitchen, and she stopped crying long enough for me to hear her explain how she thought I'd been in a wreck because the weather was so bad. "Or hit by lightning, or hit a deer, or maybe a car slid off the road and hit you…"

"Baby, I'm fine. We were very careful." I tried to soothe her, but it was obvious that it would be a long time before she didn't feel utter fear when she was away from me. She was deathly afraid to lose me and, frankly, I couldn't imagine losing her. That would certainly put me over the edge.

As time progressed I would find myself in periods where I didn't grieve or remember Josh for a few hours, sometimes an entire day; then, of course, it would hit me that he was gone and I'd hit bottom again. During those times when I'd forget him, I'd find myself thinking about Rodney and I'd question myself—did I really love Josh? Was I really happy with him? It seemed that, as his memory faded, memories of Rodney rose.

That made me feel so guilty that I couldn't stand myself.

*

August was coming to a close and we had to get back to New York so Lilly could start seventh grade. Anna and Chrissy made a case for how we should live in Jean Ville and that Lilly could go to school with them. Marianne and Tootsie tried to convince me I should consider staying because we were so much happier in Jean Ville and… anyway, they missed us.

I had read that you should not make any major decisions—move out of your home, start a new relationship, quit a job—anything drastic until at least one year after a tragic event like the loss of a spouse. I explained to Marianne that Lilly and I had to face our ghosts and deal with them, that we couldn't run away. Convincing Lilly was not as easy, though.

"We have to go back to New York," I told her that night when we were snuggled up in the pull-out bed in Marianne's sitting room.

"It's too hard being in that house without Josh." She said she was afraid to return to Brooklyn Heights.

"That's where our life is. That's where your dad is, and your mom. We have to go back." I tried to hug her but she pulled away from me. "Look, I promise we'll come back at Christmas. You'll have almost a month off from school and it'll be cold and snowy up north and warmer here."

"You promise?" She sat up in the middle of the bed and looked at me.

"Of course I promise. We'll buy our airline tickets tomorrow before we fly home." My heart broke for her, but I knew I had to be the voice of reason, the adult in the room.

"Okay, that's less than four months. I think I can do it." She lay back down and let me put my arm under her shoulder.

"That's my girl. We'll be fine, and Christmas will be here before you know it."

*

We weren't fine. The house was like a mausoleum. Josh was everywhere and we moped around most days. To break the horrible grief into smaller, more palatable pieces, we'd go to restaurants at night and shop in the city on weekends. We started staying at a hotel on Saturday nights, saying it was easier than going back to Brooklyn, but really, we were like different people when we weren't in Josh's house.

I knew I should sell it and move, but I wanted to stick to the one-year plan. I hoped I would see things more clearly 365 days after I first heard of Josh's death and my life became what would be an everlasting legacy—before Josh and after Josh. The definition of Susie Burton Ryan.

I remembered feeling the same after I'd lost Rodney; that my life was defined in those terms—before and after Rodney—yet I'd survived and thrived. I hung onto the hope that I would heal from losing Josh just as I had after I'd lost Rodney; because, as I'd learned, *hope* is the only thing that makes life worth living.

The lilies kept arriving every couple of days in New York and the house was always filled with the fresh scent, the fullness of spring in winter, and the hope of Easter, of rising and new life. Unfortunately, Lilly and I didn't feel the positive energy the lilies represented. It was much later that I realized how the sight of those beautiful, white, silky, velvet-like petals with green leaves and thick stems and the smell of flowering springtime kept the taste of hope alive in our spirits even while we didn't know it in our hearts.

I wonder today if those lilies weren't the healing balm that kept Lilly and me from going off the deep end.

Jean Ville was a good diversion for us that Christmas. It was the first time I was excited to be back in Louisiana in years and the word "home" caught in my throat when I mentioned to Lilly that we'd be in Jean Ville soon. Home had been New York for me since I was seventeen and for Lilly all of her life, yet we both felt more alive and at peace in the Quarters than we did in New York.

Sissy went Christmas shopping with me, Lilly, Chrissy, and Anna in Alexandria. We returned to Marianne's house with our rental car full of packages, unwrapped gifts, wrapping paper, ribbons, and bows. We even had a Christmas tree tied to the roof of the car. It was obvious there wasn't enough room in the three-room cabin for everything we'd brought from New York, plus all the gifts and the tree, as well all of us. In fact, when Lucy came over there was virtually no room to walk.

I told Sissy that Lilly and I would really like to get a hotel room, but there still were no hotels in Jean Ville, and staying in Alexandria defeated the purpose of us being there.

Sissy suggested that, instead, we try to find a rental house nearby, so we drove to town to meet with the only real estate agent, Mitchell Dunlap.

Dunlap said there was a two-bedroom frame house on Gravier Road, only a couple blocks from the Quarters, but it was for sale, not rent. I told Mr. Dunlap I wasn't interested in purchasing a house, I just wanted to rent for one month, but he said there was nothing available on the south side where I wanted to be. He had one listing for a clapboard house with a falling down porch on an acre of land, take it or leave it.

He led the way through the overgrown grass and weeds to rickety steps, and I was afraid to walk on the porch for fear it would give way under us. He turned the key in the lock, swung the door open, and the smell of a dead mouse or snake and the mustiness of a closed-in place hit us in the face. I didn't want to go inside but Lilly and Anna were running through the place as if it was a playhouse they'd just discovered. Once I was accustomed to the odor, I took a tour of the living room, dining room, and kitchen; each room led to the next like a shotgun house, except with huge openings between them, and no doors. Off the kitchen was a large back porch that was in a little better shape than the front porch and a huge yard that stretched for an acre to a tree line.

Back in the living room, a doorway to the right led to a hall with three doors. Two of the doors opened to bedrooms and the center door to an out-dated bathroom with rust stains in the lavatory and tub. The smell of backed-up sewage slapped me in the face and I quickly closed the door.

"I'll have to get a carpenter and plumber to come look at this place before I can make a decision. A lot would have to be done to make it livable." I made a face and headed for the front door to get some air. Mr. Dunlap was hot on my trail.

Lilly, Anna, and Chrissy were running through the tall grass in the back field and I knew they'd have chigger bites if they didn't get back on solid ground, so I yelled for them to come back to the car.

We left the gifts and other purchases in the rental car when we got back to the Quarters because there was no place to put the items inside. We definitely needed more room, but the house on Gravier was deplorable. When Sam got home from work that evening, I walked over to his house and sat in one of the chairs on the porch with him and his wife, Josie.

"I found a house to stay in when Lilly and I are in Jean Ville, but it's a mess. Do you know of anyone who can look at it for me? A carpenter, a plumber, maybe an electrician?" I was helping Josie shuck corn that she said she was going to make into maque choux, a dish of corn, corn milk, onions, celery, and sweet peppers smothered to the consistency of lumpy grits.

"I can look at it for you, Susie," Sam was smoking a pipe, rocking back and forth, staring at the pecan trees whose leaves were almost all on the ground. "That's what I do for Mr. Ducote. I'm his assistant and we build and repair houses."

"This one has something dead in it." I scrunched my nose and my eyes turned to slivers. Sam and Josie laughed.

"Probably a dead mouse in one of the walls or floorboards. I'll find it." The next evening Sam and Tom followed me to the house on Gravier Road and Mr. Dunlap was waiting in the driveway. He didn't shake hands with Marianne's uncles and it made me angry because I knew it was because they weren't white. Mr. Dunlap apparently was one of the holdovers from Jim Crow.

The Massey boys went through the house with flashlights and hammers and declared it sound.

"It has good bones," Sam said. "Me and Tom and a few of our friends can get this fixed up over the weekend." I hadn't asked Mr. Dunlap the price so when he said $15,000 I thought I misheard him. A house and over an acre of land for fifteen grand? That was the price of three months' rent on Josh's condo in Manhattan! My friends in New York would hoot when I told them. I wrote him a check on the spot and he said he'd get the deed to me the next day, and handed me the keys.

The next day was Saturday and everyone who lived in the Quarters and lots of their friends from other quarters were at the house on Gravier Road at sunrise. I gave Sam my credit card to buy supplies and he drove up the driveway with his truck loaded to the hilt at about 9:00 AM.

By the time Sam returned, the front yard had piles of debris from things the men had torn out of the house. At least ten pickups were coming and going, bringing stuff and taking trash away. Someone appeared with a couple of lawn mowers and an array of yard tools, and a group of teenage boys got to work on the yard, mowing grass, pulling weeds, shoveling mulch, planting shrubs.

It was like watching a movie on fast speed. By sundown, when Marianne drove up with an ice chest filled with beer and bags of chips and salsa, the place was transformed. The porch was standing straight and all the missing boards had been replaced, as were the boards on the outside of the house and the back porch.

An army of teenagers and young men painted the entire outside of the house white and the porch floors dark gray. Someone drove up with two rocking chairs and a porch swing, hung the swing and set the chairs, then painted them black, like the new shutters on the two front windows and the new, black, front door.

Inside, all of the wood floors had been repaired and stained. They were still wet, so I couldn't walk through the house to see what it looked like until the next day. I'd seen a new toilet, tub, and lavatory arrive, a new kitchen sink, boxes with faucets and a shower head, and new appliances. I wouldn't have known where to find those things but Sam and my credit card seemed to have no problem.

Lilly and I went to early Mass at St. Alphonse's the next

morning while Tootsie and her family were at Bethel Baptist. We got to the house on Gravier Road before the others. Lilly and I walked through with our mouths open. It smelled of fresh paint, wax, and Lysol. The hardwood floors throughout the house were a chestnut stain and had a shiny finish. The sheetrock on the walls looked brand new and had been painted a cool grayish color in the living and dining rooms, and kitchen.

Lilly's bedroom was light pink and mine was a minty green. The bathroom was beige, like the hall, and looked like a picture from Decor Magazine with its chintz shades on the window and matching shower curtain. The kitchen was modern for 1980 standards—a farm sink and stainless fixtures, a white refrigerator with the freezer on top, and an electric range with an oven. The cabinets had been totally replaced with pre-made cabinetry that Sam said Mr. Ducote kept in stock. Everything worked, everything was plumb, the drawers pulled out with ease.

Lilly and I walked through the house holding hands, not saying a word, but we heard each other's gasps and sighs as we went from room to room. When we walked out on the back porch she caught my arm with two hands and yelled. "Oh my God! Susie. Look."

The guys had manicured the lawn and it looked like a football field before a Friday night game, but that wasn't the best part. A few yards off the back porch was a huge area where they'd removed an oval of grass and built a big fire pit for roasting pigs and grilling meats outside. Four Adirondack chairs surrounded the area, and there was a swing set frame on the side with a three-person swing hanging from it. A hammock was strung between two of the half-dozen pecan trees and the shade from the oak trees screened the blazing sun from the entire area. Beyond the cleared area and the fire pit was a miniature building that looked like a tiny barn. Along the fence rows were azaleas, camellia bushes, and hydrangeas.

Already, a huge stone urn on the porch was filled with fresh, white lilies.

I inhaled the familiar Easter scent as Lilly and I stood on the back porch trying to take everything in when I heard a car pull in the driveway, then another, then it sounded like several trucks. Lilly and I didn't move. We listened to the sounds of doors slamming and people talking and laughing and squeezed each other's hands.

"What y'all doing out here?" Marianne rounded the corner of the house pulling a wagon filled with bags. Tom, Sam, Jesse, Tootsie and their families came through the house and before long everyone from the Quarters was moving around, busy doing something.

I went inside and watched Tom and Sam and their boys carry beds to the bedrooms and place a sectional sofa in the living room. Before I could ask where everything came from, a table and six chairs appeared in the dining room and a round table with four chairs in the kitchen. Marianne walked up behind me as I stood, flabbergasted, in the middle of the living room and watched the men haul stuff into the house.

"I hope you don't mind. Sissy and I picked out everything. I kept the receipts in case you want to make exchanges." She smiled, and before I could answer her, the front door slammed and Sissy walked in with huge bags hanging from her arms.

"Come help me get these beds made up." Sissy tilted her chin in the air and pointed it towards the hallway and Marianne followed her. Lilly's cousins arrived and they went into her room and helped Sissy make up her bed and hang pink curtains on the windows. I walked into the back bedroom and Marianne was putting a beautiful, gray silk coverlet on the bed and fluffing the four matching pillows. There was a chest of drawers between the two windows on the side of the house and a dresser with a huge mirror on the wall between the bedroom and the bathroom. An upholstered chair and ottoman sat in the far corner and two smart tables with lamps were on either side of the bed.

"Where? When?" I stuttered and stammered and stared at my brown sister, and felt so much love for her I could have burst.

Mari asked, "Did I get it right? Your taste? I saw what you have in New York and I thought..."

"It's beautiful. I really can't believe it." Neither of us spoke as I walked slowly around the room, running my hand over the surfaces of the furniture and the bedding, turning the lamps on and off, pulling the shades up then lowering them, drawing the draperies closed, then opening them. "I'm... I don't... well..." I couldn't find concrete words.

Marianne started laughing and I started laughing at her laughing. We became semi-hysterical and Sissy came to see what all the fuss was about and joined us; we stood there and laughed until we cried.

"I think Marianne wants you out of her house!" Sissy punched me in the side and I laughed harder.

"She won't get rid of me that easily. I'll be there tonight!"

"Oh, no you won't. I have plans." Marianne was laughing so hard she was bent forward holding her belly and it reminded me of the way Catfish would laugh when he got tickled—from the bottom of his toes to the top of his kinky head—and the thought of him made me sad, and I thought about his death, which made me think about Emalene, which made me think about Josh, and soon my laughter turned to tears. My sisters wrapped me in their arms and held me until I caught my breath.

I finally sat in my new chair and admired the small, beautiful, simple, elegant bedroom. It was so unlike the lavish Brooklyn Heights master suite, but so right for me.

Lilly loved the house and the fact that she could walk to the Quarters less than two blocks away.

Christmas in Jean Ville was better than I expected our first Christmas without Josh would be. We had our Frasier flocked to remind us of white Christmases in New York. We decorated it with white lights and new Christmas ornaments we'd bought in Alexandria. There were no memories tied to the decorations, we were building new ones and it felt good. We were still breathing when 1982 rolled in.

Every day or so, the florist arrived with a white box.

Before we went back to New York, I visited my dad. Sissy was with me when I walked into his study, the little room he'd added to the master bedroom years before that we called, "The Lion's Den.".

"Hi, Daddy. How're you feeling?" I patted his shoulder. He was sitting at his desk facing the wall on the far side of the room, his back to me. He bent over some papers and had a pencil, which he stuck behind his ear and heaved a heavy sigh.

"What are you doing here?" He didn't turn around to look at me. Sissy and I glared at each other and she shrugged her shoulders.

"I've been in town a few days and I'm leaving tomorrow. I wanted to come by to see you before I returned to New York."

"You've been here almost a month and you bought a house and had Christmas and you're just now coming to see me?" He still didn't turn around. "Don't do me any favors, girl." He pulled the pencil from behind his ear and started to scratch on the paper in front of him.

"You're right, Daddy." I started to walk out of the room with Sissy behind me, but turned around when I got to the door to the hall. "I'm sorry. I've been caught up in my own stuff." We walked into the hall and I turned to hug Sissy.

"I should have come during Christmas. I guess I was so busy I forgot all about Daddy." We walked up the hall, through the front door, and down the steps to the yard.

"You've had a lot, Susie." Sissy put her hand on my shoulder and stopped me. I turned and she hugged me. "Don't blame yourself because he's a self-absorbed ass. He didn't say anything about you losing Josh, and he knows. It's all about him. Always has been."

"How do you stand it?"

"Somehow he's kinder to me. He's never spoken to me like he speaks to you. I think it would break my heart."

"He's never liked me. And if I'm honest, I don't like him, either. But I love him. He's my dad—and like Emalene would say, 'You only get one'."

"I wish I had known Emalene, before."

"I wish you had, too."

*

That night Sissy and I went to dinner at Sylvia and Ken Michaud's home. Sylvia had grown up next door to us on South Jefferson and we'd been like sisters through high school, although she was a year younger than me. We used to have to drag Sissy with us when we drove around Jean Ville looking for boys and stopping at Dickey's, a local hamburger drive-up, where everyone hung out. Now Sissy was twenty-one and seemed so much closer to our age.

Sylvia had three children; the oldest was ten. Sylvia was a teller at the Confederate Bank, Ken worked at the local car dealership, and they lived in a white wood-frame house on Monroe Street, only a couple of blocks from the town square. We girls sat on their back patio sipping wine, talking about old times, watching the children swing on the swing set while Ken grilled chickens on the pit in the yard.

"What's it like living in New York City?" Sylvia put a platter of fried onion rings on the coffee table in front of us.

"I live in Brooklyn, really, across the river from Manhattan. I like it."

"It must be so different, the big city and all."

"Not really. Everyone lives in a pie slice. I mean, we all live in neighborhoods with grocery stores and churches and schools. It's like every neighborhood is a small town like Jean Ville." I could tell Sylvia wanted to ask me personal questions but didn't know how to approach the subject with Sissy and Ken around. When we were younger we talked about everything; everything, that is, except my relationship with Rodney, which wasn't really a relationship until I went off to college and Sylvia and I grew apart.

She asked me to help her bring some things from the kitchen to the picnic table outside. When we were alone inside the house, she turned abruptly towards me, her nose almost touching mine. Her face was red.

"What's this I heard about you and a Negro?"

"Sylvia. I just lost my husband. What's your point?" Every time I realized I'd lost Josh something hit me in the gut and took my breath away. I couldn't believe my friend would accost me about something that happened years ago when I'd recently experienced such a tragic loss.

"Look, I'm sorry about your husband, but it's hard for me to relate. I never knew him. You never brought him home."

"I brought him home, but that's not the point."

"I want to know about Rodney Thibault. *And* I understand you've been seen with a little girl who is half-colored."

"I'm not feeling well. I'm going home."

"Home? Home to that house near the Quarters? The one that all those colored people helped you fix up. What happened to your white friends? When did you become such a nigga-lover?"

"If my white *friends* are all like you, I probably made the right choice." I turned and walked out of her front door, down the street and was a block from Sylvia's house when I realized I was on the other side of town, about a mile from my house on Gravier Road. I didn't care. The fresh air would do me good and eventually Sissy would realize I was gone and come looking for me in the car.

I walked through town as the sun began to set on the other side of the courthouse. The sky was orange with pink stripes that made it look like a painting. I breathed in the cool December air and walked briskly towards the sunset and thought that if I could reach it, and touch the sunset, I might feel Josh and know he was in heaven, and know there was a heaven.

When I got to the front of the courthouse, I sat on a bench and cried. About fifteen minutes later I took off walking towards Gravier Road. It was almost dark when I heard a car behind me, and Sissy pulled up, stopped, and I got in without a word.

*

Lilly didn't want to go back to New York and, frankly, neither did I, but we had to. So we parked our rental car in the return-lot in Baton Rouge and boarded Delta Airlines for Kennedy International. We knew we'd return to Jean Ville soon. After all, we owned a home on Gravier Road that Sissy would tend and probably live in most of the time we were in New York. She was almost twenty-two and needed some independence from Daddy.

The best part about being back in Brooklyn Heights was Ruby. It was almost like having Tootsie with us every day. She sang songs and hummed and whistled tunes and kept us sane. She cooked our favorite meals and cleaned the house spotless. But she couldn't make the spirit of Josh go away and Lilly and I cried on and off every day. Ruby said no flowers came while we were gone, but we hadn't been back two days when the lilies began arriving again. It started to bother me.

Who would know when I was in New York and when I was in Jean Ville? And when I was in Jean Ville, who would know when I was staying with Marianne and when I bought the house and started staying on Gravier Road? It felt spooky, although when I talked to Marianne about it she told me I was blowing it out of proportion, that it was probably Joe, or Josh's sister, or my friends at work. So I tried to stop worrying about it.

I worried about what had happened with Sylvia and how my other white friends would treat me when I was home. I didn't want any part of the white community if Sylvia was an indication of its bigotry.

When I talked to Sissy about it she assured me that I had nothing to worry about. She had lots of friends and no one held what I did as a teenager against me. I didn't admit to anything, but I thought *if they only knew the whole truth, I'd really be ostracized.*

Lilly and I flew to Jean Ville for Easter break. We left on Friday as soon as she got out of school and landed in Baton Rouge late. We rented a car and drove the 86 miles to Jean Ville and let ourselves into the house on Gravier Road at about midnight. When I flicked on the lights, the first thing I saw was a bouquet of white, long-stemmed Easter lilies in the center of the dining room table. *How'd they get here?* I wondered, but was too tired to think about it.

I was awakened the next morning by someone knocking on the window of my bedroom saying, "Susie, get up and let me in." I peeked through the blinds and saw Marianne standing on the back porch. I walked into the kitchen and opened the door. She rushed in and hugged me, then started bringing bags into the house. I watched her stock my refrigerator and cabinets with food and drinks and all of Lilly's favorite things.

"You are an amazing aunt and sister." I hugged her as she slipped out the back door again.

"I know," she called over her shoulder. She laughed at me standing there with sleep in my eyes, barefoot, in crumpled pajamas, and my hair sticking out everywhere. When she came back inside she filled the coffee pot and turned it on. She got out two mugs and put sugar and cream on the table. Then she opened a bag that had hot biscuits with ham and sausage that she bought at the corner gas station—one of the benefits of a Cajun town—locally owned gas stations have great home-cooked food.

Lilly stumbled in, joined us, and had orange juice with her biscuit. We were both quiet while Marianne talked nonstop about her work at the hospital and about Lucy and how excited everyone was that we'd be here for Easter. When she stopped to take a sip of coffee I looked at her and grinned.

"Do you know how that bouquet of Easter lilies got into this house?"

"What bouquet?" She looked innocent and Marianne was so honest I could always tell when she was trying to hide something.

"The one on the dining room table." I tilted my head towards the adjoining room and nodded towards the flowers. "It's not like you can't smell them as soon as you walk in the door."

"Oh, that wonderful smell. I thought it was your perfume, Mrs. Ryan." She often teased me about being married to a doctor and even though I never told anyone how much money Josh left me, she knew I was financially secure, and she picked at me about how I could afford things like Haviland China coffee cups.

"Really, Susie, I don't know anything about those flowers. I didn't know where they came from when they arrived at my house, either. Maybe you should ask Sissy. She stays here a lot."

I asked Sissy, but she said the florist just delivered them the day before I arrived and there was no card. I forgot about it, except for that glorious fragrance that filled the house with sweetness and beauty and made my spirits rise.

You could almost taste *hope* when you walked in the door.

～Chapter Nineteen ～

The Book

LILLY AND I WENT back to New York after a wonderful Easter week, and there was a package in the mail. I ripped it open and a proof copy of *The Catfish Stories,* published by Shilling Publishers fell into my lap. I had almost forgotten that it was in the works and held the copy as if it were a newborn baby—MY newborn baby.

Lilly sat next to me on the sofa and we read through the 300-page paperback book with a picture of Catfish on the cover. I felt tears stream down my face as I re-read the stories Catfish had told me through the years, and which had finally become his legacy.

My life took off at the clip of a racehorse once I took the proof copy to my old workplace and handed it to Mr. Mobley, complete with red marks to indicate changes that had to be made. He ushered me into his office and I sat in one of the two leather chairs in front of his desk while we discussed a book tour he wanted the marketing department to set up for me.

"Are you up for it?" He sipped his coffee and looked at me over the top of his cup.

"I suppose I need to get myself up for it, whether I want to or not." I felt reluctant, but excited.

"This will be good for you, Susie. It'll get your mind off your sadness, give you something positive to focus on."

"What about Lilly?" I was concerned about leaving her for any length of time.

"Let's plan the tour over the summer and she can go with you." He was smiling and I could tell he was proud of the book, of me, of the company for publishing something so out of the ordinary.

The marketing people at Shilling thought it would be appropriate to launch the book in Jean Ville, where Catfish lived and was buried. Lilly and I agreed but we wanted to wait until after the anniversary of Josh's death because Father George was celebrating a special Catholic mass in his memory in late June.

*

A few weeks before the anniversary of Josh's death, my lawyer had called to tell me that the people who were leasing the Manhattan condominium were moving out. He wanted to know whether I'd like him to find another tenant. I told him I wanted to see the apartment before I decided. Lilly and I hailed a cab and I gave the driver the address Mr. Milton sent to me: 375 Park Avenue. When the taxi stopped in front of a black-glass skyscraper, I thought we were at the wrong address.

"Are we between 52nd and 53rd streets in Midtown?" I bent forward and put both hands on the top of the front seat and looked at the cabbie who smelled of stale smoke and Cheetos.

"Yes, ma'am. This is 375 Park Avenue."

I paid the fare, and Lilly and I slid out of the cab and onto the curb in front of a tall building with white stone steps across the entire front. The building was set back from Park Avenue by a large, open, granite plaza with huge fountains. Two sets of glass doors flanked a revolving entrance under a three-story portico. Lilly and I stood like Mary Tyler Moore at the opening of her television show and stared at the building, bending our necks back as far as we could, but still unable to see the top.

Lilly skipped up the stone steps and waited for me in front of the revolving doors; she got a big kick out of this and insisted on going around twice before it finally poured us into the impressive lobby of the Seagram Building.

Josh hadn't told me his condo was in the Seagram Building designed by German-American architect Ludwig Mies van der Rohe. I'd studied his works, specifically this building completed in 1958, in an art history class in graduate school. It was thirty-eight stories high with businesses on many of the lower floors. We got on the elevator and I looked at the apartment number once again: 3618.

The lobby was lavish by any standards and the building had two very stylish restaurants, The Four Seasons and the Brasserie, both designed by Phillip Johnson. When we unlocked the door to the condominium, we were greeted by the same expensive bronze, travertine, and marble on the floors, countertops, and hardware. Even the shower head was brass, and the furniture, which I presumed was part of the rental package, was glass and bronze and pure luxury. I couldn't imagine Josh living in this fancy place.

"Oh my God!" Lilly was looking out of the floor to ceiling windows that spanned the entire apartment. "People look like ants from up here." We sat on the plush, velvet sectional sofa and I clicked a remote. Music came out of the ceiling and walls and we felt we were surrounded by *Pachelbel's Canon in D.* Lilly jumped and gasped, then burst out laughing.

We walked from room to room, commenting on how we would change things to make the condo more comfortable, less formal, and we agreed that our own furniture would be out of place but we certainly could do better than the cold-feeling brass and glass stuff the original decorator had chosen.

We ate at the Brasserie and left Manhattan as darkness filtered in. In the cab, Lilly and I talked about what we might do once we reached the one-year mark of Josh's death, but decided we would wait to make any life-changing decisions until then.

*

A warm noon sun blazed as we entered the chapel at St. John's and knelt in the first row. I remembered how I had thought my life was over after I'd lost Rodney. Then I'd found Josh and learned to love again, deeply and without restraint. Maybe the memory of the pain I'd endured over losing Rodney was God's way of telling me I could survive losing Josh, too.

Joe was with us at the memorial mass and the three of us went to Josh's grave and the nursing home to visit Emalene afterwards. I yearned to have Josh back, but knew that was a dream. I felt I had started a new life over the past year, although it didn't seem real to me, yet.

We went to Marco's for lunch. Joe told us he was getting married, which was not a surprise. He'd been dating a girl named Bridgette for two years, and Lilly liked her fine. Bridgette had two children from a previous marriage and Joe had taken over being their dad. He seemed happy and satisfied with his new life. Lilly hugged his neck and told him she was happy for him, and she meant it.

"Have you told her?" Joe looked at me over top of Lilly's head.

"Told me what?" Lilly looked from me to Joe and then glared at me, steady and unwavering. "What, Susie? Tell me. I'm almost thirteen years old. I have a right to know whatever it is you two are not telling me." She had tears filling the whites of her eyes and I could see her trying to hold them back. It broke my heart when her feelings were hurt, especially if I had something to do with it. I wanted to kill Joe but, just maybe, it was time.

"You know you were adopted, right?" I was afraid Joe would spill the truth right there in the pizzeria. I kicked him under the table and he flinched.

"I was chosen." Lilly looked defiant. I had to change my strategy because she was mature for her age, having experienced the loss of basically, two parents. What she didn't know was that she still had three—me, Joe, and Rodney.

"Okay. Fair enough. How do I say this... uhm... well... Lilly, well, I'm the one who chose for you to be chosen." My heart was beating so fast I thought it would burst from my chest. We were all very quiet as Lilly tried to absorb what I'd said, while I listened to the murmur of other customers and the clink of spoons hitting the sides of glasses.

"You are the one who did what?"

"I am the one who chose your parents so they could choose you."

"You're my... you gave me away?"

"No! I gave you life, a good life, loving parents. I loved you too much not to give you the best of everything, even if it meant you couldn't be with me. I had nothing to give you."

"Why? Why not?" Her chair scratched the floor when she stood and sounded as if it ripped the linoleum. She stormed out of the restaurant. I shouted at Joe to go after her. It was like watching a movie through the floor-to-ceiling windows. Joe caught her and hugged her to him while she tried to pull away and beat her fists on his chest. She walked away, he grabbed her, she twisted out of his grip, and they moved down the sidewalk towards Utopia Park, Joe's arm over her shoulder, Lilly trying to shake it off, walking quickly until they were out of view.

I sat in that restaurant for two hours, not knowing what to do. I finally paid the bill and walked into the sunshine and strolled, without purpose, in the direction of the park. I automatically sat on the bench where Josh and I always went, where he fed the black-backed gulls and where we watched Lilly chase the birds. Back then we were carefree and unaware of the kind of pain that awaited us.

I'm not sure how long I sat there. I didn't have anything to feed the birds, so they didn't come close to the bench. I was saying to myself, *Don't feel. Don't think.* I tried not to think I might have lost Lilly, not to feel the emptiness that would be mine if she chose to hate me for what I'd done.

It started to get dark, and I could hear the diesel motors and air brakes of buses as they picked up and dropped off passengers near the park. The birds began to fly into the trees to roost for the night, and the temperature dropped. I walked out of the park to the street corner, rubbing my exposed arms to warm myself, and waited for a cab to come by.

Then, suddenly, I heard a high-pitched shout that sounded like my name and saw Lilly running towards me on the sidewalk, yelling, "Susie, Susie. Wait!" I ran towards her and she jumped into my arms and wrapped her legs around my waist as she had done when she was four or five years old.

"I'm so sorry. I thought I'd lost you. We went back to Marco's…"

"It's okay, sweetheart. It's okay. I love you so much. I can't live without you."

"I love you, Susie. I mean, Mama."

"Susie is fine. Let's not change that, okay. You'll make me feel old." I looked up and saw Joe standing about a half-block away. He waved and walked off, smiling.

*

Over the next few days, as we prepared for my book tour, Lilly had lots of questions. I told her I was only eighteen and not married when she was born. I told her it was impossible for me to raise a child while I was in college, so far from family, and that, anyway, my family couldn't know about her. I tried to explain that my dad, at the time, was mayor, then a senator, an important person and what I had done could damage him politically. The explanation sounded crazy to me, so I'm sure she thought it was insane, but she glazed over my explanations and asked about what it was like to be pregnant, alone.

I told her about Josh being with me through my pregnancy and her birth, but that once she was chosen by Joe and Emma, he stopped seeing me and started seeing her. I told her Josh couldn't keep both of us in his life, so he chose her. That seemed to make her feel good and, I think, she might have thought that Josh was her biological father because she never asked the question. There would be a time when she'd know her dad was African American and the pieces of her puzzle wouldn't fit so neatly; but for now, we were straight.

*

It's not the case that you wake up on the one-year anniversary of your spouse's death and things are different. I still missed Josh as much from one morning to the next and went to bed reaching for him every night. The house in Brooklyn Heights held too many memories and ghosts, yet I didn't want to leave for fear I would lose his memory and the sweetness of what we'd had.

In the back of my heart and soul I wondered if what I'd had with Josh was real and authentic. I was losing memories from our life together yet I could still remember every detail of each time I'd been with Rodney. What did that mean?

Lilly and I labored over our decision to sell the house in Brooklyn Heights and we had a number of soul-searching, heart-to-heart talks. We'd decide we could never leave because it would be like leaving Josh behind, then we'd decide the only way to move on with our lives would be to sell the house.

Joe came over for dinner one night and we told him about our dilemma, how we felt one way, then another. He understood, having lost Emalene, and said that moving on was the best way, because staying mired in the past would cripple us.

In the end, we sold the house and kept the Manhattan apartment. I hired a decorator to furnish the apartment with things Lilly and I loved—our beds from Brooklyn Heights, the overstuffed chair from her bedroom, the sectional sofa from our den. We put Emalene's old dining room table in the kitchen and our designer, Amy, added lots of new things. She changed the drapes and brought in pillows and comforters and all sorts of beautiful things that made Lilly and me happy and comfortable. We kept enough things from the past so that we were still attached in a small way, but brought in new things that told us, subliminally, that we had a future.

Decorating the condominium was therapeutic, but it was complicated by our travel schedule for the book tour, which began on the first of July.

We flew to Baton Rouge and drove to Jean Ville. We had four days in our little house on Gravier Road and spent that time visiting with Marianne, Tootsie, and the cousins in the Quarters. I went to see my dad twice and had long, wine-laced chats with Sissy.

*

The book launch took place at the Toussaint Parish Library where I donated ten copies of the book, one for each of the branches in the small towns in the parish. Sissy came to the launch and brought Daddy with her, which was a bit tense since Tootsie and Marianne were there, along with Sam, Tom, Jesse, and their families to whom I'd dedicated the book. I credited them with providing me with information and stories to fill in the gaps after Catfish died and presented Tootsie with an autographed, hardback version of the book.

I saw Daddy say something to Sissy as I was reading from one of the chapters and they disappeared through the door and onto the street. Later, Sissy came over to my house and said Daddy was offended that I didn't recognize him and, instead, gave all the credit for my success to a colored family.

"Not just any colored family, Sissy. Tootsie raised us! And she and Daddy…" I was angry and hurt that Daddy felt that way. After all, the book was about Catfish and his family, not about the Burtons.

"Don't get mad at me. I'm just the messenger." She hugged me, and we laughed because Sissy could make me laugh at my own insanity.

The day after the book launch, Lilly and I drove to New Orleans where we met two Shilling representatives, Billy and Cynthia, at the airport and drove to a local bookstore for another book reading and signing. From there we were off to Jackson, Mississippi; Mobile, Alabama; and Jacksonville, Florida. Every two days there was an event, followed by a day of travel, checking into a hotel, getting some rest, and meetings. Lilly became a vital part of our four-person team and helped with handouts and book supplies at the events.

We left Jacksonville on a Friday morning and drove to Charleston, South Carolina, arriving at a hotel on King Street early in the afternoon. We checked in, put our luggage in the rooms and walked to Harvey's, the bookstore downtown where the event would be held the next evening. We went to dinner and returned to the hotel.

I thought I recognized a tall man who was talking with the concierge at the hotel desk when I walked by, but Lilly was talking to me and I ignored my original impulse to speak with him. The next evening, as I stood at the microphone and read one of the stories from the book, I noticed the same man walk in through the glass doors and take a seat in the back of the room. There were fifty or sixty people in a deep room so I couldn't make out the face, but something about his presence, his swagger, his demeanor made me pause. I kept reading and tried not to stare at him.

After the readings, people queued up in front of a table where I sat signing books. As each person got to the front of the line I'd look up and ask their name, then write a short dedication, sign my name and date it. It was a long evening, and by the time the last person finally got to the table I didn't look up.

"Your name?" I took a book from Billy and opened it to the title page and started to write.

"Rodney." His voice was the same as ever—throaty and full, and I could smell his familiar scent of Ivory soap and starch and mint, orange, and lilac. My hand froze with the pen in it and I looked up slowly. A wide smile spread across his face and his eyes lit up, green with amber specks. "Rodney Thibault."

I dropped my pen and stared at him. The book slammed shut over my hand but I didn't feel it. Then my impulse was to look for Lilly and hide her. She was in the back of the room helping Cynthia pack books and flyers. Billy was standing next to me and I could feel his chagrin, waiting for me to sign the last book so we could leave and have dinner.

I stood up, and Rodney and I were eye-to-eye, the table between us. I was so nervous that he'd see Lilly, afraid of what would happen if they met each other, here, in public.

"Can you give me a phone number and I'll call you later?" I whispered across the table. He bent down and took the pen I'd dropped and wrote a number on one of the flyers.

"Will you sign the book for me?" He left the flyer on the table and stood up straight. I sat down and scribbled a note, his name and mine on the title page, and when I looked at it I realized what I'd written and blushed. He took the book and walked to the register while I sat stuck in my chair, unable to move.

I didn't call him.

We left the next day for Raleigh, then Virginia Beach, where I put Cynthia and Billy on a plane to New York and Lilly and I started the long drive back to Jean Ville. We had two weeks to recover, then we would fly back to New York for several events in the city and a review with the folks at Shilling about book sales.

My heart was still beating extra fast from the encounter with Rodney. I thought a lot about what to tell Lilly, because meeting him was bound to happen again.

Part Four: 1984

～Chapter Twenty～

Whole Again

March 1, 1984

> *Dear Susie,*
>
> *I'm sure you are shocked to hear from me. It's taken me over a year to find the courage to write after seeing you in Charleston last summer and not hearing from you. Thank you for the personal inscription. It means everything to me.*
>
> *"We are forever connected... Always, Susie."*
>
> *I've written you countless letters that I never mailed. I finally convinced myself that you would not want to find out things through the grapevine that you should hear from me, personally. We have too much history and I have too much respect for you to ever hurt you (again).*
>
> *Maria and I didn't work out. We stayed married almost two years but we were both broken, damaged people from the War, and it just didn't work. I've spent the past eight years getting myself back on track and I think I'm better than I ever was. I saw a psychiatrist for a few years, I've worked hard, and will retire as a Major—not bad for ten years in the Army and thirty-five years old.*
>
> *The main thing I want to tell you is that I'm moving back home next summer after I retire. I'm planning to go into practice with Jeffrey and Sarah, who opened their law offices two years ago in Jean Ville. It's*

simple family law, probably boring compared to what I've been doing, but it's where I'll start.

I heard you got married and that you lost your husband. I know you well enough to believe that if you married him, you must have loved him with all your heart, and I am so very sorry for your loss. I hope you are healing and that your sadness lessens every day. I have prayed for you and thought about you during your mourning.

I would like to call you to catch up when you feel ready.

Yours forever,

Rod

Lilly and I were in Jean Ville for spring break and I was opening the mail that had stacked up. I sat down hard on the sofa and without realizing it, pressed the letter to my chest. I started to cry, then I didn't know why I was crying and tried to stop, but the tears kept coming. Lilly walked in the living room and stood looking at me.

"Why are you crying?"

"I don't know, honey." The tears kept running down my cheeks unchecked and I couldn't control them.

"How can you cry and not know why?"

"I'm not sure. The tears just started coming and they won't stop." I tried to smile but it was barely a smirk. Lilly sat next to me and put her arm over my shoulder. She would be fifteen in August and was almost as tall as me, and she was gorgeous, like her dad. Her brownish, auburn hair fell in long corkscrew curls down her back and she often had to pull some of the soft curlicues away from her face with a barrette or a clip. Her oval face had high cheekbones and her eyes were as large as half-dollars, only they were shaped like almonds, pointed on both ends. Her skin was the color of walnuts, almost as light as mine, but with a tan-yellow cast to it so it was obvious she was part African American, even if only a small part.

We sat without talking for a while. I could hear the carpenters outside building the carport that I'd been meaning to construct ever since I traded our brown Torino for a navy blue Oldsmobile. I was eyeing a red Mustang fastback for Lilly's fifteenth birthday, so the garage needed to be large enough for two cars, our ride-on lawn mower and some yard tools. We didn't need cars in New York, but when we were in Jean Ville they were a must.

"What would you like for supper?" I broke the silence and turned to look at Lilly. She pulled the paper I had clutched to my chest from my hands.

"Did this make you cry?" She started to read it and I snatched it from her. She looked shocked. I'd never done anything so, well, almost violent. "What's the matter?"

"It's a letter from a friend. We don't read each other's mail, remember."

"I'm sorry. I didn't know it was a letter. I just want to know what made you sad." She looked sad and angry at the same time and I knew she was hurt and trying to hide her feelings. I hugged her close and kissed the top of her head.

"I'm sorry, sweetheart. I didn't mean to scare you. It's just that... well... it's personal. I need to digest what my friend said. You understand, don't you?"

"Not really, but it's okay. It's your mail." She got up and started to walk away, then she turned towards me. "I didn't think we had secrets." She stood there and I could tell she knew there was something I wasn't telling her, something that she should know.

"You're right. We shouldn't have secrets and I guess I've kept this one too long. Something you need to know, deserve to know, about your biological dad." She plopped down in the chair across from the sofa and slumped low, her shoulders below the back of the chair, her chin on her chest.

"It wasn't Josh? My dad... I mean?"

"No. I'm sorry. I never said it was."

"But you let me believe…" She stared at her feet and started picking at her fingernails. I was at a loss as to how to tell her.

"Lilly, surely you realize that some part of you is African American. Josh was white. I'm white. How could you justify that?"

"I don't know. Mama is black." Her eyes flew opened when she heard her own words, and she pulled in a gallon of air and held it. "That's right. Mama was not my…"

"Yes, she was. She was your mother in every way. And she was a wonderful mother. It takes more than biology to make parents."

"So; my dad. I mean my biological father. He was black?"

"Is. Is black."

"Oh." She was quiet and I felt she needed time to digest what I'd said. We sat there for a long time and I watched the darkness begin to crawl over our lawn. The birds stopped tweeting. The crickets began to chirp. I heard an owl hoot in the distance, then a car went by. I inhaled the sweet fragrance of the lilies on the dining room table.

I felt afraid—afraid to mishandle things and lose Lilly's love.

"What was, what is… was he like?" She was looking at her hands that rested in her lap.

"I haven't seen him in ten years, but he still exists," I told the white lie because I could justify that seeing him in Charleston was not really seeing him, and running into him at the Burger Barn.

I waited and tried to gather my thoughts. "I can only tell you what he *was* like… amazing, kind, caring, loving, smart, generous; all the things you'd want your father to be, and more. And he was gorgeous. You look a lot like him. He's tall, maybe 6' 4", with light skin and big greenish-hazel eyes with amber specks. He was the most gentle, interesting, intelligent person I'd ever known. Until I met Josh, I didn't think anyone else like him existed."

"Does he have a name?"

"Rodney."

"Rodney?"

"Yes. He's a lawyer, and he's been in the army for ten years. He's getting out next summer and moving back home."

"Home?"

"Yes. He's from Jean Ville. It's where we met, where we fell in love. And that's the most important thing you should know. We loved each other very much when we made you."

"Why has he never… I mean he's never tried to meet me." She looked at me and I took a deep breath. How could I tell her that I had lied to everyone? I had to blurt it out.

"He doesn't know about you." She looked at me with shock and dismay and I, too, wondered how I could have gone fifteen years without telling Rodney he had a daughter. It seemed the longer I waited, the more impossible it was to tell him. Now he was getting out of the army and moving back to Jean Ville, and he would see her and he would know.

Lilly stared at me as if she didn't know me. I barely knew myself. I couldn't remember why it had been so important to keep my pregnancy from him and then to keep Lilly a secret from him. It seemed ludicrous now, but back then it had made perfect sense. "I never told him."

"How could he not know you were pregnant?"

"I was in New York. He was in Baton Rouge in college. We couldn't see each other. He never knew."

"I need some air." Lilly got up and stormed out of the house, the screen door slamming behind her. I watched through the front window and saw her run towards the Quarters. I hoped Marianne was home. I went to the phone and called her number. She picked up on the second ring.

"Mari. Lilly is on her way to the Quarters. I just told her about Rodney. She's very upset. Would you please…?"

"I'll take care of it. It had to happen sometime. Just calm down. I'll talk to her and call you later. I love you, Susie. It'll be okay." Marianne always knew exactly what to say and how to say it.

I'd never told Marianne that Rodney was Lilly's father or that I was her mother. I'd stuck to the story of Joe and Emalene Franklin. In fact, the only two people who knew that Lilly was my and Rodney's child were Josh and Emalene and they were now both... gone.

I called Sissy. "Can you come over?" I hung up the phone and fell on the sofa. I thought about all the things Lilly would need to know now that she knew about Rodney. The Thibaults were her grandparents. They should know Lilly, and Lilly should know them. She needed to know that her best friends were actually her cousins, not only because Marianne and I were sisters but also because Rodney's uncle, Bo, was married to Tootsie's sister, Jesse.

Most importantly, she needed to understand that blacks and whites weren't allowed to date, to love, to marry in the '60s and '70s in the deep South without being punished, even killed, by bigots. Even in the 1980s, discrimination still existed in the South.

I'd have to teach her about prejudice and hate and bigotry, and I didn't want her to know any of that. The more I thought, the more I cried.

When Sissy walked in, I blurted it all out. She listened as though she'd always known and had waited for me to be honest with her. She wasn't shocked or disgusted about what I'd done. Her attitude gave me strength. When I ran out of words and tears, she got up, went to the kitchen, and came back with a bottle of wine and two wine glasses.

"Here's to honesty, and how great you'll feel tomorrow when you realize you no longer have to keep all of this inside." She opened the bottle and poured two generous glasses. We took our wine outside to see the progress on the garage, and we talked and laughed like sisters who have no secrets are apt to do.

The next day Marianne came over for coffee before daylight. Lilly had slept at her house and she'd called to tell me so I wouldn't worry.

"She'll be fine. It's time this secret came out. Can you tell me what prompted it?" Marianne took a long sip of her coffee and looked at me out the tops of her eyes. I pulled Rodney's letter from the pocket of my robe. I'd slept with it all night and had read it so many times the paper was wrinkled, the ink smudged, and the words memorized.

I handed it to Marianne and she read it without looking up. "Well, now you have to tell Rodney."

"He'll know as soon as he meets Lilly." I stirred my coffee for the umpteenth time. It was cold when I took the first sip.

"Maybe you should write him, tell him in advance. Maybe you should tell the Thibaults."

"I want to tell Rodney first. I think, deep inside, I've always wanted to tell him before I told anyone, even Lilly, or you, or Sissy. But it hasn't worked out that way. I think he deserves to know before anyone else finds out. I hope you and Sissy will honor that and not tell anyone until I can tell him."

"Where is he?" She turned the letter over as though looking for an address.

"I'm not sure. I didn't look at the return address." I got up and went into the living room and found the envelope on the coffee table, where I must have dropped it when I pulled the letter out. "Oh my God!" I shouted. Marianne came rushing to me. "He's in Brooklyn. Brooklyn, New York at Fort Hamilton."

April 3, 1984
Dear Rodney,

I'm sorry it's taken me so long to respond to your letter. To begin with, it shocked me and took a while to digest. Now that I've had time to think about things, I realize there's too much to say in a letter. I will be in New York next week and wonder whether we could meet in person. I have an apartment in Manhattan, or we can meet at a restaurant, although I think our conversation should be private.

Let me know if you are agreeable to seeing me and I'll send you all the details.

Always,
Susie

April 6, 1984
Dear Susie,
I'll meet with you anywhere, anytime. Just tell me when and where and I'll be there.
Can't wait.
Yours forever,
Rodney

I didn't tell Lilly I was meeting with Rodney. I was afraid. What if he became angry and didn't want to meet her? If that happened she would think he didn't want her. What if he didn't want her? *What ifs* were crawling around my brain at warp speed and I knew I had to tell him first and let him get used to the idea before I introduced them. It was only fair.

On Tuesday, Joe came to get Lilly to spend a few days with him and his family. Lilly and I had patched things up and had talked through things *ad nauseam*. I'd answered all her questions, explained race relations in the '60s, my dad's political position, and the dangers that Rodney and his family had been in. She had a difficult time understanding the kind of prejudice that controlled the South. She'd been raised in New York where there was no Ku Klux Klan or Jim

Crow laws, where miscegenation never existed, where she lived a life of privilege. And although things had changed in Jean Ville—the schools were integrated, the "Whites Only" signs were gone, blacks could eat in restaurants, get rooms in hotels, and ride on any train car—they hadn't changed enough. Lilly and I didn't live there. We only visited on holidays and during the summers and spent most of our time with Tootsie's family in the Quarters.

Lilly wasn't angry anymore, but she still seemed eager to get away from me and be with Joe. When I asked her how long she planned to stay with his family she said, "I'll call you when I'm ready to come back. Maybe when it's time to start school."

Wednesday morning I called the phone number Rodney had sent me. I had a meeting scheduled at Shilling, but I wasn't sure about Rodney's work schedule.

"Hi. It's me," I said when he answered the phone. I took a deep breath and tried to prepare myself to hear his voice but still, when he spoke, it took the wind out of me and I had to sit down in the chair at the breakfast table.

"Hi, yourself. It's so good to hear from you. How are you?" His voice was still low, raspy, sexy, and familiar, as if he'd spoken to me every day for the past ten years.

"I'm fine." Something caught in my throat and I tried to swallow but couldn't. I tried to speak, but words were stuck somewhere in my chest. "Uhm…"

"Are you in Manhattan? When can I see you?"

"Yes. I'm here. Uhm. I have a meeting with my publisher. Uhm. When are you, uhm, free?"

"Lunch?"

"Can we make it closer to dinner?" I was thinking that if we met for lunch and he had to get back to work that wouldn't give us much time. "Maybe you could come over and we can get take out?"

"Sure. Five? Is that too early?"

"No. I mean yes. I mean no, it's not too early. Yes, five is fine." I had to hang up before I threw up. I felt frightened in a way I couldn't remember feeling since I'd waited for Rodney to show up in Washington, DC. I put the receiver back on the hook and stared at the phone as if Rodney might come flying out of it into my apartment.

I took a long shower, washed and dried my hair, dressed in a business suit, low-heeled pumps, pearls, and a smart handbag. I went to Mr. Mobley's office at Shilling and met with the marketing team and learned that *The Catfish Stories* had exceeded expectations and there was a plan for another print run and distribution to all the bookstore chains in the country. We talked about the book signings that Billy and Cynthia had scheduled for me throughout New York and New Jersey over the next month.

"We might look at international sales at the end of the year if the book does well on the retail shelves," Mobley said. "I sure wish you'd come back to work here and find more of these types of books for us. Surely there are other nonfiction authors writing new and different narratives that appeal to the general reader."

"I'm honored that you would want me back, but my life is too full right now. I'm raising a teenager, spending a quarter of the year in Louisiana, and writing another book." I smiled at Mobley and he nodded as if he knew what my answer would be.

He asked if I'd like to have lunch with him at his club but I declined. I needed the afternoon to prepare myself, to go over what I would say to Rodney, to think, to obsess, to drive myself crazy.

I went shopping and bought Lilly some new school clothes, although she didn't like it when I chose things for her. I needed something to do to fill the time, and I reasoned with myself that we would have fun exchanging them if they didn't suit her.

I stopped at the bakery and got a freshly baked loaf of French bread and two individual cheesecakes in small pie tins. I went to the local deli near my building and bought cheese and a couple of bottles of wine. Then I dropped in at the Brasserie and asked for a menu. I told the hostess I would be calling to order dinner and someone would come down to pick it up. She knew me from the many times I'd been in there and said "No problem." I went up to my apartment, put everything away, and had nothing to do for an hour.

I changed into jeans and a silk blouse that buttoned up the front. It was a blush color, and I knew it looked good on me and hung from my shoulders to the top of the zipper on my jeans in just the right way. I brushed my hair 100 strokes until it was shiny and almost red. I brushed my teeth, reapplied lip gloss, twice, sprayed perfume on my cleavage and behind my ears, and then I paced.

Finally, the doorman buzzed from downstairs and said I had a guest, "A Major Thibault, Ma'am."

"Please send him up, Joseph." I opened the door to the hallway, then closed it. I waited in the foyer inside my apartment, then went into the living room so I wouldn't open the door too quickly when he rang the doorbell. I was so nervous that I went back into the foyer and opened the door to peek into the hall. The elevator door opened and Rodney stepped off wearing his dress blues, his hat under his arm, looking more handsome than I remembered.

Beyond my memories and even dreams of how handsome Rodney was, this creature standing in the hall staring at me was the most majestic, elegant, beautiful man I'd ever seen.

He walked up to me and our toes almost touched. Neither of us spoke. We simply drank in each other's presence and tasted the other's aura. I couldn't move. He reached his hand out and touched the side of my arm and I quivered all over. I felt goose bumps crawl up my back and onto my neck. My mouth went dry and I could smell that familiar Rodney scent.

I felt the exact same way I'd felt the last time I saw him, ten years ago at the airport in Baton Rouge when I left him behind, thinking we would meet in DC the following week to marry me.

I'm not sure how long we stood there with his hand on my arm and my feet glued to the travertine floor. What happened next seemed automatic, unplanned but natural. Both of my arms lifted as though they belonged to another body and they landed on Rodney's shoulders and my hands folded around his neck. He bent his head and when his lips pressed against mine my knees gave way and I slid, but he caught me and lifted me off the floor like a bride, carried me into the foyer, and shut the door with his foot. I heard his hat hit the floor and wasn't aware of anything else as he carried me to the sofa and gently lay me down.

He sat beside me, his butt near my waist, his hands on either side of my head. My arms were still around his neck and he kissed me again, with a passion and intensity I had forgotten existed. His tongue lightly touched the back of my teeth and I sucked in as if I could drink him, all of him, and swallow him so I'd never have to let him go again.

It all happened so fast and was so intense that later, as we lay naked in my huge bed and he stroked my hair and blew his warm breath in my ear, I marveled at the peace I felt. There was no guilt or remorse. I wasn't embarrassed or ashamed. I was happy and content as though I was exactly where I was always meant to be.

No words had been spoken. Not one.

As we lay there blissfully happy, I was no longer afraid to tell him the truth. I knew, in my knowing, that he loved me beyond measure and would forgive my mistakes in judgment.

So I told him about Lilly.

I told him about being pregnant and afraid. I told him about Josh and how he was with me during my pregnancy but left because he realized I could never love him like I loved Rodney.

I explained everything—about how, after Rodney decided not to come to New York to marry me I was so devastated I didn't know where to turn, and that somehow I felt God took me to the home of Joe and Emalene Franklin where I met and fell in love with Lilly.

I explained it all. I left nothing out because I knew now was the time for honesty and that I could never go back and say, "Oh, I forgot this part."

Every now and then, Rodney would touch my shoulder or kiss my forehead or blow his warm breath on the side of my face or push his fingers through my hair as he lay on his side resting on his elbow, his chin in his palm and his leg across mine. I was on my back and often stared at the ceiling as I talked. From time to time, he'd put his fingers under my chin and turn my head so I would look at him and he would mouth "I love you," kiss me lightly, and I would go on explaining.

"And she's wonderful, Rod. You will love her. She looks like you and she has your disposition. She's kind and sweet and beautiful. No, she's gorgeous. And she's smart. Do I sound like a doting mother?"

"Yes, and I love it. I love that you love our daughter. I love that you think she's special."

"She *is* special. You'll see. Everyone thinks so, not just me." I looked at him and felt like a little girl trying to convince my daddy I was telling the truth. Rodney laughed at me and kissed me, and pulled me to him and we made love slowly and passionately, and honestly.

And I felt like a whole person for the first time in a very long time.

*

I called Joe at work the next day, after Rodney went back to the base. I told him that I'd met with Rodney and told him everything and that he wanted to meet Lilly. I asked Joe if he could prepare Lilly for me.

"I'd like to meet him first, Susie. I mean, she's my daughter, and I should know him, right?"

"Absolutely, Joe." When we hung up I called Rodney and asked whether he could have lunch with Joe that day. Joe didn't want me there and I felt I needed to respect his wishes so it would be just the two of them, men talk.

I was nervous as I watched the clock from noon until two o'clock when the phone finally rang. It was Joe asking if he could come over. Now I was really nervous about what had happened. I tried to call Rodney but he wasn't in, so I paced until I met Joe in the hall as he got off the elevator. At first glance, I could tell that everything was okay.

Joe sat on the sofa and I stood, wringing my hands.

"He's great, Susie. I mean, I'm really impressed with Rodney and, to be honest, I didn't want to like him. Competition, I guess." Joe told me he was totally taken by Rodney's honesty, sensitivity, and his desire to know Lilly.

"He told me that I would always be Lilly's daddy; that he could not replace those fifteen years. He said he would accept any relationship that worked for Lilly—uncle, big brother, cousin. He said that Lilly was the most important person in this equation and we should all be sensitive to her feelings. He's quite a special man, Susie. I guess I should have known he would be exceptional if you loved him enough to have his child and protect him and his family the way you did."

"Is that how you see it, Joe? That I protected him? I feel like I've been dishonest with everyone." I could feel tears start to sting my eyes and I tried to hold them back. It meant a lot that Joe didn't think I was some awful liar who did what I did for selfish reasons.

"Of course. And it's how I've explained things to Lilly. I told her that you could have had an abortion and that would have made your life a lot easier. I told her you couldn't tell anyone about being pregnant, much less pregnant by a Negro, because the Klan had almost succeeded in killing Rodney's dad and brother and almost got Rodney, just because they knew the two of you had been together. So had they found out you were pregnant with Rodney's child... well, it's hard for her to understand that kind of hatred and bigotry, but she's a smart girl, and I think she's coming around."

"How should they meet? I mean, what do I do?"

"It's not up to you anymore. It's up to Rodney and Lilly. Just invite him to your apartment after Lilly gets back. Make sure they both know the other will be there. No surprises. They deserve honesty from you; that's all you owe them now."

Joe finished his coffee and got up to leave. He hugged me and told me to stop worrying, because everything would work out. I tried to heed his advice but I was a wreck by the time Rodney came over after work. I fell into his arms and shook and cried and he held me and kissed my hair and rubbed my back and said all the right things.

We had dinner downstairs at the Four Seasons and I told him Lilly would be home the next day. I asked if he was ready to meet her.

"I can't wait to meet her. Joe says she's exceptional. That makes two of you, so far. He's a good man, and I feel lucky you found him to be Lilly's dad."

"I haven't talked to Lilly about meeting you, yet. Joe is going to pave the way, so I'm not sure whether she's ready. Will your feelings be hurt if she wants to wait?"

"Of course not. We need to take this at her pace. But just so you know, I've taken the rest of the week off, and I'm at your disposal." He picked up my hand that he'd been holding on top of the table and kissed the tips of my fingers. I felt chills run down my spine and between my legs. I was still amazed by the visceral reaction I had to Rodney's touch.

We talked about other things besides Lilly and how much we still loved each other, but we didn't talk about the future of our relationship. I guess we both felt a lot depended on Lilly's reaction to Rodney.

I told him about my meeting with Mr. Mobley and that the book's sales were going well. I also told him about a phone call I'd had from my attorney, Mr. Milton, who said there was oil on the property in Texas that Josh left me and the royalties were being deposited in my bank account every month.

"When he told me my bank balance I almost fainted." I didn't look at Rodney because I was afraid he would be turned off by all of my news of book sales and oil wells.

"I'm thinking about building a wing on the hospital in Jean Ville in Josh's name, a center for cleft lip and pallet surgery for underprivileged kids. Mr. Milton thinks we should call it The Ryan Center."

"Wow. That's a phenomenal idea, and a good use of the income from the oil." Rodney was still holding my hand and I finally looked at him. He was smiling, not turned off in the least.

I told him that Mr. Milton said it was essential to find a corporate lawyer in Louisiana to handle my affairs since the Ryan Center would be in there.

"'Louisiana's laws are unusual,' Milton told me. 'they still adhere to Napoleonic laws, so you need an attorney who is versed in legal matters in that state.' You know anyone who fits that bill?" I smiled at Rodney, and he nodded, then kissed my hand.

Rodney said he had passed the Louisiana bar exam after he graduated from law school. He agreed to meet with Mr. Milton to discuss the legalities of building the center.

Rodney's brain turned me on as much as his body did, and by the time we made love that night I surrendered completely to him. No secrets. He even loved me after he discovered I was wealthy.

The only thing standing in our way now was Lilly.

*

She came home about midday Thursday and threw herself in my arms as though we hadn't seen each other in years. She told me how much she missed me and loved me, and how she hated being away from me.

"Susie, I'm sorry I've been so obstinate about Rodney and you not telling me. Daddy explained and, really, I don't understand how people could be the way they were, but I get it. I mean I do see why you couldn't tell me. I guess I still don't understand why you couldn't tell Rodney."

"I sometimes don't understand what that eighteen-year-old girl was thinking when she believed he shouldn't know. I was so afraid the Klan would kill him or a member of his family and it would be my fault. All I can say is, if it was a mistake, I am really sorry. I'm not eighteen anymore. Maybe today I would make a different decision."

"When I think that you had me when you were only three years older than I am now, I can understand how your decision-making might have been immature." She put her head on my shoulder and wrapped her arms around my waist and we rocked back and forth a little, as we had when she was younger and I'd try to soothe her boo boo or hurt feelings.

Later we sat in the kitchen and had sandwiches and iced tea, and she gabbed about her step-brother and -sister and the new house Joe and his wife had bought, and how glad she was that she didn't live there. "I love seeing Daddy, but I like being with you best. And I love being in Jean Ville. I can't wait for Thanksgiving break." She took a bite of her sandwich and it was obvious she didn't realize that what she said was profound and made me feel happy.

"Would you like to meet Rodney?" I whispered it as if afraid for her to hear and become angry, or reject my suggestion.

"Of course I'd like to meet him. You mean when he moves back to Jean Ville and we go for holiday?"

"Well, sooner if you'd like. He's stationed in Brooklyn."

"Brooklyn, New York? Across the river, where we used to live?"

"Yes. Fort Hamilton. He's a Major in the army, a JAG officer. That's a…"

"I know what a JAG is—basically a lawyer in the military. A Major? Really?"

"He's special, Lilly. I've told you that, but I guess you have to meet him and judge for yourself."

"When can he come over?" She stood up, and her chair screeched. She seemed excited, filled with anticipation.

"Whenever you say. You're in charge." I looked up at her from my seat and felt incredulous at her positive reaction.

"Well, NOW! As soon as he can. Call him." She was so excited I expected her to start jumping up and down like she had when she was a child and Santa brought her a pink bicycle and a miniature kitchen. I got up and went to the den and picked up the phone on the library table behind the sofa. She followed me and almost hung on my shoulder as I dialed Rodney's phone number.

"Hi," I said when he answered. "You busy?"

"I've been waiting to hear from you, beautiful. How's your day?"

"Pretty good, I…" Behind me Lilly was chanting.

"Ask him, ask him." She was impatient and acted excited in a way I hadn't seen her behave since she'd become a teenager. She was good at keeping her feelings in check, trying to act like an adult, but today she was acting like a typical fifteen-year-old.

"I was wondering when you could come over. Lilly's home and she'd like to meet you." I held my breath and there was silence for longer than usual while I allowed myself to second-guess everything. But Rodney came through.

"Wow. That's great. I'll take the subway and be there in less than an hour. I love you, Susie." I heard the buzz after he hung up but continued to hold the phone to my ear.

"What'd he say? What'd he say?"

"He's on his way." I hung up the receiver and felt like I was going to be sick. I went to the bathroom and vomited my sandwich. It was all too much. When I came out of the bathroom, Lilly was sitting on my bed.

"What should I wear?" She was still excited, and I had to get in gear. I swallowed my fear and helped her select jeans and a shirt from the new clothes I'd bought her. She didn't complain that I'd shopped without her or say I didn't know her taste. She liked almost everything I'd bought and chose a silk shirt that had a collar and two chest pockets. It was emerald green and brought out her eyes. She tried to tame her curls with a hairbrush but it was impossible, so she pulled it back in a ponytail and tendrils popped out around her face. She looked beautiful and innocent, and very much like Rodney.

We sat on the sofa to wait but she was fidgety and kept getting up and walking to the intercom. She would go into the foyer and open the door to the hall and peer at the elevators. Finally, she sat down again and the buzzer sounded on the living room wall near the foyer. We both jumped up.

I went to the intercom and Lilly was hanging on me, lifting herself up on her toes then letting her heels down again, over and over. I pressed the button and said, "Yes?"

"Major Thibault is in the lobby, Mrs. Ryan," Joseph said.

"Please send him up, Joseph." I looked at Lilly and her happy face had turned to a huge question mark. It scared me.

"Thibault?" She mouthed the word, then repeated it aloud, "Thibault?"

"Yes. Rodney Thibault." I walked into the foyer and had my hand on the doorknob when she whispered behind me.

"You mean Mr. Ray Thibault who owns the Esso station is my…?" She was so close I could smell the turkey on her breath. I wasn't sure how to answer her, and there was very little time to explain. I turned to face her.

"I'm sorry. Did I forget to tell you his last name?"

"That means Ellie Thibault is my cousin?" Her mind was going in a thousand directions and I didn't know how to get her to refocus on the fact that she was about to meet her father for the first time.

"I don't know Ellie. Who is she?" I was lost in Lilly's dilemma when the doorbell rang, and I jumped and pulled on the doorknob that was already in my hand.

Standing in the hall in starched blue jeans and a green and beige striped rugby shirt was Rodney. Even though I was expecting him, I was surprised. He looked over my shoulder and things happened so quickly that before I could say a word he walked past me, squeezing my shoulder as he went by, and when I turned around, Lilly was in his arms. They were both crying, her arms wrapped around his waist, his long arms around her shoulders. He was bent over and the side of his face rested on the top of her head. I watched the natural love between a father and daughter happen.

Today I wonder why I worried so much about Rodney and Lilly meeting and not loving each other. It was no different from the first time I met her. This father and daughter were so much alike— tender-hearted, caring, non-judging, smart, and they automatically loved each other without reservation.

I can't describe the reunion we had that night. All three of us were in love with each other. We floated downstairs to have dinner at the Brasserie and I don't remember what we ate. Rodney asked Lilly questions and she chattered on about her past and her visits to Jean Ville and how she was so happy to know that her best friends were her cousins and how she wanted to be a doctor when she was older and that she didn't have a boyfriend yet because none of the boys were smart enough.

She asked Rodney about his life in the military, and I learned that he'd been stationed in England and had seen all of Western Europe and parts of the Eastern Bloc. He'd been to North Africa and Egypt, and was interested in visiting Israel someday.

I was a spectator, and it was like watching the best movie I'd ever seen, listening to them talk and learning things about both Lilly and Rodney I didn't know. Every now and then one of them would realize I was there and say something to me like, "Did you hear that, he's been to Egypt." or "You didn't tell me she wanted to be a doctor." Otherwise, I sat at the table and had the most sensational evening of my entire life with the two people I loved most in the world.

Lilly and I saw Rodney every day after that evening. He didn't spend the night, because we didn't think it was appropriate, but being with Rodney and Lilly was better than making love.

The week before Thanksgiving, Rodney showed up with pizza and we sat in the kitchen with a six-pack of Cokes. Rodney and Lilly had burping contests, and I kept reprimanding them for their manners. We laughed a lot. Then Rodney asked us if we could go into the living room, that he had something serious to discuss with us. I had no idea where this was going as Lilly and I sat on the sofa, holding hands and Rodney paced in front of us with his hands clasped behind his back.

"I guess there's no other way to say this but to come right out with it." He stopped pacing and stood with his feet apart, hands still behind his back and looked from me to Lilly, back and forth. "I want to marry you. Both of you. So how can I convince you to say, 'Yes'?"

He brought his hands around to the front and had a black velvet box in each palm. He got down on both knees and flipped the boxes open. The box in his left hand held a two-carat diamond surrounded by smaller diamonds that made the stone look triple the size. The other box held a lime green peridot. It was Lilly's birthstone, and she knew it right away.

Neither Lilly nor I spoke at first, and I saw beads of perspiration gather on Rodney's brow as we hesitated. I was waiting for Lilly and, I guess, she was waiting for me. We finally looked at each other and she nodded at me. I turned to Rodney and said, "I'm convinced!"

"Me, too," Lilly jumped off the sofa and hugged Rodney's neck. He put my ring on the coffee table and lifted one of his knees so Lilly could sit on it. As he slid the ring on her finger, I was reminded of the time Josh had done that very thing when Lilly was six. I wondered if she remembered.

She looked at me and a sign passed between the two of us that said, "We've done this before. It was good then, and it's good now."

Lilly got off Rodney's knee and sat on the sofa, admiring her ring, turning it around, holding it up to the light.

He looked at me and pointed then retracted his index finger, a sign for me to come closer. I got up and sat on his knee and he slipped the diamond ring on my finger. I hugged him and we kissed deeply and passionately until Lilly said, "Hey, you two, stop it, you're embarrassing me." We all started laughing and had a group hug that ended with the three of us on the floor rolling around, tickling each other and comparing our rings.

That night after Lilly went to bed, Rodney and I went to my bedroom, made love, and he spent the night for the first time since he'd met Lilly. I thought he should be gone by the time she woke up in the morning but he said, "No secrets. We will build this family on honesty."

When she got up the next morning, he was sitting at the kitchen table reading the paper, drinking coffee. She poured a glass of orange juice and sat with us as if it was perfectly normal to get up and have breakfast with your mother and father.

∽ Chapter Twenty-One ∽

∽

Mama

L ILLY HAD THANKSGIVING WEEK off, and as much as we hated
to leave Rodney, we flew to Louisiana to spend her vacation
on Gravier Road. She was pensive during the cab ride to the
airport. After we were checked in and waiting at our gate, I noticed
how fidgety she was and knew there was something on her mind,
something she needed to talk about but didn't know how to start.

"You okay, sweetheart?" I patted her leg and left my hand on her
knee. "Want to talk about something?"

"I was just wondering about you and Rodney. I mean, I don't
want to be nosey, but how long have you known him. When was I
born? Where was he?"

Let's see, how do I begin? Hmmmm.

A Love Story
1963-present
*I'll start when I was almost thirteen years old and my dad pulled
into the Esso station in Jean Ville and I was sitting shotgun in his car.
The most gorgeous boy I'd ever seen came to the car and started washing
the windshield while my dad was in the office with the owner. I tried to
ignore the boy but my eyes seemed to be part of a magnetic field that
pulled me towards him. I knew everyone at school around my own age so
I wondered how I could have missed him.*

When he told me he went to the colored school I didn't believe him. I mean, he didn't look colored and anyway, he had such refined manners and seemed so, I don't know, dignified, intelligent, sophisticated—not that there aren't Negroes who have all those qualities, it's just that the only colored people I knew at the time were Catfish and Tootsie and well, you know Tootsie. She's just down to earth, as was Catfish.

Anyway, the boy started talking to me and even though I was too young to understand, I was attracted to him way back then. It was about two years later, when I was around your age, that I really fell in love with Rodney. I'll never forget it.

Over the next two years I saw him whenever I went with my dad to the Esso station, and we'd talk.

One afternoon, Marianne and I were in the hayloft in the Quarters and he showed up, just swung his long leg onto the loft from the ladder and scooted towards me on his knees. He reached his arms out when he saw me and I didn't know what to do at first, but when I looked at him and he smiled the most genuine smile, I moved towards him. He touched one of my hands and I shivered. He let his fingers walk up my arm while he scooted closer to me, until he could grip my shoulder. His other hand found mine and he took it into his as if he'd just asked me to dance.

All the time he stared at me and I looked over his shoulder at Marianne who mouthed, "What are you doing?" I shrugged and looked back at Rodney and thought, he's so gorgeous and the look on his face was indescribable. I can still see it today, all these years later.

He held my hand and we sat with our backs to the wall, our legs in front of us and our thighs and shoulders touching. He started to talk. I don't remember what he said, but I loved the sound of his voice. It was deep and raspy with just a hint of Cajun-ness in the twang. He wore a Dallas Cowboys baseball cap and looked masculine, handsome, and gentle all at the same time. Later I learned the dictionary has a word to describe him: mansuetude, which I translated to mean, gentle masculinity.

He had broad shoulders and seemed so big next to me, and I wasn't small at five-feet, seven-inches. I remember he told me I was beautiful. It was the first time anyone had ever told me that. I felt prickly pins run up and down my spine and was speechless. It was stifling hot and humid in the hayloft and where our shoulders touched, our skin stuck together.

He asked me to go for a walk and we climbed down the ladder and walked toward the cane fields. He held my hand and pulled me along until we got to the rows. He dropped my hand, took out his pocketknife, pulled on one of the stalks, and then cut off a rod of cane. He sliced it into three pieces and handed one to me and the other to Marianne. I'd never had a piece of fresh sugar cane so I didn't know what to do with it. I watched them suck the sugar out, but I just held mine.

A little later we sat on the ground outside the barn and talked about what we liked such as our favorite subjects in school, books we'd read. We found out we had a lot in common, especially that we loved books— high-brow stuff like Chaucer and Cheever. We agreed that our favorite place was the library.

He told me that the colored kids at his school didn't have textbooks, and it seemed outrageous to me that schools didn't provide learning materials based on skin color. Over the next few years Rodney, Marianne, and I devised a project where I would confiscate discarded books from my school for their school.

I got a volunteer position in the school library and I'd box up old discarded books, especially textbooks Rodney identified as ones they needed, and I'd leave a window unlocked on certain evenings. We'd meet behind the school and Rodney would use his uncle's pickup truck and drive under the unlocked window, then climb from the bed of the truck into the library and hand the boxes to me and Marianne.

I remember how we used to drive away with the lights off on the truck and he and Marianne would drop me off two blocks from my house. I'd walk home and say I'd been at the library—which wasn't an actual lie.

Lilly and I laughed at how I justified my whereabouts to my parents when I was in high school. She said, "Oh, Susie, you were bad." I said it was for a good cause and we laughed some more. Then we were quiet.

"Well, what happened next? I mean with you and Rodney?"

Not much until I went to LSU. Rodney was two years older than me but we graduated from our separate high schools the same year because, I guess you could say my mother had me on an accelerated program. He was eighteen and I was sixteen and we both went to college in Baton Rouge, although I was at LSU and he was at Southern. Even colleges were segregated in those days. Anyway, that's when we dated seriously. Those were the best four months of my life, even though we had to sneak and couldn't go out in public. We saw each other every chance we had.

Somehow, my dad found out I was seeing someone, although I don't think he knew who. So he shipped me off to Sarah Lawrence in New York. By then I was seventeen. The next year, Rodney saved enough money to come to New York for a week at Thanksgiving and we had the most glorious week of visiting the library, sitting in coffee houses, going to concerts. No one seemed to notice we were not the same race.

We made lots of casual friends and felt accepted everywhere we went. Until that week I don't think we ever thought there was a chance we'd ever be able to be together, but we started to believe and dream that we could be married one day and live in New York.

We both needed to finish college and he wanted to go to law school. We felt we could wait. It would be worth it.

About six weeks after Rodney's visit to New York, I found out I was going to have a baby. Josh was my doctor. That's how we met. I knew if I told Rodney about the baby—about you—he would quit school and come to New York to marry me.

It was too dangerous for his family. It's hard for me to describe the things they would do in those days to colored people who dared to even speak to a white person. Anyway, I thought about how he'd have to get a job as a janitor and would end up resenting me and...

"Well, Lilly, I can't explain all the reasons I didn't tell him or the reasons I chose to give you a better life with a couple who would be great parents," I tried not to look at her sitting next to me in the airport. "I was eighteen, scared, stupid, far away from any family support. I'm not making excuses, but I made the decision I made; if it was wrong I am so sorry. This will sound trite and you might find it hard to believe, but I made those decisions because I loved you so much."

Lilly grabbed my hand and squeezed it. She held it on the armrest between our two chairs. "Go on," she said.

"I'm not sure what else to tell you..."

Josh was my constant companion during my pregnancy and he fell in love with me, but I loved Rodney too much to even notice Josh. When you were born and I went through with the adoption, Josh thought I couldn't love him and he moved on.

When I look back, I think Josh was hoping I'd keep you and marry him, but, like I said, I didn't love him. I loved Rodney.

Josh stayed in your life. He always felt he was your surrogate dad because he had nurtured you for seven and a-half months while I was pregnant, and he delivered you.

Rodney and I reconnected at Catfish's funeral just after he'd completed law school and I'd finished grad school. We decided to get married; he would move to New York. I came back and waited for him but he never arrived. So many things happened and, in order to keep his family safe, we had to give up on our dream to be together.

I was devastated.

About six months later I met you. You were four and I fell in love with you the first time I saw your auburn curls bounce as you jumped up and down behind your mom's skirt. Finding you was the best decision of my life.

It took a while for me to learn to live without the hope of marrying Rodney. He went to Vietnam, met someone, and was engaged to be married. You were about five when Josh came back into my life. It was inevitable. He was a big part of your life with your parents, and I had become part of your lives, too. We took it slow, and as I healed from Rodney I fell in love with Josh. He was a great man and I'll always be grateful we had him for the time we did.

I stopped talking because when I thought about Josh, I still felt empty inside and missed him. Lilly had tears in her eyes, too. "I loved him, too, you know."

"Yes, I know sweetheart. And you were his little girl. He adored you. He knew you in the womb. He was the first person to see you when you came into this world. He remained in your life, the one constant person... I'm so sorry we lost him." She put her head on my chest, folded her arms around me, and sobbed. I didn't have the guts to tell her Josh's death was all my fault.

I felt her nod her head on my chest and her tears soaked through my blouse.

A couple of days after we arrived in Jean Ville, I went to see my dad. I'd made it a habit of going by every other day when I was in town. If he was hateful I left, but if he was civil I would sit and visit with him. He eventually realized that his words could run me off and he tried harder to be nice to me.

He was sitting on the front porch when I pulled up in the driveway. I stopped my car in front rather than drive to the back where I usually entered. I walked through the yard and up the front steps, went over to him, kissed the top of his head and sat in the rocker next to him.

"How are you feeling today, Daddy?"

"I'm okay. I wish I could move around better. I wish I had something to do. I'm bored." He rocked and stared straight ahead. He didn't look at me and I couldn't remember the last time he had. I stood up and faced him. I put the toes of my shoe on one of the rocker legs to stop the motion.

"Look at me, Daddy." I had my hands on my hips. He looked up, then looked immediately over my shoulder, almost like he was staring at my earlobe. "Look. I need to tell you something. It's important and I need to look you in the eye when I say it." I couldn't believe I was bold enough to talk to my dad that way. I'd always been so frightened of him. Those days were over.

"I'm getting married again." That got his attention.

"You're what?" He looked at me and his body language said he wanted to spring out of his chair and choke me, but he couldn't physically spring, or jump, or barely walk without being winded.

"I'm getting married, which shouldn't be a big deal. It's who I'm marrying that you need to come to terms with." I still had my toes on the rocker, preventing him from moving and he was gripping both arms of the chair so tightly his knuckles were white.

"Not that nigga"

"Rodney Thibault." I didn't flinch.

"Not in my town. You can't embarrass me here. Go back to New York if you want to marry a ni__er."

"You hypocrite. You had a thirty-year affair with a black woman and you have the nerve...?"

"I never married her!"

"But you had a child with her. A beautiful young woman who is my sister whom you've never acknowledged." I took my foot off the rocker and it lurched forward as if it was going to throw him out. I pushed on both his shoulders to steady him and he sat back as if the air had been sucked out of him. "Maybe you should think about that." I turned and went down the steps to the front yard and walked across the warm grass to my car.

When I walked back into the house on Gravier Road, the sweet smell of lilies from the always-arriving white flowers filled the air and I thought of how good it felt to be honest and brave.

*

Sissy and I talked about how to tell our mother about my engagement and decided that I should break the news to her in person. We drove to Houston together the Saturday after Thanksgiving. Although we'd spoken on the phone a few times since Dad's illness began, I hadn't seen Mama in ten years and wondered how she would handle our reunion.

"Look. We forgave her and have been trying to rebuild our relationships. Surely she won't judge you." Sissy was measuring the windows in the apartment I'd had built over the new garage and I was sitting on the floor turning the pages of magazines that had examples of draperies.

"Don't be so sure, Sissy. Mama is as prejudiced as the day is long. She can take up with a Mafia man, but a colored man? I don't know whether she'll be able to swallow it."

"I can't wait to meet Rodney. Lilly is really taken with him." She dropped the tape measure and it rolled over to where I was sitting on the floor. She stooped to pick it up and my ring caught her eye. "When did you get that rock?"

"Last week." I put my hand in hers and she examined my engagement ring. "I haven't been wearing it. Waiting until I've broken the news to certain people."

"Whew! It's really something."

"He's wonderful, Sissy. You'll love him." I knew I was beaming but couldn't help myself. When I thought about Rodney I smiled with my whole face. Sissy started laughing at me.

"I hope I meet someone one day who makes me glow like Rodney makes you glow." She hugged me and I hugged her back.

"I hope so, too. I really do. And I hope he's white because this is hard."

"But worth it, right?"

"I guess we'll see whether we can make it work in Jean Ville or whether we'll have to live somewhere else."

"Oh. Are ya'll thinking about living here? Are you crazy?"

"Rodney wants to come back and go into practice with his brother when he gets out of the army in May. I don't want to be so far away from him again."

"You need to think long and hard about that." Sissy turned around and didn't say any more.

*

It was about noon when Sissy and I pulled into a semicircular driveway in front of a two-story brick house in a subdivision on the north side of Houston, the address James had given us. Sissy double-checked the map and said, "This is it."

"She does know we are coming, right?"

"Yes, I talked to her on the phone last night." We drove under a portico. A doorman approached the car and opened the door for Sissy to get out, then came around to my side. I was already standing on the concrete, the car keys in my hand.

"May I have your keys so I can park your car, ma'am?" I handed him the keys and Sissy and I stepped up to the double wood-stained doors under a long veranda with white columns that reached to the roof of the second story. Six tall windows spanned the front of the house on the lower level and above us were four sets of French doors with individual terraces. The house had a regal appearance with its topiaries and massive flowerbeds filled with azaleas, camellias, holly and oak trees, and huge pecan trees that lined the driveway. Wisteria vines grew up two of the columns and made the air smell fragrant and fresh even in the hundred-degree heat.

Sissy used the brass doorknocker and laughed at the lion's head embossed on it. A Hispanic housekeeper in a starched black dress with a white pinafore opened the door and asked our names. Sissy said, "Abigail and Susanna Burton." We both giggled but it didn't escape me that Sissy didn't say Susanna Ryan.

The maid ushered us down a hall and into a solarium on the side of the house, through double glass doors that opened to a terrace that extended into a colorful garden. Mama was wearing a blue silk flowing kaftan. Her formerly mousey brown hair, now with golden highlights, had obviously been "coiffed" at an exclusive salon, swept up on one side into a flip, the other tucked behind her ear, a bit of a bang across one half of her forehead. She had on huge diamond earrings and another brilliant stone on her left hand that had to be six or eight carats. On her feet were what looked like glass slippers with one-inch heels, but they were probably some sort of plastic. Sticking out of the ends were pink toenails, recently pedicured. She wore make-up, something she'd never done, nor did I remember her having her hair done or wearing jewelry of any kind except her simple gold wedding band.

She was sitting in a wing-backed chair in front of an unlit fireplace reading a book. She looked up at us as though it were normal for me and Sissy to walk into her house, and she said, "Hello, girls. Have a seat." She asked the housekeeper if she had offered us refreshments and Sissy and I looked at each other and giggled, thinking, *when did Mama get so highfalutin?*

We didn't hug or kiss or touch. It was as though we were strangers who had come to interview her for a high-fashion Houston magazine. The maid returned with a tray of sandwiches and a pitcher of iced tea. We sat at a round marble-topped table with high-backed chairs set inside a huge bay window, picked at our food, and tried to make casual conversation.

When you've had real tragedies like I'd had, you don't have the time or patience for surface talk and suppressed truths. After an hour of conversation about the weather, Houston's politics, decorating ideas, and fashion, I became impatient.

"Did Daddy ever hit you?" I looked directly at Mama who sat back in her chair as if she'd been struck. The expression on her face went from pretend happiness to utter pain for just a second. I witnessed the curtain fall and retract before her face returned to something akin to nonchalance.

"Susanna! Why would you ask a question like that?" She took a sip of her iced tea and looked at the long, manicured fingernails on her left hand as if examining them for any sharp cuticles left behind by a negligent salon assistant. Her hands looked strange to me as I remembered her nails bitten to the quick and cuticles torn and sometimes bleeding.

"We all know what he was capable of," I said. "He beat me up so bad I had to be hospitalized, and that was just one of the many times. What about you?"

"Let's say we had disagreements that didn't turn out so well." Mama stood up and walked across the huge room to the fireplace.

"Yes, well, I happen to know that you are the one who made him beat me up the time he almost killed me." There was dead silence and her stare was blank. "What kind of mother does that to her child?"

She put both hands on the mantle and bent her head so that her forehead rested on top of the ornate, marble fireplace. Sissy got up and went to her. She wrapped her arms around Mama's waist and lay her head on Mama's back. Mama turned around and they hugged.

I watched them as if I was observing a movie. It didn't seem real, they didn't seem real, nothing seemed real. But the ice was broken and we sat down to some serious conversation where we learned of the mental, physical, and emotional abuse Mama had endured for twenty-five years.

We heard about her desperate escape from Jean Ville when Daddy was ill because it was the first time she felt he could not follow her and force her to come back. She talked about how she hid out in a small rental house that her sister, Betty, helped her pay for. Mama said she met John, the man who owned the mansion where she now lived, at a restaurant. He was introduced by a friend of Aunt Betty's husband, Rick, a shady character I didn't trust.

"Mama, I have something to tell you." I took her shaking hand in mine and held it on top of the table. She looked at me then looked at our hands. "I'm getting married."

"Again?" she pulled her hand away and reached for her iced tea.

"Yes. What you need to know is who I'm marrying." I tried to get her to meet my eyes but hers darted from Sissy to her tea to her plate and back to Sissy. We were all quiet. "Rodney Thibault. Ray Thibault's son."

"I know who he is. He's a niggra. Maybe a high yellow. A mulatto. But he's still a n__gra." She stood up and her chair almost fell over backwards, teetered, then sat upright with a thud. Mama walked out of the solarium, through the glass doors, into the flower garden outside. Sissy followed her and closed the door behind them.

Drama, I thought; *always, drama.*

I watched them talk and argue; Mama cried, wrung her hands, then walked away from Sissy. Sissy followed and grabbed Mama's shoulders. Finally, they hugged and stood in an embrace for a long time. I could tell they were whispering to each other.

When they came back inside I was sitting on the divan thumbing through *Home and Garden* magazine.

Mama rang a bell that was sitting on the table and asked the maid to set up the bar in the solarium. A few minutes later, the unnamed, un-introduced Hispanic lady rolled a glass-shelved cart with a crystal ice bucket and glasses on a mirrored tray into the room. Behind her was the butler, who carried an additional tray with six or eight decanters full of brown and clear liquids.

"Gerald, I'll have a dry Martini, two olives." Mama turned to Sissy and winked. It was the first time she resembled the mother I'd known as a child. "What will you girls have?"

"Oh, I'm not drinking. I'm driving back to Jean Ville tonight."

"Oh, Susie, please stay the night. I want you and Sissy to meet John. We'll have a lovely dinner to celebrate your engagement. You can drive back tomorrow." She looked at me as though pleading; something I'd never known my mother to do. I glanced at Sissy and she nodded. When mother turned around Sissy mouthed, "lovely," and we both cracked up.

"It's up to you, of course," Sissy finally said. "But I'd like to stay."

"May I use your phone? I need to make sure it's okay to leave Lilly."

"Who's Lilly?" Mama asked, but I was ushered to the phone in John's study by the maid, who actually had a name: Hannah.

I called and spoke with Tootsie who said the girls were fine and I should stay as long as I liked. I wanted to talk to Lilly, but she was in town with Tom's wife, Gloria, and Anna and Chrissy. Tootsie promised to have her call me when she returned to the Quarters. I gave her my mother's phone number and hung up.

"Sissy was just telling me about the little girl you adopted."

"I didn't adopt her. I have custody."

"Oh. What's the difference?"

"Mama, let me tell you the truth. She's Rodney's daughter. Rodney's and mine." I had to catch her as she collapsed, very dramatically. Her Martini hit the marble floor and the glass broke into a million tiny shards. Hannah and Gerald came running in and started to clean the mess while I helped Mama into her chair where she swooned, then came around, but we didn't talk about Lilly again.

When John Maceo came into the solarium, the mess was cleaned up and Mama was half-way through her second Martini. He kissed her on the forehead and she introduced us. He shook our hands and repeated our names as Mama said them.

"Abigail, so nice to meet you. You look like your mother. That's a compliment." Sissy did look like Mama and she could imitate anyone. Behind John's back, she pretended to shake an invisible hand and mouthed words, "Abigail, it's so nice to meet you."

Sissy is fairly short and petite with a perfect figure. I'm tall and lanky with almost no figure compared to her and we look nothing alike. My eyes are blue-grey, a dull color and are shapeless, and too big.

Sissy drew attention when she walked into a room. She had brown hair that she highlighted to a rich, honey blond and blue-green eyes shaped like sideways teardrops. Back then she wore outrageous clothes, like hip-hugger bell-bottoms and tie-dyed T-shirts. She had two pierced earrings in each earlobe and one in the top of her right ear from which she wore a dangling rhinestone thing. She went to college for a couple years but didn't like it; her forte was music and she could play the piano like a concert artist.

"Susanna, it's a pleasure." John shook my hand and looked at my ear, as if he couldn't make eye-to-eye contact. He was a handsome Italian man with dark wavy hair and a large nose, late fifties or early sixties, not an *old man* like James described him. He said he was a businessman with offices in downtown Houston, which sounded important but a bit nebulous, and his demeanor was akin to Mafia types I'd read about. His eyes gave him a Cary Grant look; long thick eyelashes that were about a quarter of the way closed. He seemed to be peering at you out of only two-thirds of his lower eyes, as if just awakened from a deep sleep.

"The pleasure is mine." *I can keep pace with him,* I thought and act formal and highbrowed. It occurred to me that I might be as wealthy as John Maceo and probably more educated. It was a fleeting thought, though, because I didn't care one whit about the money Josh left me and Lilly. I was, however, proud of my education.

John picked up a crystal highball glass and filled it halfway with bourbon—no ice, no water—that he gulped; then he poured another half-glass and sipped it. Mama was in her cups and asked Sissy to play the piano. There was a baby grand in the huge hallway between the solarium and the dining room, but all the rooms were connected because there were huge openings, no doors, and continuous marble floors.

Sissy sat down and began playing *Fur Elise*, Daddy's favorite. Mama made a face and asked her to play *Me and My Shadow*. Mama and John danced and followed each other around the room like one was the leader, the other the shadow. It was cute and I could tell they were happy together. And a little drunk.

We all sat at one end of a dining table that seated twenty people and ate steaks, au gratin potatoes, and salad. It was the first time I could remember seeing my mother laugh. John played straight man to Sissy's comedic routines and they were hysterical.

Sissy and I were ushered upstairs to adjoining bedrooms, each with en-suite bathrooms. We pretended to be queens and ended up sleeping together in the same bed, in silk pajamas Hannah brought us from our mother's closet. She took our clothes to launder, promising they'd be outside our bedroom doors in the morning.

We took showers and wrapped ourselves in robes that were terry cloth on the inside and silk on the outside and we danced around the huge bedroom like school girls.

Breakfast was pleasant. John had already gone off to work so it was Mama, Sissy, and me. I told Mama it was good to see her happy and that I didn't have any hard feelings that she left Daddy. Mama apologized, sort of, for complaining about me to Daddy.

"I had to do something to divert his anger. And you've always been so strong." She looked embarrassed, not sorry, but I took what I could get at the time.

Sissy agreed that it was nice to see Mama happy but said she was still angry at the way Mama left because Sissy became responsible for a mean, sick man when she was only fifteen.

"I'm not going to try to explain and I don't need absolution, but I will say I had no choice about how or when I left." Mama picked at her eggs and took a long gulp of tomato juice, which I thought might be laced with vodka because there were two olives and a celery stalk in the glass.

"You haven't asked about Albert or the older boys." Sissy looked at Mama but Mama was busy stirring her grits absent-mindedly.

"Albert calls me every week. I talk to James regularly and he comes here a couple times a year. He brings Albert with him. Will and Robby aren't interested in talking to me and I can't force it." She looked sad and it was the first time I considered that she might love her children; something she'd never shown. I could see the pain in her body language—the dropped shoulders, downcast eyes, fidgety fingers, shuffling feet under the table.

"Can I call you sometime?" I reached over and took one of her shaking hands. Her fingers were cold and sharp, but she cupped them around my wrist.

"I'd like that Susanna Christine." She only called me by my full name when she was angry, but I didn't see anger on her face this time, only pain. "And I'd like to meet Lilly. She's my first, my only grandchild, you know."

"Would you like to come to the wedding?"

"I might. When is it?"

"We haven't set a date or place yet, but I'll let you know." I squeezed her hand.

I got up and hugged Mama and I felt a surge of forgiveness and understanding.

"I want you to be happy, Mama. You deserve it." I was getting in the car and she was standing beside me.

"Thank you. I am happy." She kissed me on the cheek and hugged me extra long. "And don't forget to send me pictures of my granddaughter."

Sissy and I didn't talk much until we drove across the state line into Louisiana on Interstate 10 and were about two hours from Jean Ville. She said she was glad we'd gone to see Mama and that she would stay in touch, maybe even go back for a visit sometime. I told her that Emalene said, "Love your mother, you only get one."

"She also said that about Daddy," I told Sissy. "If *you* can accept what Mama did to you, maybe I should try to accept what Daddy did to me." It was starting to drizzle and I turned on the windshield wipers. The swish-thump of the back and forth rhythm was hypnotic.

"Mama seems to have accepted your engagement to Rodney. How does that make you feel?" Sissy asked.

"I'm glad, but I didn't need her approval. After all, she didn't care if we approved of what she did." I drove slowly through the rain that had started coming down harder. It sounded like it would break the windows. Sissy used a Kleenex to wipe the inside of the windshield where it was fogging up and I slowed down as the rain came down harder.

"And she wants to meet Lilly." Sissy was talking just above a whisper.

"That makes me happy. Lilly needs as many people who love her as possible."

"Anyway. It's good to see Mama happy. Don't you think?" Sissy said, her face peering out the window of the car at the rain.

"Sure." The cool water hit the hot surface of the highway and created steam that smelled musty and damp.

~ Chapter Twenty-Two ~

~

Honesty

I T WAS OUR LAST night in Jean Ville and I was in my bedroom packing when I heard the back screen door slam. I was ready to get back to New York and to Rodney; ten days was a long time to be away from him.

I heard murmurs on the back porch and could tell two people were talking. I peeked through the curtains that covered my window and saw Tootsie in one rocking chair, Lilly in another.

I didn't mean to eavesdrop but I felt protective of Lilly and didn't know what Tootsie might tell my little girl. I sat in the chair in the corner of my room where I could hear the conversation as Tootsie began telling Lilly about the Ku Klux Klan raid on our house when I was twelve and how they left our home on and marched to the Quarters.

"Your grandfather, Bob Burton, still lives in that house and he's a crotchety old man, he is." Tootsie laughed and I couldn't hear Lilly's response.

The Past is the Past
Present day by Tootsie
It started long before you was born. Long before your Mama, Susie, was born, even before Marianne. Bob Burton knowed my daddy, Catfish.

One day Mr. Burton—he was young then—he come to the Quarters to axe could Catfish get him a hog at the slaughterhouse and butcher it. I was in the field picking corn and Mr. Burton come out there and axe me how old I am. I say I was about fourteen, give or take, and he say I was the prettiest thing he ever saw and we start to walk in the field and got lost in the rows, the tall corn stalks hiding us from view.

One thing led to another and he start to come visit me when Catfish was at work. My Mama was sick at the time and she died soon after, so me and Mr. Burton would go to the fields or, if it was raining, to the barn. Next thing I know I'm expecting a baby and I tell him and he say he don't know nothing about no baby and he quit coming around for a long time.

Marianne was born, and when she was about four or five months old, Mr. Burton come to the Quarters and axe could I go help his wife. She just had her second child, and that was Susie, and the Burtons had a boy who was three and Mrs. Burton couldn't handle it. So my sister Jesse kept Marianne and I went to the Burtons' house every day and did what I could so the kids would eat and have clean clothes and take they naps and stuff.

Then a year later Mrs. Burton—she tole me to call her "Miss Anne"—well, she have another boy and few years later another one. So I stayed on to help and Mr. Burton took that to mean he could come around to the Quarters again and see me. And that's how I come to raise your mama and how Marianne come to be your aunt.

I waited for Lilly to say something, ask a question, make a comment; but it was quiet and I became nervous and caught myself twisting a strand of hair tight against my scalp. Maybe this was too much information for my daughter, I thought. Then I reminded myself that Lilly was fifteen and she'd been through what most people don't endure in a lifetime. I had to trust Tootsie's wisdom.

Okay now where was I—yes, the Klan. They was a bad bunch who tried to keep coloreds and whites apart back in the 1960s and '70s, and even before that. They thought it was their job to enforce what they called the Jim Crow Laws, which was rules the Southern whites made that said Negroes couldn't drink water at public fountains or use public restrooms or eat in restaurants or stay in hotels. It was bad in those days. Yeah, it shore was.

Tootsie stopped talking and I heard Lilly inhale. I wanted to look through the curtains to see if she was okay but was afraid to break the spell. I knew Lilly had questions; this was foreign to her, information about the Klan and Jim Crow and Southern bigotry.

Let me back up. Your mama, Susie, met my daddy Catfish when she was about six or seven. That was in the '50s, and the Klan was there then, too. Susie and her brothers caught a big ole snapping turtle and they stopped Catfish one day to give it to him and Susie and Catfish start to talk. Over the years Catfish would stop and talk to Susie when she was playing in the yard and he was walking home to the Quarters.

He had to walk right in front the Burton house to get home, and Susie would wait for him. When he retired and quit walking in front her house, she stole off to the Quarters to see Catfish. After that it come to be a regular thing. Susie would come visit Catfish and Catfish would tell Susie stories. And that's how she come to write that book with all them stories Catfish tole her.

Well, when Susie come to the Quarters to see Catfish, that's when she met Marianne. They got to be friends right away but they had to hide it because, remember, coloreds and whites couldn't be friends of no kind. One day Susie was on Catfish's porch and Bob Burton drove up and come in my house to see me and Susie seed what was going on and that's when she knew Marianne was her half-sister.

"Marianne and Susie are sisters?" Lilly's voice was riddled with surprise. It was the first time she had responded and I wanted to be with her, to put her in my lap and rock her. This was a lot of information. But I made myself trust Tootsie and I sat and listened.

"Shore are," Tootsie said. "And that makes Marianne your aunt and all those children in the Quarters is your cousins. Girl! You got lots of cousins because Rodney related to lots of folks, too, so you have cousins on both sides." Tootsie took a breath and the rocking chair rocked back and forth and I could hear Sissy and Marianne talking softly in the kitchen. I wondered what Lilly was thinking when she didn't respond.

So anyways, I think Susie met Rodney at the gas station his daddy owns over at the Y, where Main and Jefferson Street come together north of town. Anyway, Rodney would come to the Quarters when Susie was here and they got to be friends, maybe fell in love way back when they was teenagers.

When Susie found out the colored school didn't have no books for the kids to take home and that those children at Adams High School shared some ole torn-up books, she start to box up all the thrown-out books at the white school and sneak them here to the Quarters.

The Klan must have found out about Rodney and Susie. See, back then, a colored boy couldn't even look at a white woman. He had to cross the street if one start to walk his way and he had to keep his eyes down looking at his feet. Well, the way I hear tell, Rodney ran into your mama somewhere in public and he touched her, maybe just put his hand out to stop her, and someone saw him do that and they went after Rodney's daddy, and almost kilt him. They hung him up in a tree in his own front yard and burned his house to the ground.

The only thing saved him was Rodney. That boy stood as tall as he could and reached his arms up over his head for his daddy to stand in his hands until Bo and Sam got there to cut Ray out of that tree. Fact that he didn't die was a miracle.

There was a pause and complete silence. I peered through the curtain but I could only see the back of Lilly's head, which was hanging a little low, and her shoulders were slumped. "Honesty," Rodney kept reminding me, was how we needed to live, so I let Tootsie continue, uninterrupted.

"I'm telling you all this so you know how much your mama and daddy loved each other and how hard they fought to be together so they could raise you." Tootsie took a deep breath.

The Klan and Susie's daddy made sure that didn't happen. You see I think your Mama quit seeing your daddy because she thought she had to protect him and his family from the Klan. But she never stopped loving him. I believe she brought you into the world because if she couldn't have Rodney, she could have a part of him; then she saw she couldn't have you either. If her daddy had found out about you back then I don't know what would have happened.

Before she left for college, Susie would come to the Quarters all the time, maybe every week; and she would come whenever she was home from college to visit Catfish and to see Marianne. Catfish loved Susie like his own granddaughter and he felt protective for her.

Catfish used to sit on his porch in the evenings and tell me and Marianne how special Susie was. He'd repeat some of the things she said to him, and he'd say, "Now ain't that smart. That girl, she so smart."

And he thought she was beautiful and he worried some boy would take advantage of her. When she start to see Rodney, Catfish had a long talk with that boy. He was about sixteen or seventeen and Catfish sat him down and say, "Boy, you keep your zipper zipped when you around Susanna. If I hear you take advantage of that girl I'll make you sorry." Catfish would talk to Rodney about respecting Susie and told Rodney he needed to take care of her while she was growing into a woman and not take advantage like lots of boys do with girls. Catfish, now he was protective of Susie. He shore was.

I listened to Tootsie talk about how much Catfish loved and protected me and felt pride in the relationship he and I had formed. I remember Rodney telling me that we should wait until I was at least eighteen to have sex, and we did wait. I had no idea that advice came from Catfish. Catfish never told me he loved me, although I always felt it. I would tell him I loved him and he'd say, "Run off now and leave me be. You done wore me out." And he'd laugh.

Catfish was my inspiration, but I didn't know he'd also been my protector.

"Yeah, chile" Tootsie's rocker went back and forth. "You got quite a mama there. And quite a daddy, too. I know it took a long time for you to know who you are, but now that you do, you should see that you truly special. I wish Catfish was here to know you. He'd love you just like he loved your mama. Yeah, I miss Catfish. You would have loved him…

Lilly didn't say a word, and I sat in my chair and listened to the rockers move back and forth and felt my heart beat hard against my ribs.

*

Rodney was waiting at baggage claim when we arrived at Kennedy International and we took a cab to Manhattan to our condo. When we entered the lobby, the concierge called me over to the desk and handed me a long, white box with a satin ribbon tied around it. I looked at Rodney who shrugged his shoulders as if to say "I don't know anything about that."

I wasn't surprised to find six long-stemmed white lilies in the box when we got up to the apartment. I put them in a vase of water on the dining room table and made myself a mental note to discuss the lilies with Rodney when we were alone.

We spent Christmas in New York where Lilly was able to be with Joe and his family, and Rodney and I had some private time together. The lilies kept arriving, one every other day and our "house in the sky," as Lilly called it, was always filled with the fresh flowery scent. Rodney said he knew nothing about them, even after I pressed him about how they were delivered to me over the past two years, no matter where I was.

"They came to our house in Brooklyn Heights. They'd arrive at Marianne's house when we stayed there. After I bought the house on Gravier Road they'd be waiting for us when we arrived in Jean Ville, and the florist would deliver one at least every other day. After we moved into this apartment, they were delivered here. Whoever is sending them knows where I am—which house and city. It's spooky and I always thought it might be you."

"I wish I could take credit, Susie. Sorry." He kissed me on the cheek and I looked away, wondering who the heck kept sending these lilies.

While Lilly was with Joe, Rodney and I revisited all the places we had gone when I was eighteen and he'd come to visit me—the New York Public Library on Fifth Avenue, the coffee shops in Soho, the delis in Greenwich Village, the ferry to Ellis Island. We also spent time alone in the apartment, ordering meals from the restaurants downstairs and languishing in bed most of the day before Christmas Eve. We talked about where we would live after we were married and Rodney reminded me he'd promised his brother, Jeffrey, he'd go back to Jean Ville and practice law with him and Sarah.

I told him I was afraid Jean Ville had not kept pace with the rest of the world as far as bigotry and prejudice. I said I didn't think we'd be safe, maybe Lilly wouldn't be safe, in our hometown.

What is it about hometowns that beckon people back after years of living away? Rodney had not lived in Jean Ville in seventeen years—seven years in college and law school and ten years in the army. He'd become accustomed to military life, where discrimination was almost nonexistent, so he couldn't imagine that our town hadn't kept up with Civil Rights.

I knew Jean Ville wasn't ready for a mixed-race couple. I saw it in my dad's reaction when I told him who I was going to marry. I read it on the faces of my white friends like Cindy and Sylvia and their parents, too. I was deathly afraid of what might happen to Rodney or, even worse, Lilly, if we lived there as a family.

In the time I'd had my little house on Gravier, I'd experienced backlash from my white friends and my own family members, simply because of my relationship with Marianne and Tootsie. Bigotry was still active and rampant in Jean Ville, Louisiana.

I urged Rodney to consider living in New York for Lilly's sake. Finally, we compromised.

I agreed we would get married in Jean Ville so our families and close friends could be at the wedding, and I promised we would spend the summers on Gravier Road where Lilly could be with her cousins and Rodney with his family.

Rodney agreed we would live and work in New York during the school year and he would work with Mr. Milton handling my accounts. Meanwhile, Lilly would complete her three years of high school and I would finish my second book about Catfish and his stories.

"After Lilly graduates from high school we can re-assess whether it's safe to move back home," I promised. That seemed to make both Rodney and Lilly happy.

Lilly returned from Joe's house on Christmas Eve. The three of us had a private party where we exchanged gifts, then we attended midnight Mass at St. Patrick's Cathedral.

On Christmas morning, a huge box of white lilies arrived.

*

Rodney retired from the army in May and the three of us went to Jean Ville as soon as Lilly got out of school the first of June. We had lots to do to pull off a wedding at St. Alphonse's Catholic Church by the end of the month. Rodney said he would stay with his family until we were married because they missed him and wanted to spend as much time as they could with him. Anyway, my house on Gravier Road was small and would be buzzing with activities meant for girls like Lilly, Sissy, Marianne, and me as we planned and executed the wedding.

Marianne picked us up at the Baton Rouge airport and when we got to Jean Ville she took Rodney to his parents' house on Marshall Drive.

Just before dark, Rodney drove up in my driveway in his dad's car with Jeffrey, Sarah, and their two kids.

Lilly was in the backyard with Anna. I was in the garage apartment with Marianne and Sissy when I heard the car and looked out the front window. I saw Rodney get out, stretch, and head towards my front porch. I opened the window and yelled at him that I was upstairs and would be right down.

Lilly came running around the house and jumped into his arms as if she hadn't seen him in a month. It was hot and humid and I got a whiff of tar rising from the pavement on Gravier Road as I ran down the stairs.

Sissy and Marianne followed me to the front yard and I introduced everyone, including Rodney, Jeffrey, and Sarah, to Sissy. Sarah introduced us to her two children, Ward and Amber and was reasonably nice. I remembered how she'd made me feel as though I was invisible the only other time I'd met her.

Lilly and Anna took the kids to the backyard and pushed them on the swings while the rest of us went inside. Rodney put his arm around me and pulled me close before we followed the others into the house. We stopped on the porch and he whispered in my ear.

"When can we be alone?" He kissed me and I blushed before we walked into the living room. The others disappeared into the hall, Sissy and Marianne were showing Jeffrey and Sarah around the house. Rodney took advantage of their absence and kissed me again. "I love you, Susie."

"I love you, too." I kissed him back and whispered the words into his mouth and he gasped.

"We came to take you and Lilly to meet my folks," Rodney told me as the others walked by towards the back porch. "My parents are excited to know you and, especially, to meet Lilly."

"So they're okay with all of this?" I looked at him as if I didn't believe him. "Honestly?"

"Honestly! They are ecstatic." He kissed me again and wrapped his arms around me.

We all went onto the back porch that spanned the rear of the little house and talked for a few minutes then called to Lilly, Amber, and Ward to join us in the front driveway.

Sissy and Marianne saw to it that Chrissy and Anna got home to the Quarters while Lilly and I went to the Thibaults' house with Rodney, Sarah, Jeffrey and their kids. Jeffrey drove while the kids sat on Lilly's lap in the back seat, loving on her and playing patty-cake. I sat between Rodney and Lilly and I bent towards her ear and whispered, "Happy?" I watched her face light up and she nodded several times and said, "Very."

The Thibaults were waiting for us on their front porch and came to the car before we could get out. They hugged Lilly and me, then Mrs. Thibault took Lilly's hand and led her up to their porch swing and patted it so she would sit right next to her grandmother. I heard Mrs. Thibault say, "My other grandchildren call me Mamaw. Does that sound okay to you?" Lilly was smiling with her whole face as she nodded, "Yes."

Mr. Ray put his arm around my shoulder as we walked up the steps and he said, "Welcome to our family. It's taken a while, but we made it, right?"

"Right," I said, and I looked at Rodney and winked at him. He smiled at me and winked back and I knew it was... right.

*

We got married at St. Alphonse's Catholic Church on South Jefferson Street on the 30th of June. The pastor, Father Remy, was from the Philippines and had no problem with the race issue. He counseled us and ordered Rodney's annulment papers from the Diocese of Phoenix.

A Catholic Church annulment is based on proof that a couple should never have been married in the first place. Rodney and Maria both had post-traumatic stress after Vietnam and weren't in a position to make such a decision at the time, so the annulment was mostly a matter of paperwork that Rodney initiated soon after his divorce was final.

I didn't expect half the crowd of people who attended our wedding. My mother and John came from Houston. She was decked out in a long, mint-green dress and enough jewelry to sink a battleship. All four of my brothers were there with girlfriends I didn't know, all dressed in mini-skirts with low-cut tops that showed their cleavages.

Tootsie wore a long, purple dress and brought Joe Edgars, her current beau, Marianne's sisters, and their husbands or boyfriends. Marianne's aunts and uncles and their children came and filled the pews on both sides of the aisle. A number of Rodney's friends and football teammates from high school came, some wearing their old letter jackets in solidarity. It was charming.

Mr. Michel, the hospital administrator for whom I'd worked after I graduated from college, and his wife were there. Dr. Switzer and Miss Irma, and Superintendent of Schools, Mr. Ben Moss, and his wife Miss Rita came and sat on the bride's side. Even Sylvia and Ken Michaud were there and she smiled at me and winked when she saw me standing in the vestibule waiting to walk down the aisle. Several of my girlfriends from high school were there with their husbands, but lots of them didn't come, which wasn't a surprise.

Joe showed up with his wife, Bridgette. He came into the bride's room off the church's entrance foyer with a long, white box tied with a blush-colored satin ribbon. He kissed me on the cheek and walked up to Lilly and handed the box to her. When she opened it the unmistakable fragrance of lilies filled the room and she gasped. Three long-stemmed blush-colored lilies for our Lilly were lying in the white container. Joe looked at me and winked.

Lilly, Marianne, and Sissy were my bridesmaids and wore long, chiffon dresses in a bluish-gray color. Lilly handed Sissy and Marianne one of the long-stemmed lilies to carry, and kept one for herself.

My two sisters walked down the aisle and Lilly kissed me and was about to follow them when the church door opened and I turned around to see my dad walk into the vestibule.

"May I walk you down the aisle?" Daddy was wearing a tuxedo that smelled of dry-cleaning fluid. He had showered and shaved and had on black wing-tipped shoes, laced up, with black socks. I hadn't seen him dressed in anything but khakis, T-shirts, and flip-flops in several years and was shocked by his appearance. Then it hit me that this was my dad, Bob Burton, and he was offering to give me away— to a black man.

He handed me a long, white box tied with a white satin ribbon. He looked at me with a sideways sneer as I set the box on the small table near the front door and pulled on the ribbon, then lifted the top of the box. A dozen long-stemmed white lilies lay side-by-side and atop each other inside the box. They were pure white, with green leaves, and they smelled like new life, forgiveness, and redemption.

I gasped, lifted the flowers from the box, and held them in my arms like a newborn baby.

I grabbed him around the neck to hug him, pressing the lilies between us. Yellow pollen from the stamens powdered the front of Daddy's black tuxedo jacket and I used the hankie that Marianne had given me for something borrowed to wipe it off.

Lilly turned around to help and we started laughing. Even Daddy thought it was funny.

The weight of a dozen lilies was too much, so I put all of them in the box except for three, which I carried across the crook of my left arm and tucked my right arm through Daddy's.

We had been delayed walking down the aisle but no one seemed to care.

The look of surprise on Rodney's face when he saw my dad as we walked toward him was erased when he looked at me. His smile told me everything; and I knew this was the best decision of my life.

When he and my dad shook hands, Rodney reached with his left hand and squeezed my dad's shoulder.

"Thank you sir," Rodney said loud enough for me to hear. "You've made your daughter and me very proud today."

"You take care of her, Son." My dad grinned, which was as close to a smile as I'd seen on him since my mother left. I turned to look at her and there were tears running down her cheeks.

Rodney turned towards Jeffrey, his best man, and when he turned back to face me he was holding a long-stemmed, white lily. He laid it across my arms with the others.

I don't remember the ceremony, just the glow I felt throughout my body when it was over.

After we were pronounced man and wife, Rodney kissed me and we turned toward the congregation. The organ played *Ode to Joy* by Beethoven as we walked back down the aisle, our guests standing and smiling as wide as we were.

I remember thinking I was the happiest I'd ever been in my life.

We walked out into the bright sunlight through the huge double doors of the church and turned to kiss each other. Out of the corner of my eye and I noticed a pickup truck move very slowly, then stop in front of the church and a flash of sunlight hit a metal object that stuck out of the passenger window.

It all happened so fast.

I didn't hear anything—no shots, no sounds, nothing but Lilly's screams as my life turned to slow motion and I was pulled to the concrete where I landed on my back with Rodney on top of me, his face on my face.

I felt a stream of liquid run down my cheek as if tears were draining from my eyes. I noticed the stream was red and was flowing from Rodney's face onto mine.

It was surreal.

I remember thinking about Lilly. Was she okay? And I remember wondering, *How could this be happening?*

Then I blacked out.

<<<<>>>>

Other Books by
Madelyn Bennett Edwards

Catfish, A Novel

Biography

Madelyn Bennett Edwards is a Louisiana native who recently moved to an Atlanta suburb from Asheville, North Carolina with her architect husband, Gene. Lilly is her second novel, a sequel to her first, Catfish, published in 2017.

"Maddy," as her friends and grandchildren call her, went to beauty school to put herself through college, graduating from Louisiana College with a BA in journalism and English at 38—a single mom with two children. She earned an MA in writing from Lenoir Rhyne University in North Carolina after age 60. The former television health journalist started MBC, a television production company, in Alexandria, Louisiana in the 1980s, moved it to Nashville, Tennessee in the 1990s and sold it in 2003.

Maddy is presently working on the third book in the Catfish trilogy, and on a memoir about withdrawing from Dilaudid after fourteen years on an intrathecal pain pump. You can read more about Maddy and her upcoming releases on her website:
www.madelynedwardsauthor.com

CPSIA information can be obtained
at www.ICGtesting.com
Printed in the USA
LVHW031616071119
636673LV00003B/657/P

9 780999 402740